EYES WITHOUT A FACE

Betsy Ashton

Snowy Day Publications
Hardy, Virginia

Published by Snowy Day Publications

snowydaypublications@gmail.com

681 Ellis Rd.

Hardy, VA 24101

ISBN-10: 1977669468

ISBN-13: 978-1977669469

Cover designer: Kristen Houghton
Cover by 2Hopper Production & Design Studio

Dedication

For Terry, who never doubted that I could pull this novel off even when I was sure I couldn't write it

ACKNOWLEDGMENTS

First, I want to thank my husband for reading multiple drafts and being honest in his comments on what I wrote.

Mark Young, you began as my critique partner and became my best friend. You sat with me all the way through until we had That Thing's personality right. Thanks for early highlighting of the text to show me what I was doing wrong and for reading more than one draft.

To my Facebook "midwives," I thank Gareth Darby, Anne Piedmont, Shari Chernack, Chuck Lumpkin, Cat Ciric, Julie Taylor, David DuBois, preacher Larry Patton, Jon Harris and Melissa Stephens for their early ideas in our private Facebook group, "Dotting the Eyes."

To Laura Benedict's Writing Genre Fiction workshop at Tinker Mountain. I was confused about the opening chapters. Laura, Maggie Duncan, Michelle Webber, Dorothy Hassan Spruzen, Robin Haase and Sharon Higga—you were right in your comments. I hope you like the revised opening.

To those of you who helped me name characters, your suggestions remain invaluable. The winners of the naming contest are Sara Robinson, Cameron Jordan, and Pende Ford. Others contributed names too good not to use. They are Pam Pugh, Dan Dowdy, Doug Menville, Jackie Haskins.

Kimberly Dalferes, your guidance on things scientific helped me make fewer mistakes. Those that remain are all mine, CSI Gal.

To Bryan Sicher for his inspiration and demonstration in using a KA-BAR to create a sucking chest wound. To Brian Weitzman for taking me on a tour of his veterinary clinic and explaining the various chemicals I could use. To Jason, our exterminator, for an intriguing lesson on poisons I could buy at my local farm store.

To Dr. Dorothy Della Noche for turning me on to *The Sociopath Next Door* by Marsha Stout, Ph.D. And to Dr. Marsha Stout for giving tips in her book for why That Thing acts as she does. To Dave Cullen, who wrote clearly about a psychopath's mind in *Columbine*. The real psychopaths are more frightening than anything I could have imagined.

To fellow Lake Writer, Linda Kay Simmons, for telling me the story about boiling the dog on the stove. It really happened, but she wouldn't tell me who did it and when. Probably for the best. To Alan Orloff, whose book launch for *Deadly Campaign* included a wonderful misspelling on the launch cake and became a chapter title, "Deadly Camping." To Becky Mushko who owns the original Twiglets.

Wayne, my gun guy over at Blackwater Guns, who was right about the KA-BAR. It's a sweet weapon, just perfect for Bryan Sicher's sucking chest wounds. You don't have to reload it.

Kay McNulty, your volunteer work at Westlake Library led to a conversation about you wanting to be in this book. I asked if you wanted to be predator or prey. You responded, "Both." I hope you don't recognize yourself in these pages, but I was able to find a way to make your wish come true.

Writer groups provided guidance and patience when I read sections for critiques. Lake Writers and Valley Writers, you rock.

And lastly to Chuck Lumpkin for his help in publishing this book.

Thanks all.

CHAPTER ONE

WHO I AM

No matter what anyone says, I wasn't born a serial killer. I don't carry a sociopath gene, a psychopath gene, or even a serial killer gene. No such thing.

You can argue about nurture versus nature. Go ahead. Have at it. Look at the studies about psychopaths. Check me against the list of traits. I didn't wet my bed, kill small animals, or set fires. My younger brother did those things, but he didn't kill people—as far as I know. I wasn't sexually promiscuous. My sister was. She began screwing every boy and some of the men in town as soon as she got breasts.

My father was verbally and physically abusive like half the men in town. So overpowering was the old man's dominance that my mother retreated into a dark place where no spark emerged. Valium and vodka numbed her into submission.

None of this turned me into a killer. I came to this life through free will.

Back in college, I was never in touch with the lifestyles of my sorority sisters, who were into sex, drugs, and rock and roll. I knew from the very beginning that would never be satisfying. I needed something more, something different. Once I killed someone, however, I found my true calling in life.

In a way, fate led me to kill people that didn't deserve to live. Other than one time, I never, ever killed anyone without a damned good reason. Even that time, I felt justified because I was learning my craft, honing my skills, if you will. I came to killing gradually, but once I started, I continued for more than three decades.

I'm not very comfortable writing about my life. I spent the first half of it building walls, packing my emotions into boxes, and pretending to be something I wasn't. Now, beginning my sixth decade, I unpacked those same boxes onto these pages, all the while still pretending to be someone I'm not. By no means have I provided an accounting all of my kills. Representative ones, memorable ones, but not the entire list. Yet, as I record my story in black and white, I see it's not a dark coming-of-age tale full of who-gives-a-shit trivia.

My life and what I did with it matters.

If you're reading this, I'm either in a facility where I can't pursue my craft and kill anyone else, or I'm dead. You may never understand why I became a killer. At times, I don't either.

Remember, we are not all what we seem.

I have violated your trust. Telling you what I did hurt you. I'm sorry for lying. One thing I know for certain. You can't tell anyone about what I did.

Ever.

CHAPTER TWO

ADJUSTING TO COLLEGE

1985

"How old are you anyway? Twelve?" Two years into my academic career at State, and nosy students continued to ask about my age. After skipping two grades in elementary school, I was barely sixteen when I arrived on campus as a freshman. Short and boyish of build, I couldn't help looking much younger than my fellow classmates.

"Ten. Why do you ask?" I didn't get many follow-up questions.

I'd graduated valedictorian from my rural high school, where, as a straight-A student, I earned a series of academic and needs-based scholarships, which enabled me to enroll in a pre-med program in any state university of my choice. Before arriving on the State campus, my goal was to graduate at the top of my class to have my pick of the best medical schools. I saw no reason for academic excellence not to be my norm.

I took to university life, living in a dorm and studying as much as I wanted, as smoothly as ice cream sliding down my throat. No one made fun of me for being a science geek in a university full of such geeks. I kept to myself, not so much because I didn't like people but because I didn't know how to make new friends. Growing up in a small town meant kids were born there and knew each other before they began kindergarten. No one moved in; a few moved away and were lost forever. In my house, no one made eye contact with Big Chigger, who would see it as a challenge to something he said or did. As a result, I looked away from people, not at them. I had to learn to smile and gaze into people's eyes without staring or flinching. At college, I hung around almost exclusively with other science majors, all of whom I met in class, most of whom were even more socially awkward than I was.

At the start of my junior year when I turned eighteen, my faculty adviser suggested I join a sorority. "You never know how much these associations will help later in life."

To me, sororities were little more than non-stop partying full of sex and drugs. "I don't have time. Besides, that's not who I am."

"Make time. You need to fit in," she said. "It's not good for you to seem so isolated."

I liked neither her order nor the negative attention she thought I attracted by being a loner; however, her advice reinforced my decision to create an entirely new me. I'd decided two weeks into my freshman year to work on developing a new facade to mask the country hillbilly I was. The more I watched students from urban backgrounds, the more I copied their mannerisms.

"What if I can't find a sorority where I would fit? What if none would accept me?"

"You might have to rush three or more to improve your odds," my advisor said. "Although with your GPA, you'll get picked up quickly."

With that, I learned that sorority and fraternity houses had to maintain both house and individual GPAs. It turned out I didn't have to worry, because the best one, Kappa Kappa Gamma, sought me out.

"We're looking at inviting you to join our house." The sorority president studied me during an interview over tea.

I took a tiny bite of a powdered sugar donut and didn't drop so much as a dusting on my black skirt or the navy-blue carpet in the living room. Vestiges of my up-country accent told her where I came from, but my newly acquired veneer of better manners reassured her that I no longer carried the uncouth country behavior like a remnant of an unsavory past.

"You want me because of my grade point average, don't you?" I smiled to let her know I knew the rules.

"Not at all." The president tried to pretend that wasn't the reason.

"I'm okay with it." I'd never have been asked to join if I didn't have a 4.0 GPA. Did she think I didn't get it? "Really."

The country girl me answered her questions factually; the more refined me used elevated speech patterns and exercised newly assimilated behavior. Both of these constituted the public face I manufactured to adapt to campus life. Two years of observation taught me that even if I had a country accent, I could be successful in life if I made the right first impression. Sounding "Southern" was acceptable; sounding "country" wasn't.

I smiled as if I couldn't wait to become a Kappa. Mentally, I thought what a crock of shit it all was, but I played my role well. The president accepted me.

When I left the cramped double room in the dorm, I hoped to be assigned a single in the sorority house. No such luck. My new room was larger than the old one, but otherwise the beds, desks with wooden chairs, bookshelves, closets, and bureaus were pretty much standard issue. The sorority house had newer paint and better carpeting, though. The bathrooms were smaller, but with more of them, I no longer faced shaving my legs with a dozen other girls lined up at the basins. One bathroom had a tub you could reserve for thirty-minute soaks. Even the hallways smelled clean and fresh.

When I opened the door to our room, my new roommate, whom I'd learned was the other GPA pledge, sat on the edge of her bed wrapped in a towel, pink lace panties peeking out. Long legs, long light-brown hair, and hazel eyes were in direct contrast to short, dark me.

"I had to shower the dorm grit off. I hope you don't mind if I picked my side of the room before you got here. We can switch, though, if you'd rather." My new sister and roommate introduced herself. "I'm a pre-law major."

"Not a problem." I carried in a stack of boxes and set them on my bed. "Well, Pre-Law, I'm in pre-med. Nice that we're both Pre-Somethings."

I watched her rub lotion on bare legs. I'd learned about lotion when I came to State. We never had money for such foolishness at home. My mother used Vaseline or Joe's Bag Balm on her hands when they became too chapped to work, if she used anything at all. I inhaled the lotion's ginger-orange scent and wondered what it would be like to have money to spend on such frivolous items.

"I'm going to be a prosecutor like my daddy and granddaddy."

"I'm going to be a doctor like no one in my family."

I observed Pre-Law with a wariness born from years of practice. If she was offended by having to room with an unsophisticated country girl, she didn't show it. Her face, open and interested in what I unpacked, put me at ease. She pulled on sweat pants and a T-shirt.

On her bed were thick comforters and piles of pillows. A series of family photos lined the back edge of her desk. Books on shelves, posters of her favorite rock group, and a coffee pot were in sharp contrast to what little I had to unpack.

"Looks like they roomed us together for a good reason. You know what they say, nerds of a feather."

I laughed at her joke.

Because I didn't own much, unpacking four boxes took all of five minutes. I hung my clothes in the closet and filled the dresser drawers with a few sets of plain white panties and bras, socks, and one pair of pajamas. Until now, I'd gotten away with standard college garb: jeans, T-shirts, and some sweatshirts. I owned the one good black skirt and white sweater I wore to the sorority interview, an outfit I bought at a local consignment shop with money I'd earned working at the student union. I tossed threadbare quilts my up-holler granny had made years earlier on the bed, stacked textbooks, novels, and a bunch of reference books on the shelves before I unboxed a dog skeleton mounted on a varnished slab of oak.

"What's with the skeleton?" Pre-Law sat cross-legged on her bed.

"Does it bother you?"

I'd had my share of trouble in my sophomore year with a roommate who tried to convince the dorm adviser to make me get rid of the skeleton. She failed. I didn't want a year-long, whiny repeat. I placed the skeleton on top of the bookshelf where I wouldn't bump it.

"I'm not sure. I've never shared a room with one, that's all."

"He doesn't bite." I grinned and stroked the bones in the tail. "He was my first science project back in fifth grade. I found him in the woods."

"You found it? How?"

§

After a week-long mid-summer monsoon, the first sunny day found me pulling on an old jacket and worn rubber boots for a tramp outdoors. Mushrooms, toadstools, and moss exploded in a riot of colors and shapes. When I bent under a redbud tree to harvest mushrooms for a stew, a bird rustled overhead and sent a shower from wet leaves down my neck. A crow cawed and rose about a dozen yards up the ravine, which ran along the back of our property. I hiked along until my nostrils caught the distinct scent of something dead. I rounded the last bend and found a partly decomposed dog.

§

"I followed the smell. At first, I thought it might be old Hooter James, our down-the-lane neighbor, because it smelled as bad as he did, but Hooter wasn't out and about that day."

Pre-Law turned pale. She swallowed hard a couple of times. I watched her carefully. I'd have trouble if she was squeamish. Pre-med courses could be grim to anyone outside the program, and I wanted to be able to talk about what excited me. Other than school work, I had little to talk about and fewer interests.

I goofed up once in my sophomore year when I left *Gray's Anatomy* open to images of the human brain. My then roommate ordered me not to do it again. I wanted to tell her to keep her eyes on her own damned desk and leave mine alone, but because I didn't want to pick a fight, I shut the book whenever I left the room.

"As you can tell from the way I sound, I grew up in the country. I found lots of dead animals in the woods. Usually, carrion feeders and raptors got to a carcass long before I did but not this time. The crow had barely begun pecking at the rotting flesh, which was crawling with thousands of maggots."

"Eww. That must've been awful." Pre-Law's eyes opened wide behind Buddy Holly glasses.

I shrugged. "I didn't think so. I ran up to the house, got a couple of buckets and a shovel, and scooped up the remains. Back at the house, I boiled the mess in a big stew pot on the stove to get rid of the flesh."

"Double eww. That's so gross." Pre-Law went from pale to ashen. a sheen glistened on her forehead and upper lip.

When I looked back on it, cooking a dead dog on the stove was both pretty gross and pretty stupid. I should have waited for the maggots to pick the bones clean. Instead, I'd been so excited about finding a complete skeleton, I made a mistake and got in trouble.

"Yeah. By the time my mother and sister came back from shopping, I had the skeleton drying in the shed, a pile of cooked rotten flesh in the burn barrel, and too much stink in the house to pretend I hadn't done anything."

§

My family never wasted money or time collecting stuff. We made do with what we were given. My sister had a couple of dolls, I had a barn cat, and my brother had a BB gun. Other than my sweet gray tabby, Miss Snickers, this skeleton was the only thing I cared about. It had traveled with me since I left home. I ran a finger along the vertebrae.

My brother tried to grab it once to destroy it. He hit me in the stomach to make me release my grip.

"Leggo!" He kicked my shins, but my grip only tightened. He screamed his rage, which brought my mother running from the kitchen.

She grabbed him by his collar and pulled him off me. "That ain't yours. Don't let me catch you touching it again."

She shook him hard before releasing him. When she turned back toward the kitchen, he pinched my stomach hard enough to leave a dark bruise. I stowed the skeleton high in my closet where he couldn't reach it.

§

Pre-Law stood on tiptoe to look more closely. Was she looking for a collar? A bullet hole through the skull? "What'd your mother do?"

The story begged to be finished. "She puked all over the kitchen floor. So did my sister. Right after I cleaned everything up, Big Chigger—"

"Who?"

"My old man. Anyway, he came in from work and popped me a good one right across the chops."

"He hit you?" Pre-Law sounded horrified.

"Wasn't any big thing." It was, but I wasn't about to admit it to a stranger.

§

Big Chigger would smack my brother and me around whenever he felt like it, which was about as often as he got drunk, which was nearly every Saturday night. He didn't hit his favorite kid, my older sister, Princess, very often.

The old man had never said he was proud of me for anything, not even after I was accepted into a top university for free. He didn't respect me; I didn't much like him. I didn't expect a party when I packed to leave, but I'd hoped for some fleeting acknowledgment of my accomplishments. When my mother carried a box to the old car one of my aunts had given me, she slipped twenty dollars from her hidden tip jar into my pocket.

"For gas."

The Saturday I drove away, my sister was on a date, and my brother, who had outgrown his BB gun, stalked the woods with his .22. I heard two shots in quick succession and wondered if the family would have fresh meat for supper.

"I'm off," I said to the old man's back. He didn't reply.

The set of his shoulders under his tattered flannel shirt told me more than words. "Git out and stay out."

§

"I got an A on the project. It started my fascination with biology. I kept Old Rex to piss off my brother. He hated that he couldn't have it or break it."

"Old Rex? Was he your dog?"

"No. Just a dog. I named him Old Rex to give him his own identity. Somehow, Dead Dog didn't seem dignified enough."

CHAPTER THREE

SETTLING INTO SORORITY LIFE

1985

Like all students, I needed spending money. My family didn't have a dime to spare, so I worked in the student union. I spent part of my money on Aikido lessons, because I'd taken a class billed as self-defense for women early in my freshman year. While I enjoyed the forms and movements of this Japanese martial art, I was fascinated with the mental training, which included meditation. I learned to control my heart rate and to focus intently, an ability I put to its fullest effect in class daily.

Pre-Law and I shared bits of our lives and our course work in our first weeks of rooming together. My junior courses were mostly science lectures and labs; Pre-Law packed in several heavy reading courses on international law and Constitutional history.

"I need to learn as much about the Constitution as I can," she said one Friday evening when we walked across campus to the student union to clear our brains after a week of tests and quizzes. We were three weeks from midterms, so this round was a prelude for the more important exams.

"Why?" We'd talked often about her love of the law. "You're not going to be a Constitutional scholar, are you?"

"No, but it'll be important no matter where I go to law school. We'll have courses in it, and I want to be prepared."

When she brought a copy of the Constitution back to our room, I was surprised at how thin it was. A couple of days later she dropped a tome of interpretations of the original document on her desk.

"It looks thicker than *Gray's Anatomy*." We put the books side by side. Her law book won.

We grabbed ice cream cones at the student union and licked our way back to the sorority house perched on its hill. I didn't like the commercial flavors as much as our homemade ones, but any ice cream was better than none. In our room, Pre-Law pulled out note paper to write to her mother. I sorted through several books I'd bought at a local library sale. My small collection grew rapidly. Most of the time, I read mysteries, thrillers, and suspense. I also had an expanding non-fiction shelf of true crime and analyses of famous murderers.

"With your interest in murder," Pre-Law finished her letter and flipped onto her stomach before punching a pillow into shape under her chest, "maybe you should be a criminal attorney instead of a doctor."

"I don't think so. Don't get me wrong. I love Nancy Drew and modern, grittier thriller writers like Robin Cook and Lawrence Sanders." I refrained for telling her how intrigued I was with the details of violent death. That image wouldn't match the under-construction new public me. "I got interested in the different ways people killed each other."

"I read a lot of novels written by lawyers. Most are courtroom dramas by Erle Stanley Gardner or private investigator novels by Raymond Chandler." Pre-Law opened the Constitution but didn't look at it. "I asked my dad if what we watched on television or read in books was really what happened in his courtroom."

"His courtroom?"

"I guess I forgot to tell you. He's a judge."

"Oh."

"Anyway, he said the shenanigans on Perry Mason were decent theater but lousy law." Pre-Law pulled at a stray thread on her shirt sleeve. "When I close my eyes, I see myself in a courtroom sending murderers away for life."

I pushed my pillows against the wall, propped a new book about Jack the Ripper on my stomach, and plunged into a psychological analysis on what might have made him tick. How he brutalized and murdered women was red meat of legend. The more I read, the more I realized he was one sick son of a bitch. I wanted to understand why this unidentified man became "Jack the Ripper."

CHAPTER FOUR

ACCIDENTS CAN BE LETHAL

1985

My efforts to blend seamlessly into sorority life paid off gradually. I was studious, friendly, and helpful. The only area where I was noticeably different was in my dating habits. I didn't date.

Pre-Law and I went to a few parties, both on and off campus. I was always the designated driver off-campus, because I couldn't legally drink for three more years. If I got caught drinking and driving, I could lose my scholarship. I had no interest in alcohol, though, having grown up with a drunken father and a mother who kept a hidden bottle of vodka to calm her nerves.

I hadn't yet dated solo, not that I didn't want to, but the few boys who asked me out were even geekier than I was. I might have been the only girl on campus still a virgin by chance and not by choice. Because I wasn't into the frat or bar scene, I didn't know where to meet someone I wanted to have sex with. I had no romantic fantasy about the first time being special, but I did want a decent experience. The boys in high school who had asked me out hoped I was a slut like my sister, or had been as cruel as my younger brother or a bully like Big Chigger.

I wasn't even all that sure about what getting laid entailed. That wasn't not completely true. I understood the biology and physiology of sex, but I didn't know what it would feel like or how to achieve the screaming orgasms I read about in erotic novels.

After midterms, Pre-Law and I walked to a frat house hosting a post-football game kegger. We'd barely turned off the sidewalk when a chorus of hoots and whistles filled the air. A dozen half-drunk guys formed a gauntlet out front. One by one, they snagged my sisters and led them away. Only two remained. The geekiest-looking boy claimed me.

"I'll take the weird-looking one." He squinted through thick glasses. "She kinda looks black."

I glanced over my shoulder. Could he mean me?

"I've never been with a black woman before."

"And you still haven't. I'm not black."

"If you're not black, what are you?"

I didn't look like your average hill-country girl from Bubbaville, which is what I called my hometown. My skin was olive; my hair was nearly black and curly. I looked more like my granny who claimed I was a throwback to Melungeon mixed-race ancestors from Appalachia. I never knew if that was true or not, but a heritage of white, Native American, and black would explain why I looked different from the rest of my immediate family.

I bit my tongue even though I wanted to pinch his head off.

"Come on. Are you an Ay-rab? Mexican?"

"Neither."

Who the hell needed labels? I didn't care what he thought my race was. I wanted to walk away, but if I dumped him, I'd stand out by being alone. The other guys had disappeared into the house with the rest of my sisters; even Pre-Law had vanished. The geek, pudgy and wearing uncool horn-rimmed glasses, must have be the frat equivalent of me, the ringer pledged for his grade point average. I tried to edge away, but he clamped a sweaty hand on my wrist, dragged me through a filthy kitchen and out onto the balcony where he pushed me toward the rail. I twisted away, repulsed by sour beer breath. In that moment, vivid memories of my drunken father transformed the geek into Big Chigger.

"Hey, slow down. I just got here." I tried to pry his fingers loose and squirmed to get blood circulating in my hand. Jeez, what a loser. He even had a flourishing crop of zits on his checks and nose.

"You came to the best place on campus for a little one-on-one action. We all give as good as we get." Loser leaned over and puckered his lips.

I might have been a virgin, but I expected some conversation, maybe even some foreplay, before being slimed by a stranger's pudgy lips. He leered. Maybe he was flirting. Maybe he had gas. I hoped he wasn't going to puke.

"Stop it."

We were alone on a balcony dimly lit by a single bulb and overflowing with rancid trash bags, stacks of empty pizza boxes, and cases of empties. I searched the backyard for an escape route, but I only saw more bags of garbage, a mountain of crushed beer cans, and no stairway down. Loser stood between me and the only way out, the kitchen door. A prickle of fear tinged with an adrenaline rush made me hyperaware of my situation. Whether by using verbal put downs or applying my newly-learned Aikido skills, this Pillsbury Doughboy was going to be no threat if he tried to get physical.

"You look weird. What's wrong with your eyes?"

I gave him credit for noticing my eyes, so dark blue the iris and pupil were almost the same color. No one in my family, no one I'd ever met, had such singular eyes. As drunk as he was, I was surprised he could focus.

"Nothing."

"Ah, come on. I didn't mean any harm. Let's have some fun."

I couldn't imagine doing anything with him would be fun. He forced me against the railing again; I pushed him away. He didn't get the message, because he kept trying to feel my breasts. Under my shirt, no less. He pawed at me with dirty hands and pulled up my bra. One rough nail scratched my nipple. In a nanosecond, I went from wanting to get away to fury, from wanting him to leave me alone to needing revenge.

With the old man's drunken face superimposed between me and Loser, I wanted to hurt him in ways I had never been able to hurt the old man. I had to regain control before I did something I'd regret. I sucked in a deep breath and willed myself to be still. No matter that I'd come to the frat party with the hope of getting laid, this idiot quashed all desire. He wasn't going to get me into bed. Or on the floor. Or wherever he thought we'd do it.

"Why the hell did you come if you don't want some action? You're a geek, and we geeks have to stick together."

Was this bumbling invitation foreplay? How could anyone be so crude and hope to score? If I got him drunk enough, though, he might leave me alone. He was most of the way to blotto already. He crumpled his empty and clanged it onto a growing pile in the backyard.

A girl I didn't know walked out onto the balcony with a tray. "Jell-O shots."

"What?"

"Vodka and green Jell-O," the girl said. "Want to try one?"

I shook my head. Loser grabbed several and popped them in his mouth. While he was busy slurping them down, I sidled toward the kitchen door.

"How about I get us both a beer?"

"Don't forget to come back, huh?" He wiped green drool on the back of his hand.

"I won't." He was so gross my public facade almost shattered, but I managed a wink.

In the kitchen, dishes, more empty pizza boxes, and crushed beer and soda cans covered every surface and most of the floor. A cockroach skittered around the debris into a crack in the baseboard; a line of ants cleaned a smear of grease off the sink.

A crowd gathered around white powder cut in thin lines on the only clear spot on the counter top. Three people bent over and inhaled cocaine through straws. Our sorority president stepped back, giggled, and rubbed a trace on her gums. I thought about running out the front door, but first I needed to teach the creep a lesson. An open baggie lay abandoned on a table. I grabbed it, opened a Bud Light, and emptied some powder into the can. I had no idea if mixing cocaine with beer would get anyone high or not. Too bad Loser wasn't drinking Coke laced with coke. I'd have enjoyed the irony.

"Here." I handed him the can. He took a long slug.

"Braaap."

More memories surfaced of the old man and his Saturday night noises. Loser mumbled and grabbed hold of me. Whether the cocaine or beer or vodka kicked in at that moment or not, his knees buckled. He blinked twice and hit the balcony floor face down with a fleshy smack.

"Hey, guys. I need a little help here." I called into the kitchen. I threw his beer can onto the pile.

"Shit. Not again." Two frat boys carried him into the house and dumped him on a broken futon.

"He do any of the shots?"

"Yes." I pointed to the green stain on his lips.

"Man, he knows better. He can't handle hard liquor."

I pretended to be concerned with Loser's safety when I rolled him onto his back and locked his feet under the futon's wooden armrest. I knew if he puked, one of three things could happen: he could free his feet and roll over to get sick on the floor; he could foul himself; or he could aspirate vomit into his lungs and die. I didn't much care which way it went. I'd at least get even for him pawing me.

I turned to search for my roommate to tell her I was leaving when she grabbed my arm and dragged me outside.

"Let's get the hell out of this dump." She shuddered and looked over her shoulder. She didn't know about Loser.

"What's going on?"

"I stumbled into a bedroom where I saw a guy fucking a girl, her legs in the air and her hands holding his butt to keep him in tight, and two other guys naked, erect, and waiting their turns."

"Jeez."

Pre-Law shook her head. "One of the guys tried to grab me. He said he wanted more 'variety' in his round-robin sex." She had fought him off and fled.

"I saw one of our sisters draped over the shoulders of a football player with a posse of horny guys in pursuit. I'm not into group sex or rape." She took a deep breath. "I was coming to find you."

The campus was abuzz the next day. According to the campus grapevine, Clarence West, a.k.a. Loser, was found dead at the Epsilon Theta Phi fraternity house at 7:15 am on Sunday by two residents.

"Oh, hell," said our sorority president. "That house was already on probation for a hazing death earlier in the year. The national headquarters will revoke the charter after last night."

A sister wrapped in a towel walked down the hall toward the showers. "I'll sure as hell miss it. It was the best party house ever."

I looked at Pre-Law who shrugged. Neither of us knew if this was the girl Pre-Law saw on the bed.

Campus cops sent out a message that they wanted to interview anyone who attended the party. When they came to our house, this really cute cop walked up to me.

Before he could ask anything, I spoke up. "How did he die?" The rumor mill never mentioned the cause of death.

"We're fairly certain he drowned in his own vomit."

Well, now. One of the three options worked.

He flipped open his cop notebook. "This won't take long. What can you tell me?"

"He was drinking a lot." With great effort, I kept myself from blatantly flirting. The cop couldn't have been much older than twenty-one. "Beer and Jell-O shots."

"Drugs?"

"What do you think, officer? I saw plenty of cocaine." I barely kept the exasperation from my voice. "It was a frat party, after all."

"Did you drink? Do drugs?" The cop scribbled a pencil mark on a lined page.

"Look, I'm eighteen. I don't drink. I don't do drugs. It's not my thing." I tucked my hair behind one ear, exposing high cheekbones. The questions bored me out of my flipping skull, but I faked concern.

"Who else talked with him?"

"I'm not sure. We were out on the balcony where he put away a few beers and Jell-O shots. People came and went all the time. He seemed pretty popular." He was a damned nerd. Nerds don't have a lot of friends. Look at me. "I met him when I first arrived. We kinda hit it off."

"Can you remember anything else?" The cop closed his notebook.

"He passed out on the balcony. I helped a couple of his brothers carry him inside and lay him on the futon. I wanted to be sure he was all right, then left. Sorry I can't be of any more help."

I got more of a thrill fooling the cop than participating in Loser's messy demise. Why shouldn't he believe me? I hadn't done anything wrong.

§

In a corner of the campus coffee shop a few days later, I scattered an organic chemistry text and several standard black-and-white lab books on the table. Three books filled with notes and equations hid a fresh, unused one underneath.

I took a mental tally of what I'd done to lead Loser to his death and what I'd learned from the experience. I'd acted on impulse when I dumped cocaine into his beer. Stupid because anyone in the kitchen could have seen me. I had to guard against letting reactions to my old man's past behavior influence my current behavior. I'd become angry and reckless, and I'd been lucky.

I jotted notes about Loser, how I felt when he pawed me. I wrote about how he reminded me of Big Chigger. I paused and stared with unfocused eyes across the coffee shop before I added how I felt when I heard Loser was dead. Not a damned thing. I mean, nothing, nada, zilch. No remorse. No elation. No one suspected I'd wedged his feet under the futon arm on purpose.

Fooling the cop was more titillating. Mulling over the two previous days, I realized what I had done didn't satisfy me. What if merely getting even for boorish behavior wasn't enough? A crystal-clear question hung in mid-air: what would it feel like to actually kill someone?

I marked the book with a tiny scratch on the bottom of the spine.

CHAPTER FIVE

MY REDNECK FAMILY

1985

Late one night, bat-blind and brain-numb from studying, I pulled on my one worn pair of jammies, propped myself on pillows, and grabbed a novel. Pre-Law pushed the door open, twin aromas of soap and popped corn sweeping in with her. "Not a single char-broiled kernel this time."

"That's a first."

She upended an empty wastebasket and set the silver bag between our beds before flopping onto hers. She tossed individual pieces of popcorn into the air, catching them in her mouth.

"I got a letter from my mom today." She smiled at framed pictures of her family arranged precisely on her desk and pulled the letter from her book bag. She shared some of the news. "Dad finished a grueling trial. Drugs, murder, two-timing spouses. Mom said it would've made a terrible soap opera had five people not been killed."

"Did he win?" I tossed a piece of popcorn in the air. I hunted for it before finding it in my jammie top.

"Judges don't win or lose. Justice does, but the jury found the defendants guilty, so in a way he won." She shrugged higher onto her pillows. "I can't wait to practice law. It's our family tradition. I'm the oldest of four, and my daddy hoped I'd follow him into the law. I plan to."

"I'm the middle kid and the only one to go to college." I snaked out a hand to snatch more munchies. "Ever."

"You mean your parents didn't go?"

Time for me to set matters straight.

"I mean, Big Chigger quit high school in the ninth grade to support his family. He had to get a high school equivalency certificate to join the army. After he married Li'l Bit, she put on airs about being a high school grad. That didn't set well with the old man's up-holler family, I can tell you."

Pre-Law nibbled on a few bits of popcorn, her brow creased in concentration. "Did you know your whole expression changes when you talk about your family?"

"It does?" It shouldn't.

"Yes, your vocabulary and pronunciation both shift big time. Much more hill country than usual." Pre-Law laughed. "I almost don't recognize this side of you."

"It's the part of me I'm trying to leave behind. I'm not belittling my family, because they are what they are." I'd have to work harder on erasing all traces of my home town from my words and mannerisms. "I can't change them, so I set out to change me."

"Please don't get me wrong. I'm not being critical." Pre-Law tossed a popcorn kernel at me. I caught it in my hand and ate it. "You've done a terrific job creating a new personality."

"Thanks. It's hard to explain, because our backgrounds are so different." I rolled onto my side, head propped on my arm.

"That's what makes you interesting. My upbringing was pretty normal for a sixth-generation Charlestonian." Pre-Law stretched until her vertebrae popped.

"Who knows what generation those of us in small hill towns are? We've kinda always stayed where we're born."

"My family stayed put, too. My great granddaddy was a West Virginia governor and later a Senator for, like, ever. Granddaddy was a judge, and so is Daddy. He'll probably run for governor or the Senate soon. It's in his blood." Pre-Law reached up and tucked the letter into a holder on her book shelf between two framed pictures. I didn't have a letter holder.

"Did you have a choice?" I picked unpopped old maids out of the bowl and tossed them in my trashcan. "Did you have to go into law?"

"Actually, I had plenty of choices. My folks encouraged me to be myself. Except 'myself' wants to put criminals in jail. The best way to do that is to be a district attorney. That isn't making my daddy any too happy. He'd rather see me in private practice than dealing with hardened criminals."

"Not at all like my family." I remembered to drop more of my country inflections. "From childhood on I was told women were expected to have kids and take care of the house. Men were masters of their domains."

"Get real. Does that crap still exist? I thought it went out in the fifties." Pre-Law's eyes widened behind her glasses as she scoffed at my reality.

"Maybe elsewhere, but not in Bubbaville. Not in my family."

"Bubbaville?"

"That's not the town's real name. It could apply to a couple dozen surrounding hamlets. I hated it there. I couldn't wait to leave.

I call it Bubbaville to remind me I'm never going back."

I yawned and turned off my light. I wished I could turn off my memories as easily. Things I didn't want to think about or share with Pre-Law rumbled through my mind. Talking about the past opened it to scrutiny and misunderstanding.

Even thinking about my family left me feeling exposed. If I poked my head up and called attention to myself, Big Chigger would go nuclear and smack me as surely as he'd hit a fly with the swatter. He took out his frustration with being a failure as a man and as a husband by hitting someone. Or someones. Mostly, the someones were Junior and me. I made a mistake of complaining about him to my school friends one time.

"What the hell are you talking about? No one cares what goes on in your family," they said. It had always been like that and always would be. I couldn't explain to Pre-Law how the old man treated me. She'd either not believe me or pity me. I didn't want either.

I tried to pretend it wasn't a particularly bad life, except for having to go to church on Sunday with my mother. She'd taken up with a Pentecostal group before I was born. Most of the congregation were regular folks until the annual revival came to town, when they turned into snake handlers and foam-at-the-mouth fanatics speaking in tongues. This turned me off so badly I'd make myself vomit to get out of going. Princess whined her way out of attending; Junior never went because he acted out the first time he was forced to go. He was told not to return.

The old man refused to become a member after he and the pastor had a near-violent argument. Big Chigger had sat through an altar call and wouldn't crawl forward to beg the Lord's forgiveness.

"You're a sinner," thundered the pastor in his fit of weekly passion.

"And you're an ass," the old man shouted after services one Sunday.

Li'l Bit's hands flew to her mouth. She tried to pull Big Chigger aside, but he shook her off.

"Blasphemer! Leave this house of worship and never return."

My old man stomped out and drove away. No member of the congregation felt safe taking us home, so Li'l Bit and I walked five miles. Big Chigger would see any help as a slight toward himself and never forgive them. What I remember was the old man obeying a direct order from the preacher to leave and later hitting me when we finally walked into the house. Somehow, he made it my fault Sunday dinner was late, even though all Princess had to do was put the flame on under the stew pot.

My life wasn't all that different from the way my school friends lived, minus the snake charmers. We didn't know about alternatives, so we didn't much fuss about how we were growing up without. Without opportunities. Without money. Without hope.

Each of us kids had real names, but nobody used them. I didn't even know what mine was until Li'l Bit enrolled me in kindergarten. Then, she ruined everything by telling the administration clerk the family called me That Thing.

"I'm sorry. That Thing?" The clerk looked up from in penciling in letters in boxes on the school registration form. "What do you mean?"

"I mean, she don't look like Princess, her older sister. You know, the pretty little one with blond pigtails and blue eyes. She's two years older and in second grade. My husband calls this one the niggah in the woodpile. Says she must have been left on our doorstop by the devil, 'cause she's so dark," Li'l Bit said. "He called her That Thing. Sorta stuck."

In an act of self-preservation, I embraced the anonymity of That Thing, because I refused to be part of any family that didn't want me. No way was I going to quit on my alter ego.

§

Pre-Law talked so often about her family that I felt I knew them. When she tucked away her mother's weekly letter, she said, "You've never gotten mail from your folks or your sister, have you?"

"No." Hell would freeze over before Li'l Bit wrote.

"Why not? Don't they want to share your life at college?"

Share my life? They didn't give a damn about me. "The family's not much for writin,' I mean, writing."

"But…" Pre-Law got no further.

"My folks shunned me from birth and called me That Thing. When I left, they said good riddance. I don't care to hear from them."

Pre-Law went silent. My tone indicated I'd had more than enough of the conversation.

CHAPTER SIX

ABNORMAL PSYCH 101

1986

I escaped the hollowness caused by my family's rejection by throwing myself into my studies and by pretending to be someone I wasn't. I tried on different roles I read about in the novels I devoured. While the police and federal agents in many of the thrillers were interesting, I was drawn to the murderers, rapists, and serial killers. Trying their skins on was both a challenge and a deep thrill. It could also be frightening. Still, I wondered what it would feel like to kill someone.

I rejoiced when rapists were captured, because what they did to women was vile beyond words, but the serial killers were my favorites. Even those killers who acted out of blood lust had their own, often unrevealed, rationale. Too few books explored their psyches, though. Authors focused more on the "how the good guys caught the bad guys" rather than "what made the bad guys bad." I wanted to know what part of their psyches led them to do what they did.

The deeper I went into my pre-med and psychology classes, the more curious I became about abnormal behavior, particularly with the characteristics sociopaths and psychopaths exhibited. Whenever someone committed a heinous crime, journalists trotted out such terms without knowing what each meant and without distinguishing between the two. Murderers, in particular, must not have a conscience because of the often-horrific nature of their crimes, some anchors would say. They didn't know squat about what went on inside a killer's mind, nor did they care to find out. The television news mantra of the day was, "If it bleeds, it leads." Sensational reporting pushed in-depth analysis to the cutting room floor.

My introductory psych text didn't give me enough information on things like narcissistic, anti-social, or borderline personality disorders, or other commonly misused terms, so I asked my prof for outside reading.

"Check out the *Diagnostic and Statistical Manual of Mental Disorders* in the library. *DSM*'s the bible on all types of abnormal behavior." My prof squeaked back in a heavy wooden desk chair, fingers steepled under his bearded chin. He peered over the rims of his glasses. A cold pipe leaned against the lip of a crystal ashtray, the ideal prop for a Freudian look-alike. "Read the newly published research by Robert Hare, too. He's developed a great checklist of traits of abnormal behavior. He's easier to understand than the *DSM*."

"Thanks." I edged toward the door.

"Funny. I never figured you would be interested in psychiatry."

"Why not?"

"I don't know. I don't see you sitting in an office listening to people tell you their problems." He lit his pipe and sent a stream of smoke ceiling-ward. "You seem more inclined to an active specialty where you would have hands-on experience and see more immediate results."

"I don't see me being a psychiatrist either, but understanding both normal and abnormal behavior could come in handy no matter what my specialty will be."

"You're right," he said. "Keep all options open. Come back with any questions. This stuff's pretty dense."

Did he think I wouldn't understand what I was reading? Did he think I was stupid?

"Thanks. I'm sure I'll need help." The purposefully charming me smiled.

I devoured psychology books. I practiced analyzing my family background, everything about nature versus nurture, and my brother and sister who exhibited multiple abnormal traits. Sexual promiscuity was a big red flag according to both the *DSM* and Hare. My sister, Princess, got herself pregnant before graduation and didn't even know who the kid's father was. We had a real family donnybrook when Big Chigger found out.

"Whaddya mean you don't know who knocked you up? Just how many guys you sleep with?" The old man loomed over her, fists bunched, neck veins bulging.

"Don't make such a big deal out of it," Princess sassed.

Big Chigger backhanded her across the mouth, the first time I remember him hitting her in the face. She started crying and ran to Li'l Bit for support. I turned my back, glad the old man wasn't hitting me for once.

"Don't make a big deal of it? How'm I gonna get him to pay for the kid if you don't know who the hell he is?" Typical of the old man. His one-track mind reduced life to money, either the lack of it or a scheme to cadge some from anyone he could.

"Not gonna ask. Don't care." Princess stood firm. "Don't want him to know."

"Well, we ain't gonna raise your bastard." The old man stomped out, the warped screen door banging shut behind him.

The high school dropout with a snot-nosed brat lived at home where she sponged off our parents. No matter how Big Chigger threatened her, Li'l Bit protected her. Emotional shallowness and sexual irresponsibility were two characteristics of a psychopath. Princess was promiscuous and had all the depth of a child's wading pool, but she was no psychopath.

Junior, on the other hand, never lifted a finger to get a job or a life. He tortured and killed small animals for the hell of it when he was a kid. He bragged about it. When Big Chigger caught him burning a live squirrel, about all Junior got as punishment was a boot in the ass. He hit, bit, and pinched me, always where the marks wouldn't show. He exhibited many characteristics of a sociopath.

Life with Big Chigger beat the rest of them down but not me. Education was my ticket out. When I was young, my mother told me about graduating from high school and how she dreamed of going to college. After she married this handsome guy in an Army uniform, left her home in what she would later refer to as the gentility of the Piedmont, and moved to the mountains, her dreams died with the birth of her first child. By the time I came along, she dreamed through my sister. I received little overflow.

"Don't you end up like me in a dead-end job," Li'l Bit warned. The tips she earned waiting tables added to what the old man made at Sears and let us buy necessities we couldn't make at home.

More like a dead-end life. "Don't worry. I won't."

Going to college would set me free. The old man about busted a gut when I told him what I wanted to do. "You just forget that bullshit. You ain't going nowhere."

The deeper I studied the *DSM*, the more I understood that the majority of psychopaths were charismatic. Charm didn't pertain to anyone in my family, but I learned to be friendly and helpful once I got away from Bubbaville and copied Pre-Law's behavior.

Psychopaths usually possessed above average intelligence. Way above average. This I could relate to.

§

In those days, kids took standardized IQ tests that defined intelligence and placed us on career paths. Most kids didn't know how they did. We found out when we were channeled into college prep, general studies, auto shop, or home economics.

One night at dinner, Princess lit into me with no warning and for no apparent reason beyond the hormonal roller coaster caused by her pregnancy. She started carping on me as soon as we sat to eat.

"You never do anything to help around here."

I stared at her, certain her whine deserved no response.

"You should do all my chores. After all, I'm going to have a baby." Hands on her belly, Princess played the pregnancy card once too often.

"Hey, I didn't knock you up. Not my problem."

"Both of you, shut your mouths." Big Chigger slugged back his nightly beer.

Smoke curled from beanbag ashtrays next to him and my mother, who slurped her coffee. Remains of corn on the cob, fried pork chop bones, congealed milk gravy, and lumps of cold mashed potatoes dirtied plates. Princess and Junior squabbled over whose turn it was to wash the dishes.

"I did it yesterday," Princess said. "It's your turn."

"Uh uh. I did it the day before." Junior crossed his arms across his chest in imitation of Big Chigger. "It's That Thing's turn."

"You didn't do it the day before. I did," I said. "Besides I have to study for a test tomorrow."

I carried a load of glasses and tableware to the sink.

"Study? All you do is study." Junior humped plates to the counter top. "Ain't that so, Dad?"

"Don't know. Don't care." When I picked up his plate, Big Chigger blew a stream of cigarette smoke in my face. "Junior, you wash up, you hear?"

"But it's not my turn."

"Is if I say it is." Big Chigger stabbed his cigarette butt into leftover mashed potatoes.

"That Thing must be stupid to have to study so hard." Junior turned the water on to fill the sink.

"We'll see about that." I marched out of the kitchen and returned with a yellowing paper, which I unfolded and flattened on the table. I'd hidden it in the back of my panties drawer a year earlier.

I peered at the paper. "Actually, it's the other way around."

"What's that?" Big Chigger tried to snatch it, but I was at the far end of the table. He couldn't reach me without standing up.

"It's the results of our IQ tests. Let's see what it says." I smoothed the folds of the paper.

My mother turned pale, but she didn't move. "You got no right reading that. It's private."

Junior shut off the water to listen.

"Hmm. Princess, eighty-five."

She preened. Did she think eighty-five was a terrific score?

"It's not eight-five out of one hundred." I pointed to Junior. "You. Seventy-four."

"I'm smarter than you are," Princess gloated, her sing-song taunt designed to enflame her brother.

Even Junior knew he didn't have a good score. His face reddened.

"My IQ is north of one fifty." I handed the paper to Big Chigger, who read it, wadded it up, and threw it in my face.

"You guys were right all along," I said. "I can't be part of this family. I'm not borderline stupid like Junior or even slightly below average like Princess. I'm borderline genius."

I turned to Li'l Bit, who wept into a handkerchief. "So, who's my father? It can't be him." I jerked my head at the old man whose face now matched his hair.

"She called me stupid." Junior's voice rose in self-righteous anger. "I'm gonna kill her."

"Shut up." The old man bellowed over Junior's blubbering. "She told you the truth. You're one dumb son of a bitch."

Could Big Chigger actually be taking my side?

I walked outside to sit in our old, creaky rocker on the front porch. My hands shook, but inside I gloated. I'd gotten even with the entire family with one yellowing piece of paper. I rocked and listened to Big Chigger light into Junior and Princess. I heard a hand strike flesh.

Miss Snickers ran mewing from the barn and flung herself in my lap. The shouting in the kitchen formed a counterpoint to her purrs, a cow lowing in the pasture, and wet manure plops from one of the steers. I buried my face in my cat's soft fur and smiled.

CHAPTER SEVEN

DID I REALLY WANT TO BE A KILLER?

1986

One late winter night when Pre-Law was on a date, I couldn't concentrate, so I threw on a sweatshirt and a jacket and walked around campus. In the dark before moonrise, air cooling toward cold, students moved along, going somewhere, coming from somewhere else. Pools of incandescent light on the black path belonged in an Ingmar Bergman film. Colors the campus displayed during the day leached away; branches arched skyward in homage to a moon not yet over the eastern horizon. Shadows whispered secrets on the breeze.

I fell into a walking meditation, eyes downcast, my body moving on autopilot. Step by step, I emptied my mind as my Aikido teacher had instructed. Ideas arose, allowing me to examine each before deciding if this was the time to pursue it. If not, I pushed it aside. I sorted through the questions until only one remained. I couldn't believe how obvious the answer was, why I had been so restless. It'd been staring at me from the time it hung in the air at the coffee house after Loser's death.

What would it feel like to actually kill someone?

I retraced my steps to the sorority house with more haste than when I left. I lay on my bed, lights out, fingers interlaced behind my head. The remaining thought took on a second element: how would it feel to kill and get away with it?

Where I'd been tangentially involved in Loser's death, I hadn't killed him. I'd merely facilitated his demise. I needed to commit a real kill, one I choreographed from beginning to end, one where I alone was the instrument in the death of another human being, and one where I could watch it unfold. Only then could I differentiate between the idea of killing and the reality of killing. Only committing a real kill would answer the question.

I ran through a mental catalog of different ways a person could die at the hands of another, because killers differed wildly in technique. One breed staged the scene to look like the death was accidental, but I was pretty certain I wanted the police to find the body and know it didn't get there by accident. I wanted to match wits with them and feel fulfilled when they failed to find me. What if that buzz was as good as or better than the actual kill? My challenge now was to see if I could pull off a cold-blooded act.

I couldn't imagine using a gun, which was noisy and would limit the killing location. That breed of killer was showy or at least show-off-y. Besides, I had no training as a sniper. The old man kept handguns and rifles in the house and taught us kids how to use them. Part of why I didn't like them went straight to Junior, who used his rifle indiscriminately to kill small animals, both domestic and wild, whenever he felt like it. He liked to shoot close to me to remind me he could hit me any time he wanted.

I couldn't imagine anything less fulfilling than sending a high-powered bullet to explode a head in clouds of pink mist from hundreds of yards away. I wanted to be close enough to watch the change of emotion when victims realized they were about to die.

Just as quickly, I ruled out slashing carotid arteries or using a garrote. Arterial spray would be hard to control; the killer's clothing would be soaked. No modern-day Jack the Ripper could walk away from a crime scene undetected. Stabbing in gas-lit London on foggy nights was the stuff of legend. My method would be tidier.

I dismissed technique after technique until I decided that I'd strangle a woman for my first kill. At a bit over five feet tall, I wasn't imposing, so I needed to pick someone on the smallish side. The police self-defense course had taught me how to cut off the blood flow to the brain by constricting the carotid arteries until the victim blacked out. My Aikido training left me with good upper body strength and quick hands and feet.

I read about how to strangle my victim without breaking the hyoid bone by putting my thumbs in the correct position on either side of the larynx. I was uninformed enough, even naïve enough, to think that an intact hyoid would make determining the cause of death more difficult. I didn't know then the many ways manual strangulation could be detected even by a second-rate medical examiner or coroner.

If I walked up to this stranger in some deserted place and grabbed her by the throat, her natural instincts would be to scratch, kick, and scream as she tried to free herself. For protection from scratches, I'd wear gloves and long sleeves. I'd tuck my hair under a ball cap to keep from contaminating the scene.

The more decisions I made, the more excited I became. My breathing increased until I was panting. One hand slipped inside my pants and between my thighs where I discovered I was wet. I rubbed myself until I climaxed. I remained on the bed, relaxed and satisfied for a while until I could no longer lie still. I had plans to make.

After turning on the desk lamp, I reached into my book bag for the black-and-white lab book where I'd recorded my response to Loser's death. If I was going to experiment, I had to apply scientific rigor with check points and reactions.

How long do I squeeze before she stops struggling?
Will she fight? If so, how?
Will she scream?
Will her eyes roll back?
Will her final expression be one of awareness of the inevitable?
What color will her face turn?
Will her tongue protrude?
How will she look stretched out on the ground?
What will I feel?

The more I visualized how a victim would react, the more I realized a ball cap and gloves were inadequate. Man, this killing shit was more complicated than I'd thought. What the hell should I wear?

All my life I'd had no interest in clothes. My mother, Li'l Bit, gave me hand-me-downs from Princess, regardless of whether they fit or were suitable. When my sister tired of something, Li'l Bit would find a way to make her a new dress.

Where to find the perfect outfit where I can hide in plain sight? Not the mall, because I wanted a work-worn disguise. I snapped my fingers.

Ten minutes after I walked into the Goodwill store the following Sunday with nothing in my hands, I left with two pairs of jeans two sizes too big, one pair a little too tight, four plain colored T-shirts, and a well-worn dark-gray, way-too-big hooded sweatshirt.

I grabbed a pair of scratched Ray-Bans at the register before I laid bills on the counter. Once again, I was happy I'd saved money from my part time job. I tucked everything into an abused backpack and stowed it in the back of my battered Ford Escort.

I chuckled as I picked through donations from strangers. What were the odds a future victim's belongings were in the store? What were the odds I'd wear said victim's clothes when I killed her? I bought things enough like my own clothes to be comfortable, yet different enough not to be recognizable immediately if I saw someone I knew. A cheap shoe store provided a pair of knock-off sneakers. With a Caterpillar cap from the gas station, I was dressed to kill.

With the how-to-kill and what-to-wear decisions behind me, the next logical one was where. Not near State because I couldn't chance meeting someone I knew. Back at freshman orientation, one tough-sounding professor had barked at us, "Never shit where you eat."

He meant, "Don't even think about trying to date a prof."

I changed the meaning to, "Don't kill in your own backyard."

I bought a Rand McNally atlas at the local gas station and an old-fashioned compass at the student union. I put the sharp point of the compass in the center of campus and drew a radius of one hundred fifty miles. I could drive that far and back in a day. If everything went right, I'd leave before breakfast, kill, and be home for dinner.

I wiped my palms on my jeans before putting my pinkie on the hole in the map left by the compass, shutting my eyes, and spinning the map book. I let my index finger fall on a spot within the circle. A community college town, Monroe Crossing, close enough to make a trip or two to get the feel of the place before committing to it, far enough away where I would be anonymous.

I'd taken care of the clothes, method, and kill zone. I needed my victim. My pulse accelerated. The word itself was intoxicating.

My victim. Mine. How could I find her? Would it be someone I happened upon, or would I stalk her?

CHAPTER EIGHT

PLOTTING MURDER IN PLAIN SIGHT

1986

"Oh, great. Maps." Pre-Law dashed into our room after her shower the next evening and spotted the open atlas.

Shit. I couldn't believe I hadn't put it away. Had I left any other items lying around that might arouse suspicion? I scanned the room. Clean desk and bed. Lab book with the checklist closed and in my book bag. My killing wardrobe safe in my car trunk. I tidied up my thoughts and composed my face.

"Which way are we going?" Pre-Law tucked her freshly-washed hair behind her ear, leaned over my desk, and stared at the Virginia map.

I breathed in the orange-ginger scent of her expensive shampoo. I used Breck.

"I'm not sure yet."

"I can't wait for you to meet my family. They're so excited." Pre-Law had talked about little else but my upcoming visit since I'd agreed to go.

"They're excited because you'll be home for the summer." I started to close the atlas, but Pre-Law put her hand on it.

"Don't sell yourself short. They're dying to meet you. I've told them all about how smart you are and how we've become best friends." She put a slender finger on the map to trace the interstates between State and Charleston, West Virginia. She laughed and lowered her voice to share a secret with the empty room. "Besides, I have an ulterior motive. I want my own car next year. Daddy says I'm here to prepare for law school and don't need one. I hope you don't mind that I'm using you."

I'd brought the Ugly Duckling, the old Ford Escort my aunt had given me, to campus as a freshman, even though college rules limited us to two wheels, not four. I told the administrator I had fictitious relatives who were ill and implied I might have to go home on a moment's notice. No public transportation went near Bubbaville. After the administrator bought the lie, I forged Big Chigger's signature on insurance and liability waivers.

"Wait 'til he sees what I'm driving. He'll be so horrified by the Ugly Duckling he'll buy you anything you want." The Ugly Duckling might have looked like a pile of junk, but it had never let me down.

"I hope so."

Pre-Law had badgered me into visiting her family. I was curious, all the more so because I couldn't fathom how two women from such opposite backgrounds could become best friends.

"Where's Bubbaville? Will we go near it?"

She caught me off guard. I was so worried she'd see the pinhole and the faint one-hundred-fifty mile, pencil-drawn radius that

I never anticipated she'd ask where I lived.

"Um, it's way out of our way." I didn't want her anywhere near the family.

"Shouldn't we at least stop and let your folks know you're all right? Do they know you'll graduate next year?"

My face locked into a rigid mask, and I felt my eyes squint. I bit each word off. "They. Don't. Care."

"I don't get it. You've done something no one else in your family has. Aren't they proud?" She stepped away to hang her wet towel on the rack behind the door.

"My family doesn't give a shit about me." I hadn't received a single call or letter or card from anyone in three years. That Thing left home at sixteen and was all but forgotten.

After giving her suggestion a second thought, I wondered if I shouldn't show her what I'd escaped. No matter how hard I'd tried, I couldn't run away from my upbringing. No matter how hard she tried, Pre-Law couldn't understand me completely until she experienced Bubbaville in its pathetic glory. Only then would she have a clearer picture of my past. Watching her reaction to my family would be both priceless and wretched.

"You should make an effort, don't you think?"

"I don't know. I'll think about it." I closed the map and put it on the shelf next to my anatomy text. The conversation was over.

Pre-Law lay on her stomach. I stayed at my desk, a book about crime scene forensics propped up on my two-inch-thick organic chemistry text. I stared at the same page for many long minutes.

What she said about going to Bubbaville left me all churn-y inside. I couldn't let her see how upset I was. I closed my eyes and took a series of slow deep breaths. Rather than calming me, memories of how the family house smelled nearly overwhelmed my self-control. The staleness came from the wasted lives of those I'd left behind. I steadied myself to deflect Pre-Law should she ask more questions that I didn't want to answer.

"Whatever you're reading must be pretty dense, because you're not flipping pages like you do with a novel."

"It's on crime scene investigation techniques." Ah, not a question about the family. Talking about crime was a safer subject. I held it up so she could see the cover over my shoulder.

"Why would a doctor need to know about crime scenes?"

Damn. I'd opened a door I should have kept locked. "I'm leaning toward pathology. Medical examiners need to understand forensics of all kinds, especially crime scene evidence."

"Eww. I still can't get used to it."

"Can't get used to what?"

"You thinking about death and dying all the time." My roomie rolled on her side, her hair fanned across the pillow to dry, cheek resting on her forearm.

"We all die. I find that precise moment when we go from being alive to being dead fascinating." I swiveled to face her. "What do you expect from someone who keeps a dead dog as a mascot?"

"That's different." She glanced at the skeleton.

"It's not, really. I mean, I didn't kill Old Rex, but he started my interest in what happens to a body after death."

"Yes, but he's a dog." She sat up, her legs crossed yoga-style. "It's almost like you get off on blood and guts."

Almost? I wasn't about to pursue that line of thought. Time for a diversion onto steadier ground.

"Look, you're going to be a district attorney. Not all of your prosecutions will be nice and tidy. Some will be messy. You could have murderers on your docket all the time."

"Of course, unless I specialize in drug-related crimes or white-collar crime."

I leaned toward her. "Let's play this out. Let's say I'm a pathologist, and you're trying a murderer who disposed of most of a body."

"Most of a body? Eww." Pre-Law wrinkled her nose.

"You'll call in all sorts of specialists to tell you how the person died, beginning with pathologists." I rested my elbows on the arms of my chair. "As a pathologist, I'll tell you the victim was poisoned, what kind of poison was used, and describe its specific effects on the human body. I'll use my background in organic chemistry to tell you the murderer moved the body from grave A to grave B, dragging along insects and bits of organic material. Other forensic scientists will analyze the remaining tissue and the dirt residue to tell you the when, where, and how of the murder."

"I get it. I'll need all sorts of specialists. Funny, I never thought I might call you." She giggled and pushed her glasses higher on her tilted-up nose. "I have this vision of you confounding a jury with a ton of facts, turning their stomachs when you talk about decaying flesh."

"I could end up on the witness stand a lot. Pathology combines the science of dying with solving the question of how people die." And couldn't I use what I learned as a pathologist to kill more efficiently? I couldn't imagine a specialty that was more exhilarating or one more appropriate for a would-be killer.

Pre-Law yawned.

§

A week after her suggestion that we visit my folks, Pre-Law found me in the coffee house at the student union where I hung out every afternoon. By three-ish, I needed a caffeine infusion to get through late afternoon labs. The bustle of tired students seeking a jolt of something caffeine-y, sugary, or both formed the soundtrack of college. Voices raised in conversation. Laughter competed with rock music blaring from overhead speakers. The only sound missing was students quietly turning pages. My pencil taps on the table top were too light to contribute to the din.

Because I'd been swamped with planning my first hunting trip to Monroe Crossing, I left our room early each morning, usually returning late at night after Pre-Law was asleep. She materialized beside me in the student union, a fresh cup of coffee in hand.

"Have you been avoiding me?"

I looked up.

"I hope I didn't hurt your feelings," Pre-Law said.

"What are you talking about?" I stopped tapping my pencil and laid it on top of my book.

"You know, the other night when I asked about your family. About how it would be nice if we stopped in Bubbaville," Pre-Law said. "I'm sorry if I upset you."

Did she have a hidden agenda? I scrutinized her expression but saw no ulterior motive.

"I'm not upset. I've been buried under a ton of year-end assignments, that's all." And the logistics for that one special extracurricular experiment.

"I'm glad. I didn't mean to pry." Pre-Law leaned over to give me a hug. She slid into the chair opposite me.

"We're tight." I stretched, my cramped neck popping. "I kinda get why you think I'm weird because I don't like my family. They don't like me either. Why else would they call me That Thing all my life?"

I blinked several times and stared at the table.

"Help me understand." Pre-Law sipped her coffee, steam fogging her glasses. Behind those thick black frames, she studied me.

"My life couldn't be more different than yours. I got out. Of town. Of my family. Look, if kids don't leave Bubbaville and hundreds of towns just like it, they get trapped in the small-town rut. No hope. Few jobs. Hardscrabble lives. Lots of guys beat the shit out of their wives. Some go into the marines or army like the old man did. Some return home after their service and repeat the cycle.

The few girls and guys who go to college almost never return."

"Wouldn't taking your education home help your town?" Pre-Law stirred a second packet of sugar into her coffee. Her forehead folded into corrugated lines. "I'd think you'd want to."

"You're so altruistic. You grew up with parents who served your community." I dropped my chin on my hands. "I grew up with Li'l Bit serving coffee at the Drop In Diner."

"I get that your family's poor. Mine isn't. I don't give a shit about that."

"Neither do I." I swallowed a surprising lump in my throat. "This has nothing to do with money or status. It has everything to do with escaping a dying town full of dead ends. About the only job we have requiring a college education is teaching. At one time, even that wasn't true. If you graduated high school and were willing, you could teach. No training or anything."

"Yeah, we had that in West Virginia. too. Probably still do, back in the deeper hollows." This Pre-Law understood.

"We don't have many kinds of jobs, period. Farming, being a mechanic, working at Sears or at the diner. Even the local sawmill is family owned, as is the farm supply store. No future there." My eyebrows tightened into a solid line. "We ate well because my mother had a garden, and the old man ran a few head of cattle. Raised chickens, too."

"What if you opened a family practice after med school?"

That brought me upright. I'd never considered it. The town doctor was old and would retire or kick off sooner rather than later. Taking over his practice might be an option, only because it would piss the hell out of Big Chigger. Might be fun to see the look on his face when he came to my office and had to call me "doctor." And pay me. Nah, never happen. He'd demand free medical care. If he didn't get it, he'd pop me a good one.

Was I exaggerating how bad life was? Did I hate where I came from so much I couldn't see that I could do something positive by returning as a physician? Maybe something to give other folks hope?

It didn't interest me.

Pre-Law went for a snack. We continued the conversation over chocolate almond biscotti.

"Li'l Bit spends most of her energy fussing over Princess and Junior, who don't need fussing over." I licked a fingertip and picked up a crumb from my napkin. "She spoiled them rotten, gave them everything they asked for, everything 'ceptn, I mean except, a sense of responsibility. With Princess's kid in the house, I bet she's starting the cycle all over again. As long as I did my chores and kept my mouth shut, she paid me no never mind. Big Chigger plain old didn't give a rat's ass about me."

Pre-Law chewed her cookie. She worked the pencil I'd left on the table through her fingers. Shouts from newly arriving students added to the background ruckus. I took her silence as encouragement to keep talking.

"To hear me talk, you'd think our family put the 'dys' in 'dysfunctional,' but it was pretty near center of normal. Not too violent. Not too smart. Smack-dab in the middle between too poor to raise yourself up and too hopeless to care." I blinked again. "You remember I told you about skipping two grades in elementary school. I passed Princess in my first year in high school, even though she started two years aheada, oops, ahead of me. I was in college prep, and she was in trying not to drop out."

"Some of my friends have sisters like her." Pre-Law laughed. She set the pencil back on my text book.

"My folks held being smart and wanting a better life against me. They tried to make it my fault that my sister was horny and didn't have a lick of sense." I stared over Pre-Law's left shoulder, unfocused eyes recording a kaleidoscopic swirl of color.

"I still want to meet them."

"The only time you're likely to meet my kin is in court when you're a prosecutor." I gathered my books. "Look, I've got to get back to the lab."

I wove my way across campus, head lowered. People on the quad became mere patterns of movement in front and around me. Slanting late afternoon sun all but blinded me. I looked up a fraction of a second too late and plowed into a tall, kind of cute, geeky guy standing in front of the science building.

"Hey!"

"Sorry," I said. "I didn't see you."

"No shit." The geek opened the door and stepped aside.

CHAPTER NINE

BUBBAVILLE

1986

Finals battered me, leaving no time to plan and carry out my experiment. This to and fro, this go ye forth and kill, this hurry up and wait, damn near drove me bonkers. I was ready to act, but I had to do it right rather than right now. I postponed the kill until the summer when I'd have more time to explore Monroe Crossing and would be practically alone in the sorority house.

Before I knew it, Pre-Law and I packed to leave for Charleston. After much internal debate, I'd let her talk me into stopping in Bubbaville, even though my stomach soured at the thought. The day after finals, we left State early to avoid the outbound rush of students heading home. My trusty overstuffed Escort, filled with Pre-Law and her clothes, rumbled up the interstate. I took only a small bag with enough for the weekend. The rest of my stuff, including the backpack with my killing disguise, stayed in the sorority house.

"Why I let you talk me into this I'll never understand." I watched the green and white highway signs tick off the miles to the exit I needed. The closer I came to the family, the worse the idea became.

"It won't be as bad as you think." Pre-Law sucked on her shake until only air bubbles chattered through the straw. She wedged her empty cup between the bucket seats.

"No. It'll be worse."

I didn't want to pick at barely healed scabs by being anywhere near Big Chigger and Li'l Bit. Going back, even for an hour, felt like giving up, like giving in. I'd tried to finish my drink at the fast food restaurant, but I couldn't. I ended up tossing it in the trash. I swallowed bile, wishing I'd kept it. I wouldn't give anyone the gratification of seeing me get sick, though, no matter how awful I felt.

Twenty minutes off the interstate and six county roads later, we bumped along a rutted gravel trace and stopped in front of the house. The farmer in an adjacent field baled freshly cut hay. Fat brown cattle grazed in a side pasture behind the falling-down barn protecting the old man's geriatric tractor. Some steers stood belly-deep in the pond we shared with the farm next door. I now knew this released *e.coli* bacteria into the water, which could leach into our wells, but no one in small-town America gave a damn. Cattle stayed cool any way they could.

The outside, from the house to the barn to the chicken coops to the outbuildings, was the old man's world. He kept up what he wanted and let the rest go. As a result, the front porch sagged, too weary to stand upright. Pieces of clapboard siding had peeled away, revealing black tar paper underneath. Not even an eaves-to-foundation scrubbing and fresh paint would repair the leprous feel of neglect. Once brightly colored plastic toys, now sun-bleached and half-broken, littered packed dirt in what passed for a front yard. The old man piled worn-out tires and other automotive junk against the walls of a ramshackle outbuilding to prevent it from collapsing.

Could the place have become this decrepit in the three years I'd been gone? Or had it always been this trashy and I'd never noticed?

"You grew up here?" Pre-Law tried not to look shocked.

"More rundown than I remember." My heart sent blood rushing to my face. "Don't worry. We won't stay long."

No sooner had I stepped out of the car than a gray tabby meowed her way across the dirt. She rubbed against my legs, tail in the air, purring loudly enough for Pre-Law to hear. I swept her into my arms and buried my face in her fur.

"Oh, Miss Snickers. I was afraid you'd forget me."

At least one living thing was happy to see me. I introduced my cat to Pre-Law. With Miss Snickers in my arms, I led the way up half-rotten steps to the door.

"Be careful." I nodded at a hole in the next to the top step. When I knocked on the screen door, Pre-Law raised an eyebrow. "When I left, Big Chigger told me I no longer lived here. If I don't knock, they might throw me out."

I put the squirming feline on the porch, where she continued weaving her way between my legs and telling me how much she'd missed me. We waited until Princess opened the inner door.

"What the hell you doin' here?" She carried a screaming, colicky baby on one hip. A pre-schooler held the hem of her dirty shorts for support. She blocked the entry.

"Two kids? Any idea who the fathers are? Or are you still sleeping with too many men to know?" In three sentences, I fell back into ingrained patterns. I mentally slapped my face. I might have come back, but I didn't have to act like I belonged.

"What does the old man think about this kid?" The baby was darker than I was with kinkier hair. No way could it be explained away as a throwback to the Melungeon ancestors like I was. It had to be the product of a black father and white mother.

"None of your damned business." Princess scowled at Pre-Law. "Who's this?"

I introduced Pre-Law as my college roommate.

"What a cute baby." I learned a lesson watching Pre-Law paste a polite smile in place.

I pulled the screen door open and sidestepped the preschooler's sticky hands. Pre-Law wasn't so lucky. The little boy grabbed her leg. She didn't have the well-practiced That Thing moves, which kept me out of harm's way. Li'l Bit came into the living room and wiped her hands on a grimy dishtowel. She looked more worn out than ever.

"Shut that kid up."

Princess bounced him on her hip and wiped tears and snot in a vain attempt to quiet the baby.

"Thought that was your voice. 'Bout time you're home." The old rebuke came readily to Li'l Bit's lips. "I knew you wouldn't last at college."

"We stopped by to tell you I'll be graduating next year."

"So? You comin' back after? I got plenty of work for you."

When I introduced Pre-Law, Li'l Bit put on a distracted smile and nodded. Princess swayed with the baby, who took that moment to send a thin stream of watery vomit onto the living room floor, barely missing a thread-bare braided rug. Princess mopped at it with the rag she'd used to wipe the baby's nose. Pre-Law gulped and looked away.

"Ah, Ma, you know there's no room for That Thing anymore." Princess gestured toward me with the puke-soaked rag. "Me 'n the kids need the bedroom."

"Don't worry." I breathed through my mouth to keep from gagging. "I'm not staying."

"Good. You left a couple of boxes of shit in the closet. Take 'em if you want 'em. If not, I'll throw 'em out."

I left Pre-Law with Li'l Bit. My sister led the way down the hall toward the bedroom we'd shared as kids. Princess pointed to a couple of small cardboard boxes stacked in the back of the closet behind a pile of dirty laundry, two boxes containing the who-knew-what that defined my youth. I dragged them out. The older boy ran over to one and began slamming his small fists on top. I had to take it away before he broke into it.

I had no idea what the cartons contained, but I sure as hell wasn't going to open them in the miasma of the bedroom. At least, when I slept here, I kept it clean. How Princess could live in that room with two babies was unfathomable. The boxes weren't all that heavy, so I stacked one atop the other. I would make room in the back seat for the last remnants of my life in Bubbaville. I was nauseated by the time I returned to the front room.

Even on this warm day, the house was shut up tight. We'd never had air conditioning, so Li'l Bit made us leave the windows open all night to catch the evening cool. We had to close them before the sun warmed the air too much. Trapped inside were the odors of my youth: dust, cigarette smoke, fried food. Overlaying those old smells were baby puke and a diaper pail in need of emptying. Ammonia made my eyes water. I coughed and tried not to breathe through my nose.

Pre-Law and Li'l Bit sat in awkward silence on the opposite sides of the living room, Pre-Law perched on the edge of a sofa sagging so badly she'd have toppled over if she'd tried to sit back. We'd had it as long as I could remember. Three kids from my generation had broken it. It wouldn't survive the kids of the next.

"Do you know your daughter is going to be a doctor?" Pre-Law continued a one-sided conversation, which hadn't included me.

Li'l Bit shook her head.

"She's at the top of her class. You should be proud of what she's achieved." If I wouldn't brag on me, by God, Pre-Law would.

Li'l Bit shrugged because my accomplishments had no impact on the quality of her daily life.

I stacked the boxes next to the door and tried to see the room through Pre-Law's eyes. We used to have pretty, floral wallpaper, but someone had painted over it with a strange shade of gray-green. Might have been a left-over order from Sears. Old rag rugs needed cleaning at the very least, replacing if Big Chigger would kick loose some money. The squalor threatened to undermine my self-control and bury it under a cloud of despair. I couldn't imagine what Pre-Law thought.

My mother remembered she once had manners and offered us sweet tea. Pre-Law blanched again. So did I. Nothing in this house would cross my lips. I'd end up adding my puke to the reeking smudge on the floor. Slovenly housekeeping left filth thick in the corners of the room. No wonder the newest kid had colic.

The house's current condition was a stark contrast to what it was when I lived there. Li'l Bit had kept it sparkling. We might have been poor, but my mother had been proud. The looks of the place told me the old man had dragged her down so low he knocked the last bit of pride out of her.

The screen door banged, and Junior entered, drunk, even though it was only an hour or so past noon, a smudged copy of the old man. Where Big Chigger was big and packed with muscle from a life of physical work, Junior was equally big but soft, the kind of overweight kid who was bullied at school. As he grew, his mean streak kept most of the smaller kids terrified. Alcohol exacerbated Junior's volatility. He leered at Pre-Law before he turned on me.

"What are you doin' with them boxes? You ain't movin' back, if that's what you think." Junior kicked one of them. "None of us want you. This family's so much better off since you left."

"I can see that." I want to snark back at him, but I refused to sink to his level. "We're just leaving."

Junior shoved me when I bent to pick up the boxes. His bulk made him threatening; my martial arts training made me nearly lethal. Before he could shove me again, I kicked him just under the left knee cap. The unexpected blow dumped him on his ass.

"Fuck! What the fuck you think you're doin'?"

"Junior, we don't swear in this house," Li'l Bit said.

"The fuck we don't. I'll swear if I goddammed well please." Junior struggled to his feet, fist balled. Pre-Law stepped between us.

"Your sister's changed since she's been gone. I'd watch myself if I were you." Pre-Law lifted a box. I picked up the other.

Junior ran through the kitchen and banged the outside door behind him.

We piled the boxes on the back seat. I knelt in the dirt for one last cuddle with Miss Snickers. "Only one more year," I whispered into her white bib, "and I'll come get you."

When I put her down, the cat meowed. I glanced back before I turned onto the gravel road. Miss Snickers sat in the same spot, waiting.

I pulled out of the yard onto the dirt road and waved at our neighbor, who was now working his hay right next to our pasture. A blaring horn warned me of an impending collision. I swerved to avoid a rusted-out pickup. Big Chigger stared at me and flipped the bird, a humorless grin splitting his face. We passed each other without stopping.

"Your father?"

I nodded, eyes fixed straight ahead. Small pebbles pinged off the trunk. In my rearview mirror, I saw Junior standing in the middle of the road, a shotgun cradled in his arms. I started crying. Pre-Law reached over and patted my knee. We trembled until we were on the interstate.

"Now I so get it." She never mentioned my family again.

We drove out of Virginia and across West Virginia in silence. Not until I needed directions in Charleston did Pre-Law talk me through an older section of town with streets full of historic homes, all in perfectly restored condition with massive shade trees in the yards and mature, trimmed shrubbery.

Mrs. Judge, Pre-Law's mother, welcomed me with a quick hug. She called her husband to help unpack the car.

"You came all the way from State in that?" The Judge walked around the Ugly Duckling.

"We did," Pre-Law winked at me. Her father would buy her something safer. I winked back.

I was happy for her, but I wouldn't trade the Ugly Duckling for anything. Once yellow, its paint had faded to a dull tan. No matter how old it was, it started every time I turned the key.

Pre-Law's family made me so welcome I almost didn't want to leave at the end of my three-day visit. For the first time ever, I had a room of my own with a double bed, white sheets smelling of lilac, and a pile of feather pillows. I even had my own bath.

I loved The Judge, Mrs. Judge and Pre-Law's siblings, because everyone respected each other. No one yelled or threw insults. No one raised a fist. They sat around the dinner table and talked about anything on their minds. Conversations, especially political ones, were spirited, but even when someone disagreed, no one cut her off.

"Did you see how our junior senator voted on the conservation bill?" Pre-Law opened a discussion our first night. "He's trying to shut down our coal mines."

"I think the bill only addressed mountain-top removal," The Judge said.

"It's more than that." Pre-Law stood her ground. "How can a

senator from a coal-producing state be against its largest employers?"

"Read the bill, dear." Mrs. Judge sliced a coconut cake and passed around plates. "You'll find one of you is wrong."

"Don't believe everything you read in the papers or hear on television." The Judge accepted a slab of cake.

"Would Walter Cronkite lie to us?" Pre-Law had the next-to-last comment.

"Well, not Mr. Cronkite," Mrs. Judge said.

Mrs. Judge took me aside the night before I left. "If it won't hurt your feelings, Pre-Law's sister has a closet full of clothes she never wears. They should fit you. Would you like some?"

I searched Mrs. Judge's face and found nothing but kindness. I left Charleston with a carload of new-to-me clothes and an invitation to return whenever I wanted.

CHAPTER TEN

SELECTING MY VICTIM

1986

Summer, when most of my sorority sisters were back at their homes, left me free to conduct reconnaissance in Monroe Crossing. After noting the mileage and travel time in my lab book, I parked on a residential street under a tree covered with clusters of small orangish flowers. Neat white frame houses, which had stood at least a century, lined either side. I walked over to the downtown area where people strolled along the sidewalks. Alleys, crisscrossing quiet residential streets, offered out-of-sight places to kill. This not-too-small town was one where my old car and I could pass unnoticed.

In the seasonal warmth of a sunny summer day, I meandered along a quaint main street in the process of being revitalized into a trendy tourist village. Not there yet, but I didn't care. I'd be around only as long as it took to complete my experiment. I pretended to be just another visitor ambling in and out of shops, sneezing when I passed a candle boutique, and stopping to browse in a used book store.

"You're new in town." A clerk approached me as soon as I entered.

"Yes. I'm checking out the college." A lie common enough to be forgotten as soon as I was out of sight.

"It's a great college in a great town." He tweaked a couple of hardbacks into a neater stack. "Looking for anything in particular?"

"I love thrillers. Who are your favorite authors?"

Keeping in character, I engaged the bookseller in a spirited discussion about the merits of several best-selling authors before selecting two I hadn't read before.

"I hope you'll come back."

You can bet on it, but not for the reasons you think.

"I do, too. Thanks for the recommendations." I watched him put the books in a small paper bag with jute handles. "Bye."

I spotted a coffee house across the street. It would make a perfect place to rest and watch. Inside, I found a quiet corner where I had a clear view of the foot traffic on the sidewalk as well as the customers outside at wire tables or inside in air conditioning. With my back to the wall, I opened one of my new used books. Several people stopped to chat. One even asked if I was a fan of the author.

"Not yet. I picked this because the bookseller said he was good."

"The writer's terrific. You'll like it. A real hair-raiser."

I remained friendly and polite, carrying on conversations as long as anyone wanted to talk. My eyes, never still behind large sunglasses, scanned the room and sidewalk for a target. I checked my behavior since I stepped from my car. I didn't think talking with the bookseller or patrons at the coffee house would make me memorable. Wearing my sunglasses indoors, however, might have been a mistake. I scrutinized people sitting at tables and was relieved that many of them had not removed their glasses, either.

My fellow coffee sippers were a combination of students, parents, and tourists. All sought a pleasant place to rest before resuming treks around town and the campus that flowed seamlessly into it. I was about to resume my walkabout when a smallish woman entered, ordered a cappuccino, and sat at a table on the other side of the shop. Her summer dress, expensive-looking sandals, and straw handbag were a little more upscale than the rest of us. I guessed her age to be double mine because her dark brown hair was shot through with gray.

She slid a thumb under a glued flap and opened a thick manila envelope. With trembling hands, she removed several envelopes and flipped through them before she froze. Her sudden change in posture attracted my attention.

The woman tossed most of the mail aside. At last, she peeled away the dirty flap of a well-handled envelope and withdrew several sheets of paper. Her face alternately paled then flushed by the time she finished the last page. She crushed the papers and threw them toward the bin, not noticing them hit the floor.

I held my breath, praying she wouldn't put whatever upset her in the trash. With her mind no longer on her drink, she jammed the remaining mail into her large handbag and stomped out of the shop, her unfinished cappuccino abandoned on the table. On the sidewalk, I watched her ball one hand into a fist.

Alone. Distracted. Distressed.

Perfect.

I dumped my empty cup into the bin. Clumsy me, I dropped my cap on the floor. When I stood, I tucked the crumpled pages in my backpack. I tailed the woman along Main for a few blocks until she turned right down a side street. I made it to the corner in time to see her hustle up five steps and unlock the door to an old white house with dark green shutters. I noted the address. I'd come back later.

I returned to my room at State, retrieved the pages from my backpack, and read.

"You stupid bitch! How dare you think you can keep all the damn money? We planned this together, and now your stiffin' me. When I find you, your dead."

The letter ran on in this semi-literate vein for several paragraphs. The woman appeared to have stolen money from someone from whom she now hid. Why else get your mail in a secondary envelope? This someone was angry enough to threaten her. A second letter and news clipping in the wadded-up trash were more revealing.

"You brought shame to our family. Everyone knows you're a thief, but I'm glad the police haven't arrested you. Dad would never be able to survive the humiliation of having a felon in the family. Why don't you disappear permanently so we can hold our heads up again?"

It was signed "Mother."

Some fucking mother. She was even colder than Big Chigger at his worst.

A much-folded news clipping, faded and yellowed, reported a theft from a national charity a few years back. Could this be the money the writer wanted? Interesting confluence of clues: stolen money, threats from a potential cohort in crime, family shame. No wonder she was distressed. Would anyone miss her?

Damn it! I shouldn't have touched the letters without gloves. I could have dropped them beside her body, but now I couldn't. Lesson learned.

CHAPTER ELEVEN

THE KILL

1986

On an additional reconnoitering trip, I altered my appearance enough to throw off any but a trained observer. With my honey-colored skin and curly hair, I could pass for someone of mixed heritage even though I was white. I could be a Mediterranean hodgepodge: Italian, Spanish, Greek, Moroccan. A Latina. A light-skinned black. I was short enough to pass for a young boy. Or for myself. What I couldn't be was a tall anything. My only memorable feature was dark blue eyes.

Playing roles was challenging, especially when I pretended to change my ethnicity. The first trip where I identified the woman, white me. The second when I scouted locations, light-skinned black. The third and last, Latina. Not only did my combination of clothing change subtly, but my mannerisms, walk, and accent did as well. International news programs provided a plethora of accents. The more I practiced while walking around a nearly empty summer campus, the better a mimic I became.

"What should I wear?" I muttered aloud in my room one night. "Let's see. Slightly too small jeans, a plain white T-shirt, clean sneakers, and my battered sweatshirt will fit nicely." I dipped into my backpack, pulled out my killing outfit, and planned to change in a gas station about halfway to Monroe Crossing. Definitely not what I'd worn on my earlier two visits. Most definitely not what I wore to class.

§

I parked at the opposite end of the downtown area from my victim's house and hunted up and down Main. Because my family never used my given name, I grew up thinking I was an object. I wanted this woman who was important to me to have significance: She had to have a name. I called her Sad-Sack.

I strolled by her house but saw no overt signs of life: no mail in the box or papers on the porch. If she'd fled, if the semi-literate letter writer had found her, I'd have to start all over in a different town, because I couldn't risk coming to Monroe Crossing again. Two earlier trips put me in jeopardy of someone recognizing me.

I wiped sweaty palms on my thighs. I turned into the coffee house, ordered one last coffee and sank into a funk, chin on fist, back to the wall in what had become my favorite corner. I was so close, so ready, for my cold-blooded kill, but my target wasn't co-operating. If I couldn't find Sad-Sack, I had no clue how to satisfy my desire. It had all sounded so logical driving over.

"What if I fail?" I muttered under my breath.

Half an hour passed. The bells over the door rang and rang. I was about to give up when Sad-Sack entered, ordered a cappuccino, and sat at the same table as the first time. She stared out the window, tears on her cheeks. The first time I saw her she was impeccably groomed. Now, her hair was disheveled, and she wore no makeup. Either she'd started out with none or she'd cried it off. I was two tables too far to see if her eyes were swollen and red-rimmed.

She slumped; her hands trembled. Mine did as well but for very different reasons. Pumped on a surge of adrenaline, I took several deep breaths to return to a cold and calculated state from hot and bothered. Sad-Sack's head swiveled at every sound. Where she'd been distracted before, her new hypervigilance dared me to act. I double checked everything to be certain I was ready to complete the experiment.

Scraps of conversations and the roar of the milk steamer all but drowned out the occasional sniff from across the shop. I nursed my coffee as long as she did her cappuccino. When she left, I waited a few moments before following. With my hair under my CAT ball cap, my shades on my nose, and a pair of latex gloves in my sweatshirt pouch, I was ready.

In the hour I'd sat inside, the sky had turned threatening with thunderclouds building to the south, dark enough to be mid-winter. People rushed home ahead of the impending downpour. The temperature dropped ahead of the storm, so my upraised hood seemed natural. A gust of wind blew bits of trash along the street. I stuffed my hands in the kangaroo pouch of my sweatshirt, worked them into the gloves, and lagged behind until Sad-Sack turned the corner. Thunder dragons growled a warning she didn't heed.

When we came to the mouth of an alley two blocks down, I glanced at the sky, rushed forward, and rammed her hard enough to knock her face first to the walkway. Her teeth crashed together when her chin hit the concrete. Sad-Sack sprawled across the broken sidewalk, a gash on her chin bleeding profusely. She shook her head, stunned by one moment being upright and the next flat on her stomach.

"Oh my God. I'm so sorry. Let me help you," I said in a pretty good Spanish accent. She wouldn't be alive to tell anyone she was attacked by a Latina, but I practiced the con anyway. I helped her stand and steered her into the alley. She was barely as tall as I was. I dabbed at her chin with a napkin I'd pocketed at the coffee house. "Are you hurt?"

Her legs wobbled, so my firm grip on her upper arm prevented further falls. We staggered along until we came to the rear of a rundown house. I pushed her against the wall in a narrow space between two metal trash cans. Semi-hidden, the killing area would have to do.

Calculating every move kept me focused. With a thumb on each side of her larynx, my fingers found and compressed her carotid arteries. Her eyes popped wide, and she opened her mouth to scream, but no sound emerged. She struggled to inhale.

Two seconds in. she kicked for my shins; I dodged. Five seconds in came frantic clawing, but she couldn't reach my face. The long-sleeved sweatshirt protected my arms. After twelve seconds, she stared at me, shock and acceptance in her gaze. She went limp. She wasn't dead yet, but that look of resignation about what was coming next was more exciting than I dreamed it would be. I knew she knew she was going to die.

Sphincters relaxed, splashing urine and feces on the ground and on one of my new sneakers. At fifteen seconds, I lowered her unconscious body to the ground between the trash cans next to the mess she'd made.

Under my hands, her pulse slowed and stopped. I'd researched how long it took to die by strangulation. After two minutes, I released my grip and stepped back, bumping into a trash can and sending it clattering across the alley. I crouched, my heart rate accelerating for the first time since I left the coffee house. Had anyone heard the noise? The gods applauded with a huge crack of thunder. I stood, repressing the urge to take a bow. I looked down at my handiwork: a still-warm face, reddened, a slightly protruding tongue with streaks of red where she'd bitten herself in her initial struggle, and blood from the cut on her chin.

I'd killed in cold blood. I realized I was hot and wet with no way to release the tension. With no actual experience, I never guessed I'd be sexually aroused.

I staged the scene for the cops. I pulled her dress down and crossed her hands over her breasts. So many killers hid their motives behind this classic sign of remorse that it had become a cliché but a useful one for my purposes. I wasn't remorseful, not even remotely. I checked the surrounding alley to be sure no physical evidence remained. Only a urine-fouled shoe could tie the body in the alley to the soon-to-be medical student passing through town. I stripped off the gloves, folding the bloody napkin I'd used to dab her chin inside one.

The first huge splats of rain struck the pavement. I hoped a heavy downpour would clean the mess off of Sad-Sack's body. I didn't know why, but I didn't want her body defiled with her own excrement. I hunched my shoulders, pulled the hood of my sweatshirt further over my hat and sprinted down the alley. I dropped the glove without the napkin in a trash can halfway to my car to see if the small-town cops would find it. I stuffed the other in my pouch to dispose of at some gas station on the way home, where I planned to change into my regular clothes. The stained sneaker would go into a dumpster as soon as I parked in my regular lot on campus.

I slid into my car, wet inside and out. A blinding downpour kept me from driving away immediately. While I waited for the storm to let up, I squeezed my thighs together. A last clap of thunder muffled my outcry.

§

Even though I savored the kill, the feeling didn't last. Because I had more questions than answers, I conducted what the police called a post-op assessment. Like the scientist I was, I opened my lab book and reviewed the list to see if Sad-Sack had behaved as I'd expected.

How long did I squeeze until she stopped struggling? 12 seconds.

Did she fight? Yes.

Did she scream? No, my hands prevented that

Did her eyes roll back? No, she stared at me.

Was her final expression one of acceptance of the inevitable? Yes.

What color did her face turn? Red.

Did her tongue protrude? Yes, and she bit it.

How did she look lying dead? Like an insect spread-eagled on a specimen board. Dead. As in lifeless. As in nothing but a slab of cooling flesh.

What did I feel? The most sexually aroused I'd been in my life.

I chose this particular woman because she was distracted. We never interacted, never established any kind of relationship. We drank coffee in the same shop twice and walked the same broken pavement. I relished the moment when she realized she was about to die. That lived up to my expectations. Breath caught in my throat, and I was aroused again. This time, I was alone in my room where I could masturbate as much as I wanted.

§

For days afterward, I haunted convenience stores, scanning smaller local papers for any mention of the dead woman. After a week, a tiny article appeared in a sidebar on the local news page.

Sad-Sack's death warranted two measly paragraphs in a weekly paper in a small town within one hundred and fifty miles of State, almost as anonymous in death as in life.

§

The sheriff in Monroe Crossing said he has no suspects in a murder and potential rape off Main Street. "Late Saturday night the body of Kay Sullivan was found strangled behind the old Higgins's house. Three teenage boys riding their bicycles in an alley after a thunderstorm came upon the body."

The woman was fully clothed, although her skirt had been pulled up and her underwear was down around her ankles. Her purse was missing. "She was the victim of a robbery and possible sexual assault, but the results of the autopsy won't be ready for several weeks." The police were looking at Sullivan's estranged husband as a person of interest.

§

Sexual assault? Someone had to be pretty damned sick to rape a corpse. The thought was repulsive. Had someone followed me? I hadn't seen anyone, but once I put my hands around her throat, my normally acute situational awareness shrank to a tiny circle of two people engaged in a life-or-death struggle. Was it a ruse by the police to trick me, or were they too stupid to get their facts straight?

I took no lasting gratification in killing this hapless stranger who didn't have a flipping clue why I picked her. She was nothing more than a successful laboratory experiment to see if I could kill in cold blood. I could and get away with it, but so what? A scientist knows one experiment by and of itself proves nothing. I'd have to repeat it to be sure. I needed a hell of a better reason to kill, though, than mere distraction.

CHAPTER TWELVE

TRANSITIONS

1986-1987

I was officially a killer. By all accounts, I looked the same the day after I killed Sad-Sack as the day before. No neon arrow flashed over me saying, "Warning! Killer Amongst Us!" Inside, however, I savored the way I felt when she lay dead at my feet. I was special, a thing apart from and above my fellow students.

A week before our last year as undergraduates began, Pre-Law returned in a used BMW, a gift from The Judge who extracted a promise she never ride in the Ugly Duckling again. Our reverse psychology, however unsubtle, worked.

I focused my senior year on getting accepted to the best medical schools. I signed up for a heavy course load with four labs. On the first day of biochemistry, the geeky guy I'd bounced off of at the end of the spring term sidestepped me when I dashed into the lab one half minute before class started and headed toward one of the two open stools. He followed.

"Are you always in such a hurry?" He dumped his book bag on the floor.

Summer left him a little more filled out than the scarecrow I remembered. He was still tall and gawky but almost cute behind new wire rims. I took note of the unruly dark hair and clear if untanned cheeks.

"No. Hey, didn't I smack into you last term?"

"You did. I'm pre-med too. We've had several lectures together but never the same labs." When he smiled, white teeth flashed in an unremarkable face.

"I'm sorry I didn't notice you before." I put my bag next to his.

"I noticed you. You're hard to forget."

"Well, Lab-Rat, looks like we're finally going to get to know each other." I held out my hand.

The prof called the class to order. Since his opening lecture was all about what to expect, I tuned him out and looked around. Every table had spotless stainless steel tops—"I expect you will leave the lab every day just as you see it now."—and all-new state-of-the-art equipment. The smell of disinfectant wafted from air conditioning vents. I tuned back in when he talked about lab partners.

"Whoever you're sitting next to right now is your lab partner for the term."

What the hell? I hadn't expected that. I'd always picked my partner.

"You're a team. Seventy-five percent of your grade depends on the work you do together."

I squirmed and felt my face grow hot. All of a sudden, the professor messed up my plans to partner with the top student in the room. I had no idea if Lab-Rat was smart enough to be my partner, but I knew I was smart enough to be his. Hell, if I had to do ninety percent of the mutual work, I would. I had to maintain my GPA.

A couple of weeks into the first semester we worked all night on an experiment that wasn't going well. Lab-Rat asked me to coffee before we both crashed. "You study even more than I do."

We sat in the student union and chatted over breakfast muffins.

"Yeah, pre-med students have no outside lives, do we?"

Lab-Rat was likable enough. When we talked about more than our homework assignments, I learned he'd broken up with a girlfriend over the summer. I mentioned nothing about never having had a boyfriend. I wasn't about to tell him I was a virgin and damned tired of that status. The more time we spent together, the better I liked him. I watched his long fingers and wondered if their length equated to an equally long cock. Not that I was likely to find out, because he hadn't made a move on me. I'd often brush against him in the lab and touch his arm to get his attention, but he hadn't taken the hint.

We had coffee several times before he asked me out. "There's a good movie at the union this weekend. Would you like to go?"

"Sure."

I went on my first date. Even though I didn't know if we'd ever get into bed, my hormones raged by the time we stood in line for tickets. We saw some lame romantic comedy that only intensified my desire. I was so charged that *Bambi Meets Godzilla* would have kept me in the mood. When Lab-Rat held my hand in the darkened theater, I drew circles on its back with my thumb. We walked hand in hand toward the apartment he shared with three other students.

"The guys won't be back tonight."

I put my arms around him and gave him a full-body kiss. Pretty soon his body got the idea. We kissed on the stairs, at the door to his apartment. He fumbled with his keys before dropping them on the floor.

Inside, lips glued together, tongues probed each other's

mouths. Lab-Rat ran his hands over my body. We stepped apart long enough for him to pull my shirt over my head and unhook my bra. We kissed again. He unzipped my jeans and pulled them down. My panties followed.

My turn to undress him. I pulled his T-shirt over his head and struggled with his zipper. He helped. Soon, I pushed his jeans and boxers over his ass, freeing his erect cock. I hadn't seen a naked penis since I stopped changing Junior's diapers. Lab-Rat's might have started out the same size as Junior's, but seeing a real man's, not something in health science class or in a text book, made me want it inside me without delay.

Lab-Rat pushed me onto his unmade bed and fell on top of me. He spread my legs and forced his way in. It hurt, but I didn't care. He used his cock like a battering ram until he jerked. I felt a tiny tingle. Was that all there was to it? All that panting and thrusting and pounding for such a small response from my body?

After he'd rested enough to do it again, he showed me how to rub him until he was hard. We moved slower the second time with me trying to match his rhythm but bumping the wrong way several times. He shifted his weight to pin me to the bed and keep me in position. Breath coming in gasps, he sped up and finished with a loud groan.

"I had no idea sex could be so good." He rolled off.

I watched his penis slacken.

We lay on his rumpled, less-than-clean sheets. While he slept for a couple of hours, I lay awake analyzing the experience. Sore and disappointed, what made me want to scream was not my lack of reaction to the sex act itself but to being held down. He rode me one more time that night before I left to get ready for an early class. The last time we did it, I felt a slightly stronger tingle.

I returned to the sorority house confused. If what I experienced was an orgasm, erotic writers had it all wrong. I didn't feel like screaming in pleasure. The earth didn't move. I didn't die the "little death" when all sensory expression came alive between my legs. Hell, what I did in the car after killing Sad-Sack was one thousand percent better. If this was all there was, I didn't understand the fuss.

My brain linked losing my virginity with my first kill, which I'd approached in a scientific manner, the testing of a theorem. At the actual moment of the kill, I was wildly excited, but the intensity faded. Like a junkie, I needed another fix. I obsessed over my reaction to sex. Some excitement, some tingle, nothing memorable. Maybe I needed to try sex again.

Killing and screwing were a lot of work. Lessons from each included how to achieve and sustain the high, how to intensify my satisfaction. I wanted to learn. I just had to, or neither would be worth the effort.

I tiptoed into my sorority room to find Pre-Law sitting up in bed, bedside lamp on, waiting for me like my mother never did.

"Well?"

"No longer a virgin."

Pre-Law grinned and gave me a thumbs-up. "So, he was pretty good, huh?"

"Yes." Maybe in time, but not yet. at least, not for me.

"Mickey Mouse or Trigger?"

"Trigger." I stripped, grabbed my shower kit, and headed for the bathroom.

"Lucky you. Does he have a friend?" Pre-law called after me. She turned off her light and snuggled back under the covers. Her first class wasn't until eleven.

§

Working side by side in the lab gave me ample time to observe Lab-Rat. I spent most of our hours together on the knife edge of arousal. One look and my hormones were off and running. He might not be the best-looking guy, but he was the only guy I'd met who could teach me about my body.

After much experimentation, I discovered turning him on in public places was a sure-fire high. My pleasure intensified when he tried to hide his erection. Late one night, I teased him in the lab until we were both too turned on to make it to his apartment. His pants bulged; my panties were soaked. We found an empty storage room and did it standing against the wall.

The element of danger, of getting caught and possibly kicked out of State, coupled with being in lust, led to my first orgasm. When the tingle exploded, I left deep scratch marks on Lab-Rat's ass. After our first time fucking in near public, I proposed more dangerous places to get it off. We screwed behind the bleachers on the track field, at the fifty-year line on the football field at three in the morning, in a prof's office. The more unusual the location, the more intense my orgasms were.

Even though Lab-Rat was predictable, even downright stodgy in bed at times, I enjoyed being around him. Every once in a while, he surprised me, like when he invited me camping one weekend. No way did I picture him as the rugged, outdoor type.

"My dad forced me to be a Boy Scout. I don't know who was more astonished, him or me, when I took to camping," he said. "I have all the gear. It's a great way to get away. Let's try it."

"Will it be private?" I had an image of wall-to-wall people in tents and sleeping bags.

"Very."

Lab-Rat was right. Camping turned out to be a welcome break from senior year stress. We zipped two sleeping bags together and experimented with different positions. Me on top. Him on top. Doggie style. Sixty-nine. On top of a bag was the first time I pushed his head between my legs and held it there until I climaxed. We spent several weekends, just the two of us, in a national forest. I shrieked and scared a lot of birds.

CHAPTER THIRTEEN

MCAT HELL

1986-1987

The MCATs, those dreaded exams that determined who would go to med school and who wouldn't, were coming up in January, so I worked my way through the prep book. Most of the questions were straightforward; some, however, were downright tricky. I enrolled in an extra class because I wasn't going to blow my chance at getting into a top school.

Three-fourths of the way through the semester, Lab-Rat choked on a written exam. He was truly great in the lab, but tests made up twenty-five percent of our final grades. If he couldn't take a routine biochem test, I couldn't imagine him doing well on a standardized exam with his future at stake. I encouraged him to join me in the prep class. I tutored him as hard for the MCAT as I did for our class grade.

Even before we got our results, trouble arrived in all its loathsomeness. I'd combed the library for material on the three best med schools in the Mid-Atlantic and one in the East. I created a short list of where I wanted to study. My faculty adviser approved.

"You should have no problem getting into at least one of these," he said.

I left his office underwhelmed by his evaluation. Success was getting into *all* of them.

"Why don't you apply to the same schools as me? That way, we can stay together." We lay on Lab-Rat's sweaty, rumpled sheets.

I'd assumed we'd go our separate ways after graduation. Although we'd never actually discussed the question, he shocked the shit out of me when he talked going to the same medical school. I should have had "the talk" before he planned our lives.

"How can that happen? You're applying to Florida International, South Florida, Baylor, and UT San Antonio, aren't you? I'm applying in DC and Boston."

"Are you saying that my choices aren't as good as yours?"

"Not at all, but I want to go to Harvard or Johns Hopkins. Maybe Georgetown or American."

And the argument began.

"How can we practice together if we're separated for seven years?"

What? Practice together? Who said anything about that? Had Lab-Rat mistaken what was for me a temporary relationship based on sex for something permanent? His vision for our future sure as hell didn't match mine.

"We could open a practice after we graduate. Some place in the South."

The South, maybe. Private practice, not likely. With Lab-Rat, no way, Jose.

"If you go into pediatrics and I become an OB/GYN, we'd

make a ton of money. We'd never run out of patients."

Pediatrics? Where the hell had that some from? We'd never talked about my specialty.

"I've had enough of snot-nosed kids to last a lifetime." Li'l Bit had had me taking care of Junior by the time I was five. I wiped his nose, changed shit-filled diapers, and cleaned up more baby puke than I wanted to think about. Even now, if my mother had her way, I'd be back in Bubbaville taking care of Princess's brats.

"You'd be so good." Lab-Rat ignored everything I said.

I hoped keeping my mouth shut would make him forget this nonsense. It didn't. He kept after me until I hit him between the eyes one afternoon after I'd fucked him limp. "No way am I going into pediatrics. I'm going to be a pathologist."

He dared to laugh. "Dead people don't come back for follow-up visits."

Lab-Rat was right. They don't, but I didn't care.

"Dead people don't sue you for malpractice."

"Are you saying I'm going to be a bad doctor and get sued?" Lab-Rat's face turned a shade reminiscent of Big Chigger in a rage. For a moment, my father was in front of me. My anger rose and threatened a major eruption. I took a deep breath and tried to work backwards out of a volatile situation.

"That's not what I meant." I climbed out of bed and dressed.

"Why won't you see things my way?" He stood naked in front of me, arms crossed over his chest, and blocked the door.

No way could I explain the charge I got out of the art of making people dead. I tried to explain that the how and why people died was classic problem solving. He didn't care. What was important was not giving him a glimpse of the other side of my personality. He knew the public me, which was the only side he needed to see, not the private killer me, the That Thing me, which he could never understand.

"You're wasting your education playing with corpses. How can you be so stupid?"

He blithered on, but I stopped listening. I walked around him and left him talking to himself in the middle of his bedroom.

I stomped back toward to the sorority house, flames shooting out of my ears. I kicked stones out of the way when what I wanted to do was kick Lab-Rat's ass. I punched the air. I swung the door open so hard that it bounced off the wall.

Pre-Law jumped halfway out of her chair. "What did Lab-Rat say this time?"

"He wants us to open a joint practice either in Florida or Texas. Him as the OB/GYN and me in pediatrics." I threw myself on my bed and drummed my heels on my up-holler granny's quilt.

"Pediatrics? You?" Pre-Law pushed her textbook aside. "Where did he get that idea? You never mentioned peds, did you?"

"No way."

"Has he lost his freaking mind? What did you tell him?"

"That I wanted to be a pathologist."

"I bet he loved that." Pre-Law and I had talked enough about pathology for her to know I was dead serious about my choice.

"You got that right. He called me all sorts of names from self-centered right through to stupid. I left after 'stupid.'"

"I'll bet." Pre-Law returned to her assignment.

I lay on my bed and ground my teeth after I stopped drumming my heels. Who was this creep to think he could control me? To try to make me do something I didn't want to? His rage and domineering, superior-than-thou attitude reeked of Big Chigger.

I waited to see how I did on my exams, which med schools accepted me, and how I'd finish my final year. I hoped the subjects of schools and practicing together wouldn't come up again. When the test scores were posted for all to see, Lab-Rat didn't speak to me for a week. I'd aced them; he passed, but not even in the upper twenty-five percent. He had to hope his fail-safe school accepted him. I didn't give a crap where he went as long as it wasn't near me.

We waited for the envelopes to arrive. Fat ones meant acceptance; skinny ones were rejections. My mail slot filled with one fat envelope after another. So did Pre-Law's. She whooped when Georgetown accepted her.

"When you get into Johns Hopkins, we'll be close enough to get together often."

I liked the "when."

I was four for four before Lab-Rat got his first and only fat envelope from his fallback school, University of North Texas. All of his top schools rejected him.

"It's your fault I didn't test well. You didn't prep me well enough."

"That's not true."

I refused to let him blame me for his scores. Had I not planned to dump his ass, this nasty aspect of his personality would have sent me running to high ground ahead of a *tsunami* of vicious words.

"I tutored you in good faith. How many times did we go over the sample questions? You knew them cold. It's not my fault you don't test well." This endless argument grated on my nerves like hot salt on raw flesh.

"Are you saying I blew the test?" His long fingers clenched into fists.

"That's not what I said. And it's not what I meant. I think you could have done better." This argument was heading toward an irrevocable split. I tried to be kind. Hard to do when I felt just the opposite, but I didn't want to lose my first and only sex partner.

"Are you calling me a failure?" He took a step toward me, fists rising.

"Look, you're going to med school. You'll be an OB/GYN." I patted his arm before he jerked aside. I sidled away. "You know what the guy who graduates last in his class at med school is called, don't you?"

"Huh?"

"Doctor. He's called doctor. That's what you're going to be." What I may have lacked in sensitivity I more than made up for in insincerity.

"You should talk. You got into Johns Hopkins. What's a pathologist need a top school for? I should be going there, not you."

Goose bumps speckled my arms. In that instance, with Lab-Rat belittling me and constantly criticizing everything I did, I went cold. He'd never understand why getting away with transforming living people into dead people made pathology even more of a turn on than sex. I suppressed my rage when all I wanted to do was hit him upside the head. He never understood how close he came to not having to worry about med school at all.

"You have no right to leave me behind."

CHAPTER FOURTEEN

DEADLY CAMPING

1987

Lab-Rat was right: I was leaving him behind. Call me a coward, but I'd hoped we'd drift apart, letting what-might-have-beens play themselves out. I worked hard to deflect any discussion of a straight-out break up. Even with the tension between us, we were still damned good in bed. Besides, I didn't have a moment to waste finding someone else. On our way back to his apartment after dinner one night, I suggested a camping trip to ease the tension.

"We need a break. Let's get away from everything." I put my arm around his waist and pressed my breast against his arm. "We haven't scared any birds in a long time."

We went to bed. Later, we rested.

"Camping would be good." Lab-Rat lay on his back, sweat drying on his chest.

"Pre-Law has a new boyfriend." Spending two days in the woods alone with Lab-Rat had lost its appeal. I wanted other people around as a defense should he become difficult. "Let's ask them."

We'd double dated with Pre-Law several times. Unlike me, she flitted from boyfriend to boyfriend throughout her senior year. Her latest was an earth sciences major who came to class in field jackets and work boots. Because I'd never seen her flirt with someone who looked country before, I wondered if she was slumming before settling into the grind of law school.

"We're having fun without commitments. I'm not about to get tied down with anyone when we'll all be going our separate ways. Look how Lab-Rat's trying to mess with your head," Pre-Law said. "Plenty of time to find Mr. Right while I'm in law school."

"As long as you don't settle for Mr. Just-Good-Enough."

"Don't worry. I won't."

§

Lab-Rat started in on me the moment we set up the tents. We'd done this a dozen times, but now I didn't unfold the sleeping bags right. I didn't stack wood for the campfire right. Whenever he got stressed, and he was sure as hell stressed about going away to school without me, I couldn't do anything right.

I'd endured his rages and pouts too many times to count. Sex alone wasn't worth putting up with Lab-Rat's being a control freak. I'd lived with one my entire life until I left for college. Still, Lab-Rat had some redeeming qualities, so I didn't hate him like I did the old man.

Hawkeye, Pre-Law's current boyfriend, told Lab-Rat to chill before he spoiled the weekend.

"Chill? How would you feel if your girlfriend thought you were a failure?"

"I don't think you're a failure. For God's sake, you got into med school. That's a hell of an accomplishment. I've told you over and over you'll do fine." Same song, different day. Same result: boring.

"You have to help me. You're much smarter than I am. I need you to get me through." Lab-Rat had played the guilt and martyr cards earlier when we were alone. Strikes one and two. The smarts card was next in his litany. Third strike; he was out.

"You have to do this yourself."

His criticizing shredded my already raw nerves. I bit my lip to prevent anger from swallowing me whole.

"This from someone who only wants to play with dead people." Lab-Rat threw the food bag he was holding onto a picnic table and stomped off.

"Go after him," Pre-Law said to Hawkeye. "He's going to spoil the weekend if you can't get him under control."

I looked at Pre-Law, my face hot, my eyes narrowed. I fought to regain control.

"He calls pathology playing with dead people?" Pre-Law took an inventory of the ice chests. "Is he freaking nuts?"

"He's doing everything he can to change my mind. He won't shut up about us practicing together." I finished stacking firewood and dusted my hands. "That's not going to happen."

"Demeaning your choice sure as hell isn't working."

"Even if I bought into his co-practice fantasy, he'd blame me if anything goes wrong in the future. I won't be responsible for him." I shook off this latest attack. Lab-Rat had to shut up and get off my back. "I just won't."

Pre-Law said mules were more easy going and compliant than I was when I set my mind on something. I shoved Lab-Rat's behavior into a box and locked the lid.

I did a double check, twitched the ground cover in place, and folded tent flaps back to catch a breeze. Flies and small bees buzzed around discarded fast food wrappers, detritus left by previous campers. I tossed the trash in a dumpster. In mid reach for an empty beer can, I realized how much Li'l Bit had influenced how I behaved. To avoid problems with Lab-Rat, I acted the same way she did around Big Chigger. I kicked the beer can as far as I could. Pre-Law glanced at me, startled by my outburst.

"Sorry," I said. "He makes me so damned mad. I'll calm down."

I washed my hands at the tap near the bathroom before pulling marinated chicken from the cooler, along with bags of cut-up vegetables for roasting over the grill.

"Did you bring the makings for s-mores?" Pre-Law rooted through the bag Lab-Rat threw down. She found graham crackers, Hershey chocolate, and marshmallows. "Yippee."

The two of us threaded chicken and vegetables onto skewers.

"He says pathology is wasting my appointment to Johns Hopkins." I sat back on my haunches.

"Is he right? Do you need to go to there to be a pathologist?"

"No, but graduating from Hopkins will open doors neither you nor I can imagine." Pathology could lead along unmapped professional paths; furthermore, it would make me more successful as a killer. "Like going to Georgetown Law will set you up for success no matter what you want to do."

Pre-Law pulled icy-cold beer from the drinks cooler. We opened our first cans of the evening after we lit the fire. When the men returned, Pre-Law handed each a beer.

"I'm sorry," Lab-Rat said.

Pre-Law had taught me well. I pasted a smile on my lips. "No worry."

No worry at all. If he said one more word about my choice, though, he'd need the services of a pathologist.

A spring storm rolled in after dinner on our second and last night. We piled into Pre-Law's and Hawkeye's tent and played gin. We returned late to our own tent to let her and her boyfriend get it on. Lab-Rat turned away and didn't touch me, even though our sleeping bags were zipped together.

The next morning the sun rose on the freshly washed trees and undergrowth. Lab-Rat and I started out on our last hike.

"I don't understand why you're so fascinated with dead bodies." The discussion began innocently enough. "It's morbid."

I never considered pathology morbid. "I want to learn everything I can about how the human body goes from living to dead. Pathology is a good specialty."

"You'll be sorry if you don't pick a different one."

I kept my mouth shut, another trick I'd learned from Li'l Bit. Skills she'd developed to cope with Big Chigger could work for me. I didn't care why Lab-Rat thought I'd be sorry.

After the hours-long, middle of the night gully washer, we had to be careful on the debris-strewn trail. Bright sun slanted through the trees, and a distant waterfall splashed. Lab-Rat and I climbed steadily in the warming air, unseen insects singing in harmony with our boot steps.

The storm cooled the air as surely as our diverging career paths chilled our relationship. Not even the beauty of the new morning lifted my spirits. We were an hour into a six-mile hike, Lab-Rat leading the way up a steep part of the trail, when silence became too much. Over his shoulder came the familiar refrain about how I was sabotaging his future, how I didn't love him as much as he loved me, how stupid I was to go into pathology. Blah, blah, blah.

I'd had it with his shit. "You're responsible for your life, just like I'm responsible for mine. Whatever you make of it will be without me."

He stopped at a steep switchback in the trail and turned toward me. "What do you mean?"

"I mean, I'm going to Hopkins. You're not. Get over it."

"You're a cold-hearted bitch. I thought you loved me." Lab-Rat grabbed my arms and shook me hard, my head snapping backwards.

To protect myself, I clasped my hands, raised them between his arms and broke his grip. He grabbed me again, tighter this time. I shoved him harder than I had to. He lost his balance. His arms whirly-gigged, and he fell off the cliff. He screamed. I didn't.

I looked over the edge to where he lay unmoving. What the hell had I done? I'd let anger take control. I sat in the scree, head in hands, going through every second of what had happened. I didn't plan on killing him, but he pissed me off. Anger overcame reason and led to impulsive behavior. I could have shoved him less aggressively, but I hadn't. Honestly, I didn't want him dead. In my own funny way, I sorta liked him. If only he'd stopped yapping at me. I was still in the same pensive pose when Pre-Law and Hawkeye ran up.

"What happened? Where's Lab-Rat?"

"He, he fell." I covered my mouth, my eyes huge, unblinking. "The storm must have damaged the trail, because he turned too quickly near that washed-out section and lost his balance."

Three of us peered over the edge to see where Lab-Rat lay splayed about one hundred feet below us, his neck twisted at an unnatural angle. He didn't move.

Hawkeye ran back to the campground to an emergency phone to call 911. Pre-Law held my hand as we sat on a boulder and waited for the police and EMTs to arrive. I opened my eyes and focused on the mundane around me. Bees buzzed close by, and a butterfly danced among spring blossoms. A candy wrapper lay wedged under a stone. Pre-Law and I talked quietly, hesitant to disturb the hush that followed death. Her boyfriend returned with canteens and news that the EMTs were on the way. The police wanted us to wait in camp.

The police questioned us while we waited for the EMT team to hike down to where Lab-Rat lay. They called back that he was dead.

"Looks like he broke his neck. He has abrasions on his face and arms, too," one EMT shouted. "He must have bounced off the cliff face."

Hawkeye and Pre-Law drove together. Since I'd come with Lab-Rat, I'd have to take his car back to campus. I searched our tent for the keys. When I found them in his backpack, I sighed; they weren't in his shorts pocket. The EMTs had already removed the body. I followed Pre-Law and her boyfriend to the station. The cop who questioned us released them after a few minutes. About all they could say was we'd argued the first day of the trip. After that we made up and were happy. Yes, they were lower down on the trail because they had begun their hike more than forty minutes after we had. They hadn't seen him fall.

Undergoing my first police interrogation was like eating a rich dessert and not gaining an ounce. I mean, the questions I answered from the cute cop after Loser died couldn't have been called an interrogation. More like going through the motions of writing down what few facts there were. I told this cop about the argument, providing honest answers when asked, about our hike, how Lab-Rat led the way because his legs were longer. I pretended to be devastated, barely holding myself together.

"Last night's storm damaged the trails, so we were careful about where we stepped. He turned to help me over a wash-out when his boot struck loose gravel. He lost his balance and was gone before I could grab him."

No one asked if I'd pushed him, if we were arguing on the trail, if anything was wrong between us. I even produced tears when I talked about how he was looking forward to going to med school.

"It's all so sad." I wiped my eyes with a tissue I plucked from a box on the cop's desk, shut up, and didn't say anything more. I didn't want to overdo my heartbroken act.

The cop sent me home with orders not to leave State. When I

told him I was graduating and would be moving to Baltimore in a few days, he shrugged.

"Check in with me before you leave." He gave me his card.

This time was a real learning experience. I fooled the police because I played my role with the right amount of fake emotion and stuck as close to the truth as possible. It worked because the cop believed me. I filed the lesson away.

§

Back at campus, I parked Lab-Rat's car in its usual place and went in search of the head of our department. All students knew he spent Sunday evenings in his office to prepare for the week's lectures. I knocked and waited until he called for me to enter. I broke the sad news.

"That's terrible," he said. "He was so excited about graduation."

"I know." I sniffed and wiped a pretend tear from my eye.

"How are you holding up?"

"I'm a little shaky. I've never seen a dead body before." The public me lied better than a rug glued to a bald head.

"Are you sure you want to take your finals? We can freeze your grades where they are." He patted me awkwardly on my shoulder. "With straight As, you don't need to go through the formality."

"Taking them will help me cope." I raised watery eyes. I thought about flirting a little, but I didn't dare, because this was the prof who lectured us about not shitting where you ate.

On the surface, I was calm. I hadn't done anything wrong. And then it hit me. Ah shit. I had no one to fuck between now and graduation even though it was only ten days away. I'd become addicted to sex. My blood pressure rose. I breathed deeply and slowly in a fruitless attempt to keep my hands from trembling.

Back in the sorority house Pre-Law had paced a path in the living room carpet. No sooner had I opened the door than she pounced.

"Where have you been? Why didn't you come straight here?" Pre-Law hugged a grunt out of me.

"The police kept me longer than I thought. Then, I stopped to tell our prof." I hugged my friend before extracting myself from her vice-like grip. "I didn't mean to worry you."

"Are you all right?" Pre-Law pulled back and stared into my eyes.

I didn't blink. I lowered my eyes as emotion over Lab-Rat's death and Pre-Law's loving concern overcame me. Honestly overcame me. I'd never lost someone I sort of cared about. I mean, I did like him, more in bed than out, to be sure, but I didn't consciously want to harm him. When I'd killed Sad-Sack, I hadn't known her for more a minute. This time I'd had a relationship, a real physical relationship, with Lab-Rat. I felt a thrill run from my head to my toes and back. I rubbed my face with my right hand. "I can't believe he's dead."

"Me neither." Pre-Law put her arm around my shoulder. "Do you want something to eat? Maybe a cup of coffee?"

I nodded. "Coffee would be good."

That night, I lay on my bed and wished Lab-Rat was there. Once the adrenaline drained away, I realized how much I missed that bastard. God, I needed a fuck.

§

The day before graduation, the police called. The coroner ruled Lab-Rat's death an accident. He had slipped and fallen from the ungroomed trail.

"I'm very sorry for your loss." The standard police script. Lab-Rat was little more than a statistic on the list of people killed or injured in the national forest.

CHAPTER FIFTEEN

MOVING ON

1987

Three days before graduation, Pre-Law and I paraded up the stairs and down the halls at the sorority house in our caps and gowns with the other seniors. I finished at the top of my class again; Pre-Law was second.

"We're going to miss you. We weren't sure you'd enjoy sorority life, but we were wrong." The current sorority president half-hugged me before turning to others coming up the stairs behind me.

"What she means is, she's glad I didn't embarrass the house," I whispered to Pre-Law. I knew how to translate what she meant. "She sure will miss our GPAs. No house has ever had the two top students before."

"You got that right."

I wondered who the next GPA pledges would be. When Pre-Law and I joined, most other super-bright students were already in houses. Pre-law said she'd held out as long as she could before she caved to her mother's less-than-subtle nudging. She fit the house's needs on all counts: uber-smart, wealthy, and well mannered. I got in by being uber-smart.

"The nerds of a feather helped the house and each other, didn't we?" Pre-Law smoothed the tassel on her mortarboard, a golden cascade of twisted silk strands trickling through her fingers.

§

The Judge and Mrs. Judge came for Pre-Law's graduation and took us out for dinner before he returned to Charleston to hear a landmark case. A chemical company illegally discharged waste water contaminated with heavy metals and other carcinogens into the Kanawha River. He wanted it to set standards for future dumping cases.

No one from my family came.

Mrs. Judge remained behind to help us pack. The detritus of four years of college—books, clothes, television, Mr. Coffee, boom box, bedding—would fill three cars. Mrs. Judge's SUV would carry the bulk of Pre-Law's heavier boxes, with the BMW stuffed with clothes and bedding. The Ugly Duckling once again would hold everything I owned.

We moved out the day after graduation. Car and bedroom doors banged open and shut; riotous shouts from sorority sisters and parents filled corridors and rooms. No matter how careful we were, we tracked in bits of grass and grit, grinding them into the carpet. Parents and siblings humped boxes to vehicles and bemoaned the fact their students had acquired much more stuff in four years than would fit into trunks and SUVs. Parents glared at two families with envy; they'd rented U-Haul trailers.

My sorority sisters celebrated no more exams; their parents

celebrated no more tuition. Tears and hugs replaced teeth-grinding anxiety over grad school admission invitations. Animosities and petty jealousies gave way to mostly hollow promises of keeping in touch and getting together soon.

"I almost can't wait until summer is over." Pre-Law folded pajamas and stuffed them into a soft-sided bag. She scanned the room, fists on hips, before she dumped another stack of clothes on her stripped bed.

"I know how you feel." My bedding and clothing went into a few relatively clean boxes I found behind the local grocery store. I flicked a bit of desiccated lettuce leaf into our overflowing trash basket.

Lab-Rat's parents had offered me his camping gear when they cleared out his apartment after his funeral. I'd learned early in life not to turn up my nose at anything potentially useful, so I accepted their generosity. As soon as they were gone, though, his sleeping bag went into the dumpster. I kept mine.

I added books and Old Rex, my dog skeleton in his box, to my growing heap. The two cartons I'd picked up a year earlier in Bubbaville were still unopened. I'd put on fresh tape and stuck them in the back of my closet, exactly as if they'd stayed behind in my old bedroom. Although I had no reason to open them, and in fact wasn't at all curious about what Li'l Bit had sealed up, I couldn't throw them away. Maybe one day I'd open them. Maybe not.

I'd accomplished everything I set out to do academically, and yet I had little physical evidence to show for four years at State beyond my diploma. I hadn't had an actual to-do list when I arrived four years earlier, but had I, it would have contained entries for graduating first in my class, getting into the best medical schools, planning and executing a kill, acquiring a veneer of manners, perfecting separate public and killer personae, finding a boyfriend, and losing my virginity. It would not have included making one best friend.

Pre-Law and Mrs. Judge fussed over me as if I were part of their family. Mrs. Judge and I carried boxes downstairs while Pre-Law ran our various keys back to the sorority house mother and to the post office. When we were alone, Mrs. Judge gave me a card. In it was a check.

"You're part of our family. Please let us help you get settled in Baltimore."

I don't know who was more emotional, me or Mrs. Judge. I hugged her. We both cried a little.

Pre-Law dashed in from the campus post office with a crumpled envelope like the one Sad-Sack had thrown away. For a full second, I stopped breathing. Could someone have found it? I knew I'd disposed of it where it wouldn't be linked to me, but for that one long second terror paralyzed me. Pre-Law held the envelope out.

This one was addressed in Li'l Bit's crabbed printing. I didn't want to touch it. Mrs. Judge nudged Pre-Law aside. I peeled the flap off the envelope and shook out a single piece of lined notebook paper.

"We found Miss Snickers dead on the porch this morning. Junior said he didn't have nothing to do with it. I thought you'd want to know." Three sentences. No signature. The only letter Li'l Bit had ever written.

I hadn't cried, truly cried, in forever. I'd looked forward to having my own place where my cat could live with me, and Junior took that dream away. I knew he killed her. Mrs. Judge held me and rubbed my back until my sobs slowed to hiccups and stopped. I blew my nose, put the note in a box, and went to wash my face.

Finally, the SUV, Pre-Law's car, and my poor Ugly Duckling were ready. One more box appeared beside my car.

"Take the coffee maker," Pre-Law said. "I'll get a new one."

I didn't argue. I put it in the front seat where I'd hoped Miss

Snickers would one day ride to her new home. More hugs and kisses before I plopped my butt in the front seat and pointed the car's nose north. I waved a pretend-cheery hand and watched Pre-Law and Mrs. Judge fade into the haze. I drove north on the interstate and let my mind wander, thoughts clicking over in harmony with the odometer.

§

College graduation couldn't have been more different from high school, and yet in one way it was oddly similar. Big Chigger and I clashed at the dinner table when I pulled the pin and dropped the graduation grenade. He slouched in his chair after another fried dinner, a half-consumed beer beside the cigarette burning in his ashtray. I waited until he finished eating before putting a stack of papers on the table.

"What's that shit?"

"My graduation schedule."

"You ain't graduatin.'" As if the old man's words could affect my life.

"I am. I finished high school. I'm out of here. You didn't think I'd stay around until I dropped dead, did you?"

"Don't give me any shit." Big Chigger yelled. "We work damned hard to give you what you got."

"What I got? Fat lips and black eyes?" Not for much longer, you ass. I had no qualms snotting off at him.

"Whatcha gonna do? 'Bout time you got a job and helped support the family." The old man took a drag on his cigarette and blew smoke across the table into my face.

"I'm going to college. To State."

"Like hell. How you gonna do that? You ain't got no money. I sure as shit ain't gonna give you any." The old man threw his napkin on the table, where it landed on his overflowing ashtray and caught fire. Acrid smoke curled upward when he doused the flame with the dregs of his beer. "Goddammit! Look what you made me do."

"Me? I made you throw your napkin? Oh, please."

Big Chigger stood so suddenly his chair crashed to the floor. He leaped around the table, grabbed my upper arm with a stained, work-chapped hand, and yanked me out of my chair. He shook me so hard my head snapped backwards.

"Shut your goddamned mouth."

"Did I ask you for money? I have my own." I stood my ground and stared him in the face. I might have been the first person in the family not to cringe in fear.

"Oh, yeah? Where's it at?"

"In my college savings account." I'd saved every penny I earned for years working summer jobs.

"Stupid bitch. I spent that money last year to fix my truck."

"I'll go without your help." I shouted back. "You tell me all the time I'm not your kid. If I'm not, you can't tell me what to do."

Li'l Bit tried to calm his rage. "She ain't going nowhere."

"No stopping this train. Graduation's on Saturday, June third, like it or not."

Big Chigger threw me so hard against the wall my head thunked against plaster, causing bits to sift to the floor. He was bigger than I was, but I refused to be cowed. No way would I give him the satisfaction of a flinch of pain or a tear. I took a deep breath, all but suffocating on the biting fumes from the mostly soaked ashtray.

"You ain't graduating. Princess is." If the old man shouted loudly enough, maybe he could make it so. "Ain't you, Princess?"

"Nah. I flunked math again."

Big Chigger raised his fist to slug me, then dropped it when he saw my eyes narrowing. I dared him to hit me, but the coward couldn't stand up to a direct challenge. The old man never told me I couldn't do something after that.

Petty or not, I wanted my parents and siblings at the ceremony to rub their noses in my success. The old man refused to go, but Li'l Bit brought Princess and Junior. Neither of them knew what to expect or where to look. I knew what was coming: a heap of getting even.

They sat way in the back of the auditorium, but I saw them when I marched in behind the principal and the teachers. Black robes fluttered as the graduates sweated in the overheated room. After too many speeches reminding us we were going to change the world, the principal called my given name. I walked to the microphone to deliver the valedictorian address.

"What's That Thing doing up there?" Junior's voice rang out.

The principal called my given name two more times. I was the only National Merit Scholar in our high school and won the Governor's Scholarship in Science. I could go to State without any financial support from the family. That Thing, invisible and unwanted, gloated about how I'd gotten payback for years of not being good enough for the old man. On command, seniors moved our tassels from one side to the other to signify our new graduate status.

§

If high school graduation was my ticket out of Bubbaville, college graduation pushed me along my chosen paths, medicine and killing. My public distinctions, graduating at the top of my class twice, getting free rides to State and Johns Hopkins, hid a private distinction: I'd killed two human beings, one in cold blood, one in anger. Three, if you count Loser, which I didn't. On my lonely journey between my undergraduate and graduate lives, I vowed never to be mistaken for a common household killer.

Comparing me with a Sue-Bob who shot her husband for flirting with her sister at their wedding was like comparing NASCAR to push lawn mowers. Not from the same planet. I would have to select my killing methods with care to avoid falling into the same old M.O, the same *modus operandi*, trap. Variation would let me hide in plain sight and stay off police radar.

Driving north, I spent no small amount of time ruminating about how I wanted to find people who were so evil they didn't deserve to live, not unlucky ones like Sad-Sack and Lab-Rat. When I found the right victims, I'd read them chapter and verse about why I was suited to mete out justice, why I was the only person capable of taking them to task and making them pay for their crimes.

The more I thought about having a moral rationale for killing, the more excited I became. My senses sharpened. Blood raced through my veins, bubbling along like Pop Rocks in my mouth. Hair on my arms rose.

I tried not to think about Miss Snickers, even though it was impossible not to think about something once you think about it. She'd been the only one in Bubbaville that loved me unconditionally. Even though cats were supposed to be standoffish, arrogant even, she always ran to me to be petted. The former barn kitty slept on my pillow at night, purring in my ear.

Tears wet my cheeks. I kept returning to what Li'l Bit said about Junior. All his life he'd killed small animals. He got his first gun at five and began a life of terrorizing neighborhood critters. If he wanted to kill something, he did. Miss Snickers might have been in the wrong place when he aimed his rifle.

I passed the off ramp to Bubbaville, fresh tears flowing. I flipped the bird just like Big Chigger had when Pre-Law and I left the family homestead. I missed Miss Snickers more than anyone or anything. One of these days, I would deal with Junior. I wasn't sure how or when, but he would pay.

CHAPTER SIXTEEN

ON MY OWN

1987

I'd lived my entire life in the shadows of the Blue Ridge Mountains and yet I'd never driven along the Parkway. Farm and country folks I knew didn't indulge in Sunday drives with no particular destination. Gas was too expensive. Taking a ride to take a ride wasn't what we did; visiting family took place after church and chores when we drove from point A to point B and back. We never took vacations, either.

For the first time in my life, I had no schedule. No animals to feed or siblings to raise. No classes or labs. Nothing for almost three months, after which med school would start, and I'd have no life again beyond the classroom. I planned a leisurely drive northward, camping along the way.

Open car windows carried honeysuckle scent inside on warm

air currents. I remembered how the vines twisted around the rusty barbed wire along our pasture edge. I loved pulling the blossoms off and letting that drop of sweet nectar fall onto my tongue. Sun on my arms gave my skin a glow missing in winter when I was trapped indoors and wore long sleeves. When I was a kid, running free outdoors was so commonplace none of us thought about the health benefits. We didn't know we were developing muscles. We didn't know Vitamin D would help us grow strong. My sister hated the sun because she freckled. Me, I tanned like a Hispanic.

Camp grounds offered cheap overnight rates, especially during the week. I'd been in such a rush to leave the sorority house I hadn't thought through the process of camping when I packed my car. On my first night on the road I dumped everything out of the trunk and repacked it for easy access to the sleeping bag and tent. They had to be last in and first out.

Funny, but now that I was on my own, I set up the tent perfectly the first time. "Screw you, Lab-Rat. I can get along just fine without you."

Cooking on the camp stove would have been cheaper, but I had no way to keep fresh food from spoiling. I spent a bit of my savings from my job at the student union on pre-packaged sandwiches for lunches and dinner. I had to have hot coffee early in the morning no matter what. I had two choices: set up the camp stove and make instant or find a restaurant. I thought I'd find plenty of restaurants and gas stations on the Parkway, until I went hunting for my first morning cup. After I broke camp, I drove more than twenty miles before I came to a crossover at Tuggle's Gap. There, I found little more than a smattering of houses, a gas station, a motel, and a tiny restaurant that served the best coffee ever.

By my second night, I fidgeted in my sleeping bag. Although I'd planned to take my time, two days of gorgeous scenery and getting back to nature, reliving memories of the last trip with Lab-Rat and Pre-Law were all I could hack. I wanted to get to Baltimore as quickly as possible and find a place to live and a summer job.

I dropped off the two-lane highway somewhere near Roanoke and let the nearest interstate carry me north. I sang along to the songs on the radio, made mental notes of what I had to do before classes began, and looked forward to the next steps of my future. I rolled into Baltimore late one afternoon.

"Holy shit! This place is fucking huge." I gawked like the country girl I was. "I bet there isn't a campground nearby."

I was right.

Talk about naïve. I actually believed I could drive into a strange city, pick up a newspaper, and find an apartment without so much as a by your leave. That didn't happen. I spent a couple of nights curled in a ball in the front seat of my car in a parking lot behind a fast-food restaurant. I jerked awake at every strange city-night sound.

When I bought a copy of *The Baltimore Sun*, the information in the first real newspaper I'd ever read opened new worlds. I cruised unfamiliar streets. The more I drove, the less I knew about the city I was going to live in. Baltimore, with more than a half million people, contained the largest population I'd ever seen. It scared the shit out of me, but at the same time it energized me with its noise and snorting cars. More than once, angry drivers honked at the Ugly Duckling. Not knowing where I was going made me overly cautious and, therefore, a traffic hazard.

Whenever I stopped for food, I opened the *Sun*. Local crime stories reached out like a giant hand and grabbed me. Everything I needed to know about criminal activity, what kind and where it was happening, ran page after page. A target-rich environment awaited me when I was ready to kill again. I circled several stories before tossing the paper on the front seat. Time enough for research later.

With a cup of coffee on the dash and a breakfast sandwich

in my left hand, I rooted behind the passenger seat for the Johns Hopkins orientation packet, hoping for maps and guidelines on finding an apartment. If the student housing office was open this far ahead of the fall semester, I might be able to save a lot of time. I found a pay phone and made an appointment for the following day.

In spite of getting lost looking for the housing office, which turned out to be tucked in the back corner of the basement in the main administration building, I managed to arrive only a few minutes late. The student at the counter shrugged away my apology and led me to a small table where a pile of single sheets of paper was stacked.

"You're smart to get in early. You'll have the best pick." A bell dinged out front. "If you find anything you like, bring the sheets to the counter."

I thumbed and sorted and read descriptions of rooms to share, whole houses and individual apartments to rent. I ended up with four possibilities. The girl tossed the top one aside.

"Too near a really bad section of town. We never place female students there. Nasty high assault and murder rate."

Good to know. I memorized the address to cross reference with the crime stories in the paper. The thought of being close to bad neighborhoods with potential victims made the hair on my arms rise. My eyes narrowed ever so slightly. I shook my head to push the thoughts deep in my brain where the killer persona lurked. The public me had no need to bring the dark side into the light. In due time, I promised myself, in due time I would kill again.

"Thank you. I have no idea which areas are safe. I appreciate your help."

The other three apartments were in gradually-being-gentrified neighborhoods with lower crime rates. Still high but tolerable. The girl tapped one with a long, painted fingernail. "This one's within walking distance of the medical school, in case you don't have a car. I'd grab it if I were you, because Mrs. Preston's really nice and leaves you alone. If you want to check it out, I'll call her. She works nights but should be awake by now."

"I'd like to see it."

The girl dialed a number and set up an appointment. "She lives upstairs. Just ring the bell. She'll show you the place."

I thanked her and scurried to the Ugly Duckling. Ten minutes later I walked into an apartment, which turned out to be the entire lower half of a narrow brick row house. Partly furnished, it had a kitchen, bath, bedroom, and living room. Off the kitchen was a tiny utility room with a washer and dryer and a door to the backyard.

I squinted and used my imagination to see how I could make this dull place as fresh as the room I had had at Pre-Law's house. With a little time and a lot of effort, I could paint drab walls and scrub the scratched hardwood floors. A couple of area rugs would make them acceptable. Until I could afford better, clean would be enough. When I was a kid, our house was shabby but never filthy, not like it had become after I went off to State. Clean worked for me growing up in Bubbaville; clean would work for me in Baltimore.

The place smelled stale and shut in, with an underlying bouquet of rotting garbage. Not the shut-up-tight smell of the Li'l Bit's house in Bubbaville or the all-girl scent of the sorority. More like dirty sweat socks and testosterone. I took inventory of the furnishings. A double bed and chest of drawers, a bedside table, and a sofa partially filled the rooms. Kitchen cupboards contained mismatched dishes and pans. An old microwave sat on the counter next to the stove. I could make do with what the previous tenant left behind. I couldn't wait to cook for myself. A couple of end tables and lamps, a television, and bookshelves were all I needed. I already had one essential appliance, a Mr. Coffee, courtesy of Pre-Law. I could use some of Mrs. Judge's gift to fix up my nest.

Mrs. Preston and I sized each other up. She seemed friendly enough and didn't ask any personal questions. In a way, she was a combination of the aunt who gave me my car and my up-country granny. Her gray hair pulled tight in a bun made her look older than she probably was. I had no idea what she saw in me, but I wanted her to like me. I glued on the façade of the public me, the serious medical student me.

"No loud parties. I work late most nights and need my rest," the owner said.

"I'm a med student. About the loudest noise I'll make is after exams when I'll snore for twenty-four straight hours."

"If you want a roommate, let me know. No additional rent, but I want to know who's sleeping in my house."

"No plans for a roommate." I'd never find one as good as Pre-Law. I walked through the rooms again. "What happened to the previous tenant?"

"He graduated. Left a lot of junk. What with so much going on at work, I haven't had time to throw it out." She tossed a dusty pillow on the couch. "You can keep anything you want. If you don't like something, haul it out to the curb. Someone'll take it."

She named a reasonable monthly rent. "No need for a lease, since everyone I rent to is a student. Utilities are included in the rent, because I don't have a separate meter for the apartment. Figure if you don't get kicked out in your first year, you'll be here for a while."

We'll see. "Thank you very much. I'd like the apartment, please."

"I have a garage out back, but I don't have a car. You can have it for ten dollars more a month."

I wasn't sure the Ugly Duckling could handle being enclosed in a garage without feeling claustrophobic, but one could come in handy when I resumed killing. "That's very kind of you. I'll take it, too."

"One last thing. I don't usually allow pets, but the guy before you had a cat. They're okay if you keep them inside. Otherwise, my dog will chase them, and they could get hit by a car."

I swallowed a lump. Had Junior not killed Miss Snickers, I could have brought her to live with me. "No, no cat right now."

"If you decide to get one, let me know. No extra charge if you keep the place clean."

Whoa there. How would she know if I kept the place clean? Would she let herself in when I was in class? If she did, would I feel safe in my new home? My backpack with my killing clothes had lived in the Ugly Duckling for more than a year. Locked inside the garage, any items belong to the killer me would be out of sight. The public me chastised the killer me for being paranoid. No, just watchful, I told the killer me.

Mrs. Preston handed over my keys and pointed to my new mailbox. I checked out the garage before heading to the nearest store to stock up on food and plenty of cleaning supplies. By dinner time, the bedroom, kitchen counter tops, and bath were usable. I scrambled eggs, toasted a muffin, and poured a glass of milk, ready for an early evening. I shook out my sleeping bag and laid it on the bed. Time for sheets and quilts later.

The next day I scrubbed the kitchen from ceiling to floor before setting out on an archaeological exploration for furniture to fill in the gaps. My first trip to Goodwill had netted me my killing clothes. The second added a bookcase that would be fine once I sanded and painted it. I found a consignment shop on a side street that served as a recycling center for student leftovers. I picked up two end tables and lamps, a kitchen table and two chairs (for having guests for dinner?), an extra set of sheets and towels, and two area rugs. All for less than one hundred dollars. I carted the furniture home and dragged it into the house. I wiped a sweaty brow and looked around.

For the first time in my life, I not only had a room of my own, I had an apartment of my own. I sat and took it all in, enjoying the quiet. I wrote a letter to Mrs. Judge to thank her for her generous gift and telling her how I'd used part of it.

CHAPTER SEVENTEEN

EXPLORING

1987

With my apartment set up, I explored the campus. The stately buildings and the aura of self-importance that comes from being one of the best medical schools in the country soothed and challenged me concurrently. I sat on one of the benches scattered around campus and felt as small and invisible as when I was That Thing. I listened to the contrast of the close-in hush and the distant pulsating traffic. Had I known how, I might have stretched out on the manicured lawns and daydreamed. I might have indulged in watching high thin clouds filter sunlight. I might have relaxed and enjoyed the day.

Instead, I made a list of what I wanted to accomplish in the next years: in-depth knowledge of everything there was to know about medicine; making new friends, including a boyfriend; graduating at the top of my class again; and entering my residency in pathology. Here in Baltimore at Johns Hopkins I would complete my transformation from pre-med student to doctor.

Clouds thickened, erasing shadows and turning the campus into a monochrome print. Med school goals might have been clear, but the whole killing scene was muddled. Intellectually, Sad-Sack's demise satisfied my curiosity about being able to kill in cold blood. I'd done it, but immediately afterward I knew killing without reason wasn't what I wanted to do. I wanted, no, needed, a cause to kill. As if that wasn't confusing enough, the urge to find a deserving victim intensified, but I didn't know how to find one.

Whether exploring the campus, roaming through the libraries, or hiking the streets the same way I hiked in the mountains, I spent every spare minute on foot. Nothing at the State campus, which flowed into the surrounding town with no distinct boundaries, prepared me for the demarcation between the pristine campus and the filthy city streets. I'd never experienced the kind of urban grime that comes from too many people living in too small a place for too long. A myriad of different smells assaulted me and gave each neighborhood its distinct character. Italian, Hispanic, Asian, black, each smelled unique.

I memorized street names, cross-referenced them to the crime beat in the *Sun,* and sat in my apartment night after night making notes, filling a lab book with information about hunting grounds. The more I walked, the more I learned which neighborhoods were safe if I looked Latina, others where I needed to look black. I found the poorer neighborhoods fascinating, full as they were with potential victims.

Drug dens were easy to identify, what with tiny baggies, needles, and aluminum foil scattered all around. Pushers led users inside to get high. I got up enough courage one night to enter a den a mile away from my block, only to be appalled by the number of comatose users lying on floors fouled with urine and vomit. How could anyone feel safe in such a degrading dump? And how could I not find ways to clear out some of the users?

I walked the streets of murder row disguised in my trusty sweatshirt and over-sized jeans, pretending to be a black boy. I watched how young men swaggered and imitated their walks, the hem of my jeans fraying on the pavement. Too small jeans and a denim jacket I found at the consignment shop transformed me into a Latina.

I didn't limit myself to the poorer sections of Baltimore with their old buildings so full of opportunities. I drove out to wealthy suburbs where mini-mansions sprang like weeds in what used to be farmland, houses crammed so close together neighbors could hear each other belch. I roamed further afield, west to the remaining countryside with white-board pastures and abandoned barns, south toward Washington where I found a different world of neighborhoods to use as kill and disposal zones.

I analyzed my situation and decided Baltimore, with one of the highest crime rates in the entire United States, was a perfect place to kill with impunity. Sure would be a hell of a lot more convenient to walk to and from a kill scene than driving the old one-hundred-and-fifty-mile radius, especially when I would probably be working twenty hours a day to keep up with my course load.

§

After a week of settling in and urban trekking, I picked up a summer bulletin on campus and learned the job center was open in the same basement where the housing office was. I stopped in to see the clerk who'd helped me sort out apartments.

"I saw you took the duplex," she said. "It's a great place, isn't it?"

"I love it. Thanks again for the recommendation." We strolled the hallway until we came to the job office. "Now, I'm off to find a job."

I didn't feel ready to start on a killing spree. I wanted more time to blend in, more time to plan, and more time to isolate victims who needed to die. I needed money and something to keep me busy until classes began at the first of August. The science lab had an open tech position, so I walked over for an interview that afternoon.

"Have you worked in a research lab before?" The senior tech peered into various cages filled with mice.

"No." I hoped that wouldn't rule me out.

"Not afraid of mice, are you?"

"I grew up on a farm. We had mice everywhere."

"Yeah, well, you'll be working around a different caliber of mice than barn mice. These guys are worth their weight in gold." He waved toward racks of cages stacked three high. "Anyway, most of your work will be feeding them and cleaning their cages. They get fresh shavings every day after you remove the soiled stuff and pick out their crap."

"I can handle that." The lab smelled strongly of wood shavings and faintly of mouse urine.

"It's pretty easy most of the time." He lifted a mouse by its tail and weighed it before writing a note on a chart hanging by a chain on the front of the cage. He returned the squirming critter to its home. "We're doing important drug research."

I was hired on the spot. The tasks were straightforward. Top skill was paying attention to detail and not letting a cage stay dirty. I came in one afternoon to find half of them empty.

"The prof conducting this experiment euthanized the mice last night," the senior tech said. "Just dump everything out of the cages and scrub them with disinfectant and bleach. We'll be getting another shipment in a few days."

I felt sorry for the mice at first. The more cages I washed, however, the quicker I changed my mind. These mice had been killed as part of drug research, much the same way barn mice were food for barn cats.

Even though I usually finished my work by late afternoon, I worked several extra hours one day when a shipment of new mice arrived for processing. I weighed and logged in mouse after mouse. It was well past dark when I left. Rather than heat up leftover stew, I stopped for Chinese take-out.

"You must be new," the young hostess said. "I haven't seen you around before."

"I just moved in." We chatted while I waited. "I'm glad you're close enough to stop on my way home from class."

"I figured you were from Hopkins."

Did I have medical student stamped on my forehead? I asked how she guessed.

"You're walking, and you're not local. Simple guess, university student. Undergrad or grad?"

"Grad. Med school."

She raised a finely plucked eyebrow. "You don't look old enough to be in med school."

"I get that all the time," I said. "Good thing I'm not buying beer. You'd have to card me."

"I was born and raised two blocks over." She went on to tell me that her grandparents had opened the restaurant four decades earlier. Her parents ran it and were training her to take over when they wearied of the grind. "I put in extra egg rolls since this is your first order."

I thanked her and took my goldfish boxes in a sack. The wind was blowing up an evening storm. Debris-filled gutters waited for the predicted downpour to wash them cleaner. A couple of spent syringes play tag in front of me, leading me away from the restaurant. I pulled my university sweatshirt hood over my hair and hunched over. If it was going to rain, I wanted to beat it home. I turned down an alley as long as a hyphen.

I'd walked through this cut-over several times in the daylight. While not all that much different on the surface from the alley in Monroe Crossing where I'd killed Sad-Sack, the singular point of contrast was people. None in Monroe Crossing, but here gangs of men and packs of boys hung out night and day where alleys crossed streets. I realized soon enough the men were drug dealers and the boys runners. So far, I'd kept to myself and passed untouched. I suspected the streets and alleys would be more dangerous as evening wore into night, but I hadn't figured on thugs getting an early start on their entertainment.

"Well, what do we have here?" A six-foot-something shoved me before snatching my take-out dinner. "Oh, Chinese. I love Chinese."

He dumped a goldfish box on the pavement and stomped in my *moo-shu* pork. With one sneaker slimed with Chinese food, he had difficulty keeping his balance when my martial arts training kicked in, literally. I caught him unaware when I dropped him with a single kick to his gut. I heard the *pop-click* of a switchblade. He leaped up, knife at the ready. Two of his friends oozed out of the shadows, but he waved them off.

"The bitch is mine."

My eyes and lips narrowed. He must have misread the warning as a challenge, because he attacked. After some sparing and dodging knife feints, I brought him to his knees with two kicks to his midsection. He sagged toward the pavement and gave me a perfect target. I hit his sternum with an up kick as hard as I could. He fell sideways, gasping for breath. His posse melted away.

"Don't ever fuck with me again, asshole." I kicked him under his chin. Beating the snot out of him served as warning to leave me alone. "Do you hear me?"

Street-Thug gurgled. I hit him one more time on the back of

the neck. When I left, he was unconscious, face down in my dinner, which by now looked like puke. I kept his knife and the egg rolls.

Less than two weeks after Street-Thug ruined my dinner, Mrs. Preston met me when I returned from work.

"I've been waiting for you." She stared down the block. "See the guys at the corner?"

Well, well. Street-Thug and posse. "Yes."

"They've been robbing pedestrians for drug money. I wanted to be sure you knew about them and took care. Don't want anything to happen to you." She turned her back on the guys hanging around half a block up the street and walked in the opposite direction to the city bus that took her to her night job.

"I'll be careful. You, too, okay?" I called after her.

If they laid a finger on her, the killer me would have new targets.

CHAPTER EIGHTEEN

NEW NAME, SAME ME

1987

Mrs. Judge wrote to ask if she and Pre-Law could swing by the weekend before classes started at Georgetown. They were bringing the stuffed SUV to move Pre-Law into the apartment she was sharing with two other girls. I called to say yes.

During the summer, we'd kept up a weekly correspondence, so I was tuned into what Pre-Law's course load would be. God awful, just like mine. Because we were a short train ride apart, we planned to get together at least once a month. We'd alternate: one weekend in the District, the next in Baltimore.

For a few days after Pre-Law told me she was going to have two roommates, I moped around my apartment, which was too small for a roommate. Pre-Law had been the best roommate for me; I couldn't imagine settling for second best. With what I'd saved from my jobs at State, Mrs. Judge's gift, and what I earned at the mouse lab, I could afford to live alone. Barely.

I couldn't wait to show Pre-Law and Mrs. Judge my very own apartment, which by this time was neat, newly painted and furnished with castoffs from the previous tenant and things I gleaned from Goodwill and consignment shops. A new television, courtesy of Mrs. Judge, made it downright respectable. Shabby, but respectable.

I got out of bed early and swept the stoop and sidewalk clean of drug paraphernalia. Most of the street was clear of addicts at this early hour, although I spotted a woman I'd come to know from the hyphen alley. She might have been in her mid-twenties or mid-fifties, so ravaged was her face by drugs and homelessness.

I sat on the stoop and waited for the SUV to pull up and park. When it did, I was off like a greyhound chasing a rabbit. Pre-Law and I met in the middle of the street and hugged each other. Mrs. Judge reserved her physical greeting until we were all safely on the sidewalk. She kissed my cheek.

I led the way inside. "Come on in. It's not much, but it's mine."

Mrs. Judge admired my apartment, but she was horrified by the general poverty of the area. "Are you sure this neighborhood is safe?"

"As safe as any." If you don't count the thugs and drug dealers, none of which were out when they arrived. "I can walk to campus. I couldn't find anything more convenient in any better neighborhood."

"But it's so, um, rundown." Mrs. Judge looked out the window just as Street-Thug and his posse strolled by. I heard worry in her voice.

"*Baltimore* is rundown." I hastened to reassure her I was as safe with Mrs. Landlady as I'd be anywhere.

"I doubt my neighborhood will be much better," Pre-Law said.

"The law school's not on the main campus. Mom helped me find what looks like a decent place, but we haven't been there to check it out yet. That's tomorrow."

They'd seen pictures of the inside of the row house as well as a street shot taken from the opposite curb. The basement apartment had two bedrooms, a big kitchen, living room, and two small bathrooms.

"I'm going to share one of the bedrooms, I hope. If not, I'll sleep on the couch," Pre-Law said. "It's going to be weird living half underground. The pictures show windows facing the street, but most of the view will probably be legs walking by."

"Or fannies." I laughed. I couldn't imagine living in a hole. The irony of my underground life as a killer made me smile, even if Mrs. Judge and Pre-Law had no hint as to why.

§

"You know, you two need new nicknames." Mrs. Judge said over a glass of wine. We sat is a restaurant I couldn't afford in the Inner Harbor before they drove on to the District.

"True. We're not Pre- anything anymore." Pre-Law disemboweled a hard-shell crab and picked the meat with fingers smeared with butter.

"I've been thinking about that." I winked at Mrs. Judge. "What about Shyster?"

"Won't work. Shysters are con men first, defense attorneys second, although for some it's one and the same. Some are actual ambulance chasers." Pre-Law giggled. "Shyster doesn't fit with what I'm going to do."

"She still wants to be a district attorney in spite of the fact her father had the whole summer to brainwash her into going into private practice." Mrs. Judge wielded a wooden mallet to break the crab shell with a dexterity I wanted to learn.

I'd spent the last two years at State copying everything Pre-Law did to sharpen my social skills. Now, watching Mrs. Judge, I saw more I could learn through association with her. Li'l Bit had shown me how to avoid Big Chigger, but that was as far as her lessons went. Mrs. Judge could take me to the next level so I'd fit in better after I became a doctor.

"Like that worked well, didn't it?" Pre-Law laughed.

"What about Hang 'Em High?" I offered a different take on her nickname.

"Gross." Soon-to-no-longer-be-Pre-Law pretended to gag.

"How about Law and Order?" Mrs. Judge waved for a second round of wine.

"That's good. Law and Order. L-and-O for short." I wiped my fingers on my third napkin. "Sounds like that new television show coming in the fall, you know the one they advertise with the dum-dum music opening it."

"L-and-O works." Pre-Law, no, L&O, leaned across the table and squeezed my hand. "You're easy, you know. You're Doc, now and forever."

"I resemble that." Doc stepped into the spotlight as the new public me.

"Long live Doc and L-and-O." We toasted our new nicknames.

Mrs. Judge wiped her fingers on a towelette before pulling a photo from her purse and pushing it across the table. An adorable black and white Tuxedo kitten stared up at me, a paw raised in greeting.

"I volunteer at a local no-kill shelter," she said. "This little girl came in with six brothers and sisters, all so skinny we called them The Twiglets. The mother died from injuries. We've been hand-feeding all seven."

Where was she going with this? I glanced at her.

"They'll be ready for adoption in a month or two." Mrs. Judge's voice trailed off. "I call her Shamu because she's so tiny and needs a big name."

"But how would I get her?" Words left my mouth before my brain registered what I'd asked.

"I'm coming back for parents' weekend around the time she'll be released. I could bring her."

This waif needed me as much as I needed her.

"Hello, Miss Snickers Number Two." I smiled at Mrs. Judge. "Thank you."

CHAPTER NINETEEN

ORIENTATION

Orientation began one of the happiest periods of my life. I picked up my course schedule, lugged my books back to my apartment, and walked the campus to be certain I knew the location of classrooms and labs. On the last Friday of freedom, first-year med students gathered in a cavernous lecture hall to hear our professors pontificate on what the next four years would hold, what to expect from each of the instructors, what we'd study in our labs, and what we'd do in the hospital.

"You won't declare a specialty until your fourth year. You'll all follow the same curriculum. If we invite you to do your internship and residency with us—and we only invite the best of the best to continue—you'll be doing general rotations until we say you're ready to enter a specialty."

What a pompous ass. He had to have been at Hopkins since dirt was young.

"Look around at your colleagues," said another. "One in four of you will wash out before the end of your first year. Another one in four will quit before graduation. Those of you who survive will be the best of the best. Be forewarned, however. Graduation at the top of the class is no guarantee of an invitation to continue here through your internship and residency."

Was "the best of the best" tattooed on each prof's eyelids?

"I get it," I whispered to a studious-looking girl sitting beside me. She had an open notebook on her fold-over desk and was madly scribbling. "I wish they'd cut this shit."

"Hush."

This stranger hushed me? My eyes narrowed; my face flushed with heat before I brought myself under control.

§

On the Monday when classes began, I marched from my apartment in a light rain, my books safely tucked into a book bag, and took a seat in the center of my first classroom. General anatomy. Five students arrived ahead of me. More trickled in and filled empty spaces; someone settled into the seat next to me right before the doors closed signaling the beginning of class. I turned to find the girl who shushed me during orientation. Blond hair pulled back in a ponytail high on her head, she looked even younger than I did.

The second we recognized each other and grinned, the prof entered and began telling us what we would learn. "You'll study here in the lecture hall, dissect cadavers in labs, and observe autopsies."

The girl turned pale. "I'm going into plastic surgery. I'm so not keen on dissecting people."

Plastic surgery? Her Valley-Girl pronunciation suggested she'd be more suited for cosmetology.

"It's part of the general curriculum." What a ditz! "Didn't you take biology? Dissect bodies there?"

"Of course, but those were animals or insects, not someone's family." Valley-Girl shuddered. "I don't know if I'll be able to get through. The sight of blood makes me sick."

I held my notebook in front of my face and whispered. "How can you be a doctor if the sight of blood makes you sick?"

"I know. I have to get over it."

I equated plastic surgery with nose jobs, boob jobs, and wrinkle removal. I couldn't imagine anything less exciting.

"There will be no talking in my class unless or until I invite a comment, which I have not." The prof thundered over general murmuring from several students, his open palm punctuating his last four words with slaps to the side of the lectern.

My face burned. Only pages turning and the scratching of pens and pencils could be heard from the chastened students for the remainder of the lecture.

As luck would have it, Valley-Girl and I were assigned to be lab partners, much like Lab-Rat and I had been. She was smarter than she sounded, which was a good thing, because her up-talking cadence about drove me raving ape shit. It didn't take long, however, to discover she was a Navy brat who graduated third in her class in molecular biology from University of California, San Diego.

"Why come East when California has so many great medical schools?" If she was really going into plastic surgery, I would have thought she'd stay in the land famous for its search for eternal youth.

"Dad got transferred. He's teaching at the Naval Academy for two years before he takes a rotation at the Pentagon."

Naval Academy? Pentagon?

"He's in Naval Intelligence."

I filed the information away. Who knew if I'd need it? I offered to help her if she got stuck, especially during autopsies where she was, "Oh my God, like, I'm going to be totally grossed out."

"Don't plastic surgeons operate? I mean, surgeon is part of the job description. Are you going to focus on nose jobs?"

"Oh, my God, no. I want to do facial reconstruction."

I blinked. Facial reconstruction? Valley-Girl?

"You know, like rebuilding Ann Margaret's face after she fell in Las Vegas. I saw some before and after photos. From that moment, I was hooked."

Really?

"Okay, we have to get you over your blood-flight syndrome, don't we? We don't want all those injured faces going unrepaired."

§

One entry high on my check list was to make friends earlier than I had at State. The sorority gave me a better road map for life than I'd anticipated. L&O and the other sisters encouraged me to get out of my shell and into group activities. Here at Johns Hopkins with so many of us studying together, we were in danger of being little more than heads-down, sleep-deprived bodies where we knew each other's names but little else.

I hand-picked several students I wanted to hang out with. We joked around and swapped war stories about the horrors of pre-med. I hoped we'd bond as a group to help each other stay sane.

"Anyone want to go to a brew pub Friday?" I issued a general invitation.

"Which one?" One of the girls asked.

Posters stuck to lampposts all over campus advertised happy hours with free food. I gestured to one of them. "That pub has cheap, cold domestic beer. I scoped it out this summer. We can stuff ourselves with wings or all-you-can-eat shrimp on Friday nights. Buy a couple of brews, and the shrimp and wings are dinner."

"Are there any cute guys there?" Valley-Girl asked. "In case you haven't noticed, first year med school has few viable men."

Several male students groaned. She was right, though. Two of our fellow first-years were cute, but I doubted either would be a good date.

"I hear you, sister," said one of the cute guys. "Am I the only gay guy here?"

"Yes." Six voices answered in unison.

One down.

Gay-Blade threw down a challenge. "Let's make a pact. The first of us to score buys the first round of beers to celebrate the next week."

"That's my kind of celebration." A soft voice with a strong Scottish lilt belonged to the other cute guy. "The winner treats. It's usually the other way around."

"Count us in." Voices roared.

The Cruise Club, as we named ourselves, met every Friday. Or rather those who could pry their noses from their books met. The group expanded gradually until we had ten regulars and another dozen or so casual members. Gay-Blade was the first to score. He was on the hook for drinks by the fourth Friday. Shy-Scot didn't seem interested in men or women, yet he went with us every week. I couldn't figure out why.

The more I watched my classmates, the more I saw how their competitive natures pitted one against another. With slots for internships limited even for the best students, some started posturing in the first month. I didn't. I was certain my grades and soon-to-be-perfected medical skills would see me through. Time enough to suck up to the professors later if I needed it.

The weeding-out process began on our first trip to the morgue about six weeks into the fall term. Valley-Girl was terrified she'd puke. I was terrified too, not because my stomach might not be strong enough, but because I couldn't afford a new pair of good sneakers if she splashed me. We did fine. Two of the guys, however, embarrassed the shit out of themselves. One fainted as soon as the smell from the cadaver hit his nose. The other barfed loudly into a trash can.

"Both of you. Out. Now." The professor pointed to the door. "I do not tolerate students who vomit or pass out."

Barfer helped Fainting-Violet from the room. I smiled behind my mask. Their departure left more room for me at a metal table.

"Which one of those wusses will be the first of the one-in-four who don't make it through the initial year?" I winked at Valley-Girl.

"Both."

Valley-Girl was right. Both washed out halfway through the term.

Life settled into a routine of eighteen-hour days. I had little time to think about anything outside of the classrooms and the bar on Friday nights, plus my part-time job in the mouse lab. I holed up in the library or in my apartment most weekends, although Valley-Girl and I occasionally studied together. I found her rather endearing, in spite of the ditzy way she spoke. Once a month, L&O and I met on Saturdays for lunch and a break from being buried in books.

For the most part, my academic work provided all the intellectual stimulation I needed. During what little free time I had, I read more deeply into personality disorders. I was almost surprised by my utter lack of interest in killing. I didn't think I'd gone through a phase when I killed Sad-Sack, but for the immediate present I didn't feel the need to kill for the sake of killing. I didn't have enough energy left at the end of the day to plot a premeditated hunt.

I did miss a regular sex partner like I had had at State. Lab-Rat may have been a pain in the ass in many ways, but he was a delicious fuck. When my need became too great, I picked up guys in the bars, something I'd been too shy to do at State.

§

Mrs. Judge brought Miss Snickers #2 two months after classes began. Everything was ready for a new kitty, most especially me. We let her out of her carrying cage to explore her new forever home. She sampled some kibbies, drank some water, and located her litter box. She curled up next to me on the couch, one paw on my thigh, yawned, and began purring. She was home.

CHAPTER TWENTY

SO LONG, STREET-THUG

1987

Street-Thug's attack in the alley reminded me to practice three-hundred-sixty-degree situational awareness whenever I walked between campus and my apartment. All senses went on high alert the moment I stepped onto the city streets. My one physical encounter was enough. While there was no limitation on stupid in the world, I didn't think Street Thug was dumb enough to go after me a second time. Not me as me, anyway. After all, he knew me without any disguise, and he watched me enter and leave my apartment almost every day. His habits were predictable; mine weren't. A third-rate drug user was unlikely to try to take me out. Rob me, yes, if he needed cash. When scumbags like him needed a fix, they didn't think too deeply about what they'd do next and plan accordingly. They just needed a score.

The more I thought about him and his posse, the more suitable a target they became. His preying on the weak made me watch him carefully. If he attacked anyone else, I'd take him down. Or out. Mrs. Landlady told me he had robbed several elderly residents on our block. One night he sent an old man, who had been out walking his dog, to the hospital. He had no money on him to buy his safety, so Street-Thug left him unconscious and bleeding, his little dog whimpering in fear beside him.

"He should have bought a pit bull," Mrs. Landlady said when she finished telling me the story. "He'll be all right, but now his kids want him to move to a retirement home. He's lived on this block his entire life. Moving might kill him more surely than anything the users could do to him."

A local gang controlled the alley where Street-Thug attacked me. Through observation and neighborhood gossip, I knew he wasn't a gang member but a good customer. He and his posse pulled off petty attacks on pedestrians for money for cocaine. They'd get high on various stoops up and down the block, even on mine when they were daring. As far as I could tell, no one sold drugs on my street, but several clusters of users resided there semi-permanently. I'd find their fixings scattered around in the morning when I walked to campus.

The later I returned at night, the more certain I was to find Street-Thug all but passed out. Why the hell he couldn't pick a different block? His presence annoyed me.

Baltimore was in the midst of yet another cocaine epidemic, both crack and powdered. For ten bucks, you could buy a hit and get high. I had some money, but I couldn't buy enough to knock this guy off or even make him overdose. From everything I'd studied about cocaine addiction, I suspected he had a high tolerance for and equally high dependency on the drug. Mixing cocaine with another substance, a strong poison for example, would get rid of him. I turned to a text on poisons from my undergraduate days for ideas, certain I'd find one that was almost undetectable.

Back at State, we'd had a module in chemistry on poisons and drug interactions. Several students wanted to know which ones would fool the police. So did I, now more than ever.

"Don't you go thinking you know enough to hide drug usage and poisons from the police." Our prof laughed at the class. "You don't."

Not then, dear professor, not then.

When I returned one evening after dark, Mrs. Landlady's light was on. Odd, because she worked nights. I was worried enough to ring her doorbell. When she answered, I saw deep abrasions on her face and hands and a black eye.

"Street-Thug?"

"He jumped me this afternoon. I was walking home from buying dog food when he and his boys knocked me down and stole my purse. I only carry enough cash to buy what I need. I leave my wallet inside, because I don't want to lose my ID and credit cards. He got what little cash I had left from shopping." She opened the door wide enough for me to enter. I leaned over to scratch her dog's ears. He'd met Miss Snickers #2, but they weren't friends.

I made cups of tea, dressed her scrapes, and applied a thin layer of antiseptic ointment. Street-Thug picked on the wrong person. I had the reason I needed to get him off my block. He had a target on his back for elimination.

"Thanks for taking care of me." Mrs. Landlady sipped her tea.

"No problem." I set her first aid kit on the kitchen table.

Street-Thug's cowardly attack on Mrs. Landlady was nothing more than the easy robbery of an unsuspecting woman. His attack on me and the knife in his hand told me he'd have been happy to kill me, had I not gotten the drop on him. This asshole was going down. Period. End of statement.

I filled my kill book with page after page of notes. The easiest solution was rat poison, an ugly way to die, because victims bled to death internally if they ingested large enough doses. A plus was its lack of taste and odor. Mixing it with cocaine should be nearly foolproof. Traceable if anyone bothered with an autopsy but impossible to lead back to an individual buyer.

I found it odd that smaller pharmaceutical doses were used to control blood clotting and save lives. Rat poison was sold at every hardware store. God knows, no one would look twice at someone buying it. Because rats were Baltimore's semi-official mammal, I didn't bother with a disguise; I was just one more resident with a vermin problem.

"Pellets or traps?" The counter clerk said when I asked where he kept the rat poison.

"What do you mean?" I knew nothing about how the poison was sold. Cats kept mice under control in Bubbaville.

"Traps are more humane, but you have to clean them out to release the live ones into the wild or remove the dead ones. Rats eat the pellets and die in their nests. No mess, no fuss."

"Pellets."

"Got it. One box of d-CON. Anything else?"

I shook my head, paid, and turned to leave.

"Be careful handling this stuff," the clerk called out. "You don't want to inhale the dust. Even a little can be lethal. Nasty way to die."

I hoped so.

I wouldn't be the one doing the inhaling, though. I wanted Street-Thug to snort it deep in his nose and lungs. Because habitual use of cocaine numbed the mucus membranes, by the time he got a snootful, he'd be well on his way to no longer being a problem for Mrs. Landlady or me.

§

In my young black man disguise of oversized jeans that dragged on the ground and the gray sweatshirt, I bought a dime bag of cocaine in a neighborhood across town. When I mixed my concoction in the garage, I wore a surgical mask to protect my nose and mouth, Latex gloves to protect on my hands, and a lab apron to keep traces of dust from landing on my clothes. I crushed pellets using a mortar and pestle I bought at a home goods store, mixed in the cocaine, and bagged the powder. I'd pretend to be homeless to trick Street-Thug into chasing me off the block. I scattered the remainder of the d-CON around the garage in case anyone questioned me. Who knew? I might get lucky and kill a four-legged rat or two. I locked the box of gloves, mask, and apron in the trunk of my car.

§

On take-out-Street-Thug day, I left the house earlier than usual and stopped in the garage to make sure my sweatshirt and an oversized pair of Goodwill jeans were ready. The baggie was safe in the pouch. I walked through the alley to campus.

That evening, a cold, misty rain fell. Dusk was murkier than it would have been in clear weather. Perfect timing. I scooped damp grit from the alley and rubbed my face and hands. I all but ran home, ducked into the garage, and re-emerged wearing my homeless disguise over my school clothes. I trotted along the alley, rounded the corner, and crossed the street. As usual, Street-Thug and his boys were hanging out under a porch roof two doors up from mine. I pretended to look in trash cans for food, muttered aloud, and made myself a mark.

"Well, lookie here. This fool dares walk down our street." Street-Thug's Second-in-Command taunted. "We gotta teach this boy a lesson."

I moved toward a second trashcan before I was surrounded. I

produced a dry hacking cough that sounded contagious. Decomposing garbage worsened it. Street-Thug poked me in the ribs. I hung my head and babbled. If I could have drooled, I would have, but my mouth was dry from excitement. By then, I was really into my homeless person guise.

"This guy got nothin' worth stealin.' Leave him alone." Third-in-Command wasn't about to waste time on me.

"Nah. We gotta teach him a lesson," Street-Thug said.

"Yeah." Second-in-Command found his streak of bravery. "We own the trashcans and the stoops. Don't want your kind buttin' in."

I tried to push around Second-in-Command only to find Street-Thug blocking my progress. He shoved me.

"This our block. Like he say, get out, and don't come back."

I tripped and fell, the baggie of tampered drugs ending up on the pavement under me. I apologized and groveled and promised never to return. That earned me a kick in the ribs. Where I might have acted on my anger earlier, my mind warned me to keep cool and not fight back. Street-Thug kicked me a second time. Shit! That hurt. Pain burned along my left side. He might have bruised a rib or two. I dragged myself to my feet and shambled off.

"Would you look at this?" Second-in-Command held up the baggie. "Looks like someone lost his stash. It's mine now."

"Shut your face. Gimme." Street-Thug punched Second-in-Command in the mouth and snatched the drugs.

Mission accomplished.

I turned the corner and lurched down the alley; I held my side and tried to forget the pain. In the garage, I pulled my killing sweatshirt off, leaving my college sweatshirt exposed. I dumped the homeless disguise in the trunk of my car and rubbed a towel over my face and hands to remove the worst of the dirt. I struggled to stand upright, because each step sent stabbing pain through my chest. I walked back up the alley and, keeping to my side of the street, turned down my block. I waved at the posse, just like I did every day.

Around three in the morning, police cars roared into my block, sirens screaming, lights flashing, followed by an ambulance. They took three junkies away. I watched the hubbub from behind a slit in my curtains, proud of myself for ridding the world of those leeches on society. That justified the kill.

The next afternoon Mrs. Landlady had the almost but not quite complete scoop. "The guy you called Street-Thug and his boys evidently got into some bad drugs last night. They ODed. I bet we won't be seeing them again. We're safer now."

You bet we were. Street-Thug and his posse wouldn't bother us again. Their deaths rated no more than an entry in the crime statistics list in the paper, three more junkies who didn't make it. No names.

Three dead, huh?

I'd set out to kill Street-Thug; the posse was collateral damage. Sometimes, shit happens.

With killing someone just to see how it would feel was no longer on the table, offing scumbags that preyed on hapless victims like Mrs. Landlady was. My medical training must have been affecting my moral side. My heart beat as an electrical charge raced from my core to my skin, raising gooseflesh all over my body. I documented every move, every autonomic nervous system reaction.

Several times in my sophomore year, I hunted for junkies. Ever a blight on the community, they presented easy targets. I knew where all the crack houses were, both from roaming the bad sections of town and from reading the crime blotter in the *Sun*. Whenever the epidemic reached into my neighborhood, the killer me patrolled local drug dens. Sometimes I used cocaine and rat poison; other times I experimented with cocaine and powdered bleach. I never learned which concoction proved the most fatal. Medical examiners almost never autopsied drug users. Too costly to learn what the victim had ODed on.

CHAPTER TWENTY-ONE

JUMBO

1990

Fast forward to the end of my third year, where I continued to roam the brew pubs near campus with the Cruise Club. After a few beers, Gay-Blade could tell wicked bad stories about what he saw in the wards. He kept a straight face, which masked a streak of black humor. Shy-Scot remained an enigma. Fantastic student. A regular with the Cruise Club, he was not tempted by any of the women in the bar. Gay-Blade said he wasn't a "brother."

"I bet you can't get him into bed." The challenge was too intoxicating to ignore. I used every move I could, but he wouldn't take the bait.

"Damn it." I bought a pitcher of beer.

After Shy-Scot left, I found another temporary hook up.

My initial instinct on meeting Valley-Girl had been to distance myself from this cliché of a Southern California girl with her gushing speech patterns. I was dead wrong. She grew accustomed to cutting open bodies, mixing chemicals in the lab, and all the other smelly, messy things we had to do. Not once did she puke.

She became my second female friend after L&O, although our relationship remained shallower. She planned to return to California after her residency; California seemed too far away to maintain a close friendship. No matter what, she wasn't L&O.

As it often happened, talk of our future specialties dominated the Cruise Club night out. Gay-Blade leaned toward cardiology, with Shy-Scot reading up on tropical diseases.

"Aren't the local diseases fascinating enough? I mean, we have AIDS, TB, and other third-world diseases right here in Baltimore." Gay-Blade sipped his beer. "Are you going to be a missionary or something?"

Shy-Scot shot him a quizzical look. "Maybe. Doctors Without Borders always needs specialists."

"What about you?" He turned toward Valley-Girl. "Still like plastic surgery?"

"I want to be a facial trauma surgeon," Valley-Girl said. "My dad says we're going to have an influx of patients coming from Middle East conflicts over the next few years. A doctor who can reconstruct a badly damaged face will be in high demand."

"What the hell does he know we don't?" Gay-Blade reached for the pitcher, only to find it empty. He caught our waitress's eye and held it up.

"I have no idea," Valley-Girl said. "All I know is, he was pretty convincing."

"Pathology is looking better and better, if what she says is true. I'll have plenty of work, no matter where I land."

Gay-Blade's brow furrowed. "I can see why you'd pick a puzzle-solving specialty. That turns you on, right?"

That, and making people dead. "Yes. I'm fascinated with what makes a body die."

"Did you lose someone close to you?" Shy-Scot asked. "Someone whose death wasn't resolved?"

"In a way. My boyfriend at State died, but it wasn't under suspicious circumstances." I stared into my glass. "He fell while we were hiking and broke his neck."

"Seriously? That's like totally sad." Valley-Girl leaned over to give me a hug.

I lowered my head to hide the gleam of excitement the memory gave me.

§

Like L&O, Valley-Girl was a good object lesson. I misjudged her based on looks and accent, but she treated patients with such respect and tenderness that I mimicked her. Her empathy was real, though, where mine was feigned. People saw what I wanted them to see.

My copied bedside manner made me so popular I was offered weekend work at a clinic attached to a battered woman's shelter in downtown Baltimore. The mice in the lab couldn't teach me anything. Goodbye, mice.

The women in the shelter offered fodder for my growing hunger for new victims. Nurses assigned me take family histories, fill out charts with descriptions of wounds and injuries, and help physician's assistants when they set broken bones or stitched up split lips and scalps. The litany of injuries and abuse most of these women had experienced pissed me off. Repeat patients had files thick with X-rays and physicians' notes.

"We call them FFs," said the nurse with the most seniority.

"FFs?"

"Frequent Flyers. You get to know the repeat victims."

Some women brought their children for treatment of minor to

serious broken bones and other violence-related injuries. We didn't get gunshot wounds, because the law required they be treated at a hospital and reported to the police. We got everything from beatings to rape. Some of these women's stories about broke my heart. So many women were trapped in situations beyond their control. Escape seemed impossible without outside help. I would be that outside help.

"You gotta steel yourself," said the clinician, a physician's assistant with a grandiose title. "We patch them up, deliver them back to the shelter, offer counseling, and hope they don't go back to their abusers."

"Do most of them go back?"

He held up a file on the woman we'd just sent to the hospital. "She's an FF. Her old man beats her all the time, but she won't leave him. He smacks her around. She takes the four kids and runs. He calls and begs her to return. We'll see her again in a couple of months."

Some of these women were a lot like Li'l Bit, who wouldn't have considered leaving. Staying was part of her country DNA. I left before I had to fight my way out, before I had to take down Big Chigger.

"Do any of these guys kill their wives?"

"A few do. If that happens, they become the problem of the police department, and we close their files." He handed me a new chart and told me to call the next patient. "We can't change the cycle if the women themselves don't want help."

One woman came in three times in two months. Her story was similar to that of many others: knocked up at sixteen; three kids before she was twenty-one; husband had been kind, a good provider until he got hurt on the job; hard to make ends meet on her waitress wages and his disability checks.

"Does he help with the kids?" Was this woman's life like Li'l

Bit's, minus the obvious beatings? Big Chigger never beat Li'l Bit. Not that I knew of.

"He don't do nothing. Sits in his recliner all day, watching TV and playing video games. He got all fat and stinks."

I stitched up a deep cut on her hand.

"He can't barely walk, he got so big. Just goes from the kitchen to his chair and to the john sometimes."

"Who cares for your children while you're at work?"

"Their auntie. She takes them after school, so they're safe 'til I get home. He don't hit them, though. Just me."

I put a bandage over a cut and began washing caked blood from the side of her head where I found a gash too old to suture. She pulled away when I pushed too hard against the gash. "Ouch!"

"I'm sorry. I can't stitch this." I made sure the edges of a butterfly bandage were attached to her skin. "When did he hit you?"

She touched the bandage. Counting on her fingers, she said, "Seems like four days ago."

"You should have come in immediately. We need an X-ray to be sure he didn't fracture your skull." I waved to the doctor, who scribbled on the chart before I walked the woman to X-ray.

I studied the notes on the family. The husband was huge, weighing over four hundred pounds, the wife said. He couldn't support his weight without a walker. He had a host of physical problems, including high blood pressure, diabetes, arthritis, gout. She spent most of her time making sure he took his medications, tested his blood sugar levels, and injected his insulin on time.

"He eats like a hog, whole large pizzas and gallons of ice cream at a sitting," she said.

"How can he hit you if he can't walk? Why don't you step back out of his reach?"

"He keeps a bat beside his chair in case someone breaks in while I'm at work."

That didn't answer why she didn't walk away, but her agitation stopped my interrogation.

"Why do you go back?"

"I'm afraid he'll die if I don't."

Well, we'd see about that. I'd found my next victim. I had limited respect for women who were too weak or broken to do anything to better themselves; however, men who abused their wives were right down on the evolutionary scale with pond scum. If I could kill this wretched man, perhaps the woman and her children would survive.

I lifted his home address from her file and asked enough questions to know when she went to work, when she returned, and where her children were after school. I knew when Jumbo would be alone.

"Every week a nurse comes from the clinic to check on him."

I walked her to the door.

"Wish she'd check on me too, but she comes during the day when I'm at work."

I patted her arm and began planning her release.

§

I took a bus to the neighborhood and walked along the broken sidewalks. Most of the two- or three-story buildings had apartments over store-front businesses. With my sweatshirt hood covering my hair and pulled low over my brow, I melted into the mixed population living in these run-down apartments. I looked for an unobtrusive place to watch who went into the apartment house and when. I found a stoop and sat like many other men on the block.

I couldn't go daily because of classes and my work at the clinic, but I learned the pizza delivery boy came at four every afternoon. That was my way into the apartment.

I waited for everything to be perfect, but, in fact, I waited too long. As bad luck would have it, bad for the wife, things changed when Jumbo beat the shit out of her one too many times. She ended up in the hospital in a coma.

The police charged the creep with assault and battery, and then released him to house arrest in his apartment. They didn't even bother fitting him with an ankle bracelet. He couldn't roam the streets or get at his wife in the hospital. He was trapped in his apartment by his illnesses. His kids went into the system to be cared for by strangers.

My window of opportunity was brief. I checked the log to see when the next home health care visit was due. Two days out. I moved the next day. I wanted to intercept the pizza boy and deliver dinner with a side of death before anyone took notice. Everything I needed was in my pouch.

I loitered at one end of the short block. The pizza car arrived right on schedule and pulled up to the curb, large sign on the top announcing the car's purpose. I rushed forward, reaching the door a step ahead of the delivery boy.

"Haven't seen you around before. New here?" He balanced a padded hot bag on one hand.

"Sure am. Looking to move into 2C."

"Got my daily delivery for 2A." He waited for me to open the door. I didn't.

"Look, I'm going upstairs. Want me to take this for you?" I held out a twenty to cover the pie and the tip.

"Great. I hate those stairs. Be careful. The tile is broken in several spots. 2A should be unlocked." He palmed the money, shoved the box at me, and ran to his car. "Hold your breath. That apartment stinks like hell."

As soon as I knocked on the door to 2A, it swung inward. I poked my head in and almost fell backward. The stench told me the guy was close to death. The mound of flesh in the recliner, joystick in hand, eyes fixed on a video game, earphones feeding explosions and blasts into his brain, was oblivious to my presence until I set the pizza box on top of a stack of empties heaped beside his chair.

"Who you?" A voice bubbled up from the depths of his chest. He coughed and spat a wad of phlegm into a napkin, which he threw on the floor.

"Ran into the pizza guy downstairs. He asked me to bring this up."

"Money's on the table just inside the door."

I spotted the twenty and knew it would go home with me. I'd never been paid for my efforts, but I sure as hell wasn't leaving money lying around. All things being normal, he'd have had to pay for the food.

I looked at the mottled skin stretched over his cheeks and wondered what his wife ever saw in him. The apartment was filthy, but the reek wasn't from spoiled food on the floor. It came from the hulk in the chair. I'd smelled that unique sweetish odor before with a dying patient in the hospital: a combination of ketoacidosis from his diabetes and infection or gangrene from rotting feet. Plus, his adult diaper needed changing.

Dozens of empty water bottles lay on the floor, attesting to a heightened thirst, and the fruity breath wheezing between blubbery lips said this guy wasn't going to live much longer if he didn't get treatment. I could have backed out of the apartment and left him to his Darwinian fate, but I didn't. Letting nature take its course wouldn't satisfy my now-intense urge to kill someone who deserved it. He was a wife-beater, an abuser who had to be punished to protect his wife and kids.

Given what his wife had told about his diet, I was shocked he was alive. I moved close enough to see his feet encased in sticky socks. Above the knitted tops, black flesh puckered and oozed pus. If someone took him to the hospital, he'd lose both feet, probably close to the knee, but he might live. That wasn't about to happen.

I reached into my pocket and pulled out several vials of insulin and a large syringe I'd lifted from the clinic a few days earlier. We were notoriously lax in keeping track of needles and routine medicines, so I was damned sure my pilfering wouldn't be discovered. I slipped on a pair of examination gloves.

"This is for your wife. You aren't going to knock her around ever again."

"Wha-a-a?"

I pulled the tabs off the top of the vials, filled the syringe with an overdose of insulin, and stuck the needle into his belly. I shoved the plunger home. Jumbo gasped. He tried to grab the syringe but stopped. The game controller slid to the sticky carpet, bounced once, and lay still. Just as still as Jumbo was.

I stepped back, carefully replacing the syringe and vials in a bag in my pouch. I searched around the chair to find Jumbo's own supply. I filled a smaller syringe from his remaining supply and jabbed the second needle into his belly. I placed his hand to look like he had just given himself an injection. By the time I was ready to leave, he'd stopped breathing. I took his pulse. From abusive husband to useless slob to rotting corpse in less than a minute.

To erase any trace that I'd been there and make it look like he'd died of natural causes, I used the syringe I brought to drain several vials of insulin. I dropped the empties on the floor, grabbed the twenty for the pizza, and edged my way out of the apartment, down the rickety stairway, and onto the sidewalk. I lowered my head and pimp-rolled out of the neighborhood.

Later that night, I lay in bed and thought about what I'd done. I'd rid the world on one more wife abuser, one more leech on society. I wrote an extensive entry in my kill journal, satisfied that this beast deserved to die.

As I was drifting off, a thought startled me into full wakefulness. Junior could grow into Jumbo in a few years. He'd always run to fat, yet he had a long way to go to reach Jumbo's size. Could Jumbo have been a surrogate for Junior?

CHAPTER TWENTY-TWO

G-MAN

1990-1991

The clinician held open the door of an exam room to let me through the day after I killed Jumbo. We walked into chaos. One of the visiting practical nurses sat on a chair, face in hands, sobbing.

"Libby, what's the matter?" The clinician ran over and put a hand on her shoulder. "Did someone attack you?"

"No, it's not me. Bertram Dooley's dead."

"Dead? How?"

"An overdose of insulin, I think. I found a syringe stuck in his abdomen."

"Did you call 911?" The clinician asked a clerk for Mrs. Dooley's file.

"Of course. The EMTs came right away, but he was already dead and cold. They had a hell of a time getting him down the stairs. I was afraid they'd have to take him out one of the windows." The nurse pulled herself together and walked over to the drinking fountain. She took a long drink and wiped her mouth.

"Why?" I pretended I didn't know Jumbo was huge as a hippo.

"He was morbidly obese." The nurse moved toward the back of the clinic. She put her medical backpack on the shelf. "Do you mind if I leave? I don't do well with dead bodies."

"Take a couple of extra days. We'll manage." The clinician looked at me for confirmation that I'd be available for weekend duty. I'd planned to do laundry and get some sleep. It looked like Miss Snickers would have to play with her toys until I got home. Besides, I could use the extra money.

"I doubt we'll see Mrs. Dooley or her children again. After all, she only came when her husband beat her." He made a mark in the file. "Better off without him."

"How is she?" I asked.

"She's out of the coma. She'll be all right," the clinician said. "All she has to do is move in with her sister to get her kids back."

"Will the police order an autopsy on the husband?" If they did, I wanted to sit in on it.

"No need. His death certificate will read 'death by insulin overdose.'" The clinician went into a different exam room. The line of patients didn't shrink just because one woman was out of harm.

I walked home after classes ended to see police cars in my neighborhood. One officer approached me.

"Do you know anything about drug dealers in the area?"

I was wearing my college gear, so I was certain he didn't mean me. "Only that deals go down almost every night at the end of the block." I jerked my chin in the direction of the campus.

"Yeah, we know about that. How about any suspicious deaths? ODs? Anything?"

Oh shit. Had someone seen me in my homeless disguise and

followed me back to my garage? Or seen me take out users in various drug dens?

"Only three who died a few weeks back."

"Nothing else?"

I shook my head. "No one died on my stoop. I'd have noticed."

He gave me his card in case I saw anything or anyone acting suspiciously. I walked up the steps to my front door, my heart pounding, my mouth cotton-dry. Would my kill clothes be safe in my car? Maybe I should find a different hiding place. I decided against taking any action. The police weren't on to me *per se*. Their questions were part of the new mayor's crackdown on crack cocaine. I was still safe.

§

In my fourth year, I began looking around seriously for a partner. Not in killing, but for sex. I scored when I hung out in bars with Valley-Girl and the rest of the Cruise Club, but that scene wasn't resulting in a truly decent prospect for the long haul. I thought about marriage. I thought about a long-term relationship without marriage. I wasn't convinced I needed or wanted a ring on my finger to be happy. Gay-Blade and Shy-Scot were funny, but a long-term, non-physical relationship held no interest. Besides, Gay-Blade had moved on to an almost committed relationship. The guy was older, a government professional, and quiet where Gay-Blade was an extrovert.

"Who knew I'd find a great guy who wasn't part of the bar scene?"

"Yeah, go figure." Valley-Girl said.

I shocked the shit out of myself one Sunday morning when I woke up early and realized I was lonely. Miss Snickers rolled over and purred, tapping my cheek with one paw. She gave me all the love a cat could, but I was really grinding-to-the-core lonely. I had friends and one-night stands, but no one special. I should be able to figure out how and where to meet the kind of guy I wanted to have in my life, but hanging out all the time with the same people wasn't opening doors to meet someone new.

I started studying more in the library, more in the cafeteria, and sometimes in a new coffee house off campus. I talked with a lot of people, but I didn't find anyone I was remotely interested in beyond a simple conversation. I tutored medical students. Once again, none of them made me tingle.

§

One sunny afternoon, I took a study break in the near-empty coffee house and buried my face in yet another used psychology text.

"Mind if I join you?" A stranger stopped beside my table and nodded at the book lying open in front of me. "Are you a psych major?"

Tall with sandy hair, sun lines around hazel eyes. He had to be new. Believe me, if he'd been a regular, I'd have noticed.

"No. Fourth year med student. I love this stuff. I picked this up at the student book store." I lifted my school bag off the extra chair and motioned him to sit. "Are you a psych major?"

"After a fashion. Grad student in criminal justice. My undergrad work was in abnormal psychology."

Abnormal psych, huh? Criminal justice, huh?

"What does someone with a criminal justice degree and an interest in weird people do after graduation?"

I closed the book and turned my dark blue eyes toward his face. A rather attractive face it was. Strong cheek bones accented eyes that twinkled. Not handsome, but compelling. Might have been the way he looked at me with complete attention that interested me. Might just have been the way the various parts of his face fitted together. Might also have been the fact he appeared older than most of my friends.

"Law enforcement." He gestured toward my empty cup. "Want a refill?"

Hell, I'd already had three cups. "Sure." I'd deal with the caffeine high later.

When he returned, I asked, "Are you a cop?"

"Kind of. About ten years ago I joined the FBI right after I graduated with my B.A. in psychology. I'm back for my masters and focusing on profiling criminal behavior. You know, guessing what a criminal would do before he does it."

Really now. "And you can do that?"

"I'm learning."

I'd heard a little about profiling but had dismissed it as so much hocus pocus. Psychologists hadn't studied it enough to judge its value. We chatted for nearly an hour, during which time I learned more about profiling. Had I wanted to go into psychology, this might have been a perfect career behind which to kill.

"So, med school, huh? What's got your attention?"

Profound question. Deserved a profound answer.

"I'm fascinated by what makes the human machine work."

"Surgery?"

"After a fashion, as you say. I want to know what makes the body stop working, so pathology." Over the rim of my coffee cup, I watched his expression. His eyes flared.

"You'll work in a hospital? Can't really go into private practice. People frown on cutting up bodies."

"Indeed, they do. So yes, maybe a hospital or forensic lab. Where else? As you say, it's not a specialty for private practice." How would this criminal justice dude respond? Would he show Lab-Rat's disdain? Or would he be interested? "One of my premed pals at State said I was wasting my time studying medicine if I wasn't going to have a steady stream of returning patients."

"Well, your pal was right about that. No repeat business in pathology. You get one shot at finding out how someone died. I can understand your interest. It's similar to what I do—solve riddles. That's so cool."

I kept my eyes on the cover of my psychology text. I couldn't believe anyone other than me thought having but one chance to find the right answer was cool. I definitely saw synergies between profiling and pathology. I found the concept of identifying criminals and stopping them before they could act again intoxicating. My mind raced with possibilities of finding scientific evidence to support a profile. On the flip side, that same mind wrestled with kill methods and hiding the scientific evidence, even from someone trained to uncover motives and patterns of behavior.

"Yeah." He glanced at his watch. "Shit. Gotta run. Got a class in ten minutes. See ya, Doc."

"Bye, G-Man."

He loped across the coffee house and went through the automatic door. He turned at the last second and waved. I waved back.

Well, now he held possibilities. I licked my lips. He was the only man outside of the Cruise Club whose academic major intrigued me. I shocked the shit out of myself by hoping we'd run into each other again.

§

G-Man sought me out less than a week after our first conversation. I'd been hanging around the coffee house in case he returned. He did. We talked again for a long time about what we both wanted to do with our careers. Ultimately, we decided on a movie and a pizza afterwards.

"So, you've been in the FBI for ten years, you said?"

We faced each other over coffee again, a habit I found comfortable.

"Yes. The Bureau is paying for my masters." He'd graduated high in his class from University of Georgia. "I'm lucky to be doing what I love."

"Me, too."

What differentiated this man from my bar scores and Lab-Rat was I wanted him to be my friend first, my lover second. I wanted to be able to talk with him about nearly everything, except killing, of course. No matter how much I was coming to trust him, G-Man wouldn't be able to turn his back on my calling. He was too straight and narrow. Besides, he was a Fed. I wondered how he'd profile me.

Where I would practice was often part of the conversation, as was where he would be assigned. I still had my internship and residency to get through. I leaned toward forensic pathology, which required additional training.

"I'm almost finished with my masters," G-Man said one evening after we went out for an expensive-for-us dinner.

"Do you know yet where you'll be assigned?" If G-Man were going to be a far away from me, I might have to rethink how I felt about him.

"Quantico. Just south of the District. That's where the profiling unit is based."

I grinned. "Good, because I'd hate to think you'd be stuck in Omaha while I finish my residency."

"And are you thinking we're pretty good together?" G-Man reached over and tucked curls behind my ear.

"Aren't you?" I stroked the back of his hand.

Our first time in bed was slow and tender. G-Man was patient, loved exploring my body, and taught me what he liked. My reaction intensified. At last, I routinely achieved orgasms like the ones in the erotic novels. Time and again, we satisfied each other.

"Why did it take us so long to do this?"

"I'm an old fashioned kind of guy. I've never been attracted to the bar scene and don't like one-night stands." He stroked my naked breast.

"And I've spent too much time looking in all the wrong places." I licked his nipple.

"I know. I watched you."

I nearly jumped out of bed. Had he been following me? I settled for propping my head on my hand. "I never saw you at the brew pub."

"I stopped in a few times. You hang with a bunch of other med students." He kissed my breast, tongue finding an erect nipple.

I moaned but wasn't about to stop either his revelations or his mouth. "And you never came over."

"Not my scene. Oh, and you're wasting your time on the Scot."

"I'm not wasting time with you."

He rolled on his back and pulled me on top of him.

Later I wondered what he meant by wasting my time with Shy-Scot. Had he checked him out? My emotions for G-Man deepened. If this was what a normal relationship was, I liked it.

CHAPTER TWENTY-THREE

AUTOPSY

1991

The Cruise Club partied together, studied together, and graduated together. Four of us finished in the top ten. As I figured from the beginning, I was the top student, followed by Gay-Blade third, Valley-Girl fifth, and Shy-Scot ninth. Because I had no guarantee that Johns Hopkins wouldn't lose its mind and let me get away, I applied to a couple of different medical schools for my internship and residency. All were in the District. I was proud when I was invited to intern at Johns Hopkins.

Like me, Valley-Girl applied around the country, but kept her fingers crossed that she'd be accepted into Johns Hopkins's facial reconstruction program. We celebrated when we learned we were staying together. I'd gotten used to helping her and to her helping me. Shy-Scot was leaving for University of Virginia to study infectious diseases, with Gay-Blade moving north to Harvard for cardiology.

Over drinks at our last Cruise Club night, I choked up. I didn't know when I would see my compatriots again. We'd gone through so much—course loads that ground us into pulp, social highs and lows, loves won and lost—that I didn't want to lose contact with them.

"Funny how things work out." I squeezed G-Man's hand. "We all got what we wanted."

"No matter where you graduate in your med school class, they still call you Doctor," G-Man said.

I flinched when he said that. He caught my reaction.

"Hey, I didn't mean anything wrong. It's just an old joke." He rushed to apologize.

"It's okay, G-Man. I once said that same thing to a guy I knew back at State. He didn't take kindly to my words."

"Well, we're now all official." Gay-Blade raised his beer glass in a toast.

As with previous ceremonies, each of us was called forth to receive our degrees. When the medical school director called, "Father Shy-Scot," I knew why he never dated. I found G-Man in the audience. He winked and grinned.

I looked forward to my internship and residency with their grinding hours of sleep deprivation and walking dead behavior. We'd been warned the doctors would try to break us with long hours, shit assignments, and little or no praise. Shit assignments didn't bother me, not after two years of working in the clinic. I regretted having to give it up, but I wouldn't have enough hours in the day to work there, put in twenty-four-hour rotations on the hospital floor, and still find time to sleep. I all but forgot wanting to kill.

My poor cat, Miss Snickers #2, got used to me being away, but she never complained. She welcomed me home and curled up on my lap or beside me on the bed without a single meow of resentment or judgment.

After G-Man moved to Quantico, we found time to be together a couple of weekends a month. Most of the time when he wasn't around, I was so mentally and physically exhausted I could barely crawl between my apartment and the hospital. Sometimes I didn't even go home but would grab a few minutes of sleep on an empty gurney in the interns' lounge. Other zombies stumbled in and out on their appointed rounds; half an hour of uninterrupted sleep was a godsend. Mostly, I dozed and woke up feeling worse than ever.

When I officially declared my intent to go into pathology, I tried and failed to wiggle out of ward rounds or emergency room duty. With no intention of having living patients, I wanted to spend all my time in Autopsy, but internships didn't work that way. I had to do what all the others did, like it or not.

The chief pathologist, a man I'd met but not worked with when I was a mere med student, became my faculty adviser.

"I'm Dr. Charles Carsdale, 'Chuck' to my friends, 'Chest-Cracker' to my students."

I laughed. "Glad to meet you, Chest-Cracker."

I soon found out he'd call me before he called any other intern to assist with autopsies when we had interesting cadavers. Most came through the hospital, because we worked on everyone as a hedge against potential malpractice lawsuits and to confirm the attending physician's initial diagnosis into the cause of death. Cancer, accidents, cardiac events, and overdoses made up the bulk of our caseload. I learned there were many more ways to break the human machine than I'd imagined.

Occasionally, the city medical examiner would be swamped, and we'd get some overflow of murder and accident victims. The majority of the murder victims died from gunshot wounds. We learned to decipher police jargon, "single GSW to the upper chest," as easily as we identified the sex of the victim.

For me, the worst were corpses that had died by fire. The sight and stench of burnt flesh made me want to vomit. The first burn victim that ended up on our table sent me back to when I was around eight. A gas truck exploded in the town's only gas station. Five cars and two trucks, one towing a horse trailer with two animals in it, burned.

"Smells like someone charred the burgers," my old man had said.

Even then, I thought Big Chigger was crude and insensitive. I crept around behind his back to see two bodies in one car. They were burned so badly that bones were exposed. The loss of the animals affected me more than the dead, burned humans did. He slapped me a good one across my face when I threw up behind him. Putrefied flesh of a corpse long dead or a drowning victim smelled worse but didn't bother me as much.

Technicians from the Baltimore police labs came looking for insects or dirt or fibers, anything to tell the story of how and why a corpse was dead. Like a giant game of Clue, we had to figure out whether Colonel Mustard used a rope or candlestick in the library.

"We have no second chance to get it right," Chest-Cracker said.

Just like I told G-Man when I first met him.

I spent every spare minute in Autopsy and the pathology lab. I ran tests, checked results, and stored trace elements from bodies and from under fingernails. I labeled everything according to procedure and preserved the evidence until the crime scene techs showed up. More than once, I thought I might have solved a crime, but I never knew for certain.

Late that fall, I had just finished twenty-four straight hours in Emergency when Chest-Cracker called me to Autopsy. "We caught a good case. Come down to the lab. We have a lot of work to do."

All I wanted to do was curl into a ball and sleep until the next millennium. Instead, I rode the elevator to the basement. To the outsider, Autopsy was terrifying because it only dealt with dead bodies. As a result, it was far removed from living patients and their families.

"What's up?" I shrugged into clean scrubs and walked over to the stainless-steel table. I lifted the sheet covering the remains. A torso lay on the cold steel. "Jesus, what the hell happened to her?"

"We're not sure. Someone reported a body dumped in an empty lot."

In Bubbaville, occasionally a farmer would get run over by his plow. Got pretty well cut to pieces. I looked closely at the wounds where Jane Doe's legs should be. The cuts were clean, not like something you'd see from farm equipment. Not much dirt in the wounds, either, except for what might have transferred from the empty lot. The same held true for the wound on the neck.

"She didn't fall off a tractor or get tangled with a propeller." I pulled on gloves.

"How do you know that?" Chest-Cracker asked.

"I grew up in the country. I've seen what farm equipment can do."

"You're right. Someone cut her up."

Chest-Cracker made the Y-incision and peeled back the outer skin and subcutaneous layers of fat. Even a rookie like me could see there were penetrating wounds on her torso that had been hidden under layers of decomposing skin.

"Puncture wounds from a sharp, pointed weapon killed her. Get some pictures."

I reached for the camera and took a series of close-ups of the upper torso. I counted at least a dozen stab wounds, four of which could have been fatal.

"Without her head, it's difficult to know the cause of death. We don't know if she was strangled."

"Why?" I knew what someone who was strangled to death looked like. I wanted Chest-Cracker to think I'd never seen a strangled body.

"Loss of oxygen causes micro hemorrhages in the eyes. We call this petechiae."

I nodded.

"We also don't know if she was restrained," Chest-Cracker went on. "We need her hands and wrists to see if they have ligature marks."

He continued pointing out stab wounds, which were both pre- and post-mortem. "She wasn't alive when her head, arms and legs were removed, though. Looks like the fatal blow was one of the two that penetrated her heart. We'll put down 'killed by persons and methods unknown' until we have the rest of the corpse."

Maybe it was stress, or sleep deprivation, or too many long hours in the wards, but rage at the person who did this burned through me. "How could anyone do this to another human being?"

"It takes all kinds, Doc. We may never know what triggered his attack." Chest-Cracker sounded jaded as if he'd seen this depravity all too often.

I wanted the murderer to suffer the same way this poor woman must have suffered. Even if she was dead when he did his most gruesome work, she might have known what was coming. She might have been terrified.

Thinking about what it would take to find him helped bring my rage under control. I was no sleuth and, therefore, had no idea how to identify her murderer. Maybe the police would drop a clue. I was surprised when no one from the department attended the autopsy. The room should be crawling with cops, some involved with solving the murder, others off duty but fascinated by the body.

"Shouldn't we have at least one cop here?"

"Normally, we would." He shrugged. "I guess they're busy elsewhere."

I collected bits of debris from the incisions on her torso, photographed her from all sides, and washed her skin after sweeping it for additional trace material.

"Get several pictures of her back," Chest-Cracker said. "There's a birthmark on her right shoulder."

We pored over this partial corpse for a couple of hours before I stitched up the Y-incision and rolled the autopsy table into the morgue refrigerator. Chest-Cracker wrote up his report and phoned the police.

"Killed someplace other than where she was found. Death may have been from asphyxiation. No, not from the dismemberment. Yes, we collected trace evidence. Send someone over to pick it up. We'll have the toxicology screens back in a few days." He listened for a while to a voice ranting on the other end of the phone. "You new to the job? I can't rush tox tests. They take the time they need."

Chest-Cracker listened for several more minutes before hanging up. I marked vials of blood for tests for drug use.

"Do the police know who the monster was who butchered her?" I was shocked at the non-medical nature of my question.

"That's the first time I've heard you sound like you care." Chest-Cracker scrutinized me. "You're normally all business. I thought you saw the corpses as a big game, not as the remains of real people."

"Yeah, well, this one got to me."

"She was someone's daughter. Don't ever forget that." Chest-Cracker regarded me with new respect. "The police say they have several people of interest in mind. I guess they want to know exactly how she died before they make any arrests."

"Do they even know who she was?"

"If they do, they're not saying. Typical. We get the corpses, they get the publicity." Chest-Cracker threw his stained scrubs into the laundry basket. I did the same. "Let 'em stand in front of the camera. Without us, they couldn't prove anything. Hey, good job, Doc. This was a nasty one."

"I couldn't believe how much we learned from a torso."

"Always remember, we speak for the dead. We give them respect in death that their killers denied them in life."

I'd never thought about it that way. I had been more interested in the mechanics of what I was learning. My earlier experiment with Sad-Sack hadn't brought clarity to the "why" I was compelled to kill. As a result, I only had acceptable reasons for Street-Thug and Jumbo. I killed to prevent them from doing more harm. Deep inside I found unadulterated joy in kills I felt were worthy of my efforts. I only killed users in the drug den to keep from getting bored.

Chest-Cracker showed me a new way to look at our work. Yes, we did have to honor the dead. And sometimes we could honor them by getting even with the murderer.

I went back to the intern's lounge for a couple of hours of sleep, but found I could only lie rigid on the gurney. Who killed our Jane Doe and why? When I found him, I'd use a sharp pointed object, maybe Street-Thug's switchblade, to stab him as many times as he stabbed the woman. No way would I dismember him, though. I was no butcher, but I needed to know who the fuck he was. When I knew his name and where he was, his ass was grass. He was all mine.

I couldn't wait to tell G-Man about the murder. Maybe he could give me insight into the killer's mind.

CHAPTER TWENTY-FOUR

ICE PICK

1991

The newspapers didn't mention Jane Doe's death again once they reported she was a junkie.

"Too bad we can't release the pathology report." I wiped my hands on a towel.

"And give the media the truth that she was beheaded?" Chest-Cracker's eyes crinkled across the corpse we were autopsying. "They'd speculate to no end, and they'd be wrong."

"They're already wrong now about her being a drug user. We saw no indication."

"True, but as long as the media *thinks* she's a junkie, they won't hound us. Junkies aren't news." He jerked his head toward the instrument tray. "Hand me that bone saw, please."

Because the authorities hadn't released information on the dismemberment, the media had nothing to sensationalize. Without inside information from the police, I had no clue how to find the man who cut Jane Doe to pieces. The damage to the torso indicated he was filled with rage. Well, he wasn't the only one.

A couple of lab reports came back: she was dead before she was dismembered. Chest-Cracker had been right. The first tox screen showed trace elements of cocaine and marijuana but not enough to incapacitate her. No evidence in her lungs, stomach or liver of long-term abuse of any kind of substance, including alcohol or tobacco.

"Do you think Jane Doe was a date gone bad?"

"Maybe. If we had found Valium in her system, you'd be right. We didn't, though." Chest-Cracker used the bone saw to slice through the sternum. "Don't fuss over that body. It'll eat you up."

"I'm trying not to, but the violence of the desecration is hard to forget." I swiped my sleeve across my covered brow.

"Stay focused on our newest cadaver. That's your job today."

§

One morning a week or so later, I'd finished twenty straight hours on the surgical ward and was on my way out. I had a whole day off and planned to spend it in bed asleep. I stumbled through a waiting room when I heard the media report that police had identified the victim in the Jane Doe murder. A prominent lawyer in Wilmington, Delaware, had reported his daughter missing two days earlier. It took that long for the police to piece together the partial corpse with the father's description.

"She was identified by a birthmark on her back," said the police spokesman.

I'd photographed a birthmark on her right shoulder. My photos helped the police put a name to the girl: Dani Fabrizzi. Chest-Cracker's reminder that we were the last voice for the dead came true this time. My chest swelled with the knowledge that our lab led the police one step closer to solving the crime.

"Look at this photo," the police information officer said. "We want to know if you saw her and where?"

A pretty young blond woman, twenty-years old, tall, tanned, and fit, smiled full-face at the camera. We knew she was tanned because of fading bikini lines on her torso. Her belly and buttocks were toned. With her legs missing, we hadn't had any way of estimating her height.

"She had a boyfriend," the officer continued, "Dale Wainwright."

The news anchor flashed up a couple of photos of a smooth-looking soccer player from Temple University in Philadelphia. No one had seen him in the past week, either.

"He has brown hair, brown eyes, and a distinctive mole on his neck. He likes sailing and soccer. Because he may have been one of the last people to see Dani alive, we want to talk with him." The information officer said. "He may be in the Baltimore area, according to a family friend."

In Baltimore? How fortunate.

I wondered if I could find him before the police did. If he liked sailing, my money was on him being at the Inner Harbor where the deep-water Volvo racing yachts were on display. Local television news had covered their arrival for the remarkable event it was. L&O had planned to come up to see them and have lunch, but she came down with a bad cold and canceled.

I drove to the Inner Harbor, tucked the Ugly Duckling into an almost too small parking space, and ambled toward the yachts. I sat on a bench and scrutinized everyone on the pathway. An hour passed before I found him hiding in plain sight, another pretty blond girl, a carbon copy of Dani, hanging on his arm. I strolled over to eavesdrop. The mole on the side of this guy's neck matched the one on television of the man who'd killed Dani Fabrizzi.

"My father owns that one, but we can't go aboard. The crew's preparing for the transatlantic race next week."

Cutie bought the story and pressed her breast against his arm. Funny, wasn't it, how some men became more attractive when you thought they were filthy rich?

I had to figure how the hell was I going to get him to go anywhere with me. I wasn't blond. I was not his type. I retreated to my car. I had my killing backpack with me, but it didn't have any weapons in it, just a pair of used scrubs, an apron, and some latex gloves. I hadn't planned this out at all. I vowed never to leave home without something sharp again. I slapped on a ball cap, slid my wraparound shades onto my nose, and walked away from the Inner Harbor. I went looking for a hardware store.

I returned about the time the dinner crowd filtered in. Filthy-Rich sipped a beer alone at an outdoor bar. I pretended to have car trouble and asked several guys for help, but they refused. All were with dates, but my target was alone. I walked up to him and did my best "damsel in distress" act, sucking up to him, and inflating his ego.

He finished his beer and walked me to my Escort. He looked under the hood, tried the starter, and found a loose wire under the dash. Just where I'd loosened it. I asked if he'd help get the car out of the too small parking space.

"There was much more room when I parked."

I climbed into the passenger seat. Once Filthy-Rich freed the car, I pulled an ice pick from my backpack, pressed the tip into his ear, and told him to drive.

"What the fuck are you doing?" He jerked the wheel to the left.

"Drive." I pushed the pick deep enough to draw blood. "If you don't do as I say, I'll shove this deep into your brain right now. You'll be dead before you know it."

"You wouldn't dare."

Was that a threat or a challenge? I bit my tongue to contain the fury that threatened my control. I jabbed the pick in again. "Oh, I very much dare."

Filthy-Rich screamed. The pick hadn't penetrated deeply enough to warrant the amount of noise he made. Thank goodness he hadn't rolled down the driver's window.

"What do you want? Money? I have plenty."

"I want revenge. Now what will it be, drive or die here? It's pretty much the same to me."

We left the Inner Harbor area. A sideways glance told me he was afraid but searched for a way to overpower me. We headed out of town. North would do. We arrived at a country lane I'd passed on one of my get-acquainted trips. A perfect place where nobody but me could hear him scream. I told him to turn in and pull up behind an abandoned house. I grabbed the keys. I yanked him out, kicking him when he tumbled to the dirt.

"Get up, asshole."

He pushed himself to his feet. I shoved him hard enough that he had to walk or fall. I poked him in the back with the ice pick and drew blood.

"Who are you?"

"Dani's friend."

"I know all of her friends. She wouldn't have chosen you. You're not our type."

Rage flared. "What do you mean, not your type? That I'm not a killer?"

His eyes darted left and right. He sprang to one side and turned toward me. I sprayed him with Mace I carried in my front pocket. He choked and bellowed. I kicked him toward a tree and forced him to lean against it. I taped his hands together behind the trunk with duct tape from my backpack. I stood in front of him and pulled on gloves.

Filthy-Rich shook his head, eyes streaming. "I don't know what you're talking about."

"The police want to question you about Dani's murder."

"Dani's off in Florida with her girlfriends."

"You're lying."

He was a terrible liar. The police would see through him in a second, if they got their hands on him. They wouldn't, though. Not alive anyway.

"Not true. Part of her body is on a cold slab in the university morgue."

Filthy-Rich gulped.

"Her torso's there. Cut up by the pathologists. Of course, her head, arms and legs are missing, but you already know that. Enough of her body turned up in that empty lot to identify her."

"I don't have any idea what you're talking about." He tried to bluff his way out of the inevitable. "I told you I have no idea why you kidnapped me. You'll be sorry for this when my old man finds out."

I left him waiting while I walked to my car and returned with his jacket. "Let's see what you have."

I dumped his stuff on the ground. Wallet. Money clip. Lighter. Knife. Military style. A KA-BAR, I thought. I bet it would match the wounds on Dani Fabrizzi's torso. Might still have traces of her blood on it.

"You kept the murder weapon? As a souvenir? That's about the stupidest thing you can do. Fucking amateur." I spat on the ground. Oh shit. I scrubbed my foot over the saliva. I couldn't leave DNA. "You killed Dani. Then, you mutilated her body. After she was dead, you stabbed her again and again. I could give you an exact count, but you know how many times you shoved this knife into her chest. What did she do to drive you into such rage?"

"She started dating someone else. Said she wanted to break up with me. With me! Said she was sick of me controlling her."

"That was why you killed her and cut off her head? I've met my share of egomaniacal fools, but you're in a class by yourself." I extracted more things from my backpack. I pulled on scrubs over my jeans and T-shirt. If his blood spurted, I'd be protected. I had a complete change of clothes in the car, just in case.

"How do you know all of this?"

"I did her autopsy, you sick bastard. Now it's your turn." I selected a place between two ribs and plunged the pick into the hilt. "Only with you, you're going to feel every stab wound."

"I didn't touch her." His scream flushed a murder of crows from behind the house.

I thrust the pick in again. I wanted to strike this prick as often as he struck Dani, but I couldn't. Only the police, Chest-Cracker, and I knew how many wounds were in her torso.

"Where's her head?" I punctured his right lung and left the pick inside. I held his knife to his throat.

"I threw it in some wetlands near Fells Point."

"Why did you cut off her head?"

"I don't know." Stab, this time in the left side of the chest, very near the heart. "Stop. Please don't hurt me anymore."

I drew the knife across his throat deep enough to bleed but not to hit vital arteries or veins.

"I didn't think you could identify her without her head."

"Could you be any dumber? She had that birthmark on her back."

Stab, this time closer to the heart. Filthy-Rich was screaming pretty much non-stop by now. "No more questions, you limp dick."

I stabbed the ice pick through his ear and into the brain. The screaming stopped.

I looked at my work. I'd never killed with such violence before, but I felt good. No better way to kill this bastard than the way I'd done it.

I shed the blood-spattered scrubs and wrapped the ice pick inside. I peeled off my gloves and tossed them on top of the bundle. I sanitized the crime scene, once again rubbing my sneakers across the spit spot. A crime scene expert might find a trace, but it was doubtful. As far as footprints were concerned, my cheap shoes would end up in a dumpster.

I stopped at a gas station halfway to Baltimore to call 911. My voice rasped my report on where to find Filthy-Rich's body and Dani Fabrizzi's head. By now I was in my killing sweatshirt, hood obscuring my face, jeans, and sneakers like those tens of thousands of young black men wore every day. I jiggled and jived like a junkie needing a fix. All caught on the station's security cameras. I hung up and pimp-rolled behind a big black SUV where I disappeared from sight of the cameras. From there, a simple sprint to the Ugly Duckling parked at the far edge of the lot set up my escape.

On the drive to my apartment, I ran down the checklist of what I'd learned, what I'd done right, and what I'd done wrong. I sucked in a deep breath and nearly choked. What the hell was I thinking? Filthy-Rich left in my car with me. God, how many people saw us? By the time I walked into my apartment, I was drenched in a cold sweat. I'd called Filthy-Rich a fucking amateur, but I was the fucking amateur. If anyone identified me, my career as a killer would be over nearly before it began.

§

By noon the next day, a news bulletin on the television in a patient's room said the Baltimore police had identified the body of a white male found tied up and murdered out in the country as that of Dale Wainwright, age twenty-four, wanted in connection with the brutal murder of Dani Fabrizzi, whose decapitated body had been found a week earlier.

"Looks like someone did the police's job for them," Chest-

Cracker said when I came into Autopsy a day later. "Not that I'm in favor of a revenge killing, but in this case what goes around, comes around. Good riddance. At least the state won't be housing him in maximum security for the next fifty years."

"What about the death penalty? Wouldn't he have gotten that?"

"Likely not, because we haven't executed anyone in a long time. Even if the jury voted for execution, he could have been incarcerated for decades while he appealed."

"Then, I'm glad he's dead."

Chest-Cracker nodded. "Want to assist with the autopsy?"

"You bet."

What a thrill! I could help autopsy someone I'd killed and make sure no damaging evidence pointed at me.

CHAPTER TWENTY-FIVE

MARRIAGE

1991

Most couples talk about love, where to go for dinner, what to do on the weekend. G-Man and I, on the other hand, spent countless hours talking about deviant character traits.

"I can't tell you how many books I've read about the behavior of sociopaths and psychopaths." I waved at a shelf of books in my apartment. "I still don't know which is which."

"That's because they're very close. At Quantico, you'll hear both terms used interchangeably, depending on the situation and who's speaking."

"So what do you look for when you're profiling deviant behavior?" I leaned forward, elbows on my small kitchen table.

"I focus on whether the criminal we're looking for displays a total lack of conscience. So many of them feel they can get away with anything, simply because of how they think about themselves." G-Man leaned in as well. "The majority suffer either from a God complex or a narcissistic personality disorder."

"Are they always violent? I mean, are all killers either sociopaths or psychopaths?" I wanted G-Man to tell me how he worked to avoid coming under his scrutiny in the future.

"Two good questions. No, not all sociopaths are violent. And yes, most serial or spree killers are psychopaths. There are many gradations in each description, but I tend to think of psychopaths as those willing and able to take human lives. Sociopaths are less likely." He frowned for a few moments. "At least, that's been my experience to date. It could change with the next case."

"What other characteristics do they share?" I rose and put the fire on under the tea kettle.

"They manipulate others and feel no remorse or shame for their actions."

I grew silent while I waited for the kettle to boil. I stood with my back to G-Man while I processed what he said. I didn't feel any remorse for Loser's death. He might have raped me had I given him a chance. Sad-Sack was a laboratory experiment to see if I had the guts to plan and carry out a kill. Lab-Rat was different. Until he morphed into Big Chigger, I really liked him. I was sorry when he fell to his death. Street-Thug, Jumbo, and Filthy-Rich deserved to die. I poured tea and returned to the table.

"Not all come from broken, alcoholic or abusive homes." He reached for his mug. "Some do, but if everyone who grew up in a household with an alcoholic parent was a sociopath, we'd be overwhelmed with caseloads."

"My old man was a drunk and a bully."

"My point precisely. You certainly turned out all right." G-Man smiled at me. He went on to talk about how sociopaths never felt real love. "They pretend to love someone in order to manipulate them."

"Really?" My friendships with L&O and Valley-Girl and my relationship with G-Man weren't attempts to manipulate them. Especially G-Man. I cared as deeply for him as I could. I missed him when he was away.

§

G-Man met me in our coffee house near the end of my internship all abuzz about a place he'd visited. "It's called the body farm. Way the hell out in Tennessee."

"The body farm? They don't raise people there, do they?" I laughed at the name.

"Not at all. In fact, it's more a place you'd like than I did. It's a university lab where donated cadavers are left in the woods for scientists to study the stages of decomposition. I puked at the stench. I don't know how you do it."

G-Man was right. I'd be right at home. "You get used to it." I'd told him about the puking prima donna on my first trip to the morgue, and about Li'l Bit, Princess, and Dead Dog. "Any chance I can visit?"

"When you become a medical examiner, probably. Hospital pathologists don't need to learn as much about decomposition, do they? At least most of the time you deal with deaths inside the hospital or its clinics, don't you?"

"You mean, I have to wait until I'm finished with my residency and more years of forensic pathology?" When I put the numbers together, it seemed like forever. "Do I have to be board-certified first?"

"Forensic pathology? When did you begin thinking about forensic pathology, Doc?"

"You're a bad influence, G-Man. You keep talking about all the exciting things you're doing. You make me want to be part of your world."

"Wow. How cool would it be if we worked together? Is this

what you really want?"

"Forensics is more challenging than what I'm doing now." I'd read a pile of reference books about what forensic pathologists did. "It's additional training on top of my residency, though."

"Let's continue this over dinner."

We walked down the street from Hopkins to a small restaurant that had become our regular spot. We ordered from memory and settled back with a couple of cold beers.

"Hopkins's pathology department will give me the grounding I need in both anatomical and clinical pathology, plus some on the forensic side."

"You've never told me why you want to cut up dead bodies." G-Man took a long pull on his beer. "I remember once you said you wanted to determine how a body stopped working. It's more than that, isn't it?"

I'd given this question a lot of thought in recent months, because I was sure he would ask. When he did, I almost had an answer ready. "Remember when we talked about solving mysteries? Pathology is another way to solve those mysteries. Besides, I'm much smarter than the average criminal. I can find them if they try to hide how they murdered someone."

"You're definitely smarter than the criminals my group hunts. Some are too stupid not to get caught."

"Thank goodness."

The waiter brought our pizza, and our conversation turned to more appetizing topics.

After a night of sexual abandon, I watched him scan the titles of my books. He pulled several off the shelves, saying he had many of the same ones. The big difference was I had tons of mysteries and true crime books on serial killers as well. And a small pile of black lab notebooks.

"You like 'em, too." He held up a thick book on serial killers.

"I wouldn't say 'like.' They're sick, but I'm fascinated by why they do what they do." I waded into deepening water as a test to see how G-Man would respond.

"It's the why that gets me. I'd give anything to stop a serial killer."

And with that, he laid down a challenge without knowing it.

§

I finished my internship with a sense of both relief and anticipation, relief because I survived "intern hell" and anticipation because I was admitted into my pathology residency at Johns Hopkins. Had I tried to change schools, Chest-Cracker wouldn't have let me.

"You're staying here for your residency, if you want."

"I want."

I had almost two weeks before the start of more intense training. G-Man came up from Washington to celebrate.

"How long has it been since your last vacation?" We were having breakfast, a real sit-down breakfast, at a local diner.

"I've never gone on a vacation. Big Chigger wouldn't spend money to take us anywhere. Since I started school, I've been studying year round." I sprinkled hot sauce on my omelet.

"You need a week off. Let's go over to the shore and hang out." G-Man had never asked me to go anywhere other than out for a meal. "I have some time coming. We could play in the ocean, walk on the sand, and kick back. Whaddya say, huh?"

I was speechless. What the hell would I do with an entire week off? "Okay, let's do it."

G-Man looked like a little boy who'd found the toy in his cereal box. He leaned across the table and kissed me, upsetting my coffee cup in the process. It was empty.

We drove G-Man's car to Rehobeth Beach where he'd rented a small house. I had no idea what to expect, since I'd never been to a beach before. Honest. Even though I lived in Baltimore, the closest I'd been to the ocean was the Inner Harbor. I couldn't believe how good warm sand felt between my toes. I learned to play.

G-Man had a trunk full of beach stuff: towels, chairs, Frisbees, a large ball he blew up and a couple of boogie boards. I couldn't wait to try them all. If you'd told me I'd enjoy having no daily agenda and doing only what the whim of the morning dictated, I'd have called you a liar. G-Man went out of his way to make my first vacation remarkable.

"I got a new assignment just before we left." He'd be away for weeks on a task force helping local law enforcement track murderers.

We were eating a late lunch of fish tacos, when my stomach muscles tightened at his words. The crimes he investigated were often in the worst areas of the country. "Where?"

"El Paso."

"Shit. That's across from the most dangerous city in Mexico, isn't it?"

"Yes. We have an office that deals with drug running and illegal immigration. The killing fields of one of the nastiest drug cartels are right across the border." G-Man looked excited. "We don't want them to spill into Texas."

"So, you'll be working with the border control agents?"

"On both sides. It's a tough assignment." He pushed our empty plates aside and took my hand. "I might not get back to Washington for a while."

Where was this leading? Were we breaking up? Had we become a couple without me realizing it? Crap, crap, I'd miss G-Man. I really would.

"I want us to be together, Doc. We'll have distances between us because of our careers, but I don't want to lose you. What do you say to getting married?"

Married? I couldn't believe it. G-Man was asking me to marry him. I'd never told him I loved him. I did, but I never said it. The separations, though, would make G-Man just about the perfect husband for a career killer.

"Yes."

"I don't want to wait, unless you want a fancy wedding."

"I don't. How soon can we get married?"

Two weeks later, we stood in front of a judge with five witnesses: Valley-Girl, Gay-Blade, L&O, Mrs. Judge, and G-Man's best friend from the FBI. We exchanged vows; he slipped a plain gold band on my hand.

I was married. I couldn't believe it. I was the wife of an FBI agent. Our long periods of separation would let me kill as needed. Life could hardly get any better.

CHAPTER TWENTY-SIX

JUNIOR

1993

I'd been an old married lady for about two years before my family found out. I didn't tell them; I assumed they didn't care what I did. In fact, I hadn't heard anything from them since Li'l Bit's letter about Miss Snicker's death. I was shocked as shit when Junior showed up at Hopkins.

I'd finished an all-nighter in Autopsy when one of the nurses said I had a visitor. I was in the doctor's locker room getting ready to shed blood-stained scrubs and climb into street clothes. I had no idea who it might be. It couldn't be G-Man; he was away somewhere. He couldn't always tell me where. I was learning to trust him. I washed my hands and walked out to a waiting area.

Junior overflowed a plastic chair. I couldn't believe how he'd ballooned. I hadn't seen him in over eight years. He was probably three hundred plus, pasty white, and so unclean his acrid sweat permeated the room. He looked like any street junkie I'd seen in withdrawal, down to his doughy face gleaming with sweat.

"What the hell are you doing here, and how did you find me?"

"You got written up in the local paper when you got into med school. 'Local girl makes good' and all that shit."

Years ago I read how top schools issued press releases to hometown papers when they offered scholarships to their most promising students. Johns Hopkins must have a publicity department that took care of such notifications.

Junior sneezed and wiped snot on his sleeve. "That's how I knew where you was. Said you got into John Hopkin and was gonna be a doctor."

Had he been keeping track of me all these years? I swallowed bile.

"So you found me. Big flipping deal. What are you doing here?" I couldn't take my eyes off the bulk that was my brother. He reminded me of Jumbo, the bully and wife beater, who reminded me of my brother the bully, who reminded me of Jumbo…I shook my head and got off the merry-go-round.

"I need help." Junior glared at my scrubs, stained with blood from an accident victim whose bicycle had lost its encounter with a Mercedes.

"I assume by 'help' you mean money." I crossed my arms over my chest. He wasn't going to wheedle a cent out of me.

"I, um, borrowed some money from the old man to pay this guy I know." Junior's eyes darted down and to the right.

"Borrowed? More like stole. What'll Big Chigger do when he finds out?" Not that I cared.

"Ah shit. The old man'd just kick my ass."

If he wasn't afraid of the old man, it must be the guy to whom he owed money. "Why can't you repay 'this guy'?"

Junior shook his head. He leaned over his legs as far as his girth would allow. "I got no money. He'll kill me if I don't pay."

The thought tantalized me. He would be out of my life forever. The tiniest of shivers tickled down my spine. "From the looks of you, I guess this guy you owe is a drug dealer."

Junior lumbered to his feet. "Yeah."

"In Bubbaville?"

"Near enough."

"How the hell did you get involved with a dealer?" I held up my hand. "No, don't tell me. I don't want to know."

Junior took several steps toward me. "I said I need help. You got money. Gimme some."

"Why do you think a) I have money and b) I'd give you any?"

"You got married. He's gotta have money. Beside you're a doctor, and everyone knows doctors are rich." Logic as flawed as ever.

"I'm a doctor, all right, a pathologist." I looked from Junior to the stains on my chest and sleeves. "I cut up dead people."

He paled and gulped. "You got blood all over you."

"Corpses can be bloody." I pretended to wipe at my shirt. If he thought I was giving him a message, so much the better. "I repeat, how did you find me?"

"I ain't stupid. I asked around. I bin keepin' my eye on you."

This time, fear raced along my spine.

"What right do you have to show up here?"

I dropped my arms. He was too close for me to be comfortable. I got ready to defend myself if he had a mind to rush me. I still studied Aikido.

"I need money. Gimme some." He repeated his demand with dogged persistence.

That same old sense of entitlement the men in my family exhibited reared up, ugly as the day Big Chigger told me he'd spent my college savings.

"You and the old man are parasites." I held my ground, prepared if he made a move. "When I left, I broke the cycle of giving you money whenever you were in a world of shit. You got yourself in trouble. Get yourself out."

Junior started yelling. "You don't give a shit about the family."

He was right.

"You're a selfish bitch."

Right again.

"You don't care that I'm sick and need help."

Three for three.

My hands hung loosely at my sides. His behavior, his attitude, his very being disgusted me. My facial muscles stiffened into a mask; my eyes narrowed to slits. His ranting brought orderlies running to see if anyone needed help. I nodded to the largest to block the door. He crossed his arms across a barrel chest. If Junior even thought about getting violent, he'd be restrained before he could finish his thought. Weight-Lifter was a gentle giant who could bench press Junior without breaking a sweat.

"I repeat. You're not my family anymore." I set a trap. "You proved that when you killed my cat."

"How'd you know about that? It was only a fucking cat." And snap. Junior fell right in.

"Yeah, but she was my 'fucking cat.'" I'd always assumed he killed Miss Snickers #1. Here he was admitting it. That sealed his fate. He'd pay, just not yet. "So you're sick. What's the matter?"

Ranting gave way to whining, with Junior coming up with a litany of symptoms disconnected from any syndrome or medical condition. Or reality.

I walked up to him, grabbed his arm, and shoved a filthy sleeve up. Track marks. "You need money for smack? That it?"

"Hey, I ain't shooting up. Those are from blood tests. I had mono."

"Mono? You had mono when you were twelve. These are fresh."

Junior jerked his arm away, shoving me backwards against the wall in the process. Weight-Lifter took one step forward and restrained him with a hand on his upper arm, immobilizing him by pressing his thumb on the ulnar nerve, causing Junior to suffer the worst funny bone pain in his life. Took about two seconds for him to drop to his knees. That elbow was going to be sore as hell for a week. Weight-Lifter relaxed his grip and returned to his position at the door.

Irrational anger from a childhood spent being slammed against walls by the old man made my abdominal muscles as tight as my will to control my actions. Much as I would have liked to take Junior down like I did when Pre-Law and I went to Bubbaville, he wasn't worth it. My eyes narrowed further, a warning most people would have heeded. Bile burned the back of my throat.

"I still don't know how you found me. I don't like the idea you're stalking me."

"You can't stalk family." Junior clambered to his feet and rubbed the inside of his elbow. He kept one eye on Weight-Lifter, the other on me.

"Let me make this perfectly clear. We. Are. Not. Family. I don't care what happens to you. Now, leave." My face remained rigid. I wouldn't show the disgust I felt.

"I need a fix." Junior's voice varied between whine and wheedle. "You guys have drugs here. Gimme something. I'm really sick."

"We don't hand out drugs to junkies. You can go into rehab or die on the streets for all I care."

Junior grabbed for me a second before Weight-Lifter lifted him away. "She said no."

"You gotta help."

I pulled a pad and pen from my pocket. "Here's the address for the free clinic. Maybe it can help."

I handed him the paper and watched him rip it up.

"You just wait. I ain't done with you."

No, Junior, you wait. It's me who's not done with you.

CHAPTER TWENTY-SEVEN

CHILD ABDUCTION

1994

Autopsy was unusually busy one Friday afternoon. An SUV crossed the center median on I95, slammed into a semi tractor-trailer and exploded. Both were going approximately seventy miles an hour. Death was instantaneous for the four victims in the car. The trucker was on life support and not expected to live. We'd probably get his body in a few days.

"May I come in?" A voice followed a knock on the outer door.

"It's open," Chest-Cracker called.

A policeman I hadn't met before entered. "I'm Officer George Hampton."

"Glad to meet you, officer. I'd offer to shake hands, but…" Chest-Cracker lifted his gloved hands, stained black with soot and char. "This your case?"

"Yeah. I have to know if either driver was drunk." Officer Hampton paled when he caught a look at what was left of the body on the table.

"All in good time," Chest-Cracker said.

Officer Hampton protested. He needed something, anything, for his report.

"Why don't you do a whole blood test on the SUV driver, Doc?"

Chest-Cracker showed me how to use a long needle to draw blood from the femoral artery. I ran the test and gave the policeman the results. "Blood alcohol over 0.25."

"Shit." Officer Hampton thanked us and left satisfied.

We'd nearly finished sewing up the Y-incision on the young girl who'd been riding shotgun. No seat belt, major crush injuries. Her ribs punctured both lungs when they shattered. The sternum was in a dozen or more pieces, many of which had pierced her heart. I didn't know if the air bag deployed, although I doubted it.

"Well, look at that." Chest-Cracker pointed a needle laced with thick autopsy thread at the television he kept muted. "A missing child. Hope they find her soon."

I tossed my gloves in the waste bin and turned up the volume. A sobbing woman in East Baltimore pleaded with "whoever took my baby" to bring her home safely. She collapsed in the arms of a man standing next to her.

"Didn't see any tears. Did you?" Chest-Cracker glowered at the news anchor who was chirping about the missing child. A photo in the upper left corner of the screen showed a cute brown-haired girl of about six. Her smiling bald mouth confirmed that her front baby teeth had fallen out.

"No. Hope this isn't another case of a woman who found it inconvenient to be a mother and killed her kid." The press had been rife with such accounts in recent years. Hysterical mothers had become a cliché, which too often didn't withstand scrutiny.

"Let's hope not. The kid deserves better. But, if it turns out there's a body, we might get it."

Before I left for the day, I cleaned the tables, washed down the floor, and put all the bone saws, spreaders, and scalpels in the autoclave for sterilization. The television reran the woman's plea for help often enough for me to have it memorized. The closer I listened, the less convinced I was that she was telling the truth. If I was ever stopped by the authorities, I guaranteed I'd be a better actress. All the lessons I'd learned in my youth as That Thing or copying proper, acceptable behavior during college and medical school would serve me in times of crisis, should there ever be any.

I took the rest of the afternoon off, all two hours of it, to return to my apartment. I tuned the television to the news channel and began my own behavioral analysis based on what the media replayed. I didn't see remorse; I didn't see tears. I did see my next victim if the little girl turned up dead. I wasn't sure I wanted my own children, but I sure as hell hated, absolutely loathed, people who injured or killed them.

§

Five days after the little girl was reported missing, my phone rang at six in the morning.

"Doc, Chest-Cracker. We caught the child."

I was out of bed and into scrubs almost before he hung up. Twenty minutes later, Chest-Cracker met me at the door of Autopsy. He steered me to his office.

"Kids in general are bad enough, but this is the worst I've ever seen." Chest-Cracker was almost never shaken by dead bodies. This morning, though, he was practically trembling. "If you don't want to assist…"

"Let's go." I knew better than to eat anything before an autopsy, although puking on an empty stomach wasn't all that much fun, either.

The child was shrouded head to foot with a green sheet. Blood seeped through where the chest would be. This was going to be messy, but nothing prepared me for the tortured body when I folded the covering back.

Her face was a mass of fresh and healing bruises, which could only be made by a fist. Circular cigarette burn marks covered her cheeks, neck, and torso. One shoulder was at an odd angle hinting at dislocation. I took pictures of her torso, abdomen, arms, legs, and face before I pulled her mouth open to see if anything foreign was lodged inside. Nothing. She looked younger in death than her six years. I'd never seen the level of abuse this child had endured.

"Swab everything. All trace goes into bags and dishes. We need to know where this child has been."

The door swung open, and two burly cops entered. "I'm Detective Johan, and this is Detective Gonzales."

Detective Johan took a look at the child's mutilated face and puked into a trash can. Detective Gonzales backed out the door. I could hear his vomit splash on the tile. Crap. Why did they send brutes with weak stomachs?

"Where do you want me to start?"

"Scrape under her nails. Comb her hair. Send any traces of soil, skin, and dirt to the lab."

Chest-Cracker laid a small towel over the child's genital area. If she was raped, this would preserve evidence. If not, even in death the dead deserved a modicum of modesty. After a cursory visual inspection, he ordered X-rays of her entire body. "I see old burn marks, nearly healed bruises. This child was brutalized before she went missing. Maybe for years."

For years? How can anyone torture a child for years without anyone noticing? I rolled the portable unit over to the table, lifted the body onto a clean sheet, and snapped X-rays.

"She can't weigh more than twenty-five pounds. Look at how emaciated she is." Chest-Cracker stood aside and let me do my work. His voice thickened. I shot a glance at him as I positioned the X-ray machine over her legs.

"I have a grandson just about her age. If something like this happened to him, I don't know what I'd do." He cleared his throat.

I knew what I'd do.

I moved from head to foot, covering every inch of the child's body. Chest-Cracker called the lab upstairs and asked for a rush processing the film, while I shoved the unit out of our way against the wall.

We shifted the body back to the metal autopsy table. I examined her head, combed debris from her hair onto a clean piece of white paper, and photographed a penetrating injury to the parietal lobe at the back of her skull. "She was hit with a sharp object. Penetrated an inch into her brain."

"That wasn't the cause of death." Chest-Cracker pointed to broken blood vessels in her eyes. "Petechial hemorrhages. She was strangled."

The autopsy room door banged open half an hour later when the X-ray technician ran in with a fistful of developed film. He slapped them on light boxes situated around the wall. "I can't believe what I'm seeing." He pointed to old fractures of both arms, several ribs, left clavicle, and left femur.

"Do you have any idea what it takes to break a femur? Even a small child's femur." Chest-Cracker pointed to a badly healed fracture. "She wasn't treated for it, either. She'd have walked with a limp."

I counted no fewer than twelve broken bones, all healed, but none with signs of medical intervention. "Someone beat this child and never took her to the emergency room. She was off the radar. No way to catch this before things got out of hand."

When we started the actual autopsy, Chest-Cracker said, "You guys might want to leave. I won't have you puking all over my lab."

The policemen stayed and stood at the end of the table. Chest-Cracker made an incision at the back of the hair line and peeled the scalp loose to get clear images of the penetrating parietal wound. Bone fragments, dirt, and dried leaf bits filled the cavity, a place where there shouldn't be a cavity. I ignored the gagging coming from the trash cans.

"Sharp object, possibly a hammer or a small hatchet. See how the edges of the skull are crushed?" He pointed to the point of impact. "The wound is post-mortem. No bleeding. She was dead when she was struck."

I bit my lips behind my mask. My vision blurred before clearing to focus on something only I could see: the perpetrator lying dead on this same table.

"Someone hated this child." We pulled fragments of bone and debris from the brain, bagged them, and once more signed off on the evidence bags. From there, it was on to the chest cavity.

Chest-Cracker sliced through the thin layer of skin and laid open the entire chest area. I removed organs, weighed them, and set them aside for preservation. We photographed the broken ribs to document a sustained pattern of abuse. A swift vaginal exam showed an intact hymen. She hadn't been raped.

"My God! How did this child survive as long as she did?"

"Hey guys, what's her name?" I couldn't think about her as the child any longer. I needed a real identity.

Detective Gonzales, the one who'd fouled our hallway, checked his notepad. "Starr Reynolds. Age six."

"Jeez. She weighs about as much as a small four-year-old." I knew from the initial television broadcast and her bare gums how old she was.

"How long's she been dead?" Detective Johan, the one who

had made it to the trash can before dumping the contents of his stomach, asked.

"At least a week," said Chest-Cracker. "Maybe eight days, based on the rate of decomposition. She was buried in leaves and loose dirt, which slowed down tissue deterioration."

"That means she was dead when her mother went on television." Detective Gonzales said.

"Bitch." Detective Johan said.

Soon-to-be-dead bitch.

CHAPTER TWENTY-EIGHT

STARR'S REVENGE

1994

After thinking about ways of getting information on the mother, I decided to make friends with Detective Gonzales from Starr's autopsy. A quick check in the file gave me his number. He was younger and more likely to be charmed by my interest in police procedures. At least I hoped so.

"Detective Gonzales, this is Doc from Johns Hopkins. We met when Chest-Cracker and I did the autopsy on the child, Starr Reynolds." My super-friendly, eager persona took him in. "I was wondering if you'd help me learn more about how you'll catch her murderer."

"Why don't you come to the station? I'll show you how we map leads." Lt. Gonzales landed right in my trap.

"If you sure that'll be all right." My voice trailed off.

"No problem. You're part of the team, after all."

We set a date for Saturday morning, two days out.

I watched the newscasts to be sure I didn't miss an arrest or something that would throw my plans awry. The child's mother continued to weep and wail about the evil person who'd killed "my darling baby," always dry-eyed. She railed at the police for not taking her seriously. I believed the police were taking her very seriously, too seriously for my liking. I'd have to move soon. Once she was jailed, she'd be out of my reach.

The last case before I left for my weekend "date" with the detective was a stillborn found tossed in a dumpster. A passerby lifted the lid and found the infant wrapped in a bloody towel. The police brought us the tiny body.

"Why don't you verify this was a still birth?" Chest-Cracker had already cleaned up most of the autopsy room, changed out of his scrubs, and prepared to go home to dinner with his wife. I did a quick Y-incision.

"Chest-Cracker, this baby was born alive." I called the pathologist over and pointed to inflated lungs. That only happens when a newborn draws a breath. "Hope the police have found the mother."

"Okay. I'll make the call. Cause of death looks like exposure. The police will decide if it's negligent homicide or not." Chest-Cracker's face was lined with sorrow. "Jeez, why didn't she leave the baby at a church or hospital? It could have been adopted."

"Doubtful," I said. "Black babies don't get adopted as easily as white ones do."

"Still…" Chest-Cracker covered the tiny corpse, called the police, and went home. I stowed it in a refrigerator along with the others waiting pick up from mortuaries.

§

I spent a fruitful couple of hours at the police station. Detective Gonzales led me into the murder room where current cases were arranged on erasable whiteboards. Starr's first grade picture was beside a couple of the autopsy photos I'd taken. Several head shots of her mother, her father, stepfather, and three other males filled one white board.

"You have several suspects?" I flirted even though I noticed the detective wore a broad gold band on his left hand. Hell, I had a gold band on mine, too.

Could the mother not be the murderer? I couldn't be wrong.

"We've talked to a lot of people, but our experience shows it's usually someone in the immediate family, one of the parents, a stepparent. the boyfriend of the mother."

The more the detective talked, the more I realized he believed the case against the mother was a slam dunk. "We need more evidence before we can make an arrest, though."

I thanked him and let him walk me out of the station. I hated to disappoint him, but he wouldn't be making any arrests.

In the neighborhood where Starr's mother lived, the media trucks that covered the initial disappearance had moved onto other crime scenes. Ever-present scrubs helped me pose as a health professional paying a call to see how the mother, Arleen Mayfair, was coping since her daughter's body had been found.

Luck was against me that mid Saturday morning a week after I met with Detective Gonzales. I left the Ugly Duckling around the corner a block away and walked to the Reynolds-Mayfair bungalow. When I rang the bell, a frowsy woman answered. It wasn't Arleen. She was Starr's grandmother who had been with her dear, darling daughter for over a week. She was going home to West Virginia as soon as the taxi arrived. Her daughter was still too distraught to drive her to the Greyhound station.

I offered to return at a more convenient time. Convenient for me. When no one else was around. I moved my car to have a view of the front of the house. Less than thirty minutes later, a taxi pulled up, and the frowzy woman left. The waiting time let me finalize my plans. I'd overpower Arleen in the house using my trusty police choke hold. That way I could subdue her from behind. She looked like she wasn't very tall and was of average weight, so I should be able to knock her out in a few seconds. I had a partial roll of duct tape in my backpack to wrap her wrists and cover her mouth. I didn't want her yelling until she had a real reason. Like pain. Lots of pain.

I'd force her into her car, which I'd noticed was parked in the drive beside the house, and drive to another secluded spot I'd picked out where her screams would not be heard.

She let me into the house without asking for identification. I followed her into the kitchen, pulled on gloves, and grabbed her from behind. With her throat in the crook of my arm, I rendered her unconscious in under fifteen seconds. I ripped tape from the roll, bound her wrists, and slapped a length over her mouth. I lifted her to her feet and half-carried, half-dragged her to her car. A quick shove, and she slumped into the passenger's seat. She was half-conscious when the door closed with no louder sound than a small click. Her eyes met mine and widened in fear. I smiled.

I snooped around the garage, looking for a hammer or hatchet. I wanted to hit her on the left parietal lobe hard enough to fracture her skull but not hard enough to kill her. I found a hatchet with bits of dried flesh and strands of hair on it buried under a pile of greasy rags behind a battered workbench. Surgical gloves protected my hands. If I'd learned one thing from killing Filthy-Rich, it was never to touch a body or a tool with bare hands.

About thirty miles out in the country, I turned down a dirt road and pulled behind a crumbling barn. The mother was fully conscious and moaned. Loss of air by carotid artery compression often resulted in a massive headache. Her headache was just beginning.

I forced her out of the car, grabbed my backpack, and walked her to the barn. The side door was so rotten that it hung from one hinge. I nudged it open wide enough for us to enter the dim interior. Barn swallows and pigeons erupted through the broken windows, raising a cloud of dust in their maddened flight. Years of droppings left a dried powdery layer on the floor. Shafts of sunlight struggled to penetrate the gloom. I didn't need light. I knew what I was going to do.

I spread a plastic sheet I'd tucked into my pack on the floor before the mother ended up on it in a heap. Because I knew where most of Starr's broken bones were, I set about replicating some of the injuries. I ripped the tape from her mouth before I took her right hand in mine. Snap. The forefinger broke.

"Why did you kill your daughter?"

The woman shook her head, denying she'd killed the child.

Snap. The middle finger on the same hand broke. Shriek.

"Can you imagine how scared she must have been when her mother turned against her?"

The little finger on the left hand followed. Shriek.

I broke the left wrist and forearm by stomping on the arm. The resulting snapping sounds as the ulna and radius bones separated turned me on. A thumb, bent back against the broken wrist, rendered the now-terrified woman almost mute.

Hot urine stained her skirt and filled the air with a stench. Her bowels opened next. I laughed. "Is that what Starr did when you hit her and broke her ribs?"

"I never hit her."

"Well, sure as hell someone did."

"No one did. The police haven't said she was hurt. Just that she was dead."

"Just how do you think she ended up dead? Did monsters do it? Or did you?"

She babbled that she loved her baby, and no one had done anything to hurt the dear little girl. I walked back to her car and pulled the hatchet from the trunk. I held it two inches from her eyes, close enough for her to smell the rot from the blood and scalp fragments on it. She vomited all over her chest.

"You hit her with this. Right? Your fingerprints are going to be found all over it. In good time, you're going to know how it feels to die."

"How, how do you know my baby was killed?" Starr's mother begged for mercy. I nearly had an orgasm; my pleasure was that intense.

"I did her autopsy, you bitch. I'm not the only one who knows, but I'm the only one who will make you pay. You'll suffer much same way she did. Then police will find you as dead as she is."

I kicked her in the ribs, delighting in her screams. She'd strangled the child before bashing her head, but I wasn't going to bury the hatchet in her brain. I hit her with it twice, hard, right behind the ear over the temporal lobe, hard enough to fracture the skull but not hard enough to kill her. Then I knelt in the dirt behind the dying woman and placed my hands on either side of her neck. I pulled up and to the right. The sharp movement separated two cervical vertebrae, producing a delightful snap when the neck broke. She was positively, absolutely, undeniably, and reliably dead.

I dragged her body back to the car and propped her in the passenger seat. A quick policing of the barn and a rolling up of the stained sheet, and we were ready to return to her bungalow. After I parked the car in the drive, I pulled her body over until it was lying across the driver's seat, tossed the hatchet with her fingerprints all over it on the floor, and left.

No one on my watch was going to get away with hurting a child or a woman. Starr's mother joined Filthy-Rich in hell where they both belonged. I drove home totally turned on. If G-Man had been home, I'd have fucked his lights out.

§

"Did you see where someone killed the mother who cried wolf?" Chest-Cracker said as soon as I entered Autopsy the following Monday morning.

"I saw something on the news. Are we doing the autopsy?" I wanted to see the results of my handiwork naked and stretched out on a stainless steel table.

"Not this time. The state examiner is taking care of it."

Damn. I turned away to keep my disappointment from giving me away.

"Any idea who did it?"

"Not really. The police probably aren't going to look too hard, though. She left a letter confessing her involvement in the child's death. Odd, though. It's almost like we have a vigilante roaming Baltimore."

"I hope not." I knew so, but my Doc persona said act concerned.

"No matter what. Someone did the police a favor."

Yes, I did. The letter was a nice, last minute touch.

I heeded Chest-Cracker's warning. When I wanted to kill again, it couldn't be another revenge killing in Baltimore. Maybe something more random like my first kills. I couldn't present an M.O. that G-Man or his friends could follow. It would be damned hard for him to explain how he, an FBI profiler, actually married a serial killer and didn't know it.

CHAPTER TWENTY-NINE

CHANGES AFOOT

1996

"Doc, you know you have to find a real job, don't you?" Chest-Cracker and I washed up at the end of an easy day. Only three autopsies, all routine in-hospital deaths.

"Yeah, I can't hang around here much longer, unless you need another teaching pathologist." I winked. "Or unless you retire."

"I'd die in retirement."

"Then I'd be able to do your autopsy."

"Over my dead body." Our long-running joke was about to end when I moved on. Chest-Cracker laughed and threw his towel in the laundry hamper.

My lips smiled, but my brain didn't want to think about leaving my mentor and friend. I trusted him.

"I don't see you teaching, Doc. At least not at this phase of your career." Chest-Cracker leaned against the edge of the sink. "You need field experience. Besides, you have instincts that can best be honed in a high-pressure morgue or medical examiner's office."

I'd learned so much working in Autopsy at Johns Hopkins, but he was right. I needed more real-world experience. My research turned up openings at various law enforcement departments in and around the Washington, D.C. area as well as at the FBI. Like being married to an agent, being part of a legal system was too intoxicating to ignore. G-Man, of course, wanted me to go into the FBI.

"Remember when I told you about the body farm, Doc? If you joined us, you'd finally get to go there," he said one night over dinner at a lovely little restaurant off Dupont Circle where we celebrated my passing board certification and him the end of his assignment in El Paso.

"Chest-Cracker says I can go there if I'm attached to a medical examiner's office. I don't need to be in the FBI."

Having both of us in the same federal organization didn't seem like a good idea. In the behavioral analysis department, G-Man developed profiles of criminals. If we worked too close together, and if I slipped up in any way, he might sniff out my killing persona. I couldn't risk it.

"What do you say? Will you at least consider it?"

"I'll think about it."

"Great!" G-Man wore his little-boy expression, the one he used when he had a secret he couldn't wait to share.

"What?"

"What, what?" He tried to look innocent, only to fail miserably.

"Okay. What's the secret?" I studied the emotions that changed his face into that of a little boy trying to deny he ate cake when he had icing around his mouth.

He withdrew a sheaf of papers from his inner jacket pocket. I took them and laughed. Application forms for the Federal Bureau of Investigation. The same ones I'd filled out and sent in a month earlier.

"What if I want to go into the CIA instead?" I had to tweak his nose a bit. He was too cocksure.

"You won't. Spooks aren't too worried about autopsies. They clean up after themselves. Besides, they don't solve crimes the way we do in the FBI."

"From what I read, the spooks get away with committing crimes instead." Another tweak.

"Could be." G-Man paid the check. "Hey, we might even get to work together. That would be just about the coolest thing yet."

Yes, it would. As long as I wasn't the suspect. And I wouldn't be.

CHAPTER THIRTY

COCAINE WITH A KICK

1996

I focused on next steps now that my residency was successfully over, and I was a board-certified pathologist. First, get a job. I would have to leave Johns Hopkins's autopsy department in less than a month. Next, extricate myself from Baltimore, including the apartment I'd lived in with Miss Snickers #2 since I started medical school. Third, give the cops one last gift by taking down a scumbag or two.

Nothing I could do would make any law enforcement agency move on my application until it was darned good and ready. My apartment was clean and lean, so packing would be painless. I'd be moving into the brownstone G-Man had inherited from the uncle who'd raised him, so I needed very little beyond my books, clothes, the kill books, Old Rex, and Miss Snickers #2.

I wasn't sure how I felt about moving in with G-Man. I mean, we were married, but to date our lives weren't that different from before we got married. He lived in his house in Washington; I had my apartment in Baltimore.

I was committed to G-Man emotionally and physically, yet part of me was reluctant to give up my independence. More than just worrying about getting away with killing and him not being any the wiser, my bigger worry was whether I was psychologically married. I needed time to get used to being half of a couple instead of being all of a single entity. No matter what, I was moving to Washington and into his brownstone.

That left my going-away present to the cops.

During the years I'd lived in Baltimore, the cocaine problem intensified rather than abated. Even the mayor wouldn't admit how huge it was. Cocaine led to deaths. The papers rarely wrote about the death of "just another addict" any more than they had when Street-Thug snorted his last. Heroin was making a resurgence with the usual results: Addicts misjudged the strength of the hit and ended up dead. Because I wasn't a publicity hound, my kills could have little long-term impact on crime by removing another dealer or two from the streets, but it was the best I could do.

We saw our fair share of the aftermath of the drug epidemic in autopsy. Heavy drug use damaged most of the filtering organs--the lungs, kidneys, and liver; sometimes the heart failed. My fellow residents and the current crop of interns on rotation grew accustomed to eyeballing a skinny body with sallow skin and betting on what drug had done the deed.

First-timers, mostly teens who overdosed on coke, crack, or heroin at a party, required more intensive exams. That first hit, especially of crack cocaine and heroin, was often their last, so they didn't exhibit standard outward signs from prolonged drug abuse. We sent samples to the lab to identify the type and origin of each deadly overdose. When an unusual number of overdoses popped up over a two-week period, the cops asked us to analyze the drugs themselves.

"We need to know what they're taking, so we can find where it's coming from," said Lt. Gonzales, my detective friend from the Starr Reynolds's homicide who had been promoted and was on a new task force attacking the drug problem.

"Why do you think there's a bad batch of cocaine or heroin on the streets?" Chest-Cracker looked up from a sheaf of papers in his hand.

"Too many dead kids in the same area of the city."

"Isn't uncut heroin usually the culprit in the underground drug trade?"

For the life of me, I couldn't figure out why Lt. Gonzales wanted to stop distribution of tainted drugs. If word got out the street drugs were laced with evil shit, wouldn't addicts stop buying? If they didn't stop buying and overdosed, what was it to the cops? Just another bunch of junkies, and the crimes they'd commit to feed their habit, they wouldn't have to worry about.

"We'll see what we can find." With that, Chest-Cracker added drawing more blood to our daily activities.

After the lieutenant left, we sat over coffee and listed what could be mixed with cocaine.

"A lot of our dead kids aren't hard-core addicts." Chest-Cracker flipped through a dozen files of recent overdoses. "Let's see if we can spot trends before we bankrupt the city with needless tests."

"So, dealers cut coke with baking soda or sugar, right? Anything else?" I looked at the files spread across Chest-Cracker's desk.

"Any number of powdered substances. Most likely, we're dealing with someone in the shallow end of the gene pool. He's probably cutting his drugs with some over-the-counter substance more lethal than the drugs themselves."

Like rat poison, for instance, my particular favorite for targeted killings of junkies.

We studied the autopsy reports for commonality. "Hey, Chest-Cracker, look at this photo. See how the body's contorted. The spine's arched, and the muscles are spastic. We can run tests for known toxins." I found more photos of contorted backs.

"It looks like some kind of alkaloid poisoning." Chest-Cracker pulled down a thick book from the U.S. Poison Control Center. He looked up common poisons. "Could be hemlock, strychnine, arsenic, or cyanide."

"Ricin?"

"Not ricin. Besides, where would a street dealer get ricin? Most wouldn't know how to distill it from raw castor beans, even though the instructions are readily available on the Internet." Chest-Cracker shook his head. "Too sophisticated and way too James Bondish. Let's look for stuff anyone could get their hands on."

"With that criterion, we can rule out hemlock. Making a tea from hemlock leaves and getting addicts to drink it doesn't compute." I tried to imagine sitting down to tea with a dealer. No way did I see anyone making a tea from any biological substance. It had to be something that could be ground and mixed with the powered drug.

"I'd rule out arsenic. It's not as easy to get your hands on as television would have us believe." Chest-Cracker made a short list of two substances. "Okay, test for strychnine and cyanide. Neither is that hard to buy."

I pulled slides and blood vials to run through a poison-detecting toxicology analysis. It didn't take long before I'd isolated strychnine.

"Why in hell would some idiot street dealer lace his product with strychnine?" Chest-Cracker stared at the results before shrugging off the contradiction.

"Could be a rival dealer wanting to corner the market. Who the hell cares? These parasites don't matter much in the greater scheme of things." I'd never been so open in my opinion of society's bottom dwellers.

An ambulance arrived with two new bodies. One looked like a male drug user; the other was burned over seventy percent of its body. I said "its" because at first glance neither of us could tell if the corpse was male or female. An examination of the pelvis showed it belonged to a female. Once again, Lt. Gonzales showed up when we were halfway through with our autopsies.

"See you got the two freshest corpses. Any ideas?" He shifted a well-chewed toothpick from one side of his mouth to the other. He must be trying to quit smoking. Again. Common enough in cops.

"We're looking at strychnine mixed with coke or heroin. Maybe cyanide, but more likely strychnine. See how the back is arched?" Chest-Cracker pointed to the burn victim.

"Yeah. Do you only see that with strychnine?" Lt. Gonzales gestured at the contorted body before tossing a gooey toothpick in the trash. He pulled a fresh one from his coat pocket.

"Other things can cause muscle spasms," I said, "but strychnine is the most reasonable guess for now. I found traces in a couple of the earlier corpses."

"Looks like we got a drug gang war on our hands,"

"Should we assume both bodies were found in the same area?" I didn't look up from the liver I was weighing.

"Yeah. East Baltimore."

East Baltimore, huh?

"That's a wide area. Any idea where the dude works?" I pulled the lungs out and weighed them. The lieutenant looked away.

"We think he's moved into Preston, but beyond that…" Lt. Gonzales shook his head. "Could be gang-related, but usually they just shoot anyone who messes with their livelihood."

"You guys need a heads up on something new, "the lieutenant said around his toothpick. "Several major cities report a new deadly substance appearing across the country. It's called fentanyl."

"Fentanyl?" How could that drug make its way into the street drug culture?

"We think it's coming in from China," the lieutenant continued.

"That's nuts. We use fentanyl as a surgical anesthetic and to treat severe pain." Chest-Cracker shook his head. "Where would the dealers get fentanyl?"

"Where they get everything else. From other dealers. Watch out for it. It's more lethal than cocaine or heroin. Mixed incorrectly, and we'll have an epidemic of dead junkies on our hands."

Well now. Maybe it was time to rethink using rat poison.

By Saturday night, I was wired enough to try my disguise in the East Baltimore. I pulled my hair back and hid most of it under a Ravens ball cap. My tattered gray sweatshirt and an over-sized pair of jeans helped me blend in with the locals, because I wore the same uniform most of the dealers and victims wore. I pimp-rolled my way down Preston looking for a source. It didn't take long for someone to approach. I waved him off and continued down the street. I had to score soon, or I'd be too obvious. I ambled over to the next guy I saw. A quick low conversation netted me a tiny plastic bag for ten dollars. The first guy I rejected came over and shoved my dealer against a dirty, cinder block wall of an abandoned building.

"Hey, asshole. This my territory. Take you sorry ass off my street."

I didn't care if one of the new guys was selling spiked drugs or not. If he was encroaching on established territory, I could make his death look like the result of a turf war.

I went back to the neighborhood several more times, buying from the first guy and then the second guy. Each time I bought from the second guy, the first guy slammed him against a building. I amassed quite a stash of cocaine. Next, I needed strychnine. Walking into a pharmacy and asking for a bottle of strychnine might get me arrested, but outside Baltimore farm supply stores sold what I needed and didn't ask questions. In the garage behind my apartment, I ground the poison, being careful not to ingest any of the powder, and mixed it thoroughly with cocaine.

It rained for four straight days, cutting down on the foot traffic along Preston. On the fifth night when rain turned to drizzle, I returned disguised in the standard young-punk uniform. I beckoned to the second guy and asked if we could get out of the rain. He led me around the corner to a crack den. I was in luck. The addicts in it were passed out.

He jiggled and danced, too strung out to stand still for the buy. I pulled out a ten. When he reached for the money, I grabbed him and compressed his carotid arteries. He fell to his knees before toppling over on his side. I dragged him to the darkest part of the den. When he came around, I had a spoon ready. I ordered him to inhale. He was too good a customer of his own product to question what I was doing. He inhaled deeply and gasped.

Strychnine works quickly. The amount I put in the bag was enough to bring on muscle contractions and back spasms within minutes. He died in agony like many of his unwitting victims. I planted a bag in his pocket and left. I did the same thing with the first guy the next night. Different crack den, same result.

Lt. Gonzales called us a week later.

"Sending you two ripe corpses. Looks like two dealers took each other out."

The corpses were ripe indeed. I'd killed one guy on Saturday and the other on Sunday. It was Friday morning after a hot week. Maggots and worms slipped out the body bags.

You're welcome, Lt. Gonzales. I'm going to miss you.

CHAPTER THIRTY-ONE

FAREWELLS

1996

I thought I'd bade the Baltimore police farewell with my last drug dealer kill, but right before I was due to leave came reports of a rapist on the loose. The police posted an artist's sketch on television to warn a certain demographic of women to be careful, because he was reported to cruise the bar district. The public was asked to call the hot line if anyone saw or was approached by someone looking like the man in the sketch. The police pleaded with his victims to come forward. So far, five women had reported they'd been raped, but none were cooperating. That certain demographic included light-skinned black women with soft curling hair. Oh my. Me, if I put on a wig.

According to his victims, the rapist frequented two or three bars in downtown Baltimore. He used the same come on with each woman. He slipped Valium into her drink, led her away to a safe place, and bound and gagged her before raping her.

I hit the bars for a couple of nights as my public persona, as me. No disguise, no hits. I spotted him the second night when I observed how he operated. He was as confident as a squirrel in the depths of winter with a nest full of acorns. On the third night, I put on a really short black dress and red come-fuck-me high heels. I'd bought a wig at a fairly decent shop in Rockville, Maryland, and make-up at the local drugstore to complete my disguise. I hiked a bag containing what I'd need to exact revenge on him high on my shoulder.

He was in the second bar I entered. A girl I assumed he'd tried to pick up left as I arrived. She threw an angry comment over her shoulder.

"God, you're nothing but a fucking creep."

I settled on a barstool and ordered a beer. My long-necked Bud Lite and the rapist arrived about the same time. He leaned against the bar next to me, crowding into my space, and smiled.

"Hey, girl. You're new." His eyes took in everything from my curly hair to my toned legs and high heels. "I'd remember if you'd been here before."

He wasn't anything like my image of the rapist the police sought. He vaguely resembled the sketches, brown hair, brown eyes, and fair complexion. His hair was longer, and no one mentioned wire-rim glasses. Rather than standing out as a super hunk, he was ordinary in stature and appearance.

I took a sip of beer and smiled at him over the bottle. I set it on the bar, just a little closer to him than before. "That's because this is my first time."

I swiveled my stool until my thigh barely brushed his. My pushed-up breasts left enough cleavage to drag his eyes downward.

"Are you new to Baltimore or just new to the bar?"

"New to the bar." I wanted to keep him talking about himself. "What do you do?"

"I work in a bank," the creep said. "How about you?"

"I recently graduated. I'm looking for a job," I half-lied.

I scanned him. My eyes lingered on his crotch, and I caught my lower lip between white teeth. The game continued until I finished my beer.

The creep ordered another round. "On me."

Of course, it was. I took a sip before turning away for a moment. He dumped the contents of a capsule in his bottle and switched them. Idiot. Bars are full of mirrors. When I turned back, I pretended to take a long swallow. What he didn't see was my tongue blocking the bottle's mouth. He gave me time to drink more beer before he suggested we hook up someplace away from the bar.

"You're the most beautiful woman I've ever seen." His hand reached out and tucked a curl behind my ear. He leaned closer, his lips brushing the same ear. "Let's get out of here. I have a place nearby where we can get it on."

I slid off the stool and grabbed for my bag. I stumbled a little and reached out to steady myself on the bar. He took my hand, led me around the corner, and down a couple of blocks before turning into a sleazy apartment building. By the time he unlocked a door into a one-room apartment with a poster bed equipped with handcuffs and a gag, his grip changed from supportive to vice-like. A normal pickup would have been alarmed when she saw the bondage setup, but what I saw was an easy way to keep him restrained while I got vengeance.

He yanked me around to kiss me. He didn't get a chance. He found himself looking into the nozzle of a small aerosol can. One push of the button and he took a blast of hair spray directly in the eyes. He sucked a deep breath, and a lungful left him choking. He fell backward. I jumped on top, straddled him, reached for the gag he'd left tossed on the blanket, and stuffed it in his mouth. I didn't care if he choked to death, although I preferred to kill him myself. He thrashed and tried to sit up, but I threw my weight on top of him. I yanked his left arm over his head and locked one handcuff. He swung at me, fist grazing my collarbone. I secured his right arm, cut his shirt off, and unzipped and lowered his pants.

"Too bad. We could have had so much fun if you hadn't raped those other women." I slapped his penis hard. I used the cuffs he had attached to the bottom bedposts to keep him spread-eagled.

My victim lay bound arm and leg, gagged, and ready for his punishment. I'd kept Street-Thug's switchblade, not so much as a souvenir but because I thought it might come in handy one day. I snicked it open and waved the tip in front of his eyes to give him a good look at the weapon before I started carving. His eyes flared. He flung his body from side to side, but the restraints were tight.

I pulled on a hospital gown and Latex gloves, climbed on the bed, and straddled my victim.

"Just so there's no mistake, I'm getting even for the five women you raped." Five that the police knew about.

I moved the knife tip to the top of his chest and carved a capital R into a pectoral muscle. He screamed, but the gag reduced the noise to a moan. A followed. More moan-y screams. Blood oozed from the fairly deep cuts. I finished with P, I, S, and T. He farted. Leaning back on his legs, I waved away the smell and admired my penmanship. He was sobbing, his eyes pleading for mercy, something he didn't give his victims, something he wouldn't get from me.

I climbed off the bed and stood at the end dead center between his legs. I took his balls in my left hand and severed one. Testicles don't have major arteries running through them, and veins bleed but don't pump blood. They leave little spatter. Blood dripped as I dotted the I. I looked from his penis to the switchblade. Too much gristle for such a slender blade. Besides, the knife was made for stabbing, not for sawing.

I walked around to the side of the bed and raised my arm. “Good-bye, you asshole.”

I struck hard. His eyes followed the point of the knife into his chest between two ribs where it lodged in his heart. His final cry choked to silence. I watched his eyes dim. I left the knife in his chest.

If anyone saw me enter or leave the hotel, he’d remember a light-skinned black woman with curly hair wearing come-fuck-me heels. Most likely, he’d remember the shoes, which were red going into the room and red coming out.

I walked several blocks away from the bar district and caught a cab to my house. The danger of what I’d just accomplished demanded a private evening with my vibrator. In the cab, I sent a silent message to Lt. Gonzales.

“Sorry, Lieutenant. You guys couldn’t take this bastard down, so I had to. Too bad you’re on the drug task force, or this would have been my personal going-away present, not two scumbag dealers.”

I spent several hours writing in my journal to capture how I felt, what I did, why I killed the rapist. Once I began, I couldn’t stop detailing every move I made, every thought and the ultimate rationale of dotting the I with his testicle, the only action I improvised. My tone in the kill book was as smug as I felt.

§

G-Man and I were ecstatic when the Office of the Chief Medical Examiner, or OCME, offered me a job in the District, thanks to a glowing letter of recommendation from Chest-Cracker.

“Saw-Bones and I go all the way back to medical school. I told him if he didn’t hire you he’d be certifiably insane,” Chest-Cracker said.

No need for certification. A warm letter of acceptance signed Dr. George Haskins instead of "Saw-Bones" welcomed me to the team.

To my shock, Chest-Cracker and a couple of the original Cruise Club threw me a small going-away party at our favorite brew pub before I moved to Washington. Competing emotions yoyoed: sadness because I wanted to stay in Baltimore, my comfort zone and a great killing field; joy because I would be working in one of the most exciting morgues in the country, scoping out new hunting grounds.

Gay-Blade came down from Boston where he was a new cardiologist in a growing practice. He and his partner had adopted an adorable Haitian boy two years earlier.

"Hi. Etienne."

The boy ran into my arms and gave me a sticky kiss. I pretended to taste the red Tootsie Roll Pop he held out to me. At three, he was a perfect age to love unconditionally.

Valley-Girl had shocked the shit out of us by landing a position as a facial reconstruction surgeon at the Cleveland Clinic. So much for my initial impression that she was slated to make fabulous money doing nose and boob jobs in Southern California. No matter how much I tried to hide my cringes, her trademark way of up talking still drove me nuts.

L&O, her husband, Thurston, and their four-year-old daughter, Libby, drove up from Georgetown. She had delayed her return to Charleston, West Virginia, by taking a job in the Justice Department where she specialized in prosecuting organized crime.

"The Judge was nearly apoplectic when I said I was going to work at Justice." L&O's father continued to disapprove of her doing anything except entering a law firm in Charleston. "Mom, on the other hand, is so proud. Dad will change his mind when he sees some huge indictments coming down soon."

"Libby will help bring him around, I'll bet." I hoisted her little girl and nuzzled her freshly shampooed hair. I couldn't wait to live closer to L&O to renew our monthly lunches.

Thurston, a lawyer for a conservative political action committee, was a good sport about the verbal beating he took from the Cruise Club, which remained unabashedly on the liberal side of the spectrum. Only Father Shy-Scot missed the party, because he was with Doctors Without Borders in Chad or Mali or Niger. Somewhere hot in the Sahel.

I filled my time between the party and leaving Baltimore with getting rid of anything I didn't want to take with me to my new life. Mrs. Landlady said I could leave whatever was usable in the apartment, just as I'd found it nine years earlier. Once again, everything I owned fit in the Ugly Duckling. Unlike when I moved to Baltimore, Miss Snickers #2 would ride in her carrier next to me on the front seat.

Mrs. Landlady and I went to lunch before I turned in my keys. "I'll miss you, Doc. You're the best tenant I've ever had."

"And you're the best landlady any woman could wish for. I'll miss you, too."

CHAPTER THIRTY-TWO

SOUTHEAST

1996

I reported to the Office of the Chief Medical Examiner two weeks after I took out the rapist.

"Welcome." Saw-Bones scrutinized me. We'd met during the interview and vetting process, but now I felt stripped bare. "Chest-Cracker says you're the best student he ever had. Is he right?"

"I don't know about the best ever, but I'm the best of the latest crop."

"We'll see what you don't know."

"I'm sure there's plenty I never ran into at Johns Hopkins. I can't wait to get started." I smiled. Saw-Bones would have to be incredibly good to be better than Chest-Cracker. With time, I'd decide which was the better pathologist.

"No matter how good Chest-Cracker thinks you are, you're going to have to prove it to me."

I nodded.

"You'll start at the bottom and take directions from me and any senior pathologist until we can assess your skills."

"I understand."

I settled into my new job at the same time G-Man and I settled into life under one roof in Southeast Washington. Until we moved in together, I hadn't realized how much I wanted a normal-seeming married life. Not only did our sex life improve through availability and proximity, but we could also talk about everything important over dinner. Everything, that is, but my killing side line.

Although G-Man traveled much of the time, my job had more regular hours. I spent time with Miss Snickers #2 and explored my new home, a two-story row house off Capitol Hill, and the neighborhood around it. The house G-Man had inherited from his uncle was in an area struggling with gentrification. Sometimes gentrification won; sometimes it didn't. The neighborhood's high crime rate made us vigilant when we were out on the sidewalks.

We walked back toward our house after a Friday night dinner at a small bistro off Pennsylvania Avenue. An angry horn disrupted the evening calm. We watched self-important drivers in expensive cars bully their way through jammed traffic. A rattletrap, out-of-state VW bug from an earlier era didn't jump a green light quickly enough for an impatient limo driver whose staccato blasts echoed down the street. Washington traffic reduced the high and mighty to little more than annoyed specks on the planet.

We chatted about what to do on the weekend. We settled on a visit to the Air and Space Museum and a lecture at the National Gallery on freedom of the press. No sooner had we turned onto our block than screams replaced horns. We ran around a second corner and found a woman surrounded by five men with knives. Another woman lay face down in the gutter.

"Stay back!" G-Man called.

"Like hell!"

G-Man charged the crowd only to be blocked by a burly knife-wielding brute. Cool in combat, he dodged the knife and threw several punches, connecting with facial bone and flesh. I ran at the guy slashing wildly at the upright woman. He didn't know I was there until I smashed his left forearm with doubled fists. He turned toward me, knife in his right hand.

The bloodied woman crumpled to the ground next to her friend who lay in a widening pool. Dark liquid seeped from several wounds on her neck and back. Knife-Guy lunged at me.

Stupid move. It took so little to disable a thug rushing you when you knew what to do. I sidestepped a second before he reached me, thrust a foot in his path, and watched him hit the pavement face down next to the unmoving first victim. He struggled to his feet.

I dropped back a step to give Knife-Guy room to stand. Before he could take a step toward me, though, I was on him, the palm of my right hand cocked to connect with his nose. Whether it was a myth that you could kill someone with a strike to the nose or not, it didn't matter. The blow snapped his head backwards, and my left elbow to his throat sent him reeling. His full weight carried him onto a wrought-iron railing. The resounding snap of his neck was so sweet, so satisfying. He was dead before his body slid to the sidewalk.

G-Man had a thug in an arm lock. The other three had fled. Once we were out of immediate danger, I looked at the two women. I was ninety-five percent certain the first was dead based on the amount of blood pooling around the body, and her absolute stillness. The second was alive but was bleeding heavily from her throat. My doctor's instinct took over. I dropped to my knees, pulled the woman to lie against my torso, and applied pressure to the neck wound. Knife-Guy missed her carotid arteries because blood was flowing, not spurting, out of her body. I pressed her jacket to the wound and held it tight.

My vision gradually widened now that the attack was over and the adrenaline stopped boiling through my veins.

G-Man struggled with the thug who seemed intent on breaking the arm lock and following his cowardly pack. G-Man wrenched the arm higher, forcing the man to his knees in the blood. Without handcuffs, he had to drop his full weight on the guy's back. The two fell to the ground, one with breath, one without.

G-Man stared at me.

"I'm all right. It's not my blood."

"Jesus, where did you learn to fight like that?"

"Later."

"Get away from the woman," thundered an authoritarian voice from behind me. Two police cruisers blocked the street, flashing lights painting the houses red and blue.

"I'm a doctor. If I move now, she'll bleed out." I kept my hands on the victim's neck.

"I said, get away from her." The patrolman, young and visibly jittery, put his hand on the grip of his sidearm.

G-Man shouted at the testosterone-flushed officer. He fumbled in his pocket for his FBI credentials. "Cuff this man."

"Who the hell are you giving me orders?" The patrolman refused to budge.

"FBI."

"What the hell's going on?" A second officer walked up and stared at the scene.

No one seemed too excited about blood all over the sidewalk just off Capitol Hill. Or about the two dead bodies lying on the pavement. The bleeding woman a little more so; the now handcuffed man, less so.

"I'm with the OCME. I need an ambulance right freaking now

unless you want this woman to die."

G-Man freed my ID badge from my jacket pocket and waved it under the younger cop's nose. I refused to release the pressure on the woman's neck. Her other wounds could wait. More squad cars rolled up, followed by a couple of ambulances. The leading EMT took charge of the woman. I made a futile attempt to wipe her blood off my hands with a couple of tissues, but I looked like a chainsaw massacre survivor.

The first officer nudged the dead assailant with the toe of his shoe. "Who did this?"

"I did."

CHAPTER THIRTY-THREE

INTERROGATION

1996

"What the hell happened? Looks like a butcher shop." A different EMT offered a clean towel. It helped a little.

"Are you sure you don't need medical treatment?"

"I'm fine. Who are these guys?"

I turned to G-Man, who shrugged. He put his arm around me for comfort, as much for his sake as for mine. He was breathing hard; he didn't realize I wasn't. In fact, my pulse was slow and strong. No one had better take my blood pressure. They might think I was going into shock.

G-Man jerked his chin down the block. "I heard the third man drop something metallic when he leaped the curb across the street."

The first patrolman bundled us into his cruiser with a request (order?) not to get blood on the seats. I touched the door handle, leaving a sizable smear. Served him right. "We need to get your statements."

I couldn't wait. I knew the drill. I'd be in a room separate from G-Man if the police thought we'd done anything wrong. If not, we'd be together. After all, there were two dead bodies on the streets in a city that hated mess and tourist-damaging publicity. Imagine how arresting an FBI agent and a District medical examiner would look when the cops realized the perp was dead, courtesy of me, and one of his buddies was in handcuffs, courtesy of my husband.

At the local station, we were ushered into a stale-smelling interview room. Even years after smoking was banned, accumulated nicotine lent an undercurrent too pervasive to be washed or painted away. A short, skinny detective entered.

"I'm Detective Hamilton." He took in my sodden blouse and jacket. "You're a mess. Go wash up. Bathroom's just around the corner."

I nodded and went to wash my face and hands. Blood spattered my left arm, the one that crushed Knife-Guy's larynx. My blouse was hopeless. The outer door opened, and a police woman came in.

"You might want to change." She held out a clean police T-shirt and a plastic evidence bag.

"Thank you." The T was large, but it was dry and not stiff with "biologicals." I stuffed my saturated blouse and bra in the bag. "Why the evidence bag?"

The policewoman shook her head. "Detective Hamilton's orders." She took it away.

"You look better," G-Man said when I returned to the interview room. He too had cleaned up. He walked over and gave me a huge hug.

"You, too. Okay, Detective, shall we get started?"

Detective Hamilton ran through the basics: name, address,

phone number, etc. He checked our driver's licenses. Mine raised the anticipated question.

"Okay, miss, do you still live in Baltimore?"

"It's Mrs."

"Right. Do you still live in Baltimore?"

"No. I recently finished my residency at Johns Hopkins and moved into our house off Capitol Hill." Give up as little information as possible. Let him ask the questions.

"Residency? You're a doctor?" He didn't look like he believed me.

"I am."

I'd learned with Lab-Rat's death that answering a question directly and with no embellishments was the best way. Detective Hamilton waited for me to add something. I didn't. From the corner of my eye, I saw G-Man raise an eyebrow.

"Okay, you're a doctor. What kind?" His question came out a little sharp. I kept my eyes on him all the time, not staring, just not looking away. Did he expect me to spill my guts?

"She's a pathologist," G-Man said.

"Really?"

"Yes, really. I was at Johns Hopkins from med school through my residency. As part of my training in pathology, I performed autopsies for the Baltimore police department on every type of body you can imagine. Maybe on some you shouldn't imagine. That's why I tried to help the woman. I didn't want her body to end up on my table."

"Your table?"

"Did you not hear what my husband said? I'm a pathologist. I'm with the OCME."

"And when did you move here?"

I didn't like his attitude. G-Man and I had done the Metro Police Department, the MPD, a huge favor and here he was, copping (pun intended) a stupid attitude.

"As I said, about a month ago. I haven't had time to change my driver's license, Officer."

"It's Detective, Miss."

"It's Doctor, Detective." I smiled as genuinely as I could. I wanted to wipe his attitude all over the interview room floor. His face flushed an angry red leaving old acne scars pronounced.

"So, a pathologist surveyed a crime scene and knew immediately that two people were dead?"

What a stupid question. Any idiot could see the woman had bled out by the time we got there.

"One. I was certain the woman on the ground was already dead because the blood pool was substantial. I couldn't help her. I was more concerned with the woman the man with the knife was attacking."

"Why didn't you tell her to stay back?" Detective Hamilton swung abruptly to G-Man.

"You don't tell my wife to do anything. She does what she thinks is right." G-Man smiled with pride.

"So, two of you took down five armed men? I don't buy it."

What was this asshole's problem? He acted like we were slugs that didn't walk upright. "Let's get the facts straight. We took on five men. We took down two, one alive, one dead." G-Man shot back. My attitude was rubbing off, because he jerked the pompous asshole's chain, too. "I'm sure you don't want to get any facts wrong, do you, detective?"

"You FBI guys think you have all the answers, but this is my town. I ask the questions." Detective Hamilton's face contorted.

"Fine. Ask the right questions, and we'll give you the right answers."

Detective Hamilton didn't have a chance to respond before G-Man continued.

"Being an FBI agent had nothing to do with what we did. I caught one guy who's in your lockup with blood all over his pants. Probably on his shoes, too."

"His shoes?" Detective Hamilton asked.

"I'm sure your crime scene techs will find at least two different sets of bloody footprints at the scene, not including ours. I saw them before your officers rolled up, so I'm pretty sure two guys stepped in the blood pool." G-Man sounded a little exasperated. "I do this for a living, detective. I've been around too many crime scenes not to notice details."

"So have I. Why didn't you call the cops?" Detective Hamilton raised half of a unibrow.

"We were a little busy."

"Okay, doctor, tell me what you did." What did this jerk have against doctors? I knew what he had against the FBI. My gut told me he'd applied and been rejected.

"When I ran toward the struggle, I saw a woman in the gutter, a seeping blood pool, another woman backed against a wrought iron railing, and a large man lunging at her. When he turned toward me, I saw he had a knife. I hit his forearm, numbing it." I was positive I broke the radius bone. "He stumbled to his knees. Check for blood on them. He got up and came at me. I hit him in his nose, hoping to slow him. It didn't, so I hit him again across the throat. He fell backward and hit the base of his skull on the railing. He broke his neck."

"How do you know that?"

"I heard it." I leaned forward in my chair and put my elbows on the table. "It makes a distinctive sound, detective. Once you've heard a neck snap, you never forget it."

Shit. I hoped G-Man didn't pick up on that. He'd be all over me wondering how I knew. I couldn't tell him about killing Starr's mother. My expression didn't change, but my heart rate accelerated.

"With all that noise, you heard his neck snap?"

"Detective, I was unaware of anything but what was going on inside a six-foot radius. I heard the woman sobbing and the cervical bones breaking. Nothing else." It was true. I had been in a cone of silence.

With that, Detective Hamilton stopped asking questions. For the life of me, I couldn't figure out why he disliked me. I knew why I disliked him, but me? I hadn't done anything to upset him other than pull his chain when he took on an attitude. Maybe he thought all women should be shrinking violets. Maybe he hated his mother. Maybe his wife had just left him. At any rate, we wrote out our statements and signed them. We were free to go. We left the police station and looked for a taxi. It was late, and the streets were empty. We walked home.

"Hey, Doc, you never told me you studied karate," he said.

"Aikido. It started with a few self-defense courses at State, and I found I liked it. I thought it might come in handy. I have a black belt. Funny. My Baltimore neighborhood was much rougher than Southeast. I used my skills more than once to protect myself. Tonight was the first time I used them to stop a crime. What the hell was that, anyway?"

"Most likely a robbery gone bad. Could have been a domestic dispute with backup. At least one guy's in custody. The police will get his two buddies and charge them all with murder. Too bad about the first woman. Hope the other one makes it."

"Me, too."

CHAPTER THIRTY-FOUR

AFTERMATH

1996

Three mornings later I opened the door into the morgue and checked the log to see what autopsies were waiting, which were urgent, which we could delay. When I began my residency, I thought the dead were a patient lot, but I soon learned that none of them liked lying around waiting for their autopsies. Homicides and violent deaths took precedence over "died of natural causes."

Three new cases, a woman dead of knife wounds, a man dead from a broken neck, and a woman killed in a wreck on I395, had a primary or senior pathologist assigned to each, with a second pathologist assisting. Saw-Bones had my name beside the broken neck along with his. All three bodies, laid out on stainless steel tables, were covered with green sheets.

"Hey, Doc. I need you on this guy." Saw-Bones had his protective clothing already on. "Could be a homicide."

Before I could respond, the outer door opened, and two policemen entered. A scrawny police officer in a rumpled suit identified himself as "Detective Hamilton. Here for the two homicides." The other policeman, Officer Kingsford, was to observe the accident victim's autopsy.

I faced away from the door when I tied the gown on. I grinned at the sound of Hamilton's cigarette-roughened voice. He'd been such a shit with me in the precinct house that I couldn't wait to get a little payback for his attitude Friday night. His reaction to my presence was going to be fun. I grabbed gloves and a hair cover before turning around.

"Good morning, Detective Hamilton."

The detective glared at me for a moment before his eyes darted around the room as if looking for a place to stuff me. "What the hell are you doing here?"

"As I told you Friday night, I work here. I have to recuse myself from your autopsy, Dr. Haskins." I walked over to the accident victim.

"Okay, what's going on?" Saw-Bones looked from me to the detective and back.

"She was involved in the murders." Detective Hamilton's words were clipped.

"Murder singular. Self-defense, also singular." I adjusted the light over the accident victim on the third examination table.

My table was the farthest from Knife-Guy. I was the junior pathologist working with a more senior doctor. Dr. Thom Swift, second in command to Saw-Bones, had the murdered woman. I began the routine processing of my corpse.

"You were?"

I gave Saw-Bones a two-second recap of Friday night's extracurricular activities. I glanced at Detective Hamilton, who'd crossed his arms across his chest.

"Get her out of here." The order was blunt.

"My lab, my pathologist, my rules," said Saw-Bones with equal bluntness. "She stays. She'll do the autopsy on the accident victim."

"I want her out of here."

"Is she a suspect in any of these three cases?" Saw-Bones waved a bloody scalpel at the bodies.

"No." The syllable was drawn out.

"Then, there should be no problem if she does her job." Saw-Bones waited for Hamilton's response.

"Duly noted, but she stays away from the other two."

Saw-Bones cut me a look which Hamilton couldn't see. He winked over his mask before making the first chest incision.

My partner, Dr. Gretchen Tong, and I took up our positions on either side of the accident victim; Officer Kingsford stood at the foot. I turned on the microphone, gave my name, Dr. Tong's name, and that of the officer. We made the Y-incision, took blood samples for tox screens. Not much of a mystery with this woman. Young, drunk, face and torso smashed from hitting the steering wheel and windshield.

"She wasn't wearing a seat belt, was she?" Dr. Tong asked.

"No. And the airbag didn't deploy either," added Officer Kingsford. "Single car accident. She lost control on a curve and hit the guardrail at"—He flipped open his notebook—"about sixty miles per hour."

"Cause of death is a ruptured heart. We'll know if she was drunk when we get the tox screen." I turned off the microphone, our job finished pending the results of the tests. I told him I'd write up the preliminary report and send it to the appropriate precinct. Officer Kingsford left.

"Jeez, Doc. Look at this larynx." Saw-Bones waved me over. I stood at the head, opposite Detective Hamilton, my gloved hands clasped behind my back. "It took a lot of force to do this much damage."

"Yeah, an elbow thrown in just the right way can be lethal." I smiled behind my mask. Looking at the damage, I was damned proud of how I gotten rid of Knife-Guy.

"Look at his neck. I think he broke C3 and C4." The assisting pathologist pointed. The numbers referred to the vertebrae in the cervical part of the spine, the neck.

Saw-Bones looked at the X-rays. "C4 and C5. You're off by one."

"So, did she kill him when she hit his throat or when his neck struck a wrought-iron railing following the blow?" Technically, Detective Hamilton was correct: I had killed him. His tone made it sound like I was a homicidal maniac instead of a concerned citizen with a black belt in martial arts.

"You really did this?" Saw-Bones stared over his half-glasses.

"I did."

Saw-Bones turned toward Detective Hamilton. "Can't tell if he was alive when he hit the railing or not. Either the blow or crashing into the railing would have been fatal."

Detective Hamilton made a strangled sound. He wanted to dispute the cause of death but couldn't. Saw-Bones had ruined any chance he had of charging me or anyone else with homicide. He left, but I had a suspicion I'd made an enemy.

"Good girl."

"He doesn't like me." I didn't give a shit if the asshole liked me or not, but I wanted to keep up pretenses of having a conscience. I threw away my mask.

"Hamilton doesn't like anyone. Man has a serious attitude problem." Thom walked over to look at the body.

"If Hamilton doesn't want to cross my path in the future, then the MPD will have to reduce the murder rate."

"Great work, Doc.," Thom said. I knew he meant the kill. I was relieved the detective hadn't heard me being praised. I swept off my hair cover and bowed.

CHAPTER THIRTY-FIVE

WHITE COLLAR CRIME

1998

One night at dinner, G-Man and I watched coverage of a white-collar crime back in the news after a two-year hiatus. A couple had run a Ponzi scheme to rob their closest friends of literally billions of dollars. When the husband was sentenced to multiple life sentences without the possibility of parole, spectators in the courtroom cheered. The wife was given a lesser sentence and allowed to remain out of jail, pending her appeal. The public went nuts. People picketed her million-dollar house in the Kalorama neighborhood for weeks.

"I don't buy her story. Do you?" G-Man said.

"About her not knowing what her husband was doing?"

"Yeah. She had to know. I don't see how you can be married to someone and be as fooled as she claims to be." He reached for the wine bottle and refilled our glasses.

Interesting insight about our marriage.

The news droned on in the background. Mrs. Money-Bags's attorneys sued her husband's defunct business for millions to support her, saying she was as much a victim as his friends were. They asked for understanding and sympathy, because Mr. Money-Bags's illegal activities had turned her lifestyle upside down. She was about to lose her mansion.

"Understanding? She was as much a leech on society as he was. Sympathy? My ass. She can say what she wants, her lifestyle shows how she profited from her husband's thefts." G-Man stared at the screen.

"How would you profile her?" His answer might be a clue as to how he would analyze me if he knew my darker side.

G-Man was silent for several seconds. "She suffers from narcissistic personality disorder and exhibits a strong sense of entitlement. She believes what her husband did was right and she should continue to live the lifestyle he gave her."

I leaned back in my chair, a fine Shiraz making spider tracks down the sides of my stemmed glass. I gestured for him to continue.

"Think back to what we saw of her arrest and how she behaved at his trial. She never once showed remorse for her complicity in her husband's crimes. Her only emotion emerged when faced with the loss of the money the two of them had stolen. Even Mr. Money-Bags showed a modicum of remorse and apologized to his victims when he faced the judge at sentencing."

I poured a bit more wine into G-Man's glass. He was so deep into his analysis that what I did didn't register.

"She sat in court smug and confident that the money was well hidden. Only when the prosecution revealed numbers for their offshore accounts did she become emotional. It'd been all about her from day one."

Good analysis.

"I'm sure her friends have abandoned her. No more lunches at the Willard. No bridge clubs. Nothing. I expect she's become a social pariah."

"As she should. Remember, she's living in luxury compared to the victims, who are ruined financially. Her husband's in prison for life." I took a sip of wine.

The story concluded with a report on how events had piled on this woman. Her eldest son committed suicide in her house, her daughter was in rehab for drug abuse and severe depression, and her younger son turned against her when he testified for the prosecution at her appeal. No one wept for her. She suffered the first level of punishment. The second would come soon enough.

"Someone needs to get even for the pain she and her husband caused." I pushed my empty glass aside.

"Don't you think justice will prevail?" G-Man finished the last of the wine. "Traditional justice, I mean."

What did he mean by "traditional justice?" Through the courts instead of vigilante justice?

"My heart bleeds." I couldn't have put any more sarcasm in my voice. "What would be a fitting punishment other than prison?"

"How about living in a double-wide in West Virginia?"

I nearly choked with laughter. "She'd give double-wides a bad image, don't you think?"

§

The role of vengeful killer grew on me. Mrs. Money-Bags was a perfect target. No longer satisfied with removing drug dealers from society, I used the move to Washington to expand my scope, to up my game, so to speak. I could select victims with great care, because the District had a higher caliber of victims in addition to general scumbags. A target rich environment, I recommitted myself to taking out victims who wronged others and who couldn't take action for themselves.

While I couldn't return the money to Mrs. Money-Bags's former friends, killing her might provide them some vicarious satisfaction, or at the very least a sense of relief that she couldn't hurt them again. With her under house arrest and wearing an ankle bracelet, I knew where to find her.

I hadn't decided how to kill her. I could incapacitate her with my serviceable choke hold but then what? I toyed with strangling her outright, suffocating her with a pillow or stabbing her in the ear with my old friend, the ice pick. Whether Saw-Bones ruled her death an accident or homicide was immaterial. What mattered was that she'd be dead when I left the house.

When G-Man went out of town for a week, I had my chance. The *Post* reported her house had been sold as part of repaying some of her husband's thievery, but she was refusing to vacate the premises. She had five days, or the marshals would physically remove her. I waited until the middle of a Sunday afternoon, when most people would be back from church and planted in front of football games. I should have the street nearly, if not totally, to myself. I raised the brass lion-head knocker and let it fall. Mrs. Money-Bags opened the door and held onto the jamb to keep from falling. She was shit faced.

I introduced myself, pushed inside, and walked into the living room. I almost didn't recognize the ruin of the well-dressed woman I'd seen on television. She'd aged a decade in two years. Her formerly perfectly coiffed hair was dry and stringy, an inch of brown and grey roots showing above the bottle-blond color. Her manicure was chipped. I guessed her pedicure was in similar shape. That figured, because she was under house arrest and couldn't keep her regular spa appointments. Nor could she afford them. She blinked mascara-smeared eyes to bring my face into focus.

Her being drunk cleared up how I'd kill her. I improvised. Vodka and ice on the end table, throw cushions on the sofa and chairs. I had enough to work with.

"Who are you?" Her slurred speech would have been difficult to follow except I'd grown up with a drunk in the house.

"The bankruptcy court sent me to make sure you'll be out of the house by Tuesday. You can't stay here now that it's in been sold."

She fell into her recliner, knees too shaky to hold her upright. On the table was a glass half full of ice and a bottle of cheap vodka.

"Get me more ice."

Who the fuck did she think she was, ordering me around? I went into her kitchen, pulled on my ever-ready latex gloves, and filled her glass with crushed ice. I returned to the living room and topped off the tumbler with vodka. Before she could register what I was doing, I grabbed a large throw pillow, shoved it against her chest, and held it there with pressure from one knee.

I grabbed her head and pinched her nostrils to make her breathe through her mouth. Then, I tipped her head back and poured the entire glass of ice and liquor down her throat. She choked and tried to pull away, but I forced her chin up and clamped her mouth closed. She opened alcohol-blurred eyes, comprehension of her pending death almost overcoming her stupor.

I leaned in, my face close enough to see the broken capillaries like a plague of caterpillars marching across her nose. I eased the pressure on her nostrils long enough to grab the vodka bottle. Pinch, pour, clamp. I poured straight liquor down her throat. As long as she breathed, the vodka would enter her lungs. I loved each labored breath, each gagging sound. More, I savored the terror in her eyes.

Mrs. Money-Bags stopped struggling. Her pupils became fixed.

I wasn't positive she was dead even though I couldn't find a pulse. It might have been too faint to detect. I fetched more ice from the kitchen and pushed some into her ear. If she were alive, the ice would have triggered eye movement or any other involuntary response. She was dead.

The autopsy would show she choked to death on vodka, physically drowning in the drink that was supposed to relieve her psychological pain. I merely hastened her demise. She'd have liquid in her lungs, in her mouth, in her windpipe, even in her stomach.

I slipped out of the house, gloves tucked into my pocket. Where the street had been nearly empty when I entered the house, couples walked dogs or pushed strollers along the sidewalk as if the entire world was out enjoying a sunny afternoon. A police car cruised by, windows rolled down, the driver's arm resting to the window edge.

I took a deep breath and nodded to several people who spoke to me, all the time praying no one would remember I'd been in the neighborhood. The policeman never looked my way. My heart pounded until I was back home. I wiped sweat from my brow. I'd come too close to making a mistake for my peace of mind.

§

Mrs. Money-Bags's body wasn't found until a real estate agent and her client came to do a final walk though of the house. The odor hit them as soon as they opened the door.

"I thought the place had been cleaned out," said a pale Re/Max agent.

The news cycle shit-storm lasted a couple of days. Saw-Bones ruled death by drowning. After a quick series of interviews with her attorneys and the district attorney, the story died as surely as she had.

Case closed. Another notch on my bedstead, another entry in my journal. Life was good. So was death.

Before G-Man returned, I sat up late into the night writing in my kill book, noting how I felt, how I selected this victim, how deliciously ironic the idea to drown the drunk in vodka was. G-Man's assessment of her narcissism was correct. She had been the center of her own universe. I documented page after page with details until I was satisfied that I'd accurately reported how I felt a moral imperative to rid the world of parasites like Mrs. Money-Bags.

CHAPTER THIRTY-SIX

DECOMPOSITION AND SKELETONS

1999

To continue studying for my certification as a forensic pathologist, I asked Saw-Bones to send me to the body farm. Ever since G-Man told me about it years ago, I'd wanted first-hand exposure to how bodies decomposed and in what time-frame changes occurred.

"Doesn't the FBI have a body farm?" I thought G-Man had said it did, but I couldn't remember for certain.

"No," Saw-Bones said. "If you're thinking about the one in the Patricia Cornwell novel, it's a university lab over in Knoxville. I'll give them a call and see if I can get you in one of its week-long classes." Saw-Bones jotted a note on a sticky pad.

Within two weeks I was set to drive to Knoxville with a warning from Saw-Bones: "Be sure you shower extra-long each night before you go to dinner. If you think the smells here in our lab cling to clothing, you ain't smelled nothing yet."

I knew what decomposition smelled like. After all, I'd boiled Old Rex's skeleton in the kitchen before mounting him for my bookshelf.

G-Man and I spent a couple of days at home doing normal things. Shopping, eating out, cleaning the house, screwing our brains out.

No matter how cavalier I was with Saw-Bones, nothing in my experience either in a lab or on the farm prepared me for the intensity of reek that wafted over the facility. I breathed deeply, aware that I might be the only person in the world who thought the smell of decomposition was an aphrodisiac. I drove up to the front of the main building, parked, and walked in. A man whom I took to be a researcher walked over and introduced himself.

"Dr. Rigby. I'm in charge here. You must be the pathologist from D.C." He held out a slender hand.

"How did you know?" I took his hand before giving him my paperwork.

"I know George well." He released my hand. "He'd said you'd have an air of authority most students lack."

"Thank you. Everyone calls me Doc."

"Everyone calls everyone 'Doc' here. You'll fit right in." His cell phone buzzed. He shrugged an apology before turning to take the call. He waved to a younger woman who carried a stack of file folders. He covered the phone with his hand.

"Sandra, Doc here needs to get oriented. Can you help?" Dr. Rigby waved before moving down the corridor.

"I'm Sandra Warfield, the coordinator of the students for all the summer sessions." She nodded me toward an office with a desk and two chairs. "Let's go over what to expect before you settle in."

I already knew I was going into student housing and expected to be in a dorm. Instead, I was surprised to learn I'd be in a house much like the one I was in at State. "Call me Sandra" gave me a fistful of papers about the courses, maps of the campus, tram schedule from housing to the labs.

I signed the release forms. Sandra stood and led me to the door. "If you take the tram to your housing, you can settle in."

"I drove. Just point me in the right direction, and I'll find my way." What I really wanted to do was poke around the farm itself, not unpack in a sorority house.

Students gathered for a group dinner around seven. Dr. Rigby talked to us about what would happen over the next week. "I expect you to do your best, learn the most you can, and not puke on the bodies."

Nervous laughter around. Each student was asked to introduce him or herself, talk about what course they were taking, where they were in their studies, and what they wanted to get out of the courses.

"I'm with the chief medical examiner's office in Washington, DC."

Murmurs of "oh wow" and "oh my God" floated around the room.

Sandra was right. I was the only medical doctor in the group, although several students were doing post-doctoral work in forensic anthropology. I wondered how many chose this field based on watching too much television.

Multiple courses went on concurrently. From general human decomposition to DNA degradation to entomology, the lab offered overviews of everything you needed to be a successful medical examiner. I'd chosen identification of skeletal remains.

"I've done enough autopsies to be comfortable with soft-tissue wounds, but I don't know enough about skeletons. I need to learn to recognize the difference between man-made wounds and predation marks."

The next six days passed as if one. We had a routine from the first morning: up early, to the lab for assignments, field work, guided lab work, and one-on-one meetings with the course leaders. Before long I could recognize the difference between knife cuts on bones and marks made by animals, but I hadn't been able to determine the nuances of different types of knives. I mentioned this to my advisor. He set me up with a password to the university database of images and reports.

After dinner and long talks with G-Man on the phone, I spent several more hours poring over photos. Late one night, I realized I was learning how to avoid leaving marks on my victims as much as I was about how to identify the weapon of death in future autopsies.

§

"So, was it worth it?" Saw-Bones greeted me when I reported for work my first Monday back.

"Oh, my God. Was it ever!" Over coffee I'd brought in from Dunkin' Donuts, I told him about my experience.

"And you didn't puke, did you?" He reached over and tapped my upper arm.

"I didn't, but some of the grad students did."

"Let's get busy. We have a couple of accident victims and one shooting." We moved to gown up. "Thom's out of town working with the Fairfax PD on the shooting case."

"Why us? That's in Virginia." I dressed, tied a mask on, and settled a clear plastic, protective shield over my eyes.

"Our body is from a similar drive-by in the District last Sunday. Thom went to look at the evidence in Fairfax."

"Serial?" That could be interesting from an autopsy perspective but not as an example of how I wanted my next kill to go down.

"Could be. Could be spree. Could be a coincidence." Saw-Bones rolled a body out of the cooler.

CHAPTER THIRTY-SEVEN

SHOOTER

2000

We didn't hear anything from the shooter for almost six months, during which time life settled into a routine balance of work and play. We didn't know if the two original victims were happenstance, if the shooter had moved to a different state, if he was in jail, in a hospital, or dead. We didn't know squat until Saw-Bones called me at five in the morning. "Our shooter has been busy, Doc. Five bodies overnight."

"I'll be there in about twenty minutes."

"The shooter again?" G-Man rolled ever when I hung up.

"Looks like it."

"I might see you later." He fell into a deep sleep.

After my intern and residency years, I thought I'd get more sleep, but that hadn't happened. As long as the murder rate continued at its current pace, it didn't seem likely that I'd get more than four or five hours at a stretch. I shrugged into street clothes when a memory rose. My intern group whined about our collective state of exhaustion. Shy-Scot shut us up with, "Sleep is highly overrated." It might be, but it was also in short supply. I rushed down the street toward the Metro.

Five new corpses, huh? Up until now, this shooter had only killed two that I knew of, if it was even the same man. My money was on him killing out of state.

I'd fallen into the assumption trap Saw-Bones set for us. He called the shooter a male because the majority of snipers were men. I couldn't challenge him without proof. Men killed from a distance; I killed up close. Then again, I wasn't a sniper.

I walked into controlled chaos in the morgue. One pathologist was already moving his cart of instruments toward a body. I glanced at the work ahead of us. Five tables, each bearing a body not even covered by sheets. Still clothed, wounds stiff with drying blood. In the locker room three other pathologists pulled off shirts, shrugged into surgical smocks, and grabbed helmets and safety goggles or shields.

"Get in here as soon as you can," Saw-Bones called out. "We'll have cops swarming all over us, all demanding answers. The more we can give them, the sooner they get out of our faces."

I shed my civilian clothes as quickly as I could, suited up, and walked into the autopsy suite. "We have to stop meeting like this, Saw-Bones. G-Man is getting jealous."

"Tell that to the shooter. When he stops, we return working normal hours. Until then, G-Man will have to cope." Saw-Bones winked at me over his mask.

"Want me to start at the far end with Thom?" I saw my second-favorite pathologist had rolled a cart beside the gurney. "If this is the same shooter, where's he been?"

"Could be a different guy," Thom said. "We haven't heard from that shooter in months."

"The signature looks the same. Police don't know who he is, where he's going to strike next, or even how he identifies his targets." Saw-Bones took several pictures of his victim's head wound. He jerked his chin down the line of tables. "Three white males, one black male, and one Middle Eastern female. All shot with a high-velocity rifle from long range. The damage indicates large caliber bullets."

"I have an exit wound." Thom wielded the camera, getting close-ups of a white male with a chest wound so gaping I could have buried my fist in it. "This one was hit in the chest. Weren't the earlier wounds head shots?"

"Pretty sure you're right," Saw-Bones said. "I'll check when we take a break."

"Might be a copycat." I flicked on the overhead lamp, cued the recorder, and inventoried instruments on my tray with a single glance. "Did all these happen in the District?"

"Your guy was shot in Southwest when he was coming home from work. The other two white males left a bar over near Chinatown around midnight. Don't know where the black male was, but the female was waiting for an early morning bus to take her to work in Northeast."

Thom clicked a few more frames of the chest wound. "Turn him over, Doc. I want shots of the entry wound."

I bagged clothing, cleaned under fingernails, and combed debris out of hair, none of which would be of much value if we had a random shooter. Still, I followed protocol by rote.

Police officers and detectives arrived, asked questions, hung around for a while and left. All but Detective Hamilton, my least favorite Metro cop. He arrived about eight and didn't leave. I don't know why he was so condescending whenever we worked together.

He'd been disgusted with me since I killed the street attacker. I guessed he'd wanted it to be murder so he'd get another notch for solving a crime. Instead, he had me on self-defense and a dead knife wielder that didn't net him any points toward promotion.

Saw-Bones and I had almost finished the second victim, the black male who looked like he might have been in his forties, when my phone vibrated. G-Man. I yanked off a glove.

"Hi, Doc, got a second?"

"I'm kinda in the middle of a series of autopsies." I moved away from the table.

"That's why I called. You working on the shooter's victims?"

"What else? I'll most likely be here until further notice. Did they assign you to the case, too?"

"Yes. We're trying to pull together a profile and see if we can figure out where this asshole is going next."

"We'll do what we can to help."

"Oh, and tell Saw-Bones to stop calling you at an obscene hour. No man should call another man's wife at five in the morning." G-Man laughed before muffling from the phone. "Gotta go. May have a witness. Keep me posted."

"G-Man says they might have a witness."

"Frickin' Feebs always think they have a witness."

One thing I could count on with Detective Hamilton was a disparaging comment about the FBI.

"Let's hope so. This shooter is one mean dude," Thom said. "Will you look at the damage done to this female? Bullets basically blew her head off."

"Bullets?" Detective Hamilton leaned in for a closer look. I gave him credit for one thing: he never paled nor vomited, no matter how juicy the corpse was.

"He got in two shots?" I asked. Could a standard high-powered rifle be fired twice in time to hit a human head before the body fell to the ground? "Same caliber?"

"Yes. No. Oh shit. Two shooters." Thom held up the second bullet, which clanged as it dropped into the metal specimen pan. "Smaller caliber."

"Jesus. We'll have a panic on our hands if these guys are lining up random victims and firing together." Detective Hamilton said.

I returned to the first victim. "No second bullet here."

I needed a closer look at the black victim. Saw-Bones and I worked on him together. I made an incision across the base of the skull and peeled up the scalp. Two entry wounds about three centimeters apart. Off center in the back.

"These guys are good." Saw-Bones whistled.

"Trained snipers." Detective Hamilton gave his assessment through clenched teeth. "We gotta keep this quiet. No one needs to know we have a pair of shit heads."

"I agree. Call G-Man." Saw-Bones waved me toward my phone.

Detective Hamilton growled.

§

For three days straight, new bodies crawled out of the woodwork. A search of an area in Rock Creek Park turned up more, all shot in the head from the side or behind, and all in varying stages of decomposition. Saw-Bones, Thom, and I performed more than a dozen autopsies on the new corpses.

"These guys have been active far longer than we originally thought."

Our serial shooters had about half as many kills as I had, although they'd been working only for a year or two. I'd been killing for well over a decade in different jurisdictions. With another multi-jurisdictional manhunt underway, I didn't see how these guys could escape. Eventually they would make a mistake.

Part of me admired the thoroughness of the killers. More of me was repulsed by their randomness. Saw-Bones had no clue about a motive. Neither did G-Man nor the rest of the task force. Did the two shooters have the same motive? I couldn't see a pattern among the victims except the very randomness of it all. I had specific reasons for each of my kills. I had about a million questions, all of which congealed like clotting blood into one: "Why?"

"Crap and double crap." I'd never heard Saw-Bones sound angrier. "The bastards hunted these people. Rock Creek Park's a favorite jogging and biking spot inside the District. We have fragments of exercise clothing and sneakers. Metro police said they found all the bodies hidden in thick brush along a mile or more of pathway."

"How did they find them?" Thom made a fresh incision in a woman.

"Joggers complained about a stench." Detective Hamilton, our ubiquitous cop, had oiled his way into the lab without me seeing him. "We sent in a canine unit. Cadaver dogs found the bodies."

Just like me and Old Rex, they followed the smell.

On the third day, G-Man showed up at the door of the autopsy room. When I looked up from one particularly gruesome head wound, he beckoned me to join him in the corridor. I knew from experience his stomach wouldn't take kindly to the maggots crawling out of the victim's mouth. I threw my soiled gloves in a trash bin and hung my rubber apron over a hook near my table.

"Be right back, Saw-Bones."

"Take your time. No one's going anywhere."

I followed G-Man outside. God, the fresh air smelled good. I'd been in that stinking room far too long. Forget that I loved what I was doing and that the smell of decomposition was an aphrodisiac. Even pathologists and serial killers need a change in venue occasionally. We sat on a wall in the sunlight.

"Anything new?"

"Like you, we think these guys are trained snipers. The

ammunition is military grade." G-Man rubbed his unshaven chin. That was so out of character and so against the FBI code that I had to comment on it.

"Getting kinda fuzzy, aren't you?" I stroked his whiskers.

"No one gives a rat's ass about now. Most of the task force hasn't shaved for days. Our room is ripe, although not as bad as yours. Anyway, we're too busy checking military records to worry about beards. Someone's monitoring postings on websites. Somewhere, someone knows who these guys are. Maybe we'll catch a break, and someone will brag about this."

I leaned against him.

"We have a narrow list of potential civilian shooters, too, but that's not helping. Whoever these assholes are, they're always two steps and one shooting ahead of us." His shoulders slumped. G-Man put his arm around me. "Sometimes I wonder if we'll ever find them. The entire task force is out of ideas."

I'd never seen G-Man deflated before. I leaned into his chest hoping he wouldn't notice the stink on me. "They need transportation. Even if they're lying in wait like they did in the park, they have to get away. Any idea what they're driving?"

"We have more sightings of the vehicle than you can imagine. Everyone's seen it. Green truck. White van. Blue sedan. Tricked out black Cadillac SUV. Even a UPS truck." He laughed at the last. "Wouldn't that be a hoot, though? Using a UPS truck as a getaway car. No one would think twice about it being in a neighborhood or on a city street."

It would be a perfect getaway car. Hide in plain sight in a vehicle no one notices. Could be a FedEx or Post Office vehicle. Or a cop car.

"Good catch on the second bullet." G-Man hugged me tightly. "We tried several military weapons and even our best sharpshooters couldn't fire fast enough to hit a head twice before the body fell."

I loved this analytical side of G-Man's job.

"Two different rifles. Definitely. No prints because the killers don't leave shell casings. Or, we haven't found them yet." G-Man lifted me off his chest and rose. "I need to get back to the command post at Metro police department headquarters. They're in charge of the investigation."

"Why not you guys?"

"Even though the FBI and Metro police department are both federal law enforcement organizations, we defer to the local cops whenever we can."

I stood, too. I needed to get back inside to Maggot-Mouth.

"We're trying to get prints from the latest round of unidentified victims, but that's hard when most of the fingers have rotted away." I looked up. G-Man was white and sweaty. "Now, don't go getting sick all over me."

I pushed him toward his car and went back inside. Maggot-Mouth and his crawlies hadn't gone anywhere. I peeled off the scalp, scraped the worms away, and looked for bullet holes. I wasn't immediately certain if the lack of face was from insect infestation or if the bullet had been a through-and-through. I searched the skull for entry marks. Finally, I found a hole in the left parietal lobe area. I removed the brain for further dissection.

"Got a bullet. Looks like the shooter was almost out of range. This one penetrated the skull over the parietal lobe, ricocheted around for a while, and lodged on the inside of the skull in the frontal lobe. No exit wound." I picked up the bullet and listened to the satisfying clang it made when I dropped it in a pan Saw-Bones held out. "Death was instantaneous."

"I'll get it to the FBI. It's in pretty good shape. It might help identify the type of rifle."

"G-Man's going to be happy. We can't tell him it came from the maggoty head, though. He'll barf."

CHAPTER THIRTY-EIGHT

NO ISLAND PARADISE

2001

The shooters went silent again. The task force was no closer to finding where they went when they disappeared. All any of us could do was wait until they killed again.

G-Man and I decided to slip away for a quick vacation. We boarded a plane to Puerto Rico in April of 2001. In the past, vacations had too often been interrupted or postponed by either his work or mine. A few days in San Juan romping in the ocean and drinking rum-laced drinks would be perfect to recharge our batteries. Saw-Bones said he'd get along fine without me.

We settled into our room overlooking the ocean. I'd never been in the tropics before, so I had no frame of reference for what I saw out the window. Clear blue sky, soft blue-green ocean, palm trees. Flowers, most of which I couldn't identify, bloomed in shades of salmon, red, lavender. A few seconds after we unpacked, we were in swim suits, racing along the path to the private beach hand in hand, and plunging into the water. G-Man plunged; I waded. He swam out into the depths while I settled for knee-deep water closer to the tide line. He tried to coax me to join him, but I couldn't swim. We dined that night on island fish and each other.

G-Man wanted to check in with the local FBI office in San Juan. We dropped in long enough for him to catch up with some of his buddies from Quantico and to introduce me. We spent two wonderfully peaceful days lolling by the pool, basking in the tropical breeze-cooled sunshine. Death was the farthest thing from our minds until an airliner exploded and crashed just off shore. G-Man's cell buzzed before dawn.

"Yeah?" He wasn't a morning person. I never spoke to him until he was on his second cup of coffee. "Where? How many? On my way."

"What happened?"

"Plane crash. Don't know how bad it is, but the Bureau wants all agents to report to the airport."

I grabbed my phone when an incoming call chimed.

"Doc, Saw-Bones here. Are you up to speed on the plane crash?"

"I just woke up. The FBI are sending a car for G-Man. It's one of those all hands come in to help situations." I flicked on CNN, which already had wall-to-wall coverage but few hard facts about an explosion off the coast of San Juan. I told him what little I knew.

"The local police called me. They don't have a medical examiner, just coroners who are really doctors with no forensic training. I volunteered your services. I hope you don't mind."

"No problem." It wasn't the first time Saw-Bones "loaned" me out. "G-Man's already gone. Where do I go?"

"Hold on a sec." The line went silent. Saw-Bones must have been talking with authorities, because he came back immediately. "Be downstairs as soon as you can. A squad car will meet you in front of the hotel. Oh, sorry about interrupting your vacation."

"Tell it to the victims." I rang off and dived into clothes.

I called G-Man to tell him I was coming in, too. He relayed what little they knew: An Avianca flight from Bogota exploded on approach to Luis Munoz Marin International Airport, scattering flaming debris and bodies or body parts across a couple of miles of ocean and land. Agents were to report to a special area at the airport where a temporary morgue was being set up. I would do whatever was needed.

I ran out the front door, flashed my ID, and jumped in a squad car waiting under the portico. From the hotel to the temporary morgue was about nine miles. Lights and sirens seemed superfluous on the near-empty, pre-rush hour streets. Two days ago, I would have noticed the palms and jacaranda (a new tree for me), but now all I saw were industrial buildings blurring past and leading into the airport. We made the trip in five minutes. The car pulled up in front of a remote hanger at the edge of the international airport. I was out of it while it was still rolling.

I felt the smell before it hit my nostrils. Burned flesh, offal, blood. I had never become accustomed to burned flesh, not since I was a child. I was going to have to shrug it off this time.

The plane went down no more than three hours earlier, but already body bags littered the hanger floor. I walked through bagged corpses to a makeshift autopsy area set up at the rear. I saw several places where I could be of service. I asked around until I found a doctor standing with hands on hips. He had the "where the hell do we start" look on his face, just like I had had when the Rock Creek Park bodies flooded in. I introduced myself.

"You're from the District's OCME, aren't you? Dr. Haskins

told me to expect you. ”

I handed him my card and showed my ID badge. “My husband and I were vacationing when we both got called. He’s with the FBI around here someplace.”

“I can’t thank you enough.” His eyes darted from body bag to body bag. “I don’t know where to begin.”

“I do.”

We talked about where to start, how to process the remains, what the authorities would need from autopsies.

“Can you lead that group over there?” He jerked his head at several U.S. Army medics, perhaps a Naval corpsman or two, a couple of local doctors, and a nurse milling around. We didn’t have nearly enough resources for the volume of casualties.

“How many were on board?” I called over my shoulder while I shrugged into protective gear stacked on tables at the side of the hangar.

“About three hundred twenty-five. We don’t have the manifest yet.” A nurse’s pale face told me she wasn’t used to autopsies.

I moved to the first stainless steel table. “Ever done this before?”

The nurse shook her head.

“Not to worry. I have, just not in this volume. Hand me what I ask for, don’t vomit on the table, and keep the floor washed clean. We’re going to be here for a long time.” I turned to the others. “What about you folks? Any high-volume trauma experience?”

“Triage in Kabul,” said an Army medic.

“Me, too,” said another.

“I helped identify the fallen in Baghdad,” said the last medic.

The Navy corpsman had hands-on experience in Kandahar.

“Unfortunately, we won’t be doing triage.” I indicated that one of the medics should hoist the first body bag onto the table. As soon as I unzipped it, burnt flesh smells erupted. So did the nurse’s breakfast. She turned her head in time to vomit on the floor. The corpsman flushed it with a bucket of water.

I set the people on my team to different tasks. One medic became the photographer; another took fingerprints where there were fingers; the corpsman helped keep the area clean; the nurse steadied herself and took blood and DNA samples. We scraped, swabbed, photographed, inked, and searched for identification in what clothing remained. The doctor I met when I first arrived set up his team beside me and copied everything I did.

Many of the corpses were badly burned or dismembered. Some looked like they'd died from blunt-force trauma, probably from hitting the water. We didn't find many wallets or passports, but occasionally we got lucky. Each opened body bag helped us put together a grisly picture of what happened on the plane.

"Looks like an on-board explosion and fire," said one of the Army medics. "Saw this in Afghanistan."

Hours later, a couple of experts from NTSB, the National Transportation Safety Board, which had jurisdiction over transportation-related accidents. arrived with a copy of the manifest. They taped a chart of the plane's interior to the hanger wall so we could match the bodies we could identify with their locations on the seating chart.

G-Man came in late in the afternoon. Navy divers recovered the black boxes, because the principal parts of the plane's carcass lay in fairly shallow water. Teams of volunteers collected every scrap of debris on the beach and a ship with a huge strainer was on its way from the other side of the island. A different NTSB team oversaw the distribution of the parts in a nearby hanger where it would reconstruct the plane.

"Any theories yet?" I glanced at G-Man's sweaty face. I shook a finger in a gore-covered glove at him. "Don't you dare puke."

"Too late. Already did. Three times on the beach. Now I know why you never eat before you start an autopsy."

"Theories?" I opened yet another bag. A child. The little corpse was badly charred so my first task was to determine its sex. Given the extent of the injuries, the kid had to have been sitting close to the source of the explosion. I turned to the NTSB agent. "How many kids were on board?"

She scanned the manifest. "Seven children, plus three babies in laps."

"How many boys?"

"Four."

I cut away the last fragments of a diaper. I had a male toddler. Two, maybe two and a half. Only one child matched the approximate age and sex. The agent put a tick mark next to a name and an X on the chart.

G-Man roamed between my hanger and the parts hanger. Each person who came in had a bit more information, a bit more speculation. Some amateur video captured the actual explosion. Even though it occurred around two in the morning, a videographer shooting the end a wedding reception caught the instant the plane blew up. The video and the black boxes were on their way to Washington for analysis.

Fifteen hours in, a second team arrived from D.C. and relieved G-Man and me. I had been wearing scrubs and gloves, but the charred-meat smell clung to my hair and skin. I couldn't wait for a hot shower. We grabbed a lift to the hotel with promises to return the next morning. The night shift took over. A sense of urgency hung over the morgue hanger. The immediate worry was bodies decaying in the heat. We had maybe one more day before the remains had to be refrigerated.

Day two was more of the same. More body bits turned up to be processed. We finished the main work and watched as the autopsied remains were transported to refrigeration units aboard a Navy hospital ship which had arrived from the other side of the island. On day three, the local FBI and Puerto Rican authorities dismissed us with profuse thanks. The rest of the case would be worked between San Juan and Washington. Leg work would continue in San Juan; lab work of all kinds would be handled stateside.

Our vacation was ruined, no matter how hard we tried to pretend it wasn't. We left. Exhausted though I was, I couldn't sleep on the flight. My brain chewed on why anyone would want to commit wholesale murder. The NTSB hadn't ruled out an explosion based on mechanical failure, but I didn't think that was right.

Suicide by pilot was possible but didn't need an explosion to accomplish that goal. Flying the jet into the ocean would have worked equally well.

We hadn't had a terrorist attack on a plane since Pan Am 103 blew up over Lockerbie, Scotland back in 1988. This felt evil; someone had to be behind the destruction. Regardless of who brought this plane down and what his reasons were, I wanted revenge for the toddler. My worst nightmare was the killer died on the plane.

CHAPTER THIRTY-NINE

FAMILY MATTERS

2001

We filled the weeks after our foreshortened vacation with an endless crop of autopsies for me and G-Man's continuing search for the snipers. I was less frustrated than he was—I could arrive at definitive causes of death most of the time and close my side of a case, where G-Man and the sniper task force continued to have too few actionable leads and too many false sightings. We kept our ears tuned to reports on the search for the Avianca bomber coming out of the Bureau and NTSB, but that task force had as little luck as we did.

The image of the charred toddler never left me. The more I thought about the loss of his future, the more I wanted to hunt and kill the bomber. That fact that I had no way of finding him led me to go on a small but intense hunting spree in the District drug community.

Saw-Bones and I relaxed in his office at the end of a rare easy day. He showed me a letter he'd received from the lead coroner in San Juan, thanking me for all my work. "If she's ever ready to more to Puerto Rico, we can put her to work immediately."

"That sounds interesting."

"No, it doesn't." His tone told me not to consider leaving.

I was fairly certain he was joking, but his words triggered a near-Big-Chigger reaction. He threatened my loss of control without knowing it. My breathing accelerated, and my heart pounded.

"What? Me leave? And give up the excitement of mounting body counts?" I rose to go home. I wanted to stop for a latte on the way.

"I could loan you out on more exciting cases. It would give the office and you great exposure."

Getting loaned out might be very interesting, but it had to be for my benefit. I'd had enough of letting myself be used. Big Chigger had used me too many times in the past for me to acquiesce without more thought.

"I'll have to think about that."

I exited the Metro station, grabbed my coffee, and thought about Saw-Bones's proposition. G-Man would support my decision to take limited assignments away from the medical examiner's office, I knew, and I wanted Saw-Bones to be proud of my work in a way I'd never wanted anyone else to. Not even Chest-Cracker, who'd been replaced as a mentor and friend by my current boss. What better way to showcase me than by working occasionally in other jurisdictions?

I mused about a fairly recent stealth visit to Bubbaville, something I did a couple of times a year so to keep current on what has happening in the town that housed Big Chigger and Li'l Bit. My last trip, a week before our Puerto Rican vacation, reminded me of where I started and how far I'd come in escaping the suffocation and boredom of small town Virginia. Sitting over a cup of coffee at the local gas-and-go let me eavesdrop on the latest gossip. Common in all towns, gossip was mostly interesting to those repeating it.

I picked up a tidbit that Big Chigger had been injured in a forklift accident at Sears and was on disability; Li'l Bit still worked at the Drop In Diner. I wandered over to see if she was on duty. She was, but I didn't sit at her station. I watched her hustle plates of greasy food back and forth to a variety of booths. If she'd taught me one life lesson, it was focus. Short of a fire or gunshots, whatever happened in the diner outside of her four booths and five tables went unnoticed.

I left without her seeing me, a metaphor for my life in Bubbaville. I shrugged. I'd made little impression on the town or family until I left with scholarships to State, and even that was short lived. I'd faded from the town gossip mill.

On the way back to the District, I congratulated myself on escaping. Had the townsfolk given me a second thought, they might have said I'd turned out good by becoming a doctor. They'd have said I turned out bad if they had known about my vocation.

I walked the few blocks from the Metro station to my home, where I looked forward to the coffee and a hot bath. I didn't expect two men to be sitting on my front stoop.

Someone must have seen me in Bubbaville, because Big Chigger and Junior waited for me on the stoop of our row house. I hadn't had any contact with the lard-ass since Junior was thrown out of Johns Hopkins during my residency. The last time I saw the venal old man, he flipped me off when I took my two boxes containing remnants of my childhood away the year before graduation from State.

My eyes narrowed as I stared at each in turn. Junior was still the squishy frog he'd always been. Long on fat, short on muscles. The biggest change was in Big Chigger. His large frame, which had once sported thick muscles, was flabby. His skin was gray and damp. Had I been able to turn and walk away, I would have, but turning my back on Big Chigger had never been wise. It had earned me many a hit on the head or worse. I stopped on the sidewalk.

"How did you find me?"

"Hooter James saw you at the diner a few weeks back. He called," Junior said. "By the time I got there, you were leaving town. We hopped in his truck and followed you."

"And you waited this long to show up? Why now?"

"We came a couple of times, but you weren't home. Ain'tcha going to let us in?" Big Chigger licked cracked lips.

I didn't move. No way were these two losers getting into my house to trash it looking for drugs and money. "No."

I'd rarely told Big Chigger no, but I no longer needed to filter my words to stay safe. Nothing he could do to me now was worth continuing the pretending I'd done as a child.

"Oh, big hot shot doctor forgets where she came from, forgets to respect her father." Big Chigger lurched to his feet and advanced down the walkway, fists balled.

"Did you forget you told me from the day I was born I wasn't your kid? That someone else was my father because I didn't look like you?" More than a little venom burned the back of my throat.

"I never." Big Chigger shook his head, but nothing cleared his confused thoughts. "I was a good father."

"Is that what you mean by being a good father? Rejecting me from the time I could remember? Well, you can't say anything I give a shit about." I braced for an eruption.

"She's right. You called her That Thing all the time." Junior stared slack-jawed at his father. "Have you told yourself these lies so often that you believe them?"

"Don't you call me a liar, asshole." Big Chigger turned on his son. I had to stop this before we had a fight on the street.

"You called me That Thing to show how much you loved me? Get real." I sidled over a couple of steps to get a clear shot at Big Chigger should he make a move toward me. I'd been waiting for this since my first Aikido lesson. He was toast if he so much as raised an eyebrow in my direction.

He lunged and swung wildly at my head. Fool. Toast. I kicked his shin. He yelped and bent over to grab his injured leg.

"Leave him alone." Junior used the railing to pull himself to his feet, swayed, and stepped up beside the old man, who used to be capable of taking care of himself. The closer I watched them, the more I realized that both were using drugs. How had Big Chigger fallen so low as to get hooked on something other than anger and beer? Junior elbowed his way in front of his father. "I need some medicine. I'm really sick."

"You're sick, all right. I told you last time I saw you in Baltimore I wouldn't give you a penny for drugs. I didn't then. I won't now." I dismissed him and turned toward the old man. "And you. From what I've heard, you don't work. I bet you don't do anything around the house to help your wife. You didn't before I left home, so I doubt you changed your lazy stripes in the years since."

"Don't give me any sass, girl, if you know what's good for you." Big Chigger straightened up and took another step toward me. "I got hurt real bad. Been in lots of pain. I ran out of medicine. It's not my fault I can't work."

I took the lid off the coffee cup. If he took one more step toward me, the next move would be extra hot latte in the face. That should be enough to stop him. I sure as hell didn't want a noisy scene with Detective Hamilton running me in for assault, disturbing the peace, or living on the block. I was tired and cranky. I wanted them gone.

"We need money. Your ma don't earn enough. My disability don't buy much." Big Chigger changed tactics and whined. He sounded like Junior when he confronted me at Johns Hopkins. He went from threatening bluster to whining wheedler in a single sentence.

Maybe he thought he could guilt me into helping. Fat chance. Any sense of obligation I might have felt toward the family died the first time he struck me. In this unfair battle, these two half-wits combined didn't equal a whole me.

"You're a big time doctor. You make a lot of money. Time you be sharing with the family that raised you."

"Looks like you have enough for booze and smokes. Why don't you give Li'l Bit some money to buy decent food?"

"I give her my disability check, don't I, Junior?"

"Nah. You drink it before she gets home. You don't give me nuttin,' either."

"Daughter is only good for popping out kids. She's so stupid she only got two of the daddies to pay child support. And she don't share." Big Chigger couldn't suppress a sly leer. "I know where she keeps her stash, though. Help myself to it when I need it."

"Just like you did when you stole my college fund?" If Princess had money, why did he drive halfway across the state to harass me?

"Hey, you know where she keeps drugs? Why didn't you tell me?" Junior turned on his father for holding out on him. He shoved the old man against the wrought-iron railing.

"Not drugs, stupid. Her stash of cash." Big Chigger smiled. "I just made a poem. Not as dumb as you think I am."

"I don't think you're dumb."

"Princess got nothin.' I took it all. It should be mine for all I did for her." Once again Big Chigger looked confused. "I'm hurtin' real bad. I need pain killers."

I moved to the center of the walkway, blocking any run for

cover Big Chigger or Junior might make. "I repeat. I'm giving you nothing."

"That Thing gotta be rich, her a big shot doctor and all." Big Chigger wiped snot off his upper lip.

"If you think I'm a big shot doctor, why don't you make an appointment?" I smiled at an image of Big Chigger, cold and stiff, waiting for my scalpel to open the Y-incision. "Come to my office, and see what I do for a living. Hop up on my table, and let me work on you."

"Huh? What the hell kind of doctor are you?"

"Pathologist."

"You look up assholes all day?"

"Not a proctologist, fool. A pathologist. I cut up dead bodies. Want to come down, and let me cut on you?" I turned sideways to let them pass. "You and Junior are dead to me."

Big Chigger finally got it. He wasn't getting anything from me. He swung a ham fist at me and missed. I didn't. A blow to the side of the head stunned him.

"Get out, or I'll call the cops. They like me. I'm one of them."

"You a cop?" Junior looked around as if expecting to see men in blue running down the street, guns blasting.

"I'm a medical examiner. I work with the Metro police and the FBI. I know every law enforcement officer in town, so go ahead. Try something." I picked up my cooling latte. Damn, I'd have to nuke it. "Now get the fuck off my street. If I catch you here again, I'll have you arrested for stalking. Or being a peeping tom. That ought to go over real well back in Bubbaville."

Junior must have seen something in my eyes, because he dug his fingers into Big Chigger's arm. Together they staggered back to their rattle-trap pickup parked halfway down the block. The truck coughed to life and backfired away from the curb. Jesus, they weren't smart enough get into witless protection. The waiting list was too long.

"One of these days, Big Chigger, you're going to be on my table. And I won't be gentle when I cut you open."

"Cut who open?"

I turned to see G-Man get out of a bureau car. He waved at the guys inside. I did, too.

"Big Chigger."

"Your old man? That was your old man?" G-Man stared down our street, empty but for exhaust fumes from a rotten muffler.

"Yeah."

CHAPTER FORTY

BIG CHIGGER

2001

Since Junior dragged Big Chigger off my front porch, he'd left messages on my office voice mail at least once a week. "Dad's in a bad way. He needs pain meds for his back, but the doctor won't give him no more."

Doctor must be my kinda guy. I wanted Big Chigger to live without drugs, not because I didn't believe in them, but because I wanted him to suffer. I wanted payback for the years of pain he put me through. I was inattentive one afternoon and answered a call without looking at Caller ID.

"I need something to knock down my drug habit." Junior plunged in.

"What, no hello? No, how are you?" I snotted back at him. The sound of his voice took me back to a childhood I had no desire to revisit.

"If you don't help me…"

I cut him off, sick of his mewling and his toothless threats. "Why don't you get off your fat ass and go into rehab?" I wanted both him and Big Chigger out of my life. I hung up with him in mid-word.

I forgot about the exchange until Li'l Bit left a message. I hadn't heard from her since she sent the letter telling me about Miss Snickers' death. "Your father was in a car accident. You gotta come home."

Nothing else. Just an accident and come home. I hadn't called the house since I left for college, because I made it a cardinal rule never to reach out to them, but this time I called the house. A male with a deep-ish voice answered.

"Yeah? Who's this?"

"Doc."

"Who's Doc?"

I had no idea who answered the phone. "I'm trying to reach Li'l Bit or Princess. Who are you?"

"Princess's oldest son. Big Chigger called me Kid One."

That explained nothing except this wasn't Li'l Bit. I hadn't seen this kid since L&O and I stopped in Bubbaville. He wasn't much more than three at the time. Time to see if he could give me any information.

"Is your mother there?"

"Nah. She took off several months back with a trucker. She left me and her other two kids with Li'l Bit and Big Chigger."

Okay. I was getting somewhere. Slowly, but somewhere. "Li'l Bit left a message that Big Chigger was in an accident. That true?"

"Yeah. He was on his way to the gas-and-go for a six-pack. Some asshole ran him off the road."

"So, is he all right?"

"I don't know. Li'l Bit's at the hospital. She left me with Kid Two and Kid Three. I'm waiting to hear. All I know is he's hurt really bad. They took him to the hospital. They won't let me in cuz I'm not eighteen yet."

"Is Li'l Bit at Regional?"

Regional took in most of the poverty cases. Well, that fit Big Chigger. No money, no insurance. No choices.

"Yeah."

"Any idea why she called me?"

"She says you're a doctor. Maybe she wants you to check on him."

I hung up and went into Saw-Bones's office to ask for the afternoon off. I told him about my father's accident.

"Go. Family comes first."

Well, not really.

§

After hours of fighting Beltway traffic and the tedious drive out Route 66, I stood at the end of Big Chigger's bed. I'd identified myself as a doctor, as the patient's daughter, and as a medical examiner. I asked the nurse for professional courtesy to review his chart. Li'l Bit nodded her approval.

I flipped through the pages and scanned the results of the X-rays and other tests. Pretty much what I expected: severe damage to his torso when he hit the steering wheel. He must not have been wearing a seat belt. Then again, I don't remember him ever wearing one. Heavy smoker, diabetes, high blood pressure, cardiac arrhythmia, a spider-web of broken capillaries on his face, indicating a pattern of heavy drinking. That combination should be enough to kill him. Unfortunately, slowly, unless he got help.

I'd just finished reading the chart when his doctor came into the room. I knew him. He'd been one of the interns a few years behind me when I was doing my residency.

"Hey, Wound-Stitcher."

"Doc, how the hell are you?" Wound-Stitcher enveloped me in a massive hug. He'd always been demonstrative, even in his first year as an intern. "You're his daughter? I didn't connect his name with you."

"Yes. I lost track of you when you left after your internship. Where did you finish?"

"Georgetown."

"And you ended up here?"

"I figured I could do some good. If we only could get to these people before their life styles put them onto a downward slide."

We chatted for a few minutes until Li'l Bit shifted in her chair. Wound-Stitcher went back to being all business. "We wired your father's crushed sternum together and stopped the internal bleeding. That's all we can do. The rest of his problems are more likely to kill him than the accident. How long has he been this rundown?"

"I haven't a clue. I left his house at sixteen. I rarely go back. Since his accident, he can't even work the farm. What's he going to have to do when he's released?"

"Once the injuries heal, exercise and stop smoking. Lay off the fat and red meat. Those three things will help get his diabetes and cardiac problems under better control. It's all up to him." He looked at the machines and noted something on the chart. "Oh, and wear his seat belt."

"Has anyone else been in to see him?"

"Your brother." Wound-Stitcher shot a glance at Li'l Bit. "Anyone else in the family able to take care of him?"

"Only my brother Junior, but he's dumb-assed useless. My sister's oldest kid says she took off leaving three kids behind. Oldest is about fifteen, maybe sixteen."

"Kid One is seventeen." Li'l Bit's voice echoed from the depths of despair.

"Big Chigger wouldn't listen to them if his life depended on it."

"It does." Wound-Stitched shot another look at Li'l Bit. "They all live in the same house?"

"Far as I can tell. I live in the District."

Wound-Stitcher made some cryptic notes in a spidery doctor's handwriting. He stared at Big Chigger, glanced at Li'l Bit, and finally looked at me. "He'll need care. I'll advise he get into a nutritional program, maybe AA. What do you think?"

"He won't eat healthy food and won't go to AA, but you'll have documented your recommendations."

Wound-Stitcher flipped the chart closed. He stopped in the doorway. "We should have coffee together soon. Catch up."

"I'd like that. Lots of changes between Johns Hopkins and now."

"Where do you practice?"

"I'm a medical examiner at OCME."

"I'd make a joke about getting this guy soon, but he's your father. I hope he makes it."

I don't.

§

On the drive back to D.C., I found a way to help Big Chigger get the hell out of my life. I stopped at several drugstores and loaded up on nicotine patches. If he used them as recommended, he might quit smoking. If not, he'd likely die. I read the warning material.

Do not apply to broken skin.
Do not apply more than one patch at a time.
Do not smoke while using the patch.

I dumped them in a baggie, along with a few Oxycodone

patches, and waited for the next whiny call. When it came two weeks after Big Chigger was released from the hospital, I made it to Bubbaville in record time. I knocked and pushed the door open. Big Chigger and Junior slumped in recliners in the living room.

"Whatcha doing here?" Junior slurred his words.

"He called." I jerked my head at the old man.

"What did he want?" Junior struggled to clear his vision. He was as befuddled as Big Chigger had been when he wobbled on my front stoop.

"Help." I held up a baggie full of patches.

"Gimme." Big Chigger snatched the bag.

"Let me show you how to use them." I snatched the bag back. "Roll up your sleeve. We need to put one on your shoulder."

Big Chigger pulled off his sweat-stiffened shirt. I went into the bathroom and returned with a dull razor and some shaving cream. "I need to clean a place for the patch. It won't work over all this hair."

I shaved a mohair thatch from Big Chigger's shoulders on both sides. I peeled the backing off one patch and applied it on top of a small nick from the razor.

"It's not working," Big Chigger whined. "I still feel awful."

"Be patient. Just because you have a patch doesn't mean it'll work immediately. Never use more than two at a time, or you'll overdose." I turned away from the hulks of both men.

Junior dipped his hand in the baggie and dragged out a couple of patches. He slapped one on each arm and leaned back, waiting for an instant high from the opiate. He lit a cigarette and stared at the television. Big Chigger also lit up.

"You shouldn't smoke with these patches."

"I don't care. Gimme another one. I really don't feel good."

"I'm the doctor. I said don't use more than two at the most."

"Hell, you work with dead people. Whatcha know about real

people?" Big Chigger added a third patch. His breathing was labored. "My heart's racin'."

First rule of a doctor is do no harm. First rule of a serial killer is get rid of those who deserve it. The rules were in conflict. I left the baggie and walked out the door.

"What if I need more of this shit?" Junior called after me.

"Don't worry. You have enough."

More than enough.

CHAPTER FORTY-ONE

RESOLUTION

2001

For the next few weeks, my attention swung between FBI and the joint task force being no closer to identifying or capturing the shooters to worrying about the Avianca bomber to wondering why I'd heard nothing about Junior or Big Chigger.

The shooters killed sporadically, sometimes two at a time, sometimes once a week, sometimes nothing for an entire week. Their lack of predictability left the citizens in the District and the surrounding counties in Virginia and Maryland jumpy as hell.

I didn't approve of their killing technique or the randomness of their choice of victims, but I had to admire their audacity. While I preferred personal reasons and in-your-face killing, the shooters' reign of terror had the average person hiding behind his car when filling up at a gas station. Men and women rushed home from train stations like broken-field running backs dashing for the safety of the end zone or a front door.

"Why can't the police find the man who shot my husband," a distraught woman sobbed on national television. "They're not doing anything. They talk big but don't do squat to find the killer."

She was wrong. The task force worked around the clock following every lead. It kept one important piece of information out of the news: it knew there were two killers. The public thought it was only one.

A body turned up, shot once in the head outside a strip club in Maryland. Three men left the club together; one was shot.

"Either this was a copycat, personal, or only one of our killers took a shot." G-Man said right after the body was found.

FBI crime scene experts, along with Maryland police, swarmed the street looking for a bullet that missed. Search though they did, they found nothing.

"I hope these creeps haven't split up," G-Man said late that night. "Our profile has a dominant and a submissive shooter working together. If they split up, it will be harder than hell to find them."

"I know. I keep hoping we'll get a bit of luck and find something."

As far as the Avianca bomber was concerned, he might as well have vanished in the downed airliner. All we heard was crickets.

Around six one Monday morning, the phone rang. Saw-Bones. "Hey, Doc, are you up?"

I wanted to joke that he'd never ask one of the men the same question, but he didn't sound like he was in a joking mood.

"Why are you giving me a wake-up call?"

"I wanted to hear your cheery voice," he said. A joke, feeble, but a joke. Must be another sniper attack. Saw-Bones was more reliable than an alarm clock. I didn't know why I bothered to go to bed sometimes.

I held the portable phone in one hand, swung my legs over the side of the bed, and walked into the bathroom. I'd be damned if I'd go to work without showering.

"You sound beat. Have you been working all night again?" I peered at my reflection in the mirror._When had my eyes packed such puffy bags under them?

"I couldn't sleep, so I came in a couple of hours ago."

"Did you even go home last night?" I pulled the shower curtain aside and turned on the water. "Give me an hour. Want me to pick up coffee on the way?"

"Please. We'll need a lot of it." His non-answer to my question told me he'd not made it home. We were supposed to be closer to a nine-to-six outfit than a team that pulled all-nighters. Yeah, right.

Exactly one hour later, I walked into the morgue and put a go-box of coffee in the break room. "Coffee's here. Get it while it's still hot. What's up?"

"Two different sets of bodies. One set looks like a poisoning. Three people dead in two separate apartments in Chinatown. I have no idea why the cops are snarly about it."

"And the other?"

"A series of overdoses from west of here."

"Where is 'west of here?'"

"The mid-Shenandoah Valley."

"How come we're catching these cases? I don't mean the poisonings but those from out in Virginia."

"The state crime lab is backed up."

"And we aren't?"

Saw-Bones rubbed tired eyes. "We are, but the locals specifically asked for us. No, for you."

"Why me?"

"Guess your reputation is spreading."

We sat long enough to drink a coffee and fill in two more pathologists, who'd gotten delayed by a power outage on the Metro, on what the day's workload was.

"I'll take the Chinatown case." As second in charge, I could pick my cases most of the time. "If it's poison, we'll have to wait for lab tests. Let me get that out of the way before I help with the drug overdoses."

Saw-Bones turned to the other two pathologists, one barely more than an intern, the other who'd worked in the OCME longer than I had.

"You're with me." He beckoned to the junior pathologist. "We'll start with a white male, middle aged, dirty. Probably homeless. Most likely an overdose."

"We've had so many heroin ODs lately that I'm getting bored," whined the intern. "Even the five who injected pure Fentanyl were more of the same."

Saw-Bones ignored him.

I uncovered the body of an ancient-looking Chinese man, emaciated, nearly skeletal. Could he have died of old age? His body showed signs of severe dehydration, so I examined his throat where I found broken blood vessels. Signs of violent vomiting. His buttocks were covered with smears of bloody diarrhea. I removed his stomach and emptied the contents into a beaker for further testing.

"Saw-Bones, this isn't food poisoning. It's something else."

He walked over and listened to my explanation. Liver damage, kidney damage. "Call the lab. Get the guys working on an expedited tox screen."

I covered the body and pushed it into the refrigerator. I removed a female body from the fridge next. A repeat of the male:

elderly Chinese female, emaciated, signs of vomiting, and bloody diarrhea.

"Looks like the old man and woman consumed something that contained poison. We're they found in the same apartment?"

"I'm not sure. We'll ask when someone from the police department shows up."

"Come look at this," Saw-Bones said. "Here's something we don't see every day."

The intern rolled the male body over to expose the back. At least five trans-dermal patches overlapped on his shoulders.

"Peel those off. Let's see what he was taking." Saw-Bones told the intern.

The skin under two of the patches was rough and red, broken in places. I put one under the microscope. Nicotine replacement. Hmmm.

"Where'd you say this body came from?"

"A small town called Criglerville in the mid-Shenandoah Valley."

Two hamlets over from Bubbaville. Could Junior be selling the patches as Oxycodone? He and Big Chigger were supposed to use them themselves. What idiot would be stupid enough to sell or buy smoking cessation meds as Oxy?

"He a smoker, Saw-Bones?"

"Heavy. Don't tell me."

"Yeah. Stupid guy used multiple nicotine patches while he was smoking."

Saw-Bones raised an eyebrow. I'd been sloppy in voicing such a harsh assessment of the victim. Our role was to find out how they died, not pass judgment.

"Looks like he didn't read the warning labels. The one I peeled off brought a chunk of skin with it. His heart's enlarged, probably from long-time problems, exacerbated by the multiple patches."

Saw-Bones shook his head. "Hypertension, untreated diabetes. What doctor would give a patient nicotine patches in his condition?"

One who wanted to get rid of her father.

I heard a knock at the outer door. "I'll get it." I didn't bother to take off my apron.

"Probably another ambulance. Have them off-load the bodies in the cold room."

Two ambulances waited. "Got two stiffs in each, Doc," called out one of the EMTs. "All from Virginia. Two more dead coming in from Bluefield, West Virginia."

Bluefield? That was pretty far south for Junior.

"Guess they want all the bodies autopsied at the same place to see if there's a pattern."

"There's another in Regional. Young guy, but he's not likely to make it. Full cardiac arrest when we got there," the second EMT said.

The EMTs unloaded the body bags onto gurneys and rolled them into the cold room. I signed the paperwork and unzipped black bags one after the other. A teen and Big Chigger.

I told Saw-Bones the last corpse was my father.

"Go home." Saw-Bones came around the table and reached out to pat me on the shoulder. He pulled his hand back before he smeared body fluids all over my scrubs.

"I want to stay."

"You need to leave." Saw-Bones was adamant. "At least get some air. Take a walk or something."

I walked up to the National Mall and sat on a bench to watch carefree tourists snap pictures of the Capital. Like the students at State years ago, they had no idea that death sat in their midst. I closed my eyes, face upturned to the sun.

For years I'd joked about having Big Chigger on my table. Finally, I did, and I couldn't bring myself to do his autopsy. No matter how much I wanted to fillet his flesh as he had filleted me verbally all my life, the son of a bitch was still my old man. I was glad he was dead. I really was, but I couldn't cut him open. Maybe Li'l Bit would have a chance to heal from decades of his abuse, if she wasn't too beaten down. I returned to the office.

"I sent you home."

"I have to see what happened."

In the hour I'd been gone, Saw-Bones had finished the young overdose victim. The teen had multiple patches on his arms and shoulders. Time for Big Chigger. I stood at the end of the table where we usually had a policeman observing. Big Chigger had the same crop of patches as we found with the other corpses. Saw-Bones filled out the death certificates: Accidental Death from Nicotine Poisoning.

"You know, he'd be just as dead if it had been Oxy instead of nicotine." I pointed to Big Chigger's body.

"ODing on Oxy is a lot less painful than the way these bastards died." Saw-Bones looked at me. "I'm sorry. I didn't…"

"It's all right. Look, even though Big Chigger was my old man, he was a class A-One prick. He threw me out in my teens." I stowed the bodies in the refrigerator. "I've barely talked with him in the past twenty years."

"I'll let the police know what we found."

I wanted to leave contacting Li'l Bit to Saw-Bones, but I couldn't. I expected tears when I got her on the phone, maybe from relief. I looked for some sign, some emotion for the loss of her husband of nearly forty years.

Instead of asking about her husband, she said, "Junior's in the hospital in bad shape. You'd better come home."

I left a message for G-Man and drove out to meet Li'l Bit at Junior's bedside.

§

"How many of those patches did he use?" More than he should have.

"I don't know. Six. Eight, maybe. Like your dad, he just wanted to get out of pain."

Time for the gut check. Time for Li'l Bit to learn how stupid her husband and son were.

"Those weren't pain killers. Both Junior and Big Chigger put nicotine patches on and kept on smoking."

"Nicotine patches?" Li'l Bit had difficulty focusing.

"I told them how to use them, but they knew better than I did. Misuse killed Big Chigger and will probably kill Junior."

"What am I going to do without them?" Li'l Bit's work-roughened hands lay curled in her lap.

I had no words. After the hell these two men had put her through, Li'l Bit was worried about what she'd do without them? "Maybe you can have a life."

"Hey, Doc," came a familiar voice from the hospital room doorway.

I spun around. "Hey, G-Man. What are you doing here?"

"You left a message, and I talked with Saw-Bones. I figured you'd need me." He walked into the room and crushed me in a hug. "I'm G-Man. You must be Li'l Bit."

My mother turned reddened eyes toward my husband. "Glad to meet you."

The first time my husband met my mother wasn't how I expected it. I didn't think they'd ever meet. I leaned into his chest, grateful to have someone to hold onto. I brought him up to speed on my father and brother. We were talking with Li'l Bit about next steps when a sheriff's deputy showed up.

"Are you 'Doc?'"

"Yes."

"I came to your house after your mother dialed nine-one-one." The deputy pulled his hat off. "I'm very sorry for your loss." He nodded at Li'l Bit. He looked at G-Man, an unspoken question in his eyes. "You too, ma'am, sir."

"This is my husband, G-Man."

The deputy tipped his hat.

"What can I do for you?"

"I want to talk with your brother. He's under suspicion of being in possession of a controlled substance." He looked as uncomfortable as anyone could in uniform. He tugged at his twenty-two-pound-plus belt.

"What controlled substance? Junior was selling drugs?"

"Not my baby. He'd never do that." Li'l Bit held a tissue to her lips.

"Be quiet." I looked at Li'l Bit. "Junior's been dealing something or other since high school."

I turned back to the deputy. "What do you think was he dealing this time?"

"Oxycodone. Got a lot of it flowing through here lately. I've run Junior in for low-level possession and dealing, but no one's died until now. The deaths change the charges."

"And you're sure Junior was dealing Oxy?"

"We've had a series of deaths from overdoses. Looks like Junior here got some bad drugs. We'll take him in as soon as he's able." The deputy looked smug.

Time for a smack down.

I walked out to the nurses' station and asked to see my brother's chart. It took some finagling, but a nurse handed it over. I returned to Junior's room. A quick flip of the pages told me the deputy was going to eat his words, with or without mustard.

"So, Junior was high when he was brought in?"

"Yeah. We found three bodies, all with patches all over them.

Gotta be Oxy. What else would it be?" He fidgeted with his belt again, rearranging his gun so that it hung to the right of his cock.

"Nicotine." I pointed to the entry on the chart where an ER nurse noted removing multiple patches.

The deputy looked sick. I had him wiggling on a hook. Time to reel him in.

"My office conducted autopsies on men brought in from Criglerville. Cause of death in each, including my father: cardiac arrest due to nicotine poisoning. Looks like Junior is guilty of being stupid but not a drug dealer."

"This time, maybe. But he's dealt before and will again. We'll take him in to see if he can tell us who his source is."

"That would be me. I gave some patches to my father after his accident, because his doctor told him he had to quit smoking and lose weight. I wanted to help." And help I did, thank you very much.

"We'll be keeping an eye on your brother to make sure he doesn't deal again." The deputy turned on his heel and stomped to the door.

"You probably shouldn't leave. I don't think Junior'll last the night."

He didn't.

CHAPTER FORTY-TWO

GOTCHA

2001

One week after we sent the stomach contents of the two Chinese corpses to the lab for a "rush" analysis, we knew what the toxin was: Amatoxin, found in poisonous mushrooms not native to the U.S. Because the majority of the victims lived in Chinatown, teams of police took samples from grocery stores, herbal medical practitioners, and organic markets across the District. A month later, mushrooms from two groceries and one herbal medicine distributor tested positive. The health department shut them down. Total dead: nine. Total sick but recovered: thirty-one.

If the poisonous mushrooms had been mixed with healthy mushrooms on purpose, we had a case of product tampering. Unlike the Tylenol scare in 1982, this didn't receive widespread news coverage. Was it because the tampering was localized or because the victims were minorities?

"Was it an accident or murder?" I prepared for a new week.

"The police don't know." Saw-Bones picked up the list of cadavers. "Quiet weekend. One new female victim from Chinatown."

"What else?" I pulled on gloves and fetched the cadaver. Saw-Bones's list had more than a single entry.

"A smattering of auto accidents, heart attacks. Pretty normal stuff."

"At least, the snipers weren't active."

"Indeed. Turn the Chinatown autopsy around as soon as you can, will you?"

"Sure."

An hour later, I finished and walked into Saw-Bones's office.

"Everything points to Amatoxin."

"Our latest victim probably had some bad mushrooms in her kitchen cabinet. The known distributors haven't reopened." Saw-Bones said.

"I'll call the detective in charge. He can add one more victim to the case." As assistant medical examiner and the second in command, I made as many calls to the police as Saw-Bones did. I poured a cup of coffee. "What's next?"

As one series of lightly-covered deaths wound down, the other major news story did not. The media firestorm fueled panic with endless speculation on where the snipers would strike next. Shootings in three states, well, two states and the District of Columbia, seemed random. Police in all three jurisdictions, the Feds, including G-Man, various coroners' offices, and our lab were no closer to a capture than when the first bodies appeared.

Eyewitnesses emerged from the gutters, each claiming to have seen the shooters or know them personally. They were white, black, Asian, extra-terrestrials. They drove cars, trucks, walked or teleported from kill site to kill site.

"I'm glad I'm not you, G-Man," I said over a rare dinner together. "You have to chase every clue even when the report is too outrageous to be credible. I have to get the cause of death right the first time, but no one can rush some of the tests. Gives me more time to think about what happened to a specific corpse."

"One credible sighting," G-Man said, "is all we need. We'll get the bastards."

Not many weeks after Li'l Bit, the three boys, G-Man, and I buried Big Chigger alongside Junior in the family burial plot, the Medical Examiner's office received a body shot in the face from close range.

"This doesn't fit the pattern of our snipers. The earlier victims were shot in the back from a distance. This shot came from maybe a couple of dozen yards away." Saw-Bones pointed to what was left of the back of the skull, most of which was missing.

Later in August, after a long stretch of high temperatures and higher humidity, tempers flared, and people died. We were hit with a flurry of murders. In the course of twenty-four hours, nine bodies piled up in the morgue, only one of which might have been from our shooters. Maybe two. At least seven didn't match the current M.O. Our shooters had always killed with long-range head shots from a rifle, not close in with nine-millimeter bullets to the face or torso.

"Not hard to figure out that these bodies don't have the wounds we expect." I rolled an autopsied body into the refrigerator. "I wonder if the snipers have moved on."

They hadn't. They hit again. Twice in two days. One victim in Bethesda, Maryland, one in Purcellville, Virginia.

"We have a solid lead on the vehicle. Several eyewitnesses came forward after the Bethesda homicide." I put G-Man on speaker phone in Saw-Bones's office. "They saw a post office truck nearby. Something no one would notice. We're checking on everyone in the area."

"SNIPERS USE P.O. TRUCK," screamed the *Washington Post* headlines. Television stations broke into local broadcasts with breathless breaking news reports.

"The FBI has confirmed it is looking for a postal vehicle in conjunction with the Sniper Shooters." A serious-looking national television anchor stood in front of the Hoover Building. "Police confirm they are close to an arrest."

"Fat chance of that," I said. "Is that anchor trying to reassure a jittery public that they are almost safe, or is he going for a boost in ratings by being the first to cover the story?"

"Both, probably," Saw-Bones said.

Media outlets condemned the authorities for not doing enough. A dozen people saw the shooting at a gas station in Purcellville. All saw something different, though, and not one saw a post office truck. Neither did the now ubiquitous traffic cameras. We processed the body almost before it stopped twitching.

As luck would have it, the Purcellville shooting was the break G-Man's task force needed. "We had it all wrong. When we analyzed the traffic camera footage in both Purcellville and Bethesda for a post office truck, we found a squad car that didn't fit."

"A cop? The shooters are cops?" I'd never considered that angle. If true, the media would have new grist for the outrage mill for weeks to come.

"I said the car was a police car. That doesn't mean the shooters are police. The plate number is from a car stolen six months ago in Pennsylvania." G-Man sounded tired but hopeful. "Things should happen fast."

CHAPTER FORTY-THREE

WRAPPED UP

2001

Events tumbled faster than they could be reported or made up. Facts piled up. A tip came in for a cop car tucked behind an abandoned warehouse in Manassas, Virginia. A night watchman said the business had gone bankrupt, and no one was supposed to be there. SWAT teams and negotiators descended on the property.

G-Man was wired into instant updates. "You won't believe it. SWAT surrounded the warehouse. When they broke in, they found a man sleeping on a filthy mattress. We had him cuffed and stuffed before he could reach for his rifle."

The second shooter was in the wind. G-Man didn't hold much chance he'd get away. "Most likely he'll end up dead, a suicide by cop."

"You mean 'We haven't quite decided whether he committed

suicide or died trying to escape.'"

"Huh?" G-Man must have been distracted, because he usually caught all my classic movie references.

"*Casablanca*, silly, after Peter Lorre's character dies in police custody."

With one shooter in custody and the news outlets no wiser to the presence of his partner, G-Man told me the crime scene professionals were combing through the police car.

"It wasn't a real squad car, after all." G-Man and I ate breakfast like a normal couple. "Actually, it had been one, but Newark, Delaware, decommissioned it and sold it at auction. The buyer was supposed to repaint it."

"How did you figure out it was bogus?"

"The idiots hadn't changed the medallion on the door. We never called in support from any state outside of Virginia and Maryland. Once a traffic camera captured a clear image, our experts were able to identify the medallion. A quick contact of the auction site gave us a buyer's name."

"Add the stolen license plate, and it wasn't hard to put out a BOLO, was it?" I spread lemon-lime marmalade on half a scone. "Did the 'be on the lookout' work? Did the tip line light up quickly?"

"It sure did."

G-Man's phone rang. He listened, spoke briefly, and hung up. "It's getting weird."

"How? Hasn't it always been weird?"

"The auctioneer said the car was sold to a woman."

A woman? Hmmm, that added an unexpected twist.

"The second shooter could be female, huh?" I grinned. "We are the more dangerous sex, after all."

"I don't buy it, but if female DNA turns up in the car, we'll have to adjust our profile yet again." G-Man ran his left hand through his hair. "We don't dare release any information to the public. Everyone is getting back to normal since we arrested the only known shooter."

I looked out the kitchen window at sunlight slanting through our cherry tree. All along, G-Man thought they were looking at a dominant-and-submissive team. The man in custody exercised his right to remain silent, until he couldn't not talk. Like many spree or serial killers, he wanted the world to know who he was and why he'd done what he'd done. Nothing G-Man had seen convinced him that he'd been the leader.

"If you're looking for a woman, is she the dominant partner?"

"She could be, but no one on the task force foresaw a woman shooter. We're waiting for forensics."

"Why do you profilers never think first about a female serial killer? All you talk about is 'he.'" I wasn't asking for equality between the sexes, but law enforcement in general dismissed women in many of their profiles.

"Because few women have been serial killers over the last century, and most of those fall into discrete categories." G-Man popped the last bite of toast in his mouth.

"Such as?"

"Black widows who killed their spouses for their money. This extends to women who killed boarders for their pension or Social Security checks last century."

So far, so good.

"Angels of death. Most of these work in the health care industry and kill terminally ill patients."

Okay.

"But aren't some angels of death also male nurses or orderlies?"

"That's what I mean. It's so hard to jump to any conclusions about female serial killers." G-Man stood and carried his cup to the sink. "In a way, I'm kinda glad we don't know more."

"How so?"

"Because that would mean we had a lot of first-hand knowledge to work with. We don't, so we assume the killers are male."

"But why jump to conclusions at all?" Anger crept into my voice. "Why not keep an open mind?"

G-Man put a soapy hand on my cheek. "Are you taking up the feminist cause for equality among serial killers?" He pecked my forehead.

"It's a thought." The FBI's stubbornness of "we know best" grated. G-Man was so supremely confident that his profile was right. I wasn't. "Want to go for a run in the park?"

"Yes."

§

Forensics came back with female DNA. The FBI ran it through CODIS, the Combined DNA Index System, where it identified an AWOL Army sharpshooter charged with murdering civilians in Iraq. G-Man had a name, local addresses, and phone numbers.

"She's armed and considered extremely dangerous," read the release that went out to all local law enforcement personnel. "Approach with extreme caution."

Meaning, shoot on sight. That was what I would do, and as it turned out, exactly what a rural sheriff's deputy did when he encountered her on a back road. One shot through the windshield of her Jeep into her left eye.

G-Man swung past the medical examiner's office when he knew it was over. "Local sheriff out in rural Maryland took the shot. She's down."

"Has the surviving shooter said anything more?"

"Oh, he won't stop talking. We have his entire life story from birth until today."

Saw-Bones had his feet up on his desk. "What's their connection?"

"Same company in Afghanistan. They shot up a village on a sure tip that a Taliban leader was there. He wasn't. They murdered everyone, men, women, and children. Shades of My Lai and Lieutenant Calley. Both are wanted by the Army." G-Man flipped open a file.

The woman went AWOL in Kandahar province, made her way to the States, and kept in touch with the man, who went AWOL when he walked away from his home base in Virginia after he rotated out of the field. They met over drinks in a bar in Manassas, argued about who was the best shot, and dared each other to prove it. Rather than go to the shooting range, they hunted for several weeks in Rock Creek Park, each taking out a series of joggers and bicyclists.

Saw-Bones glanced at me. "We thought that killing field might have been practice."

The pair began hunting at random, shooting from greater and greater distances, challenging each other to fire simultaneously.

"I get all that," I said. "I understand tests of skill, but I don't get the sheer randomness of their victimology."

"According to the man, competition was what it was all about."

"Any sexual element to it?" Saw-Bones asked.

"He hasn't mentioned it, but I imagine the shooters were a couple. Probably got off on the kill as well as the shooting," G-Man said. "He said the challenge and hitting the targets were fun."

Saw-Bones choked, spraying coffee over the legs of his scrubs. "Fun?"

"I can't imagine random kills would be fun." I needed a connection to my victims. I bit my tongue before I said anything incriminating.

"Some spree killers live for the excitement of the crime itself. Go figure." G-Man stood and left the office.

Yeah, go figure.

CHAPTER FORTY-FOUR

QUESTIONINGS

2002

During the year following Big Chigger and Junior's deaths, G-Man mentioned how I'd changed. I didn't feel any different.

"You seem lighter," he said, "almost as though that chip on your shoulder is gone."

I no longer feared phone calls or unwanted visits from the old man. Until he was planted, I was unaware how he'd controlled my behavior my entire life. I thought I'd escaped his domination when I left home, but G-Man saw it differently. Now, with me out of Big Chigger's reach, I could be me.

I didn't blame the old man for driving me to become a killer, but he couldn't tarnish that claim to fame. Had I been avenging what Big Chigger did to me and Li'l Bit all my life? My most satisfying kills were getting revenge for people who were too weak to defend themselves. Like Li'l Bit. With him gone, though, the need to take revenge lessened.

I went through multiple rounds of self-examination. I never believed I was a psychopath or a sociopath, but was I little more than a screwed mess of a woman with daddy issues? I had no idea. What I knew was, I finally felt free.

I sought out my mother to see what, if any, advantages she was taking with her new-found freedom. She'd wept and moaned so much when her husband and son died about not knowing how to go on that I worried she'd give up, that she'd continue living in the shadow of his influence. For that reason, I called once a month.

G-Man convinced me we needed to go to Bubbaville six months after the twin deaths to see for ourselves if she and the three boys were all right. He'd talked with Li'l Bit quite a lot at the funerals. Because he'd only been to the house one time, I navigated. We almost didn't recognize it.

The once-falling down house, nearly overrun with trash and castoff machinery, looked like people lived there who cared. The yard was empty of long-unused toys. Someone had hauled away piles of broken car parts and worn-out tires Big Chigger had thrown against a shed. Even the rotten truck was gone. Instead of the air of neglect that had hung over the place like fog from a fen, fresh paint and a mended porch presented a new face to the world.

"What the hell happened?" I turned to G-Man before I opened the car door. "Did Li'l Bit move and not tell me?"

"I don't think so," G-Man said. "Her car's in front of the barn. Let's go in."

I steeled myself against negative memories and climbed the steps to the porch, no longer having to move around the hole in the second to the top step. Someone had rebuilt the porch and its railings. I knocked.

The door swung inward on oiled hinges. Kid One opened the

screen and ushered us into the living room. I walked into an altered reality. The house smelled of fresh paint and cooking, not puke and rancid diapers. Used but serviceable chairs and a couch replaced the broken-down furniture of the past. They anchored the same old rag rugs, which were clean once again. Li'l Bit came from the kitchen and wiped wet hands on a dishtowel.

"I'm so glad you came out." She stood awkwardly in front of me, uncertain if she wanted to or should hug me. I leaned in and kissed her cheek quickly. G-Man shook her hand.

"As you can see, we've been busy." Kid One brought iced tea. We sat on the unfamiliar furniture.

"What happened?"

I couldn't stop looking around. Big Chigger's absence loomed over every change, as disapproving in death as he had been in life. No ashtrays. No rotten recliners. No painted over wallpaper. No filth and grime in the corners. Had the old man been here, he wouldn't have allowed my mother to make any changes.

Kid One took a long drink of iced tea. "We happened. Two, Three, and I decided we couldn't live the way Big Chigger and Junior made us, so we talked Li'l Bit into putting a bit of effort into making the place livable."

"You succeeded," I said. "It reminds me more of the way the house was when I was a little kid."

"It took forever to get the stink out. With your father and Junior smoking and drinking in here all the time, the house smelled worse that when you boiled down that rotten dog." Li'l Bit laughed. "Remember?"

"She still has it." G-Man grinned back. "The skeleton, I mean."

"Her sister got so mad, because I wouldn't make her get rid of it." Li'l Bit looked a little nostalgic, a little sad. "And Junior tried to steal it."

"Has anyone heard from Princess?" No one had mentioned

her after Kid One told me she'd run off with a trucker and left the three boys behind.

"Nope," Kid One said. "She's been gone a long time. She hasn't called. I don't think she's coming back."

I glanced at G-Man who stared at Li'l Bit. My mother wasn't mourning the loss of three members of her family. I should have been surprised but realized she was happy not to have any more leeches hanging around.

"All us kids are doing well in school, "Kid One went on. "And in case you're wondering, we decided to keep Big Chigger's names for us almost out of spite."

"Like Michael Jackson's kid being called 'Blanket,'" G-Man said.

"Or me staying That Thing, at least in the family"

Kid One had an after-school job at Sears and contributed most of his pay to the household budget. Kids Two and Three did odd jobs when they weren't working to clean up the outside. The boys were responsible for the chickens in the new coop beside the barn and the cows fattening on grass in the pasture.

"We figured if we were going to stay here, we might as well return this to the working farm it once was. We even expanded the vegetable garden."

"Several of the neighbors helped. Old Hooter James—you remember him, don't you—gave us a couple of starter cows to rebuild the herd. He's been plowing the fields and mowing the hay for a split in the crops. Turned out to be a pretty good neighbor," Li'l Bit said.

"Does he still smell worse that the dead dog?" Hooter had a well-earned reputation even when I was still in Bubbaville.

Kid One laughed. "Well, we don't let him in the house, and he doesn't ask to come in."

G-Man and I stayed for dinner. One bite of Li'l Bit's chicken and dumplings brought a flood of good memories, no matter how hard I'd painted a totally negative picture of growing up in Bubaville. It hadn't been all bad. Mostly, but not all.

"Not what you expected, was it?" G-Man drove us home to the District.

"Not at all."

"So how do you feel?"

How did I feel? Relieved my mother and the boys had found the guts to go on? Sad that my sister still represented all that was irresponsible in the old family? Of course. Glad I got out? Without a doubt.

"Good. I feel really good."

CHAPTER FORTY-FIVE

THE INTERSTATE KILLER

2002

2002 dragged on with no high-profile cases for either G-Man or me. Contrary to what people outside law enforcement think, most of an FBI profiler's work was routine: paperwork, monitoring open cases, waiting for the next serial something to come along. G-Man specialized in serial killer and rapist crimes; he wasn't an expert on bank robberies, hostage situations, cyber or white-collar crimes. In between cases, he trained new agents and filled out reams of paperwork.

In the ME's office, I autopsied cadavers which had died of natural causes, were victims of domestic violence, or died in vehicular accidents. I was in limbo, because I couldn't hunt with G-Man at home. Even when drug overdoses from batches of bad methadone, heroin, or fentanyl filled our tables, the police weren't overly excited.

"Let the bastards kill each other," one new detective said. "As long as tourists and politicos aren't victims, the brass doesn't break a sweat."

When G-Man was out of town periodically, a dealer would turn up stabbed by a KA-BAR or ice pick. A few died from using drugs heavily laced with fentanyl. You're welcome, Metro PD.

§

I was in the kitchen finishing dinner when G-Man called from the living room. "Doc, you gotta see this."

I carried two bowls of pasta, meatballs, and sausage into the dining room. From the table, we could see the television. G-Man turned up the volume when CNN came back from its commercial pod.

"Police in Tennessee have discovered body parts dumped in trash bins at rest stops along I-40. They believe the killer is working his way eastward. Truckers and other travelers should be on alert when they stop or stay overnight at rest stops."

The news anchor went on to say three bodies, one male and two females, had been found dissected. Police recovered parts wrapped in black trash bags in dumpsters or behind buildings for dozens of miles along the interstate.

"Ah shit. Three similar victims makes him a serial killer." G-Man poured each of us a glass of Pinot Noir. "I hope this isn't another Ted Bundy wannabe."

"More like Jeffrey Dahmer. Bundy decapitated some of his victims, but I don't remember him dismembering the bodies."

"Maybe it's Dahmer meets Hannibal Lecter." G-Man leaned back in his chair, brow furrowed. "Plenty of other lesser-known serial killers dismembered bodies. Back in the 1930s, a guy out in Cleveland butchered a bunch of drifters, cut off their heads, and chopped them up."

"It's just not that common, you have to admit."

"You're right." G-Man pushed a fork-load of pasta into his mouth. "Mm, good."

"Do you know how hard it is to dismember a body? It takes a lot of strength if you don't know where to cut. Bones are incredibly dense."

"You should know." G-Man and I listened to the end of the report. "You cut people up for a living."

"I do not. I don't dissect them. I do autopsies. But, that doesn't mean I don't know where to cut if I wanted to." I spooned shaved Parmesan onto the pasta and dug my fork in. "Betcha we both get assigned to this one."

"Only if this creep crosses state lines or comes toward Washington."

"Or if we get 'loaned out.'"

The thought of working with G-Man on a case as grisly as this one turned me into a wild woman that night. He reached for his pajamas, but I pushed him onto the bad, went down on him until he was hard, and climbed on top where I could control our timing. I came three times before I brought him.

"Where the hell did that come from?" G-Man sprawled across the sheets and panted.

"Guess the idea of us working together was too sexy to ignore." I rolled on my side, one leg across his belly. "Want to do that again?"

"After I rest."

We finished slower the second time. I'd have mounted G-Man again had he not fallen asleep.

§

The Interstate Killer, as the media named him, left behind bodies as he steadily marched into North Carolina. By the end of the first week, the count was four. Another week led to three more bodies discovered in North Carolina and Virginia.

Unlike me, this guy appeared to kill indiscriminately. He found his victims, men and women, vacationers and truckers, along the interstates, killed them somewhere other than where he kidnapped them, and dumped the remains, leaving no discernible clues to his selection process.

"Hi, Doc," G-Man called at work. "You guessed it. I'm leading the profiling team. This has all the earmarks of being as hard a case to crack as the snipers were."

The FBI asked Saw-Bones and me to help. As a result, we soon had parts of several bodies scattered on gurneys and in cold storage. We didn't have much to work with, because the Interstate Killer did a right fine job of giving us only body parts. Most hands were missing, as were the heads. Our task was to match body parts where possible to identify a single victim. It proved difficult. We received a black female body, for example, but no black hands.

"I'm glad I studied different kinds of blades and their marks at the body farm. It's going to come in handy." I took DNA samples and photographed marks.

"Who the hell is this guy?" Saw-Bones looked at a clean cut through a shoulder joint. "He has some knowledge of human anatomy."

"Look here." I pointed at an arm with no hand from another corpse. "He left stutter marks before the final cut. Looks like he wasn't certain where or if he wanted to cut."

"To do a job this thoroughly, he needs a safe place to work without interruption. Otherwise, he risks exposure." Saw-Bones shoved his gurney back in the cooler. "No matter how many times we see the results of the worst of human nature, something this brutal always gets to me."

"We see worse depravity than this all the time." I turned the arm over. I peered at a patch of unmarred skin and wondered if I could use some of the latest techniques to lift the murderer's prints. I tried. Nothing. "He wears gloves."

"I can't see any pattern beyond kidnapping people along an interstate. No pattern except he likes to cut people up. And no other pattern except he has an endless supply of black plastic bags." Saw-Bones threw a glove into the trash.

Body parts continued to trickle in. We used DNA to identify three of what were now eighteen distinct bodies. According to local missing persons' reports, one was a young mother of two moving from Oklahoma to North Carolina to take care of her ailing father. Her babies hadn't been found. Another was a trucker taken from a stop outside Nashville. The latest was a beer delivery man kidnapped near Bristol, Tennessee.

"Could he be practicing to get something right? Like working on his technique?" I understood practicing.

"Could be. If we can figure out what he does with the heads, we might have the answer to that question." Saw-Bones pulled off his apron. "We're done for the night. Time to GTFOH."

"Huh?"

"Get the fuck out of here."

We moved toward the outer doors, switching off the work lights. Safety lights came on automatically and cast a dim glow over the gleaming tables.

"What happened to the children from the female victim?" I locked the door.

"Why don't you ask G-Man?"

I met G-Man for dinner in Adams Morgan that night, where we talked about the case over a glass of wine and steaks. I wasn't in the mood to cook.

"He knows how to cut up a body." I ate a bite of rare steak.

"He could be a doctor. Or a butcher. Someone who has a decent knowledge of anatomy and the right surgical or dissecting tools." G-Man added two pats of butter to his baked potato.

"Have any people gone missing with kids in the car?"

"Why do you ask?" G-Man put his knife and fork down.

"We identified one of the early victims. Her mother said she had two kids with her. We have no children on our tables." I continued eating until I realized G-Man had stopped. "What? Don't tell me there are more missing kids?"

"There's that look again." G-Man stared at me. "When you get upset, really upset, your eyes are narrow and flat."

Flat, huh.

"Well, I'm pissed off. I'd love to get my hands on this bastard."

Oh. you bet I would. Ice pick in the ear felt right.

"So would I."

"Because of the kids?"

"Keep this between us for now. We're looking for seventeen children, all under the age of ten."

My turn to lay my silverware on the table. I had to restrain myself to keep from throwing the knife across the restaurant. I lay it next to my plate and dropped my hands into my lap, where I clutched them until I cut off circulation to my fingers. How could seventeen children go missing and no one figure out why? My eyes narrowed even more.

"I asked Saw-Bones if the killer was keeping trophies. Could he be keeping the children?"

G-Man toyed with his knife, drawing crude body outlines on the table cloth. "We think they're alive, because we haven't found signs he's killed them."

"You've done the profile. Do you have any idea about his motive?" I shoved my plate aside.

"Glad to see you think this monster is male."

"I'm all for equal opportunity serial killers, but like you I really don't see this killer as female."

"Given the brutality and precision of the dismemberments, we're looking for a white male between thirty and forty. He's strong and probably works in a profession where he works with dead animals." G-Man rubbed his temples. "Beyond that, we're waiting for more evidence to turn up."

"Then, he could be a butcher or a hunter."

"He's definitely a butcher, whether he earns his living at it or not." He glanced around the restaurant. "Keep your voice low. We don't want anyone to overhear us."

I agreed. The average diner didn't want to listen to law enforcement talking about blood and guts in a steak house.

CHAPTER FORTY-SIX

ON LOCATION

2002

Four months into the Interstate Killer's multi-state rampage, a farmer out plowing a fallow field he intended to plant with winter wheat uncovered a skeleton. He called the local sheriff, who in turn called the state police, who in turn called the FBI.

"We may have a dumping ground." G-Man called my cell as soon as I got to work.

"Did they find any children?"

"I don't know. I'm heading down to Danville to set up a crisis center. I'll know more when I get there."

"Danville?" I tossed my tote in my locker and reached for a gown.

"It's the closest town to the farm."

"Okay. Let me call you back."

I dropped the call and went to find Saw-Bones. He took one look at my eyes and waved me to a chair. He was on the phone with our primary FBI contact and offered my help. If we had a lot of skeletons, we'd need a portable lab and forensic anthropologists. I listened to his side of the conversation briefly before I started working my phone. Dr. Rigby, who had been the head of the body farm in Tennessee when I was a student, had become my mentor for forensic anthropology before retiring four years earlier. With his departure, Dr. Sandra Warfield, who had shepherded me through my workshop, now ran the farm. We'd kept in touch.

"Sandra, Doc here. You've been following the Interstate Killer, I assume." I gave her a thumb-nail recap of the issues. "What I need are a couple of top forensic anthropologists or pathologists to help sort bones."

"Two of our grads worked on the World Trade Center identification team, but I can't ask them. They suffer in varying degrees with post-traumatic stress."

"I understand."

Sandra suggested three anthropologists who would be good. "When do you need them and for how long?"

"Last week and who knows."

"Where are you setting up?"

"Danville. My husband says there are a couple of motels there, but not much more."

"Text me the name of the motel where you'll be staying. I'll meet you there. You're going to need me." She rang off.

I hadn't expected the leader of the body farm to drop anything and move to Danville, but if she was managing the bones, they would be in good hands.

Saw-Bones finished his call and grinned. "I secured a state-of-the-art mobile lab so you can do most of your work in the field. I'm not sure how many people know this beast exists. You'll love it."

I told him what Sandra said. We didn't discuss loaning me out on this case. No way would anyone keep me back.

"Go home and pack. We'll get by without you. The other pathologists can handle the workload until this is over." Saw-Bones had a distant look in his eyes. Once, he would have been the one heading out to the field instead of me. His responsibilities kept him tethered to the ME's office. He returned from wherever his mind had taken him. "You've got that 'this asshole's mine look.' You won't rest until he's caught."

Or until he's dead.

"Yeah, well. Some killers are too evil to survive. I want this one dead."

"Go get him, tiger."

Little could he know how much I wanted to deliver the death sentence personally.

§

I went first to the garage housing the mobile lab. The amount of equipment packed into something the size of a school bus overwhelmed me. I looked at the printed inventory of supplies and specialized equipment, and saw nothing missing. Three hours after I entered the garage, I walked into my home, picked up Miss Snickers #3, and snuggled with her. I was going to miss this current incarnation, a solid-colored blue kitty. Much as she loved both me and G-Man, she loved the house sitter more. And why not? The house sitter often spent a week at a time spoiling her.

My phone buzzed continually with calls from G-Man, Saw-Bones, and Sandra, all of whom needed immediate answers. Of the three anthropologists, two were available and would join the team before the end of the week.

I plugged Danville into my GPS and pointed one of the ME's cars down I-95. It looked straightforward, but traffic was a bitch. I used the drive time to receive and convey information to my team, some of which would soon be in route. Sandra was on her way from Tennessee, two scientists from the FBI lab in West Virginia, two anthropologists from Alabama and Florida, all were packing for a lengthy field trip. The lab van would be about half a day behind.

G-Man fed me steady updates. "It's definitely a dump site, but we're not sure whose. We think it's the Interstate Killer, but some of the partial skeletons look way older than the few months we know he's been active."

G-Man must have turned away from the phone, because his voice was muffled for a moment. "Hey, don't touch anything. The anthropologists need to see the bones where you found them."

I had images of the farmer and his backhoe digging trenches and scattering evidence. "Did the locals cordon off the area to keep everyone away?"

"Yes."

The state police set up roadblocks around the property and stretched crime-scene tape across each entrance to the field. The farmer and his wife were allowed to stay in their house because it wasn't adjacent to the pasture and because he had to feed his cattle and chickens. The police stationed a patrol car on every country lane within a three-mile radius. They checked drivers and logged license numbers.

"These deputies are pretty good. They're putting a paper on the dashboard of every local car that leaves the area. When the car comes back, they match the license plate to their records."

"Sounds thorough." I swerved around an eighteen-wheeler poking along in the left lane. "Asshole."

"Me?" G-Man asked.

"No, the driver of a semi texting and driving in the fast lane." I was tired of traffic slowdowns, so I flipped on the flashing red light and watched cars scatter to the side of the highway. "How many skeletons have you found?"

"Can't be sure. Maybe four. Two are small. Could be children. No heads, just ribs, vertebrae, and long bones." G-Man muffled the phone again to warn someone who'd wandered too close to the pit. "We haven't touched anything."

"Good. I should be in around six or seven tonight. Shall I meet you at the motel?" I glanced at the clock on the dashboard. I'd lost an entire hour getting around Fredericksburg. At this rate, I might hit rush hour traffic in Richmond.

"Yes. We'll have dinner together."

"Will I meet with the rest of the team tonight?"

"Yes."

Following dinner, the team gathered in a conference room at the Courtyard Hotel. White boards covered with maps and photos of the dump site gave me a decent picture of what we knew. After fifteen minutes of listening to G-Man, I realized we knew damned little. There appeared to be one mass grave and several individual ones. Some bodies had been tossed on the ground and not buried. Predators had stripped all flesh from the unburied and dragged partial skeletons in an ever-expanding radius.

"You'll notice different colored pins on the map. The main dump site is circled in red. Kidnapping points are in blue, body parts not in the dump site in yellow." The trail ran straight across Tennessee into North Carolina before turning north and east into Virginia.

"How early can we get to the pit tomorrow?" Sandra stood in front of a group of photos. "I need better images before anyone begins digging."

Clint Kitchen, the DNA lead from the FBI lab in West Virginia, was the first to answer. "Seven-thirty. We need full daylight."

"We haven't set up work lights, but we can, depending on the hours you need to work," G-Man said. "We ordered several."

"You won't have to send anything off site, because my lab is due in late tonight. We can use it for initial victim identification. I also have the DNA results from the victims we autopsied at my office but whom we haven't identified. If we find the rest of the body parts, we should be able to make some matches."

Clint waved for Sandra and me to remain after the meeting broke up. "Doc, I want to take an inventory of everything in your lab and see what else we need."

"You'll find it's remarkably well stocked."

We divided the tasks among the DNA team, the anthropologists who would recover the bones themselves, and forensic pathologists who would identify cause of death. I headed up the latter team, with Sandra heading up the anthropology group. Clint could handle the DNA testing.

CHAPTER FORTY-SEVEN

STORIES IN THE BONES

2002

Before sunup, Sandra and I joined a convoy of techies, my lab van, and trucks filled with materials to the dump site. We found several large tents erected around the field, the largest protecting the grave site, a smaller one over what would become the autopsy and sorting area.

A state police deputy, maintaining traffic and access control, waved us to a makeshift parking area. We headed to the smaller tent for what would become our daily morning briefing. More introductions of people we hadn't met the night before, identifying who would be assigned to which team, and getting a pep talk from the task force leader, Clark Kent.

"I've had a lifetime of jokes about my name, so spare yourselves the effort. You won't come up with anything original." He paused to glance at the dump site. "I don't have to remind you how important your work is. We must apprehend this guy before he can kill again. You're the best in your fields. It's an honor to work with you. Now, let's get started."

We didn't join hands and pray. We didn't high-five the group. We didn't sing *Kumbaya.* We didn't send up a Marine Corps "Hoo-rah!" We separated into our teams and got to work.

Sandra introduced me to the two forensic anthropologists who had arrived in the middle of the night. The scientist from Alabama rubbed his hands together.

"Holy shit! This is bigger than anything we had at the body farm, isn't it, Dr. Warfield?"

Sandra jerked her head toward the grid. "Welcome to the real world, Tide."

"Tide?" I was lost.

"'Bama grad. They called me 'Tide' at the farm."

"I'm Gator," said the second anthropologist.

"Florida, right?" I shook hands with both men.

"You got that right. What about you?"

"State undergrad, med school at Johns Hopkins"

"Holy shit again." Tide faked a hillbilly drawl. "We got us a certified genius, huh, Gator?"

I led Sandra and Clint, who nearly tripped over my heels like a pair of over-eager puppies, to the forensics van. The driver unlocked the door to the toy store and stepped aside.

"Oh, my God." Clint exhaled a deep breath.

"Holy crap," said Sandra.

I took a book off a shelf and paged through the inventory. Things I took for granted in my lab were neatly arranged in bins and drawers. I wouldn't need scalpels and bone saws used in autopsies on flesh, probably, but we would use the DNA identification equipment immediately. I asked the driver to back the truck closer to the autopsy tent. I wanted it no more than a couple of steps away.

"How much did this sucker cost?" An FBI tech working with Clint joined the group.

"Somewhere between 'higher than my pay grade' and 'holy shit,'" I said.

Tide's voice rose from the grave site. "Do we have sifters? Without digging, I can see lots of fragments. We don't want to miss anything."

The Danville chief of police and the Pittsylvania county sheriff walked up to introduce themselves. Sandra repeated the question about sifters.

"I have one in my trunk," said the country sheriff. "If you need more, we'll borrow them from adjacent jurisdictions."

"We have one in Danville. I'll have it sent out." The chief of police added his support and reached for his phone.

Clark Kent waved the local men into the autopsy tent for a quick update. I left Clint and his team to get acquainted with the lab; Sandra and I walked to the dump site. Forensic anthropologists stretched strings tied to stakes to form a grid. Wherever they spotted bone fragments, they marked locations with colored flags.

"We have a hell of a lot of work to do." Sandra looked at the field of flags covering more than an acre, some flags under the tent, most in the open. "Start with the unprotected fragments. If weather sets in, we don't want to lose anything."

With the anthropologists bending to their jobs, I returned to the autopsy tent to set up tables and stack empty plastic storage containers, because the bones would need to be sorted and attached to as many single bodies as possible.

"What?" G-Man moved beside me.

"What do you mean?"

"You have that look again. It's as if you can imagine the killer standing in front of you."

And me holding my ice pick. I'd decided on the way down that the KA-BAR was too quick. I could wield a mean pick to inflict maximum pain before the death thrust.

I faced G-Man. "Don't you? Don't you wish he were standing here? Wouldn't you like to take him down?"

G-Man turned away. "I've never seen you like this."

"Like what?"

"Like you want revenge."

"I do. I want him dead on my table." I put an arm around his waist. "I look like this more often than you can imagine. Ask Saw-Bones. I used to freak him out, but he's gotten used to me. Remember, we haven't worked this close since the bomber brought down the Avianca jet in Puerto Rico."

I received a hug in return, but it felt ever so slightly different from others. Oh, shit. Did I reveal too much? The last thing I needed was G-Man to go all wiggy on me.

By the time a lunch truck from Danville showed up shortly after noon, we had the site organized and each team heads down doing its job. I gazed over the grid lines. Each box had a covered bin in it; each grid was numbered. Sandra and I already had three such boxes in our tent waiting for sorting. Using one of the four worktables, we laid out bones from one box to piece together. A quick inspection from Tide told us the bones were mixed up and belonged to more than one corpse. He sorted pieces by function: arms, ribs, legs, pelvises. Still no hands or heads.

"Just like the autopsies I did back in Washington." I grabbed a sandwich and bottle of water from the truck and sat on a folding chair. "What the hell is he doing the hands and heads?"

§

Clint closed the first week by identifying DNA from four partial skeletons. We had distinct profiles but no names. The task force leader assigned a young female agent to notify the jurisdictions where people had disappeared to secure hair and saliva samples for cross-indexing. The more we had on hand, the quicker we could make positive identifications. The local police would interface with the families.

Deputy sheriffs expanded the original perimeter by walking an unmarked grid to see if there were more grave sites. More skeletons turned up a quarter of a mile away. I walked over and stared into a gully where bones jutted out of a dry stream bed.

"Fuck." I glanced at Sandra, whose face said she agreed.

"I see four pelvises." She scrambled down the embankment and worked her way around the bone pile. "All female. Photograph and collect as many as you can," she said to Tide, "in case the rains predicted for the weekend actually fall."

We'd had several scares, but so far autumn rains had missed us. I called out to two men to move a sifter and several bins to the edge of the gully. I looked around for G-Man before finding him with Clark Kent.

"Hey guys, we just located another bone pile over in a stream bed. From the looks of the ground, the stream handles runoff after heavy rains." I nodded toward Sandra's people who were already taking pictures and rushing the collection process.

Clark Kent watched more men scurrying away with empty bins. "What's the hurry?"

"Rain in the forecast, for one. Two, I don't think the bones were dumped there. Looks more like the bodies washed down from upstream and were trapped in debris piles. We'll know more when we get them on the table."

He looked skeptical. "Are you an expert on topography and water flow?"

"I was raised on a farm. We had runoff channels at the edge of our property and in the nearby woods. I grew up sifting for 'buried treasure.'"

"Find anything?" The task force leader wasn't convinced.

"Only a dead dog."

§

G-Man headed back to the District on Saturday to prepare for a Monday meeting; I worked through the weekend. The more unique individuals we identified, the more complicated the picture became. We set up two more tables when the volume overwhelmed our initial setup. Because the skeletons were scrambled, we continued laying out bones by type. We tagged each with a code indicating location where it was recovered. Gator and I set aside any with cut marks. If we could identify the tools the murderer used, we would have one more essential answer.

I worked alone in the tent for most of a rainy Saturday and nearly overnight into a stormy Sunday morning, eyes half-focused, seeking patterns in the bones laid out on the tables. I stepped back and simply stood. Only my eyes moved. That's when I saw it: a group of small bone fragments than had made no sense when we found them. We'd assumed the murderer pulverized a body, whether out of frustration or for some other cause. He hadn't. He'd killed a pregnant woman.

I wiped a place clean and began reassembling a child. I had a partial skull, shattered, but identifiable once it was pieced together. Tiny ribs, arm bones and even fingers fit.

"Son of a bitch." Rage built. My hands trembled for a second or two until I controlled my emotions. I wanted the bastard to die as horrible death as anyone I'd killed, including the rapist. I called G-Man.

"A pregnant woman? That doesn't fit the profile."

I sensed I wasn't alone by the time I'd pieced most of the tiny body together. "He had to know the woman was pregnant when he kidnapped her." I didn't turn.

Clark Kent stood behind me. "How far along was she?"

"Thirty-two or -three weeks, I think. This baby would have been viable."

Clark Kent rubbed his eyes. "He's more of a monster than we thought."

"How many kids do you have?"

"Four."

"Always hard when it's kids and women, isn't it?"

He pinched the bridge of his nose. "I have to look at our list. It's possible we can identify the fetus, at least. Let me know if you can put together the woman's skeleton." He walked away, shoulders slumped enough to show how human he was.

"A fetus?" Sandra had looked for me at the hotel. When she didn't see either me or my car, she came out to the site. She stood aside and stared at my work. "Where are you with the mother?"

She knew I'd go after the mother next. Based on where the fetus was found, I struck gold with a partial skeleton from an adjacent grid. As soon as Clint came in, I'd have him process samples for a DNA match.

"My God. Look at the damage done to these ribs." Sandra pointed to a shattered ribcage. "He chopped this woman to pieces."

I ground my teeth. "Son of a bitch used a hatchet or a cleaver based on the size of the cut marks. The fetus may have been partially dismembered in the womb, because I haven't found all the pieces."

"I've never seen such brutality concentrated on one body."

"Unfortunately, I have."

Sandra put on a gown over her sweater and jeans and pulled on gloves. "Let's see how much of the mother we can find."

We worked in silence until I lost track of time. When the team arrived, we had most of a female skeleton pieced together. I gave the forensic anthropologists an update before Sandra sent them back the same grid box for a second search. Clint took samples to the lab van. We hoped the woman was the baby's mother.

Knowing that we put together the two nearly complete skeletons energized the group. I asked the autopsy team to reexamine all pelvises and rib cages for signs of irrational violence. By noon we had two more, both men. Over sandwiches and hot coffee, we recapped what we'd learned.

"We don't know what sets him off, but proof of his anger is on these tables. He destroys some of his victims nearly entirely." Gator waved a Reuben sandwich. "Think about it. If he pulverizes large portions of bodies, he has to have a place where blood won't be noticed. And he had to have something he can use to transport crushed bodies."

"Yeah. Crushed bodies can bleed out pretty quickly if he cuts arteries or ruptures the spleen or heart." Tide turned to Clark Kent. "What do you think he's driving?"

"Hey, you're on a roll, Tide. What do you think?" Gator didn't give Clark Kent a chance to answer.

Boos came from all around. Gator smiled and took a bow. He'd worked hard to fit "Roll Tide" into the conversation. Collegiate rivalries had sprung up at the beginning of football season, with chants of "Roll Tide" or "Go, Gators" echoing across the dump site. Grads from other schools showed up in school colors, bringing an illusion of normalcy to an otherwise grim and dark task.

"Hey, Doc. Why don't you wear school colors?"

"Oh, but I do. I graduated from State before I went to Johns Hopkins. I wear surgical green in honor of Hopkins."

I wasn't going to get off easily. I had the feeling I'd find a sweatshirt from State on my table in the near future.

"Okay, back to the question," Clark Kent said. "Anyone have ideas on what kind of vehicle this creep is driving?"

"Some kind of a van."

"Some kind of delivery truck."

"A hearse." My voice was quiet, but everyone gaped at me. "A hearse."

Clark Kent leaped from his chair, cell clapped to his ear. "Hey, G-Man. Get the team in Quantico to check all funeral homes in a one-hundred-mile radius from the dump site. We may be looking for a hearse. Also look into delivery trucks and vans.

"Yeah, I know. It's pretty broad, but he dismembers bodies, so he has to have a place to work.—

"Good idea. Butcher shops, deer processors, and taxidermists, too. When are you getting back?—

"Okay. Check in with me throughout the day. See you tonight in the war room." Clark Kent returned to the tent. We'd overheard what he had ordered checked out.

"More likely a deer processor around here," a Henry county deputy said. "All of us hunt. I'll get a list."

CHAPTER FORTY-EIGHT

BALLOON KID

2002

"Hey, Doc. Got a minute?" The Danville chief of police stood in the doorway of the tent. The morning was cold and getting colder, but we kept one flap of the tent open at all times. We had space header run by generators to keep the chill off, but we were always cold.

"Sure, chief. What's up?" I stripped off my gloves.

"Um, I need a favor. Can you step outside?" He edged backwards to let me pass.

We grabbed coffee and settled on the rear bumper of his squad car. "We don't have a medical examiner, and our coroner is a dentist."

"This doesn't have anything to do with the Interstate Killer, does it?"

"No. A kid came in early this morning. I need someone to perform an autopsy."

"And you figured because I'm from the District ME's office, I'd know how to do one." I ducked back into the tent. "Hey, guys. The chief has an emergency not connected with this case. I'll be back as soon as I can."

Shit! I hated to work on a kid. They didn't deserve to die. Their parents, certainly, but I'd never met an evil kid. I listened while the chief gave me all he knew. "About ten-year-old male. Right now, it's death by cause unknown."

"Isn't that what I usually get to say?" I sipped my rapidly cooling coffee.

"Yeah, but I want to know the cause. There's a sicko out there."

"The world is full of sickos, chief. Sometimes we find them, sometimes they find us."

The chief drove quickly but without lights or sirens, because this really wasn't an emergency. What little traffic on the highway moved aside when his car crowded bumpers. The body had been found off a rural road some twenty miles west. Badly decomposed. He'd never seen anything like it. He led me into the coroner's office where I found scrubs, booties, gloves, and a head cover. I could smell the child. I asked the chief to help lift the body bag onto the table. The contents shifted. I heard sloshing liquid.

"You might want to step out. This is going to be really messy," I said.

My stomach flipped when I unzipped the body bag. Made of heavy black plastic, these bags usually sealed in smells and kept liquids from leaking. No way anyone wants to face a pissed-off transport EMT with a ripped bag. Cleaning a "bus" takes more scrubbing than most of us want to think about.

The chief retched into a trash can. He wiped his mouth, swirled some water, spat, and applied a thick layer of Vick's Vapor Rub under his nose.

"A little late, huh?" I reached for the jar and greased my upper lip. It helped a little, but the stench of decomposition was already in my sinuses. I don't know why I bothered. I'd smell this kid all day.

"What the shit killed him?"

I turned the corpse over to look at the back. White kid. His pathetic little body was broken. His belly was distended. I saw abrasions on his hands, knees, and buttocks. Blood had pooled under the skin where he lay after death.

I pulled off my gloves and flipped through a rudimentary report for a description of the crime scene. The trucker who found the body hadn't touched it, but the highway patrol officer had nudged it onto its back. I tossed the report aside. "The body's been moved. No pictures of where he was found. Wonder what the hell caused these weird bruises."

I pointed at several broad marks, sharp on one edge, smoother as the bruise moved outward. I used a scalpel to make the Y-incision. The chest cavity was full of congealed blood.

"What the hell?" I heard rather than saw the chief bend over the barrel again. I was in for a morning where vomited coffee stink mingled with rotting-kid-stink. I mopped blood and insect larvae from the chest cavity.

"I have to open his abdomen to see what caused this bloat."

I had never seen such damage done to internal organs. Even a cursory examination revealed ruptures in his colon and lower intestine. His liver was bruised. One kidney was so damaged I couldn't immediately identify it. The kid's abdomen had burst like a balloon.

"Jesus. This kid was tortured." The chief mopped a pale, sweaty face.

"Where I grew up, we'd have kids and men get liquored up on a Saturday night. They'd joyride and wreak havoc on someone they didn't like if they had a mind to." I moved the child onto his back.

"Nowadays, they're usually high on home-cooked meth," the chief said.

"Same results, different substances."

I'd seen a lot of evil done to people over the years in my lab. I'd done some of it myself, but what this kid went through was the worst ever, worse even than the charred toddler from the plane crash. That child still haunted my dreams, but his death was instantaneous. The body before me was alive when the damage was done. Something had been shoved up the colon and torn it to shreds.

I lifted ruined organ after ruined organ from the destroyed torso, weighed them, noted damage. and asked the chief to photograph everything. I needed his help, because I couldn't manage the camera and the body. I found tearing around the anus but no metal shavings. No wood. No glass. This kid wasn't raped with the usual objects: crowbar, wooden bat, bottle.

"Am I looking for a sadist?"

"Possibly. Did you happen to notice his face and ears? We took lots of photos but never talked about his face."

"Whaddya mean?" The chief wasn't following. "Lots of damage. Broken nose. Scrapes. Swelling. What am I missing?"

He'd asked the right question. I looked for a reference book I hoped would be in the coroner's office. It was. I found what I wanted, thumbed through the index, and opened to the right pages. Laying the book on the desk, I pointed to a picture.

"Down Syndrome?"

"Think about his face. Slanted eyes. Fairly flat cheekbones. Low-slung ears. Where did they find him?"

"Out off Smith's Store Road. Kinda a crossroads with a few failed businesses, some houses. There's an abandoned shop out there."

"What kind?" I asked.

"Auto repair." The chief rubbed his chin. Some color had returned.

"Back to the body." I turned and trotted into the autopsy room. I peered again at the kid's face, his ruptured colon, the perforations on his internal organs and the large bruise on his back.

"You're looking for one or two men who have access to an auto or truck repair shop." I pointed to the pattern of bruises. "Those probably came from a truck tire. My gut says the boy was thrown away on a pile of tires while he was still alive."

The chief leaned in. "Yeah, could be a truck tire made the bruise. Any other ideas?"

I knew how people in rural areas talked about people with mental retardation. Brothers, fathers, or uncles who hated the kid would see his condition as a reflection of something wrong with them. Kinda like Big Chigger calling me That Thing because I didn't look like him or Li'l Bit.

I didn't know if people around the crossroads would recognize the physical symptoms of Down Syndrome. "Have your deputy see if anyone knows of a 'retard' who went missing."

"You grew up in a rural area, didn't you?" The chief said.

"I did. Bigger than your crossroads, but it had the same kind of people. This kid had to be gotten rid of."

"But what about the initial ruptures?"

"Look for a garage with a high-pressure air pump." I turned the kid over again. I scraped the inside of his anus with a cotton swab and sniffed. "We could send this out for a lab test, but my nose says it's a combination of feces and grease or oil."

The chief looked at me with even more respect than he had before. "How the hell did you come up with that?"

"Hell, I don't know if I'm right, but it's a theory. Air leaves no trace. If they blew this kid up through his anus, he'd pop like a balloon. It was a very painful death." I threw my gloves into the trash.

"These are just theories, but if you find the guys, they'll squeal like pigs."

I covered the poor little body and rolled the gurney into a refrigerator just big enough to hold it.

"You know, sometimes I wish we had a vigilante who would hunt these types down," the chief said. "Give them a dose of their own medicine. Oh shit. I didn't say that."

"I didn't hear a thing."

And I couldn't do a thing.

CHAPTER FORTY-NINE

EYES WITHOUT A FACE

2002

The chief dropped me at my hotel so I could wash away some of the dead-kid stink. No amount of scalding water, however, could remove the smell in my nostrils. I pulled a State sweatshirt over a fresh long-sleeved tee. As I had suspected, one day shortly after our discussion about wearing school colors, I returned to the hotel to find the sweatshirt neatly folded at the end of my bed. G-Man swore he had nothing to do with it.

I caught a ride back to the dump site with one of the FBI techs who had worked almost all night. I was in no mood for idle chatter; I'm glad he didn't say anything. I sat as far away from him as possible, because I was afraid I still smelled.

Autumn had given way to bare trees, the last of the dry leaves covering roads and ground. The team wanted to clear the site before winter set in with its even shorter days, cold rain, and penetrating winds. The dump site yielded fewer and fewer remains.

The immensity of the Interstate Killer's rage was getting to all of us. We needed a break in the case or a long weekend away. I was more exhausted than I'd ever been. Taking revenge on the dead child I'd autopsied wasn't possible, because the police would have no trouble finding who killed him. I couldn't solve the problem, but someone would talk, and talk soon.

The monster we sought, this Interstate Killer, was the challenge I needed, but I was stuck in the midst of the investigation. No way could I slip away like I did so many times in Washington or Baltimore to hunt. With a large number of kills to my credit, and no longer living in fear of Big Chigger, I wondered if I was I losing my edge. I'd taken revenge for so many people. What would it be like to find and dispatch one more? If I could hunt, would I take revenge for the victims of the Interstate Killer or the one who popped the kid or both?

Was I no longer an active serial killer but a retired serial killer? The idea was disconcerting. A huge chuck of my secret identity was tied up with my calling. If I was no longer a serial killer, what the hell was I? I rededicated myself to my legitimate work until I could work this conundrum out.

Sandra quizzed me on the autopsy. "I can't imagine what kind of monster would blow up a kid."

I stared off in space for a moment or two. "Someone in the kid's family did it." I told her I suspected the boy had Down Syndrome. "Back country folks would see him as a stain on the family. I'm surprised he wasn't 'disappeared' when he was a baby."

Gator stopped sorting ribs. "That's ridiculous. You can't 'disappear' a child today. We have laws to protect them."

"Laws work when people acknowledge and obey them. Otherwise, they might as well be written on toilet paper."

"I know, but…" Gator got no further.

"Look, where I grew up, more than one baby 'died in its sleep' over the decades. Had there been the kind of autopsies we can do today, coroners would likely as not have found suffocation."

"Hard to believe," Gator said.

Sandra broke in. "He's not 'country,' Doc. Big-city boys have different kinds of monsters to deal with."

"Don't I know it," I said.

I walked over to Gator's table where he'd pieced together a male torso. The pelvis had been shattered, but he'd salvaged much of it. Broken ribs, clavicles in three pieces each, vertebrae dislocated from the spine.

"The damage is all post-mortem." Gator picked up a rib. "See, cut marks but no sign of healing."

"Do the cut marks match the others?" They looked similar. I'd need to see them under a microscope before I could be certain.

"What was done to the bones screams murderous frenzy. This body was attacked and crushed much like the pregnant woman and her fetus were." Gator ground his teeth.

"Why are some skeletons virtually destroyed when others were barely touched?" Sandra asked. "It doesn't make sense."

"If the murderer is looking for the perfect something, whatever he deems imperfect could send him into a rage, culminating in violent destruction." Gator glued another bone fragment onto the pelvis.

Sandra stared at the bones on her table. "What kind of perfection?"

I shrugged. The shattered skeletal remains had to have something in common, but what? The answer was in the bones; we hadn't asked the right questions.

Sandra had finished gluing a ribcage together when a black FBI Suburban hurtled down the road and skidded to a stop alongside our autopsy tent. Waving away a cloud of dust and crushed leaves, Gator, Sandra, and I dashed to the car, Tide a couple of steps behind. G-Man threw open his door and shouted, "We found a trash bag." He picked it up. We heard dry rattles.

Gator carried the bag into the tent; Sandra and I moved tubs of unmatched bones onto the dirt floor. Under the vigilant eyes of the entire team, he cut open the bag and displayed its contents. "Hands. The missing hands."

"Oh, my God." Sandra bent over the table. She lifted several from the bag. "We have wedding rings."

Clark Kent demanded photos as soon as possible. The DNA team would take samples to match to other body parts. Many hands showed signs of mutilation, twisted fingers, and broken metacarpals. Maybe my mojo wasn't completely gone after all. I wanted to kill the bastard.

Sandra pulled me aside. She scrutinized my expression before she asked if I was all right.

I shook knots from my neck and shoulders and tried to relax my facial muscles. "I'm going to be fine."

"Why don't you go back to the hotel and get some rest? You've barely left the site since we arrived." Sandra put a hand on my shoulder. "You don't have to be here every minute, you know."

I picked up a camera and ran off a series of digital images for Clark Kent. "You couldn't drag me away from here if you tried."

My fatigue vanished. Finding the hands brought a renewed rush of adrenaline. Gator had proven himself the best at identifying bones by sex when possible. He sorted hands by size. Large arthritic hands we decided were most likely male; smaller, more delicate hands, female. Sandra and Clark Kent moved those with rings to a separate table. After thoroughly examining, photographing, and tagging each one, Sandra removed the rings, placed them in sealed evidence bags, and gave them to the team leader. I sent the pictures to his e-mail account. Clint took the bags and all but ran to the portable DNA lab.

The lab housed our files: DNA, police reports, crime scene photos. From where I leaned over a table of female hands I could look out the open tent flap and see Clark Kent shuffling file folders. He set aside a dozen.

I grouped five left hands together. On three, distal and proximal phalanges showed deliberate breaks, the joints between them dislocated, the finger bones themselves in multiple pieces. "The Interstate Killer tortures some of his victims before killing them."

Tide came over for a closer look. "Pretty sure he pulled these out of joint before breaking them." He pointed to several with excessive damage.

I thought back over the number of missing children. If these were mothers trying to protect their children, I could understand the damage.

"Hey, Gator. Any children's bones?" The lack of any trace from the children remained an enigma. If he was torturing them as well, I wished the worst kind of death on him.

Preferably one by my own hands.

"Nothing even close. Several male hands most likely belonged to physical laborers, athletes, maybe even boxers, but nothing small enough to be a child." Gator held up a fairly intact hand. "Look at the arthritis in this poor guy. He had to have been in chronic pain."

Bony knots between every finger joint revealed a man who had injured his hand frequently. Like many of the farmers where I grew up, if you broke a finger or toe, someone would pull it back into place, tape it up in a makeshift splint, and send you back to work. Gator's arthritic hand could have belonged to Big Chigger, or Junior, had he lived long enough or done any physical work.

Clark Kent returned to the autopsy tent. "I called the local jurisdictions for descriptions of rings. We should have several by tomorrow."

The anthropologists and forensic pathologists bobbed their heads like those old-fashioned drinking birds kids won at fairs. I laughed.

"What?"

"Huh?"

"We look like those silly toy birds that dipped their plastic beaks into water and bobbed up. It struck me funny." I blushed. I wasn't normally given to levity at times like this. Acerbity, to be certain, but not levity.

"Guess we all need a laugh. Let's stop early, have dinner, and get a night's rest. We'll make better progress in the morning." Clark Kent took three steps toward the opening in the tent when another black Suburban roared down the road, an FBI agent at the wheel, horn honking madly. "Guess we don't stop."

All the scientists lined up to see what he had. The driver slammed out of the SUV the instant it came to a complete stop. "Another bag. Much heavier." He opened the back of the van.

Tide and Gator elbowed him aside. The two men hoisted the bag and carefully carried it into the autopsy tent. They set it on the last empty table. "You keep finding stuff like this, and we're going to need bigger tables."

Tide cut it open with a pair of scissors. The smell rose like a miasma, filling the tent. My eyes watered.

"Skulls. A dozen or more." Sandra said before I could utter a word. "And what looks like parts of two heads with flesh still on them."

I carried one head to a hastily cleared spot at the end of the hands' tables. Female. Face smashed in. Frenzy again, only this time recent. "This head is only a few days old, I think. Sandra, do you see any predation or insect infestation here?"

The leader of the body farm poked and prodded. "No animal

predation. No sign of human predation, either. Either this guy is eating his victims, or he's carving the flesh from the bone skillfully enough to avoid leaving a trace." She reached for a pair of tweezers. "Dead fly larvae. Not yet in the pupa stage. Something interrupted the development. If I had to guess, he left this head lying around for a day or so until maggots appeared. Then…" She peered closely at the larva in her tweezers. "Christ. He froze the head."

"We're looking for a site with a freezer large enough to hold bodies." G-Man shouted to the field investigation team. "Either a mortuary or a butcher shop."

"Not a mortuary," Tide yelled. "They don't freeze bodies."

Gator finished pulling skulls from the bag and lined them up. Hollow eye sockets mocked us, as did lipless grins. He set the bag on the ground. It clunked softly. He reached in and pulled out what looked like two marbles.

"What the hell are these?" He turned the objects over in his hand. "Do we know if any of the missing persons had prosthetic eyes?"

When he held one up, G-Man and I had our answer. "They're eyes without a face. Our guy is a taxidermist."

CHAPTER FIFTY

DOMINOES

2002

The sheriff turned all of his deputies, all five of them, loose to visit every taxidermist within a fifty-mile radius. Three days of searching and knocking on doors turned up nothing. Was the taxidermist idea another dead end?

We gathered in the war room at the hotel after dinner. I'd miss this team; we'd grown close over the weeks we'd spent digging and sifting dirt, cataloguing bones, and assembling skeletons. The last to arrive was the sheriff. Odd, because he was usually the first to arrive and the last to leave.

"I'm missing a deputy," he said even before he shut the door behind him. "He hasn't checked in since a call in the middle of the afternoon. He went to visit the last place on his list."

Clark Kent frowned. He stood in front of the map. "What sector was his?" Each deputy had a specific area assigned to him, so no one would waste time overlapping efforts. Or skip an area.

The sheriff tapped a thick finger on the map. "He was right outside Martinsville. Smaller town than Danville, but with lots of empty buildings and an extended rural community surrounding it. I'm going to drive out there. I'll call later."

"Probably took off early," Clint said.

"No, he wouldn't without checking in first," the sheriff said. He walked to the door and left.

Each team updated Clark Kent on its status. From the positive reports, it looked like we would wrap up the dump site by the end of the week.

I was headed to our room when I saw G-Man and Clint huddled over a piece of paper. I stopped in mid-stride.

"What?" I didn't like their expressions.

"Let's go to the bar next door." G-Man steered me through the automatic doors.

We sat in a booth at the far corner of the nearly empty bar, ordered drinks, and waited while Clint laid several DNA charts on the table. He looked at G-Man who looked at me. Clint's assistant had run DNA on all skeletal fragments to match them with the missing people. He had found a familial match with one set. G-Man cleared his throat.

"Several weeks ago, police in Greensboro, North Carolina, located an abandoned tractor-trailer. When they ran the plates, they found out it had been reported stolen. No one had heard from the driver, who had an untarnished record. One of the local FBI agents, who'd seen reports on a kidnapped trucker and probable victim of the Interstate Killer, decided to check it out."

I'd done the autopsy on an unidentified male before the dump site had been discovered. That torso was locked safely in the coolers back at the ME's office. Saw-Bones and I initially thought he might be the missing trucker, but without a name to put with the body, he remained a John Doe. According to the FBI, the trucker was Eric "Rick" Carter, a regular guy his fellow truckers said.

"The agent called Clark Kent after he found blood traces on the door and front seat." Clint picked up the narrative. "Long story short, we had a crime scene team go over everything. They found hair from a female as well as a male."

Clint shifted the charts to give me a better view. He pointed to the results of samples from the truck itself. Definitely one female and one male. He pulled another sheet from his pocket. "We matched the male DNA with your torso back in D.C. and with one of the skulls."

"That's great news. Positive ID?" I asked.

"Yes," G-Man said, "but there's more. Go on, Clint."

"We matched familial DNA to you. Remember, we ran DNA on everyone on the task force to rule out cross-contamination. I tested your sample. I'd swear in a court of law the female is related to you. Most likely your sister." Clint slid a pair of test results across the table.

I couldn't believe what I was hearing. I wanted to shout that the evidence must be wrong, but I knew how thorough Clint was with his testing protocols.

"There's even more," Clint said. "That fetal skeleton–it belongs to the woman you reassembled."

"And the DNA's a match to me, too." The statement came out as flat as I felt.

Clint and G-Man nodded.

"I called Li'l Bit this afternoon. She thought Princess might have been pregnant when she left, but she didn't know for sure." G-Man reached across the table and took my hand.

I stopped listening. I couldn't take in another thought. I may have despised my sister for her crappy self-destructive behavior when we were growing up, but I never wished her dead. She'd done nothing to me. Really.

G-Man held my hand and squeezed. "I'm so sorry."

I stared out at nothing. The bar vanished into the darkness that came with this new knowledge. I wanted to wallow in pain and sorrow. I wanted to talk to my mother and see how she was taking the news. I should have been the one to tell Li'l Bit, but I found myself grateful G-Man had already done so.

A commotion in the parking lot snapped me out of my trance: cars pulling out, horns honking. G-Man threw some money on the table, and we bolted outside. Two of the Suburbans were already on the move. G-Man flagged down the last one and threw himself in the shotgun seat.

"You stay here."

He slammed the door before I could grab the handle. The car spun away. I watched G-Man wave the driver to leave me behind. Clint took my arm and steered me into the war room.

"We're not field agents. Let's wait until they call or come back."

I had to go from finding that my sister was lost forever to being a scientist in a matter of minutes. And being dumped by G-Man. I should have been riding with him. I packed my emotions into a box and slammed the lid, much like we'd done with the skeletons.

Clint and I took up residency in the war room along with Gator, who'd been reading in his room. Two hours passed. Sandra wandered in and paced. I remained frozen in my chair. I couldn't turn off the idea that my dead sister was a shattered skeleton we'd worked on. I had put her back together without knowing who she was. Her baby, too.

I stared at my hands, so skilled at assembling pieces of puzzles. They lay idle in my lap. My brain, on the other hand, churned. The more I thought about Princess, the more I wished she'd had the guts I'd had and gotten out earlier. Her life, except for her three boys living with Li'l Bit, had been a total waste. I hoped she'd found happiness with her trucker at last. Midnight came and went before one by one the Suburbans returned.

"Well?" Clint asked before Sandra could. "Did you find the deputy?"

G-Man rubbed tired eyes. "We did. He's dead. It looks like he stumbled onto the killer's trail when he was making a routine check on an amateur taxidermist not quite an hour from here. The sheriff found his car parked in the drive of a residential house. A plain old brick ranch. Nothing remarkable. He checked a large garage or barn in the back where he found the deputy's body, which had been pulled inside the door. He also found a commercial-grade standing freezer, a smaller chest freezer, and tables clean but stained with blood."

"How did he die?" I couldn't see this young deputy, this little pup of a man, mixing it up with a wanted killer.

"He was stabbed in the back with a skinning knife," G-Man said.

"Oh, man." Clint's expression made me think he secretly wanted to be a field agent instead of one of the best DNA experts in the FBI.

"On one side of the garage was a complete taxidermy shop. Not only did this guy mount deer, he also mounted fish."

"Why is this important?"

No one answered my question.

"What was in the house was more important." G-Man the Unfazed was fazed. I wanted to fire questions at my husband like bullets from an Uzi, but I knew enough to let him work the words out at his own pace. He took a deep breath.

The inside of the house was spotless. Not what he expected from someone as ruthless and cold hearted as the Interstate Killer. Shelves lined the walls of the living room and main bedroom.

Dolls of all kinds sat next to stuffed human heads.

"I can barely wrap my brain around what this guy did. He displayed mounted adult and children's heads like they were trophies."

"Male and female heads?" Sandra asked.

"No. Only female."

"What about the taxidermist? Did you find him?" Clint asked.

"We did. Clark Kent has him in custody," G-Man said. "The guy didn't put up a fuss at all. We broke in and found him in the living room holding his wife's hand. He looked tired and, in a funny way, relieved we'd found him."

The murderer's story was nothing like G-Man's profile. Yes, he was a white male, but not in his thirties. Closer to mid-fifties, he lived with his wife in a pin-neat, normal-looking house. Except for the human heads.

"What did his wife say?" It didn't seem possible she wasn't aware of the crime spree. She had to have known what kind of monster her husband was. "Was she his partner?"

"Not in the traditional sense. She had no idea what her husband was doing."

"Really?" I didn't believe a word of it. Of course, the people I worked with had no idea about my extracurricular activities, either.

"Wives know what their husbands are doing, just like husbands know what their wives are doing," Sandra said.

"His wife has no idea about anything. She had a massive stroke two decades ago, according to her husband, and hasn't spoken since. He's her sole caregiver." G-Man massaged his temples. "He's been trying to reach her through dolls. When they didn't provoke a response, he moved on to live dolls. He kept the children alive for her to play with. When she didn't respond, he killed them and preserved their heads."

I shivered. No way my vivid imagination could have created this scenario. All this time we were looking for a man who loved his wife and wanted her to be happy?

"But what about the rage we saw in some of the skeletons?" Tide wandered in.

"He was pretty skilled at mounting deer, but he had to learn new techniques to mount human flesh. Fish made a good substitute, because scales have to be handled differently from fur. They're much more delicate. When he turned to humans, he practiced on men he kidnapped. When he ruined a specimen—his word, not mine—he flew into a frenzy and smashed his work. But the more he worked mounting fish and human heads, the better he became."

"I know amateur taxidermists back in Alabama. When they want a perfect mount, they cover the object with Vaseline before slathering on dentist's alginate," Tide said.

"What's that?" Gator asked.

"The stuff they use for temporary crowns. My friend would make a cast of the subject and use it to cut carving foam like you get in high-end camera cases. Finally, he'd stretch the preserved skin over the foam."

"That's just what this guy did."

"Does this guy have a name?" Sandra asked.

"Jackson Grimsley."

"We thought he'd be hiding in the mountains somewhere," Gator said, "not living down the highway in plain sight in Martinsville."

"Did you count the heads?" Gator asked. "I mean, do we have any idea how many people he killed? Over what period of time?"

"Well, he didn't keep written records." Clark Kent massaged his temples. He frowned. "He began a couple of years after his wife's head was hit by a Mac truck. His description of her condition, not mine. That puts him beginning to kill around 1990."

"Jeez." Clint sucked in a deep breath. "If he killed at least once a year, that would give him a body count of over forty victims. We haven't found them all."

Clark Kent pushed himself out of his chair. "We won't. He said he dumped them all over interstates and back roads, in pastures, pig sties, and rivers. Not that we need every body, but it would help families who are still in limbo about their missing loved ones get—"

"Don't say 'closure,'" Tide cut in.

"—answers, Tide. I was going to say answers." Clark Kent waved and left the room.

"Doc, this guy was as normal as you and I are," G-Man said. "To look at him, you'd never know that he was insane. He won't go to trial. He's not competent."

"Except in killing. He was more than competent there." Sandra followed Clark Kent out of the room.

In a way, the Interstate Killer was a soul brother. I hid in plain sight. Since the murderer lived in a normal neighborhood and had a normal life, our connectedness was stronger than I could have imagined.

"Where will the FBI take the heads?" My job wasn't over.

"To the main lab in West Virginia. I assume you'll want to finish there?" He looked at me, his brow furrowed. "Or can you turn the final work over to other experts?"

He should have known better. Of course, I'd lead the autopsy team.

"We found children's bodies neatly wrapped and stacked in the chest freezer and six adult bodies in the standing freezer. Five women, one man. I think our presence in his backyard spooked him. Once we'd found his dump site, he couldn't get rid of the remaining bodies."

The next morning, the FBI pathologists, Sandra, Gator and I drove to Martinsville. Clint followed in my van, so we could do some basic identification at the site. A large refrigerated truck was on the way. We'd pack the heads and any bodies or body parts for transport to the lab.

I steeled myself when I walked into the living room. Glassy eyes stared unblinking from the preserved faces. They looked so real. I walked over to touch one. Mortician's makeup kept the faces looking life-like. I shuddered. The men had been right; I didn't see many adult heads.

"Where is the wife?"

"She's been taken to a hospital for observation," G-Man said. "She'll never see her husband again."

I walked along the macabre trophy room. Six heads from the end I recognized Princess. I reached out to touch her cheek. So lifelike, so dead.

I started screaming. Once I started, I couldn't stop.

CHAPTER FIFTY-ONE

EPILOGUE

2004, two years later

The fact you're reading this means I'm in a place where I can't hurt anyone again. It also means you found the clues I left about the existence of my kill books. You may never understand why I turned to killing, except I felt compelled to remove people who hurt people who couldn't stand up for themselves, couldn't protect themselves. I killed strangers when I really wanted to kill my old man. I accept that now.

I had a ripping good run for a long time. I knew before the first kill no one would ever catch me. Night after night I'd lie in bed thinking about past and future kills. I planned each one step by step. Well, most of them anyway. I learned patience. And patience made each kill divinely satisfying, deliciously exciting. Planning and execution almost canceled each other out, but not quite. Execution was always the better part.

You're going to analyze me to see if I was a sociopath or a psychopath, but I never cared for labels. Since I'll never go to trial, labels are irrelevant.

I'm uncomfortable writing about my life. I spent most of it building walls, packing my emotions into boxes, and pretending to be something I wasn't. Now, I have to unpack those boxes in these pages, because I want you to understand me.

I've written often that I'm smarter than everyone else. Always was. Still am. No one caught me. I just got tired and found a safe way out. I planned this exit strategy for a long time. Once Big Chigger was dead, I realized I didn't want to continue killing the rest of my life.

I studied examples of psychotic breaks both in popular literature and in psychiatric journals. I needed an excuse, a cover, if you will. The Interstate Killer gave it to me. Everyone thought it was because Princess was a victim. Not true.

Shit, even serial killers get tired.

The Interstate Killer turned out to be certifiably insane. He looked and behaved in a normal manner, caring for the love of his life, killing strangers to see if he could shock her back to awareness. I, on the other hand, have been acting all my life. I pretended to be outraged by man's inhumanity, all the while taking steps to stop that inhumanity in my own small way.

Is this a pretend break? It could be. I don't want to go on trial and face execution. Killing no longer satisfied me as it once did. One day it just wasn't fun anymore. It wasn't enough. Finding my sister was the excuse I used.

I'm in an institution for the reasons listed above. I don't speak. I make limited eye contact. I respond to oral or physical commands when I want to. Mostly I sit and watch and listen. I'm sure I was hospitalized against my will, although I no longer care. Being here suits my purpose.

I baffle the doctors. They wonder if I could I be in a catatonic stupor? Could I have a neurological disease? Could I be bi-polar? No one has suggested my psychosis could be fake. I'm a world-class actress who was never nominated for an Oscar. I might be faking it. I might not be. I might have had a true psychotic break.

Doctors have tested me for everything they could think of. They went down the bipolar rat hole for a while. They tried a stew of drugs with no success. They tried therapy. Do you have any idea how useless it is to try to analyze a selectively mute subject?

They ran a boatload of tests to see if I had a disease. I gave up gallons of blood in their search for the Holy Grail. Lyme disease. Negative. Malaria. Negative. Syphilis. Negative. HIV. Negative. Encephalitis. Negative. I drove them crazy.

Next, they tried a variety of anti-psychotic drugs. Thorazine. Haldol. Serlect. Clozaril. Risperdal. Since I'm not psychotic, it stands to reason the anti-psychotic drugs wouldn't produce their desired outcome.

The doctors see promise in my behavior. They hope I'm emerging from my stupor, because I choose to dress and feed myself. I can walk to the common room to watch television. I finger books but don't yet read. I can have visitors and receive mail. Li'l Bit and the boys have come over. So have L&O and her family. I have cards on my shelf from the Cruise Club, including one touching prayer sent from Shy-Scot, who is still in the Sahel. Chest-Cracker and Saw-Bones, Sandra and Dr. Rigby have sent long letters of support.

I pretend I'm coming out of a dark passage from insanity to sanity. I cannot tell you how much fun it is, fooling the fools who think I'm crazy. I pretend to be improving to win a slackening of restraints. I can walk around the hospital without alarms going off. I can't go outside, but that's no problem. There's plenty to do inside.

Knowledge that I hunted for over three decades without anyone giving me a second thought, that I did it while a member of the criminal justice system, would be unbearable to my friends, family, and colleagues.

I worry about the political implications of what I did. If the truth came out, it would destroy careers and overturn cases. The FBI would have a collective coronary. Everything I'd touched in Baltimore and the District would be grounds for exoneration.

Let my confession be a cautionary tale, for we are not all what we seem. I've violated your trust with what I did. Nothing you could have done would have made me stop killing.

One thing I know for certain, G-Man. You won't tell anyone about what I did. Ever.

AFTERWORD

Richmond—Henrico County authorities have been called to the private Hughes Psychiatric Hospital to investigate a series of unexplained deaths. While administrators at the hospital will not go on the record, privately one said, "It's probably someone who works here. It's not hard to lose your perspective when you work with psychotics." The Angel of Mercy syndrome has often been cited when medical personnel kill patients. Police are investigating the deaths as possible homicides.

Where I Hang Out

Contact me through my website to reserve time for your book club or to chat about anything on your mind:

http://betsy-ashton.com/contact-me/

Sign up for my newsletter to receive advanced notifications of new books, contests, and other rather cool stuff

http://betsy-ashton.com/

I blog twice a month on the home page above as well as at www.rosesofprose.blogspot.com on the 17th and 27th of each month.

Follow me on social media. I'm Betsy Ashton on each of the sites below:

Facebook
Twitter
Pinterest
Instagram
Goodreads
LinkedIn

CPSIA information can be obtained
at www.ICGtesting.com
Printed in the USA
BVHW030153080420
577170BV00001B/125